The Playdate

The Playdate

CLARA DILLON

SANDYCOVE

an imprint of

PENGUIN BOOKS

SANDYCOVE

UK | USA | Canada | Ireland | Australia
India | New Zealand | South Africa

Sandycove is part of the Penguin Random House group of companies
whose addresses can be found at global.penguinrandomhouse.com.

Penguin
Random House
UK

First published 2024
001

Copyright © Clara Dillon, 2024

The moral right of the author has been asserted

Set in 13.5/16pt Garamond MT Std and 11.2/16pt Gill Sans MT Pro
Typeset by Jouve (UK), Milton Keynes
Printed and bound in Great Britain by Clays Ltd, Elcograf S.p.A.

The authorized representative in the EEA is Penguin Random House Ireland,
Morrison Chambers, 32 Nassau Street, Dublin D02 YH68

A CIP catalogue record for this book is available from the British Library

ISBN: 978–1–844–88659–3

www.greenpenguin.co.uk

MIX
Paper | Supporting
responsible forestry
FSC® C018179

Penguin Random House is committed to a
sustainable future for our business, our readers
and our planet. This book is made from Forest
Stewardship Council® certified paper.

To Peter, Jemima and Charlotte

Prologue

More wine, Adam?

You're struggling again this evening. We both are. At dinner you pushed your plate away and said, yet again, that you wished I'd never gone ahead with that playdate. You'd told me not to, you said, but I wouldn't listen. If it hadn't been for the playdate, none of this would have happened.

Or would it?

'How did it come to this?' you've asked, bewildered. So many lives destroyed. There are so many gaps, you keep saying. Things you wish I'd told you before.

I did try, many times; you know I did. But you were away such a lot with work, and then distant or distracted in other ways. Even when we did talk I often felt that you didn't really believe me. Or thought I was exaggerating.

'Bunch of dramatic housewives' was how you described us. 'Too much time on your hands.'

But in all the years you've known me, have I ever been a person for drama?

No. Well, then.

To be fair, I can't blame you. I find it difficult myself to comprehend Vanessa's behaviour, the sheer irrationality of her hatred. That there are people in the world who can act in such a way. You and I – Lexie too – we have all been affected; 'traumatized' is, I think, not too strong a word; I think even you would admit that now.

So perhaps I need this conversation as much as you do. To sit here with you in this rosy August evening in our tiny back garden with a bottle of something you've picked up on your travels in Paris or Madrid or Milan. To go through it all again, to fill in all the gaps, to – yes, to admit that there were times when each of us let the other down. So that hopefully in time we can repair the damage to our relationship and move forward. Because if there's one thing I've learned from all of this, Adam, it's that when it truly mattered you stepped up for Lexie and me, and for that I will always be grateful.

I

You're saying you want to go over the playdate again. You still haven't grasped that the playdate was not the beginning. Well, so be it. We've discussed that day already of course, with the police, the lawyers and God knows who else – and it's still very hard to talk about – but if you think it will help, then I'm happy to oblige. And this time you've asked for all the details. All the background, the petty school-gate trivia that always bored and exasperated you before, now you are prepared to sit through all of it. You want to properly listen. To understand.

All right then.

Earlier this year, the first Friday of April, to be exact. You were away again that day, at a meeting in London. Here in Dublin the sky was heavy and low, blurry at the edges like smudged charcoal. There had been a yellow alert on the radio that morning as I recall, forecasting heavy rain.

You were surprised to hear I had invited Polly.

'Vanessa's kid?' you said on the phone. 'Didn't you say she'd been giving Lexie a hard time in the playground?'

'They used to get on well,' I said defensively. 'I'm hoping they might again if they have a nice afternoon.'

'But why? You keep on complaining about these people. Why doesn't Lexie just find some other friends?'

I'm not trying to be critical, but this happens to be a good example of how these conversations usually went. No matter how many times I tried to explain the background to you, it never seemed to get through.

All the same, you had a point.

'Polly's coming?' Lexie had said the night before, stiffening on the sofa. 'But . . .' Her fingers rose to her mouth. 'But I thought we'd invited Imogen and Mia?'

'We still have.' I reached to tuck a wisp of her hair behind her ear. 'But Polly's mum has to be somewhere tomorrow afternoon so we're helping her out.'

Lexie said nothing; confrontation, as you know, not being her way. But the tension, denied an outlet through her voice, travelled down her body like toothpaste in a tube, popping out at her bare feet, which twisted and clawed around each other. She chewed her thumbnail. Her eyes, large and worried, moved from side to side. I could see she was thinking.

'Imogen and Mia will be happy,' she said finally.

'Yes, they will.'

'We could go on the trampoline.' She was starting to get excited now. It had been her dream – it was the dream of every third-class girl – to have Polly Mayhew over, and even before the recent . . . difficulties . . . with Vanessa, Lexie never had.

I remember once you used the word 'valiant' to describe Lexie. I can't remember the context, but it struck me at the time how apt it was. Such a good child always, so kind and willing to please, no matter what the cost to her. You were right. I should have left things alone.

At two fifteen I leaned against the railings outside the school, digging my hands into the pockets of my parka. A sharp breeze flicked briskly at the magnolia leaves. From behind the red-brick buildings an enormous slate-grey cloud rose like a wall.

The bell rang. I pushed myself off the railings. Smiling, I went to the gate. The doors opened; a horde of under-twelves in primary-coloured coats streamed like M&Ms into the playground. Four of them came clustering around me. Lexie, with ink on her chin, tripping over the open flap on her backpack. Her two friends, Imogen and Mia. And Polly Mayhew –

4

Imogen and Mia, I saw, could hardly believe that Polly was coming with us. They huddled together, staring at her in awe. Lexie hopped and fidgeted, tugging at her sleeves, brightly looking from one face to the next. Only Polly seemed composed. She stood a few feet apart from the others, swinging her backpack, calmly gazing into the distance.

'How did the Gaeilge Fair go?' I asked.

'Good.'

'Did you buy everything through Irish?'

'*Tried.*'

'What did you buy?'

'Haribos.' Imogen uncurled her fingers to reveal a sticky empty packet.

'A chocolate-chip bun,' Mia whispered to her trainers. 'And a second-hand Malory Towers.'

'And I got *this*.' Lexie hauled a grubby blue stuffed dog out of her backpack.

'Lovely.' I looked towards Polly to include her, but she stared away, her pretty face bored. The school Gaeilge Fair was done and dusted, in the past, not worth all this fuss.

'Okay, everyone,' I said. 'Let's go before the rain starts.'

There wasn't much conversation between them as we crossed the road, but that wasn't unusual at the start of a playdate. Mia, tiny and delicate and prone to chest infections, was so shy that it often took an hour or so for her to speak above a whisper. Imogen, taller and sturdier with long brown hair in bunches, had more to say and usually dominated their three-somes. But today she was more subdued, walking deferentially behind Polly, the undisputed leader, with her sunny ponytail and lithe dancer's gait. She looked older than the others even though dressed in the same green crested school tracksuit. It was her absolute confidence, the self-possession that came from years of being told she was beautiful, clever and admired,

5

and of confirming every day with her own eyes that this was the case.

'How much longer?' she asked in her strong, clear voice.

'Five minutes.'

'When I have a playdate, my mom always drives.'

'Mine too,' Imogen put in.

'Well, not far now.'

'We live up there.' Polly pointed across the Green, to where a wide road lined with cherry trees curved towards the summit of the estate.

'I know.' I smiled down at her. 'You're lucky. You have a lovely view. We're in here to the left.'

'In there? To the *little* houses?'

'Sure,' I said pleasantly as Lexie's face flushed. Polly didn't mean it like that; she was barely ten. 'And here we are!'

The first drops detonated in giant, saucer-sized splotches as we all crowded under the porch. The light was strange, the sky so dark behind the bright yellow-brick houses that the street looked like a negative.

'Just in time,' I called as the door gave and everyone fell into the hallway. The porch roof began to roar.

Lexie chewed her sleeve. Now the trampoline was a non-starter.

'I'm starving.' Polly rubbed the front of her tracksuit.

'I'll heat up some pizza. You girls leave your wet things in the hall and play in the TV room.'

In the kitchen I switched on the oven. The place had seemed perfectly clean that morning. Now, in the harsh light from the patio doors, I saw crumbs on the table and a sticky patch on the counter. I found myself grabbing a cloth and scrubbing tensely before catching myself. *Sara – she's a child! She won't care!*

The brutal truth was I had forced this playdate. We'd all been at Spoon the previous day, fifteen or so third-class mums gathering around scones and flat whites to raise funds for the new AstroTurf. Vanessa and her mates were putting in a rare appearance as Erica, the class PA rep, was responsible for collecting the ten-euro donation per mum. The shriek and rattle of the coffee grinder meant that I had to strain towards Vanessa's end of the table to hear about the outfit she was planning to wear to an upcoming charity lunch.

'. . . so in the end I said, you know what, I'll just go with the Jimmy Choos.'

'Oh, *super* choice, Van!'

'Well done you!'

'They'll look amazing with the Jil Sander!'

'What's the lunch in aid of?' someone asked from further down the table.

Vanessa looked surprised. 'It's Milly O'Driscoll's charity? My best friend who works for Google? All over the *Business Post* last weekend?'

'Oh – of course.'

'So!' Vanessa popped her sunglasses on her neat blonde bob. 'Think of me tomorrow, ladies, when I'll be in the Merrion, raising a Prosecco to you all.'

She rose, plucking her little bag from the seat beside her. People scraped their chairs back quickly to let her out. From my end of the table I saw Orla Mooney change colour, her scone suspended halfway to her mouth.

'Tomorrow, Van?'

'Yes. That's why I asked you to take Polly after school for me. It's going to be absolutely super!'

After some confusion, however, it transpired that Orla had thought Vanessa's charity lunch was *next* Friday. Tomorrow she had to take Sadbh to Crumlin Children's Hospital for her ENT appointment. They'd been waiting six months.

'Vanessa, my God. I'm so sorry! I was positive you said the lunch was next week.'

Vanessa stood holding the tips of her fingers to her chest. 'Gosh, Orla, I don't *think* so? I'm sure I wouldn't have got this wrong. Tomorrow is one of the most important days of my best friend's career.'

'But look – I have your text . . .' Orla tried to show her, but Vanessa ignored it, staring ahead, as astonished as if Orla had tried to hand her a dog turd.

'So – sorry, Orla, not blaming *you* or anything – but this puts me in quite a difficult position. What am I going to do about Polly? Ernestine will be away. She took the weekend off as we thought everything was covered.'

'No, no, we'll sort something out.' Orla swung to Erica. 'Any chance you could . . .'

'My car's full tomorrow,' Erica said grimly. 'I'm doing Oliver's rugby run.'

'Hang on. Let me see . . . maybe Crumlin . . .' Orla began to jab at her phone. The whole atmosphere of the café had changed. Now they were all turning to each other: 'Could you –' 'How awful.' 'What if . . .' while Vanessa simply stood there, wide-eyed and helpless in their midst.

Weird, weird, this hold she had over them all. As if they were in some kind of cult.

'She sounds ridiculous,' you'd scoffed, soon after we'd moved here. 'Like a South Dublin Cruella de Vil.' Later, though, when you met her, you were bewildered. 'But she's nice. Nicer than you made her sound.' As if my description of her had led you to picture a monster instead of the neat, pretty hostess in the elegant dress. But that's the way she worked. If she had looked like her true self no one would have gone near her.

'Just find some other mothers to hang out with,' you said, bored, when I complained.

8

But the trouble was, there weren't any others. Practically the whole kit and caboodle of them seemed to be well and truly under Vanessa's thumb. If it was just me, I would have been more than happy to steer clear – I'd come across Vanessa's type before – but for Lexie, new to the school and to Dublin, I'd had no choice but to make an effort. And slowly, surely, my sycophancy had begun to pay off. Lexie had begun to settle, to make friends. Until that disastrous dinner party at Vanessa's house when I had discovered to my cost exactly what happened when one got on her wrong side.

Or rather, Lexie had. Because not only did Vanessa control the mothers; through her daughter Polly she controlled what went on in the playground too.

This, Adam, was what I had tried to make you understand. The real reason behind Vanessa's iron grip on the social life of St Catherine's primary school. If you were in favour, then so was your child. But if you were not ... And so the ghastly merry-go-round went on.

Up until then I had been half listening down my end of the table, idly flicking at a sugar sachet, but now, as something occurred to me, I sat up straight.

Sara – this is your chance. To help Lexie. Take it. Take it! Before someone else cancels their child's heart surgery to step in.

Brightly, I said, 'I'll take Polly tomorrow.'

Silence. Vanessa stared all around her in a puzzled way as if wondering where this strange voice could possibly have come from.

'That's so kind,' she said when she finally looked in my direction. 'But I don't want to put you to any trouble. Isabel will do it.'

'Vanessa – oh my God, I'd love to, but it's the one day – it's Ross's dad's seventieth and they're coming up specially from Fermoy . . .'

Vanessa tapped her nails on her bag strap. I knew what was going through her mind. She really, really, did not want to let me do this. To be put in the position of owing me after the appalling way I had – apparently – behaved. She waited for someone – anyone – else to step up, but no one did and slowly, like a rusty hinge, her reluctant gaze creaked towards me.

'Well,' she said. 'This is extremely kind of you, Sara. Where did you say you live again?'

She knew perfectly well where we lived.

'Twenty-four, Brookfield Terrace,' I said. 'Just down the hill from you. Lexie would love to have Polly. And no need to hurry. We'll give her dinner if you're late – just something simple, if that's all right . . .'

Why was I gushing? Why did she always have that effect on me? Even now, even when I was the one doing *her* a favour? But really, it was the other way around, and both of us knew it.

'Really *very* kind,' she said. 'Thank you so much.' She popped her sleeve up and looked at her watch. 'Oh my gosh, I'm super-late for tennis now. So sorry to rush off – but if you all don't mind . . . Byye! Byye!'

She swished out of the café, followed by Erica, Isabel and Marina, who had been quickly and quietly gathering up their things. The door tinkled shut behind them, leaving the rest of us sitting facing their empty end of the table, so vibrant and colourful mere seconds ago, now dingy and abandoned, the music from the radio no longer mellow but tinny and jarring and the scent of Jo Malone replaced by the reek of old gravy.

'Thanks so much, Sara.' Orla, hunched over her cappuccino, chuckled miserably. 'You saved my bacon. My God – if she'd had to cancel that lunch.'

How? I felt like giving Orla a shake. *How* would Vanessa have had to cancel the lunch? What about relatives? Neighbours?

Childminders? But there was no point in saying that to Orla, who'd had Stockholm syndrome since Junior Infants.

'It's no trouble,' I said. 'Honestly.'

'No, but it really is nice of you. Especially considering how Vanessa's been to you ever since the . . . well, you know. And the way Polly –' Orla lowered her voice. 'I mean, I don't know if you know this, but Sadbh says she and Lexie haven't been getting on so well lately. Little tiffs during breaktime, that sort of thing.'

'Yes, I –' The sachet I had been fiddling with split, scattering granules over the table. 'I know. That's precisely why I've invited her.'

'I mean, it's just girls messing, you know, but – Sadbh said she felt a bit sorry for Lexie the other day. Polly dared them all to pretend Lexie smelled. No one was allowed to touch her or speak to her. Whenever she tried to talk to anyone they had to hold their noses and run away. Lexie wasn't crying or anything, Sadbh said. Just standing quietly on her own. It was only Polly being high-spirited, of course, but Sadbh said she was glad when the bell rang. She didn't like the way Lexie looked. Kind of white, she said. Like a ghost.'

Silence from the living room. I went to peek around the door. Usually on playdates the girls rummaged in the toybox, built forts with chairs and sheets, played schools with Lexie's blackboard. Today there was a lot more standing around. A lot more, 'What'll we do?' and '*I* don't mind!' Like her mother, I realized: when she smiled, we all smiled; when she was dissatisfied, the sun went in and all was subdued and grey.

'Will we do a dance competition?' Lexie asked eagerly. 'I have some medals. We can take turns being judge.'

Polly shrugged, looking around our tiny living room with its orangey laminate flooring and black pleather sofa. I felt the ridiculous urge to explain: *I didn't choose this decor. We're just renting here.*

'We did that *last* time, Lexie,' Imogen said.

'What about my dog collection?' Lexie ran to the windowsill, where her beloved china dogs were arranged in rows. 'I have seventeen breeds. See how many you can guess.'

She was trying so hard, and my heart ached for her.

'You *play* with those?' Polly raised an eyebrow.

Lexie flushed again. 'Not really.'

I stepped in. 'Anyone like to design a mug?' From the shelf I pulled the emergency pack of white ceramic mugs and acrylic paint pens.

Imogen and Mia perked up at once.

'We can draw on those? Really?'

'And keep them afterwards?'

'Of course!'

Even Polly seemed intrigued. They converged on the pack, like lionesses on a kill, ripping it open and sharing out the contents. Lexie looked gratefully over at me. From the doorway I gave her a discreet thumbs-up.

Back in the kitchen, I blew my hair off my forehead and glanced at the clock. Two hours to go. I removed the pizzas from the freezer and began to cut off the packaging.

In fact, the mugs seemed to have done the trick. When I next checked, the four of them were kneeling around the coffee table on the brown shag-pile rug, busily designing. Lexie seemed relaxed, the tip of her tongue poking out, absorbed in her picture of a puppy with a red collar. She was good at art. Just to see her like that, so content, filled me with happiness. Relief, too. Today had been a gamble, but it looked to have been the right call. Polly was having a pleasant enough afternoon. I was under no illusion that this would be her most amazing playdate ever or that she and Lexie would ever be close friends, but the point was, Vanessa would be grateful, or whatever sensation passed for gratitude in her world. At the very least, surely now she would forgive me for what had happened at her dinner party, call Polly off, and Lexie could get on with her life without being targeted.

Polly's eyes were narrowed as she shaded in her graphic of birds flying across a moon. The birds could have been drawn by a teenager. Polly did everything well.

The thing was, I had often thought, away from Vanessa's influence, Polly was not that bad. Sometimes I felt sorry for her. Having Vanessa as a mother must be a challenge. The rampant competitiveness, disguised as concern: 'We don't know *how* she won that gold! The youngest child ever! I mean, it's supposed to be *fun*, isn't it? Not all this *pressure*.' When in fact Lexie had told me that Polly attended two gymnastics classes per week, in addition to having a private tutor who went to their house. The Mayhews had a dog, a large, non-shed Labradoodle who I'd heard spent much of his time alone in the back garden. 'My dad hits him when he barks,' Polly had told the girls. 'You have to show a big dog like that who's boss.' Lexie had thought Polly seemed troubled by this. I couldn't picture Vanessa reading to Polly and her two older sisters, chuckling with them over a board game, shivering on a freezing bathroom floor in the early hours while a child vomited into the toilet. It would be difficult, I imagined, to be a child in that house. Vanessa simply did not *see* people.

That morning at drop-off I had made sure to confirm the playdate arrangement. Vanessa had been put on the spot yesterday in Spoon but she'd had plenty of time since then to come up with an alternative. And if she had, the first Lexie and I would know of it was when we saw Polly leaving the school that afternoon with someone else. 'Oh my gosh,' Vanessa would say in surprise. 'Did I not tell you? I've just been so busy.'

To forestall this for Lexie I made my way to Vanessa's spot in the playground, where, face freshly coated in Desert Sunset or some such, she stood chatting with Orla, Marina and Erica.

'. . . so I said to him, I don't think you realize who . . .'

Orla saw me and waved. 'Hi, Sara!'

Vanessa turned. '*There* you are, Sara! Thank you *so* much again for having Polly today.'

'No trouble at all. Hope the lunch goes well.'

'Oh, I'm sure it will. Milly's events are always amazing. Not meaning to be rude, but I must rush. I've got an unbelievable amount to do before this afternoon.'

'Of course. Have fun.'

As she moved off I remembered something I'd meant to ask her.

'By the way . . .'

'Ya-hah?' She was already several feet away.

'Polly's EpiPen.'

'Her what?'

'Wasn't there something on the class WhatsApp at the start of the year? She gets a serious reaction to peanuts?'

'Oh, that. It's in her bag.'

'How does it work?'

A teeny frown. 'Do you not know?'

'No – sorry. I've never seen one.'

'Oh. I thought everyone – no, no, of course.' She stopped and exhaled, making a little noise. 'Polly – would you mind? Could *you* show Lexie's mum how to use an EpiPen?'

'Sorry to delay you,' I apologized.

Polly removed the pen from the pocket of her backpack and competently showed me how to operate it. It seemed very straightforward.

'Great! Thank you.'

'You're welcome.' Vanessa smiled, walking again. 'Just don't give her nuts and she'll be fine. She knows herself, don't you, Polly?'

'And is it just nuts, or –'

'Just nuts,' she trilled, by now halfway across the playground. If I wanted to ask any more questions, I'd have to run and trot behind her as I spoke. I gave up and simply waved.

The pizzas were in the oven. I had double- and triple-checked the ingredients on the boxes. Definitely no nuts. I had even re-scrubbed the kitchen table where you'd had that prawn satay the previous week, just in case. I was taking no chances.

I was doing some work on my laptop when I became aware of a small face poking diffidently around the door.

'Em . . . Lexie's mum?'

'Hi, Mia. All okay?'

'I . . . I need to go to the bathroom.'

'Sure. You know where it is? First door at the top of the stairs?'

'Lexie's in there.'

'I'm sure she won't be long.'

'She's been up there for ages.'

'Let me check.'

I went up the stairs and knocked on the bathroom door.

'Lex?'

Silence.

'Lexie!' I knocked again. 'Is everything okay?'

The door opened. Lexie appeared, looking pale. At the sight of me, her lip began to tremble.

I squeezed in and shut the door.

'What's the matter, sweetheart? Aren't you finishing your mug?'

'She said it was boring,' Lexie whispered.

'Who?'

'Polly. Her and Imogen are watching TikTok. On her phone.'

Polly had brought a phone?

'She said . . . she said my house is tiny and horrible and my stuff is babyish. She said she's never coming here again, and . . . and Imogen said she wasn't either.'

I knelt. I didn't know what to say, what to do. I just hugged her, held her close. My gentle, funny, clumsy little daughter. Sunlight glittered and flashed on the taps.

'Hey, look.' I nudged her. 'Rain's stopped. You can play on the trampoline, after all.'

She stirred at that, rubbing her eyes.

'Go on.' I smiled into her tears. 'Wash your face and get bouncing. We've got this.'

She sorted herself out while I pottered in our bedroom, giving her a chance to recover. When we came downstairs again I hung back a little, allowing her to go on ahead to re-join the girls while I tidied the pile of schoolbags in the hallway. Then, adopting my best brisk but cheerful attitude, I marched into the sitting room.

'Okay, girls. Phone away, please.'

Polly looked defiant, but I no longer cared. 'Mia, the bathroom's free now. And, great news, the rain has stopped so you can all play in the garden.'

'I'm starving,' Polly said sullenly, rubbing her abdomen.

'The pizzas are nearly ready. They'll taste all the more delicious after some fresh air.'

I left them to retrieve their coats and shoes from the hall.

'And no climbing on the tree,' I warned as they came trooping into the kitchen. 'It'll be too slippery after the rain.'

Once they were outside, I filled a jug with water, imagining myself dumping it over Polly's head. You'd been right, Adam. Only I hadn't listened and now I'd made things even worse. *Were* Lexie's things too babyish? *Should* I get her a phone? Let her sit glued to teens with vocal fry giving shopping and make-up tutorials instead of being her usual active, busy self, always up and about, interested in her surroundings? Well, whatever happened, we weren't doing this again.

The smell of warm dough and cheese filled the kitchen. The trampoline squeaked. The grass sparkled; the air looked like washed glass. One of the girls called something. Mia responded in her silvery little voice. Then came the sound of Lexie laughing.

My spirits rose again. Being outdoors always helped. I'd never yet hosted a playdate that wasn't revitalized by a dose of fresh air. Perhaps this afternoon wouldn't be such a disaster after all. They'd play out there, eat the pizza, then leave. And then – job done. Never again! I looked again at the clock. Forty-five minutes to go.

I was setting out plates and tumblers when I heard the screams.

At first I thought there'd been an argument. Or someone had seen a spider. I went to the door and hauled it open.

It took me a second. A small figure in a green tracksuit, lying motionless on the grass. Directly under the branches of next-door's pear tree.

You know, Adam, what I thought. What you yourself would have thought. My feet seemed to leave the ground.

Not Lexie! Not Lexie!

As I flew past I saw her standing on the trampoline. Her hands were at her mouth.

'Mummy,' she cried when she saw me.

My breathing restarted. The spinning of grass and sky slowed. The child on the ground, blonder than Lexie, came into focus.

'Was she climbing?' I turned on the children. '*Was she climbing?*'

'I don't know. I don't know.'

I dropped to my knees. She was on her back, one arm out, the other twisted behind her. Her eyes were closed, her face pale. So very pale.

'Polly,' I said sharply. 'Polly!'

I think I thought if I was mummyish and firm enough she'd stop messing about and sit up. But she didn't. Her eyes stayed closed. Her skin was white, strangely smooth, like a doll's. Unreal. None of this was real. Around me, yet far away, voices surged and retreated. Was she breathing? I leaned in, trying to hear.

'Hello there!' Crouched beside me was a woman. Angela from next door. At the time we didn't know her well.

'I heard the screams and came over the wall. Can I help?'

'I think we need an ambulance.'

Angela felt Polly's neck. As we now know, Angela used to be a nurse. All we knew back then was that she was rather strict, taking a hard line against children entering her garden or kicking balls near her hellebores.

'There's no pulse,' Angela said.

No pulse. Beneath me the ground seemed to fall away. On the trampoline, the children wept and whimpered.

Angela pressed on Polly's chest while I dialled 999.

'There's a child.' My voice was high. 'Fallen from a tree. There's no pulse.' It was as if someone else was saying it.

Then I helped Angela with the CPR, taking over the chest compressions while she did the breaths. I'd done a course while pregnant with Lexie. *One-two.* It came back to me quickly enough. *Seven-eight.* The rhythm of it brought the blood back to my head. Angela was so calm and sensible. Thank God she'd been here! Any minute now, Polly would respond to the CPR and wake up. We'd help her to her feet, go inside and have the pizza – bloody hell, that was still in the oven. Probably burned to a crisp by now . . . *Fifteen-sixteen*. The white face, so unearthly. Such a beautiful child. Good at everything. Vanessa hadn't wanted her to come, but I had made her . . . *Nineteen-twenty*. The rain was back. Drops were streaming down my forehead. *No pulse*, Angela had said. A child in my care. I was on my knees in the rain and a child . . . I'd thought it was Lexie and I . . . and now the trembling in my hands had started up again. Something inside me was roaring, rising. And Vanessa . . . Vanessa was coming at five.

2

I'll stop there. There's a lot more, as we both know all too well. But you're looking away from me now, putting your hand to your face, the way people do when something is difficult to hear. Anyhow, I think that sums up the main events of the afternoon.

Your glass is empty. Another? I could do with a drink myself.

What happened at the playdate was shocking and traumatic. For the Mayhews, for Lexie, for us, for everyone involved. A cruel, icy blast of water – but into a vat already filled with poison, a toxic acid that had been pooling, needing only a few drops to explode . . . You're staring at me now. Where has it come from, you're wondering, this anger and passion that I so rarely show?

Vanessa, of course, is the . . . but look. Why don't I rewind a bit? Choose a point at random and keep talking. Perhaps that way, in time, things might become clearer to us both. Have some more wine. Stop me anywhere you like.

The first time I ever met Vanessa was on Lexie's first day at school, three weeks after we moved here.

Unfortunately, you had to miss her big day due to having to be in London again. I took lots of photos of her in her new green tracksuit, gap-toothed and adorable, her fair hair uncharacteristically neat in two wispy plaits. You FaceTimed her during breakfast. I could see how moved you were, how proud. You touched each other's fingertips on the screen.

The previous week, when Lexie and I had walked past St Catherine's the red-brick buildings had been peaceful, glowing in the evening sun, statues of robed saints casting long shadows across the playground. This morning there were children everywhere, racing around, screaming and shouting in their Irish accents. They all seemed to know each other, even the tiny ones. Lexie had been chatty and excited over breakfast but had grown quieter and quieter as we walked past the Green and down the hill of the estate.

'Look!' I drew her attention to a cluster of little girls, dramatically darting from group to group, shrieking and hugging each other, all the while looking over each other's shoulders to see who else was around. 'They look about your age. Maybe that's your class.'

Next to the girls a woman in a long, flowery skirt was ticking things off on a clipboard.

'Excuse me,' I said, approaching her, my head doing that poky little tortoise movement that people do when they're unsure whether to intrude. 'Are you the third-class teacher?'

'Yes! Hello!' She looked up, pushing back her hair. She was young and very smiley with a harassed, distracted air. 'Miriam Brennan. And this is . . .'

'Lexie Carey. She's new.'

'Oh, yes! Lexie! Welcome to St Catherine's, Lexie. Where have you come from? England?'

'London,' I said, when Lexie hesitated and looked at me. 'We just moved here a couple of weeks ago. But Lexie's dad is Irish. And my parents are Irish too, so . . .'

'Lovely! Lovely to be back home! Well, Lexie, the bell's just about to go. Your leena will be here beside the steps.'

'Her . . .'

'Her leena.'

I was baffled, but Ms Brennan's gaze had already skittered past me to the queue building up behind. More parents were hovering, drawn to the flowery skirt, seeking the nectar of talking about their child. I withdrew to leave her to it.

'She seems nice,' I said to Lexie. 'Friendly.'

Lexie pressed against me, her fingers kneading my leg, seeking my touch. Her expression was neutral, but I knew what was going on in her head. She was eyeing all the chatter and noise and activity and quailing at the thought of having to get to know all of these girls, to have to banter, to fit in. The mums, too, stood in groups, talking and talking, their mouths opening and shutting, everyone festooned with lunchboxes, scooter helmets, pushchairs and cockapoos. A few feet away from us stood a thin, pale woman who also seemed to be on her own. Her long black puffy coat was zipped to her chin even though the day was warm. With her was a girl of about nine or ten.

'They look new too.' I nudged Lexie. 'Hey. Maybe they'll know what a leena is.'

When the woman happened to glance our way I gave her a little wave. 'Hi there!'

She reared back in a startled-filly way, as if I had just burst a crisp bag.

'Are you new here?'

The woman looked very surprised. 'No.'

'Well, this is Lexie. She's starting in third class. I'm Sara.'

'Edel,' the woman said reluctantly after a pause. 'And this is Imogen.'

'Is this a nice school?' I smiled at Imogen, who had a surly expression and very long hair down to her waist.

She shrugged and kicked the ground. Lexie pressed harder against my leg. Edel, meanwhile, was staring all around the playground as if trying to catch someone's eye. Possibly I was boring her. *Don't be ridiculous*, I thought. *Of course you're boring her. She hasn't seen her friends all summer and here you are, standing in her way.*

'Well.' I smiled again at them both. 'Nice to meet you. Hope to see you around.'

At first I thought Edel was going to walk off without responding. At the last second she glanced back and, grudgingly, a corner of her mouth twitched. Then she turned and vanished into the crowd. A moment later, however, I spotted her on the other side of the playground, standing again with Imogen, just the two of them.

O-kay. At least she had smiled. *Baby steps*, I thought.

The bell rang. A flurry of hoodies and lunch bags, a surge towards the steps. Lexie and I stood back so we could watch where to go. Gradually from the chaos the girls organized themselves into a series of long, straggly lines – *leenas!* – each with a teacher at the top.

A sound behind me made me turn. We were standing just then beside a low gate that led to a car park. A slim blonde woman in a white tracksuit was at the gate, about to open it from the car-park side. She was talking on her phone.

'*Beep-beep!*' she said to Lexie, who was standing in front of the gate.

Startled, Lexie leaped to the side. Without so much as a glance in her direction, the woman strode through the gate, still talking.

'Yes, yes, so then *I* said –'

Lexie's backpack, unbalanced by the leap, swung down her arm and bumped against the woman's elbow. Unfortunately, the woman was holding a takeaway coffee cup in that hand. Brown liquid flew from the hole in the lid and spattered all over the woman's white leggings.

The woman stopped.

'Oh. My. God.'

'Sorry. I'm sorry.' Lexie's hands flew to her mouth.

The woman was standing with her arms up, looking down at herself, phone in one hand, dripping coffee cup in the other. A tiny bag dangled on a chain from her elbow. The coffee had left a stain – not large, but distinct against the white, and the leggings did look expensive.

'I'm so sorry.' I stepped forward. 'Can I –'

'I'm fine. It's fine.' Her tone said it wasn't fine at all, but then we had just ruined her outfit.

'I've got some tissues –'

'It's fine. Really.' Mirthless smile. 'You're very kind, but please don't worry.'

I stepped back and she walked off, talking again into her phone.

'Yes. Still here. No. Some out-of-control child has just rammed into me – I *know*!'

As she reached the centre of the playground three or four women materialized at once from several different directions as if they had been watching for her arrival, and swarmed around her, hiding her from view.

'It was an accident,' Lexie whispered, her eyes huge.

'Of course it was, sweetheart.' I knelt, smoothing back the wisps of hair that had already escaped from her plaits. 'Don't give it another thought, okay?'

I kissed the tip of her nose. In return she managed a quivery little grin that pinged at my heart.

'Don't let it ruin your day,' I said. 'Let's go and find this leena of yours.'

She gripped her backpack, visibly firming her chin. Brava, Lexie! We set off towards Ms Brennan, who was beckoning brightly and a little frantically from the steps. On the way we passed the coffee woman. She seemed to have recovered from her trauma and was at the centre of a large group of women, all of them talking and laughing loudly. Around them the playground seemed suddenly brighter, more colourful and vibrant.

I found myself watching the woman. Something about her . . . She was attractive in a groomed, high-maintenance way.

24

Her hair was perhaps slightly too blonde, the eyebrows several shades darker, giving her face a rather hard appearance. Or perhaps that was just my perception after her behaviour at the gate. Which was unfair, I knew, because it might well not be easy to get those stains out.

Anyhow, probably because she seemed so much at the centre of things, I assumed that her child or children, wherever they were, would be further up the school than third class. Unlikely, therefore, that Lexie or I would have much to do with her, and I remember feeling glad about that. And with that, as I gave Lexie a final hug and waved her off to her *leena*, I put the woman and her spotless white leggings out of my mind.

Lexie was overjoyed to see you that evening.

'Daddeee!' She raced out to the hallway at the homely sound of your key in the door. She was in her pineapple-print pyjamas, worn out from her day but wide awake again at the sight of you. You knelt to greet her as she flew into your arms. The two of you looked like a competitive Christmas ad for a department store.

'So, princess.' You put a hand out to stop yourself toppling to the floor. 'How was your first day?'

'Fine!'

'What did you do?'

'Can't remember.'

I had managed to get a bit more out of her earlier, when she was less tired and it was all still fresh in her mind. So, while the two of you snuggled on the sofa, her tucked under your arm, her eyes shadowed and over-bright, enjoying us all being together, I sat on the armrest and filled you in. Ms Brennan, apparently, was 'nice'. The girl sitting beside her was also 'nice'. She couldn't remember her name. They had done some Gaeilge and she had learned her first Gaeilge word: *marda*, meaning 'dog', which had pleased her, as she loved all animals.

'Not *marda*,' you said. '*Madra*.'

'Whatever.' She stuck out her tongue.

'Well.' You tousled her hair. 'It all sounds fantastic.' Her plaits had come out, leaving her hair all crinkly, which she loved because she thought it made her look like a mermaid.

You put her to bed while I prepared dinner. Lamb and pistachio burgers from the Ottolenghi cookbook; we've both always liked our cuisine. But back downstairs you were quieter. You'd been up since five; I could see you were exhausted. You shovelled in mouthfuls of lamb, clearly without tasting it, all the while checking messages and taking calls, scribbling on pieces of paper.

'Yes. No. I'm back in London on Friday. Talk then.'

I sipped my Rioja. Outside, it was getting dark. The tea-lights on the kitchen table and counter gave off a cosy glow. Your shirt collar was open, your messy Tintin quiff and rosy-cheeked baby-face belying your sharp intelligence, the ambition and determination that had driven you to ditch your flashy City job to set up on your own. Lexie and I had hardly seen you since we'd moved here. While you pitched and travelled, we had unpacked on our own, explored our new neighbourhood, located the bank, the supermarket and the school. We had visited your parents in Stillorgan, where your mum hugged and fussed over Lexie, plying her with mini choc-bars.

'Sorry! Sorry!' you said, coming off your phone. 'Sheesh, this is a lot more of a ball-ache than I expected. Trying to do everything on my own from two different countries. Once I land a couple of key clients things should settle. I'll be able to spend more time here.'

'It's fine,' I said. 'We knew it would be tricky.'

'Mmmm.' You stared out at the garden, your left leg hopping restlessly up and down. 'That tree next door is annoying. The way it hangs over our patch, blocking all our light. Neighbours should prune it.'

'I don't mind. It gives the garden some character.'

'Well, it certainly needs that. All the houses round here are like identikit blocks of cement. No imagination. English architecture is so much nicer.'

'It's early days,' I soothed. 'Just do what you have to do. Lexie and I will be fine.'

But you were still on edge, checking and sending emails until finally, in bed, you shut the phone off and chucked it on the nightstand.

'Whooo.' You rubbed your eyes with the heels of your hands. 'I'm wrecked.' Then you turned to face me, giving me your full attention for the first time that evening. 'So. Lex's day went well?'

'I think so. She was nervous going in but, as you saw, quite happy tonight.'

'Didn't I tell you? You've been fretting over nothing. She's not as sensitive as you keep making out.'

'I hope so.'

'I know so! Now! Come here!'

You sat up, tugged me over on to my back.

'Legs – check. Still nice and long. And . . .' You spread my hair out over the pillow.

I was happy to lie there passively as I knew you liked. In the early days it had given me a charge to hand over the power like that, allowing you to position me whichever way you wanted. The stomach-swooping, free-fall sensation of giving up control. But – and I think I had mentioned this to you a couple of times – maybe Lexie's arrival had changed things, or perhaps I had just realized it over time anyway, but often it seemed as if you were talking to yourself *about* me rather than *to* me. You rarely looked at my face or expected a response. But with the

27

recent move and all the commuting you'd been doing I was just glad to have you home, so I relaxed into it.

'Remember that night at Hakkasan?' you said, stroking my foot. 'Those high heels and that glittery little dress of yours. Ballard and all those gobshites couldn't take their eyes off you. I love it when you get dressed up.' Your fingers trailed up my calf. 'I miss those days. Sometimes you can be a bit casual, you know, in your parka thing and your jeans. Your mum clothes.'

'I *am* a mum!'

'I know, I know. I just . . . I loved your work clothes. Those tight black skirts all you City ladies wear. Shimmying along the Strand.'

'Well, when I get a chance to apply here for –'

'Mmmm.' Your hand had reached my thigh. 'Because these legs . . . still so, so hot . . .'

'And you . . .' Smiling, I went to put my hand out, to touch your face, but you moved aside and went on staring down at me. Scrutinizing.

'I'm glad you haven't put on weight like a lot of women your age.'

'My age?' I laughed. 'I'm only thirty-nine.'

'No, no, sure. But some older women, you know, you see them starting to . . . But not you. You're still so – except for . . .' You touched the small roll of flesh on my abdomen. 'But that's from the pregnancy, obviously, so it's worth it.'

Later you slept, as soundlessly as if you had been switched off. The sleep of the utterly exhausted. So silent were you that it was as if you were abroad again and I was alone. I was thinking again of Lexie. So trusting and sweet in her green tracksuit, a half-size too big. She could be anxious at the best of times and today was a challenge she had looked forward to and dreaded in equal measure. The haughty coffee woman – who of course I now know was Vanessa – was back in my mind.

That niggly feeling again . . . and then I got it. She reminded me of a girl I had once known at school. Grace. Grace Gillespie. The name in my head made me lie still.

I don't know if I ever told you about Grace Gillespie?

Anyhow, that was who the woman reminded me of. Not so much in looks – although there was a resemblance – but in the imperiousness, the way she had more or less ordered Lexie to move out of her way without even bothering to look at her. As if Lexie didn't matter; as if she was invisible.

3

From time to time I'm still amazed to think I have ended up living in Ireland. With a child who is one hundred per cent Irish. Even with both of my parents being Irish, before I met you – you probably remember me telling you this – I had never spent more than a few days in Ireland. Once, when I was ten, we had stayed with some cousins in a town called Drum-something in County Clare. It had rained almost literally without stopping. Their bungalow, which looked like a mobile home that someone had flung gravel on, was surrounded by bare tarmac. The garden had breezeblock walls and a stripy lawn with a soccer net at each end. We had played pool in their garage and they had watched Irish sport on TV all day long. After that we never saw them again. My mother had never got on with her family – my mother rarely got on with anyone – and there had been some argument or other during the holiday and we had never gone back.

We weren't in touch with any other relatives and, growing up in darkest Surrey, we didn't come across many first-generation Irish people. Not that anything about my childhood had inclined me to seek them out, or to yearn for a country I knew little about apart from that even the Romans had found it too wet and dreary to conquer. As far as I was concerned, I was English, and Ireland was a small, provincial, rain-drenched rock to the west, of no interest or relevance to me whatsoever.

So I had never expected to marry an Irishman.

We've tried to remember – was it Janina's cousin or your friend Ben's who introduced us that boozy night at Radio

Rooftop? Anyhow, our two separate groups had ended up coming together thanks to whoever's cousin it was who knew people in both. Being tall, you stood out from the sweaty hordes at the bar. You had just come from work and were wearing your dark grey Brioni suit, which sat perfectly across your shoulders. *Smooth*, I thought, as Janina led her band of hens across the floor to where you and your rugby mates were necking shots and ribbing each other. It struck me how much fun you were all having. From a distance you'd looked like a student, but up close you were older than I'd thought, around my age, with faint lines around your eyes. I remember feeling conscious of you as I chatted to a random hedge-fund manager on my other side, and felt that you were the same, both of us looking-without-looking as around us the drunken banter raged on.

Our first conversation, when we finally found ourselves alone, was, thrillingly, about work. Manways & Co. LLP, where Janina and I checked our souls in at reception each day, was much less prestigious than your glitzy Berger & Fleischer – or Bragger & Flasher, as everyone called it – but we both knew what it was like to work extremely long hours. 'Making other people's money for them,' as you drily remarked. You explained your plans to set up your own RegTech company as soon as you had the contacts and experience.

Your confidence and vision were intriguing. A chronic fence-sitter myself, I never knew how to take people who were extremely focused and sure of themselves. Whether I should envy them or despise them for being unable to see any other point of view but their own. But you I found intelligent and interesting. The fact that you were so attractive didn't hurt. I could tell from your accent that you were Irish, but the topic barely came up. After having lived for almost eight years in London you seemed more London than the Londoners themselves; I assumed that you had left Ireland for good, and so did you.

The Irish market was too small, you said. You had educated yourself out of ever being able to work there again.

Yet, eleven years later almost to the day, here we sit in our Dublin back garden, huddled and shell-shocked in the tiny parallelogram of sun that we receive for maybe twenty minutes a day. Fine-tooth-combing a year that began with a house move and a sweet little community primary school and ended in a nightmare.

You always loathed this house. The first time you laid eyes on it, I remember, you stopped dead in the road. Your mum was disappointed. She had offered to househunt for us as we were so busy and had gone to a lot of trouble to find something suitable. It did fit all our requirements – close to her and your dad and fewer than forty minutes by car from Dublin airport – but as I watched your shoulders slump I sensed, as clearly as if you had shouted it, your panicky longing for London, the story-rich ancient buildings, the bridges lit up over massive black water.

I had always loved that view too. From our balcony we could see Westminster and the London Eye. The first time I visited your London flat I'd been captivated. The views, the gleaming industrial design, all polished concrete floors and floating staircases – oh yes, and the enormous waterbed beside the floor-to-ceiling window. We were too high up for anyone to see us, though we joked about it. You stroking my face, doing your thing with the positioning. 'I can't believe it,' you said. 'I can't believe a woman like you is in my bed. I feel like I discovered you in some mysterious hidden cavern and scooped you out before anyone else could find you. This silky hair. These long, sexy legs. You come from good stock.'

'Good stock?' I laughed, mocking your accent. 'What am I, a prize mare? Is that how all Irish men talk to women?'

You often made admiring but functional comments like that,

as if you were appraising a Charolais beef breed, or a car. You liked showing me off, your hand in the small of my back as your friends made silent-whistle faces at you when I, apparently, wasn't looking. I'll admit it, I enjoyed the attention.

I was different from other women, you said. I was a challenge. A mystery. You'd had to work hard for me.

If you had, I hadn't intended it that way. People said I was aloof. It wasn't shyness. I could be perfectly confident when I wanted to be. But in general I found people tiring. I was happiest on my own, reading, swimming, hiking for miles in the South Downs.

'But you're in LONDON,' you said, as if I owed it to all the people who didn't live here to see everything. You yourself acted as if you only had three days left to live. Briskly ticking off *Time Out* lists, booking flights or Eurostar tickets for any weekend you were free. Your interest in the world around you was phenomenal, passionate. I was not a passionate person, not about anything; it was as if a gene in me had been deleted or failed to express. I was quite proud of this. In my view my detached view of humanity was a good thing, cleanly puncturing through all the mawkish bombast and self-interest. It took meeting you to make me see that by living constantly in my own head I was missing out. Your energy whooshed me up off my quiet little rock and showed me the sunset horizon. You loved beautiful things, Michelin-starred restaurants, expensive clothes, five-star ski chalets, like your boss Sanjay's that he let us use for free. Things I might previously have sneered at as being shallow and materialistic but was surprised at how much I enjoyed once I came 'crawling out of my own arse', as you put it.

Anyhow, it wasn't materialism just for the sake of it. The experiences brought us closer. Both of us loved to travel, even if I liked to seek out peaceful hidden gems and you preferred to have crowds around you. You had a huge circle of friends from all over, all as frenetic and high-achieving as you. But what I also liked about you was that, perhaps due to your having grown up in Ireland, you seemed more grounded than some of your more pompous, entitled colleagues. When Johnny Ryan moved to Hong Kong and you bought out his share of the flat I jumped at your offer to move in. We had some wonderful nights out and trips away, and during that time – you know this, Adam – I was the happiest I had ever been.

Inevitably, things change. Bosco, your other wingman, married Catherine, and they left London for Galway. And in the same month your dad had his stroke.

Thankfully, he recovered, but you were deflated. I hadn't seen you like that before. Pacing morosely, pondering your mortality. What was important. Family, old friends. In bulletins from Ireland 'the lads' were reporting that Ireland was a different place these days to what it had been in the late nineties. Nicer to live in, more going on. People had moved on, Bosco said. Everyone there was matching and hatching, forming new friendship groups around children and schools and GAA clubs. He and Catherine had moved back 'just in time'.

I remember the night, almost eighteen months ago, sitting under the heater on our balcony, Lambeth Bridge and the London Eye lit up like something out of a fairy tale. You, holding my hand, leaning forward in a supplicating way, as if you were afraid to ask this of me.

'I know it's a hick town, a village compared to here. But is there any chance – any chance at all – that you'd consider it?'

'Adam.' I was completely floored. 'I never thought you'd – I mean, wow. Dublin!'

'I never thought I would either. It's just crept up on me.'

'Adam – I'd like to support you. You know I would. I realize you want to be closer to your parents. But . . .'

'I know.'

'Apart from anything else' – my heart was sinking because it was already clear to me that even though the decision was ostensibly mine, whatever choice I made would alter the future of our relationship – 'it's taken me so long to slog up the Man-ways ladder. All that arse-licking. I'd have to start all over again.'

'But accountants can work anywhere, can't they? Someone with your experience would get something easily.'

Glittering boats drifted eastwards towards the Houses of Parliament. I said, 'I know no one in Dublin. No one at all.'

'You know my parents.'

'Okay, but . . .' I twirled my coffee spoon. 'What about Lexie?'

Lexie. Our precious, beautiful, life-changing little Lexie.

4

Lexie had been an unexpected pregnancy – well, as unexpected as one can be when you've been having sex most nights beside a picture window overlooking the Thames. Once we'd got over the shock I was surprised by how conservative you were about popping the question, super-keen to set a date. You've denied it, but I still strongly suspect your mum's influence. Breda, always looking me up and down when we flew to Dublin to visit, whispering ostentatiously to you when I wasn't quite out of the room.

I'm sorry. I'm being an arse. Your parents were always pleasant, if a little distant, the few times I had met them. Maybe she thought I was going to keep you in London away from her for ever. But if anything you sided with me rather than your mother – the opposite of most Irish men, I'm told. I sensed that you were embarrassed by her the time they came to London and I thought it would be a treat to take them to dinner at our local Michelin-starred restaurant. 'Very nice,' Breda had said faintly, prodding at the Tandoori scallops starter, hiding them under the cavolo nero when she thought I wasn't looking. You made a discreetly apologetic face at me, which of course I found flattering.

The silence from the phone when you broke the news to her about her impending grandchild. How we laughed when she and Jim stuttered out their congratulations and hung up. Their attitude was so fusty and old-fashioned. All the same, I found that I didn't mind. If you were rushing us into marriage because of Breda it made you seem family-oriented, which I liked. Seeing as my own family was altogether lacking in that regard.

'I never thought you'd be the maternal type,' my mother said, watching with her lips pinched together as I breastfed Lexie. *That's because you weren't*, I thought, but I didn't say it; I had no need; I just didn't care any more. Even if Lexie had been a surprise I loved her from the second I saw her. This astonished me, and still does. I had braced myself to think of her as a duty. I don't know if I told you this, but I even blurted out to the midwife when I was eight centimetres dilated, 'I hope to God I can love her!', and the midwife had looked taken aback. But when she was born and she came out, solemnly gazing around her with her wide, dark-bright eyes, it was as if everything I had ever cared about or thought of any value was swept away like trash and this glowing jewel unearthed. She was my life now. I was amazed by it, the sheer love I felt. Lexie was a good baby, a wonderful little baby. She slept through almost straight away, did everything she should. And so beautiful, so enchanting . . . well, anyhow. I could go on, and I know you feel the same.

In fact, that night on the balcony, I suspect you were just waiting for me to bring Lexie up so you could pounce with her as your Dublin trump card. 'It's Lex I'm thinking of,' you said. 'My parents are getting older. I'd like her to get to know them better, before it's too late.'

'But how would she cope with a move?' I asked.

'Oh God. Not this again!'

'Not what?'

'You keep on with this sensitive stuff. I don't get it. Lots of eight-year-olds hate loud noises. And being away from their parents. She's just a normal, loving little kid.'

'It's more than that.' I couldn't explain it. Mostly Lexie was sunny and placid but occasionally, out of the blue, she would become abruptly very emotional – deeply, inconsolably upset, shaking and crying – and it would be hard to understand from her what had caused it. When particularly stressed she stuttered.

Lately it was happening more often. I thought perhaps it was because you and I were working such long hours and we were on our third nanny in two years. She had started to drag her feet about going to school, even though the teacher reported that she seemed perfectly happy while there.

'See?' you'd said, but I wasn't convinced. The school had a high staff turnover and the teachers didn't seem to know the pupils very well. I had begun to research other schools. The expense of some of the better ones was eye-watering, but we could afford that. What bothered me was how far away they were, how much time Lexie would have to spend commuting on buses or Tubes with yet another new nanny as the old ones ticked the London box and moved on.

'She likes things being the same,' I said. 'Change makes her anxious. How would she handle a whole new country?'

You leaned forward, excited now, as if this, my main objection, was easily overcome. 'You were going to change her school anyway, weren't you? So, what's the difference? Irish schools are generally very good. The likelihood is we'd have an excellent school within walking distance.'

'But you'll be trying to get CareyComp off the ground. You'd have to commute between countries for a while. What if I was alone and got stuck late at work? Or Lexie was sick?'

'My mum would step in,' you said impatiently. 'Come on, Sara, what's with all the dithering? You're like me, you know you are. You like a challenge. You'd hate to live in the one place all your life, mouldering away. Anyway, you wouldn't be working in Dublin straight away, would you? You'd have to register there or whatever. Look for a job. So you'd be there to settle her in.'

'Yes, but –'

'You've been going on about not seeing enough of Lexie – well, now's your chance. Spend as much time with her as she needs. You'd never be able to do that here.'

I sipped my Nespresso. I needed time to think, to keep control of the conversation. I'd seen you like this at work, putting on the pressure, the hard sell, to nail a client. Once you got an idea in your head you were like a dog with a bone. My mother had never had anything good to say about Dublin. Crime, litter, dilapidation, derelict buildings, lots of pubs and swearing . . . From somewhere on the river a horn sounded, plaintive and low. The whole of London was there before me, reflected in the water. It was like being at the centre of the world.

Neutrally, I said, 'Let me think about it.'

Truth be told, I didn't at that point take you very seriously. You've always been a person for impulses, that pass again as quickly as they arrive. Often as soon as you achieve something you lose interest in it and move on to the next challenge. Best, I thought, to nod and smile, and this latest notion would soon be overtaken by the next one.

That night Lexie came to our bed again, crying quietly, winding her skinny arms and legs tightly around me like an octopus, even in her sleep. Something was troubling her and neither she nor I had any idea what it was.

If moving to Dublin was another one of your impulses, the itch was taking a while to scratch. A month later you were still going on about your ageing parents, the fantastic Irish schools, the super-great sense of community. I asked around. Talked to your Irish friends and to people at work. The consensus did seem to be that despite some excess tarmac and swearing, Ireland was a good place for children.

'Kids over there are more innocent, like,' said Deirdre from Cork, over cortados in the Manways cafeteria. 'Less pressure on them to grow up.'

I knew what she was referring to. That morning we'd had our latest bunch of teenagers on work experience. The boys interested in one thing and one thing only: how much money we made. The girls not even caring about that, shrugging, dead-eyed, perma-bored. It was probably just the Manways effect – a stint at a commercial accountancy firm would suck the soul out of any teen – but I compared these sophisticated, jaded children to Lexie, carefully lifting moths off the lampshade to release them from the balcony, weeping over a dead bird she had found in the park, and this glimpse of her future troubled me.

Well, something in London wasn't making her happy, so perhaps it was time for a change. A couple of times she had remarked that when she was grown up she wanted to have five children and a dog and live on an estate with lots of neighbours where everyone would know each other. It sounded like my idea of hell . . . but . . . central London was so very transient. Our block of flats was full of workaholics, the windows rarely lit until midnight or later. Or not at all, as many of the flats were empty year round, investments for owners who barely remembered they possessed them. There were no children for Lexie to play with. I had wondered if part of the reason she was unsettled was that she was lonely. It wasn't just your Irish friends who were emigrating. Several of my own work and university friends with young families had left London for villages with cricket clubs, high-speed broadband and the WI. I had no family, unless you counted my parents, who between them had minimal interest, and Steve, who was . . . Steve. True, Lexie would know no one in Dublin, but people said it was friendlier than London.

'People there are so genuine,' your Irish friends enthused, raving about their sheltered, happy childhoods. Of course most of them had fled from there the minute they'd turned eighteen.

These were all the things running through my mind when

over dinner one evening I said to you, 'All right. Let's do it. Let's give Dublin a try.'

'What?' You almost choked on a chickpea. 'Seriously?'

'A try,' I said firmly. 'Depending on how Lexie settles. *And* if Manways agrees to give me some leave.'

'Fuck.' You leaped from your chair. 'Wait'll my mum hears! She adores Lexie. We'll find somewhere close by. They can see each other every day.'

'Well. Hmm. Let's see about –'

'Thank you, Sara.' You came to me and wrapped your arms around me. I stood facing your neck, smelling the residue of your Tom Ford cologne and the faint tang of sweat from a crowded Tube journey. 'You won't regret this. I swear.'

When your mum phoned a few weeks later to say she'd found us a house on a nice local estate with good schools and transport, I thanked her and said we'd be there by August. A nice local estate. Lexie's dream, if not mine. Well, if it made Lexie happy. Perhaps, I thought, if she met some of the neighbouring children before school started it would smooth the transition for her. It would be easy, I imagined, to get to know people on a Dublin housing estate.

'Too easy, probably,' you said gloomily. 'Irish people are very nosy. You can't sneeze without everyone knowing your business.' Now that our moving date was approaching, it was, just as I had anticipated, you, not me, who was having last-minute cold feet about cash flow and living too close to your parents. But we were in it now and might as well see the year through.

The day arrived when we flew over and met Breda at the house. She came bustling out of number twenty-four, all beams and frosted lipstick and big, arms-wide hugs for you and Lexie. A more formal nod at me as we still didn't know each other very well. The house, midway along a gabled, yellow-brick terrace shaped like a Toblerone, was smaller than it had looked online. A streak of rust trailed down from a vent in the wall. A bent pink hula hoop was propped against a lamp post.

'Not quite Chelsea, is it?' you said, your hands hanging at your sides. 'I knew prices had gone up here, but is this seriously all we could get for our budget?'

Breda's face fell. 'Well, you know yourself. There's been a baby boom. Everyone wants a house with a garden. I was lucky to get this. I didn't like to pay any more, seeing as you'll be needing to keep up the London flat for your commute – and of course now that you'll be the sole earner . . .' A glance in my direction. Whether a pointed glance or not I couldn't tell.

'I like it,' I said firmly. The house was certainly small – just two bedrooms and, yes, a little bunker-like and unimaginative – but there was a big sunny common across the road with mature trees, some with rope swings attached. We were a twenty-minute walk from the sea and a forty-five-minute bus or car journey from Wicklow, which, according to TripAdvisor, was the 'garden of Ireland'. On first impressions, Dublin was not quite as bad as I had feared. On the common some boys were playing, kicking a ball across the grass. Lexie was staring at them, transfixed.

'Of course,' Breda was saying in the posh voice she put on sometimes. 'This isn't the kind of place *you're* used to, Adam. Very different, obviously, from where you were brought up. But once you've had a chance to settle . . . find somewhere more suitable . . .'

'It's hardly downtown Caracas, Mum,' you said perversely, looking as if you wished it was. You curled your lip at the trimmed box-hedges, the polished black stone at the estate entrance with 'Brookview' carved on it surrounded by geraniums.

I had been prepared to make the best of things for Lexie's sake and yours, but over the following fortnight, the more I got to know the area, the more I found that I genuinely did like it. While you were abroad Lexie and I fell into a pleasant rhythm together. I liked the way shop cashiers and mums with toddlers on the common – I learned to call it the Green – smiled at her, keen to offer advice about schools and places to visit. I liked how Lexie blossomed, enjoying spending so much time with me instead of with a nanny. How she could pootle for hours on the local beach, which smelled slightly of sewage but was scenic and full of rocks for climbing. We took the Southbound Dart towards Greystones and were astonished to emerge from a tunnel and find ourselves curving high above a wide blue bay that made us both gasp with pleasure. There was nothing like this in London.

I watched Lexie gaze, wide-eyed, out of our living-room window at the children on the Green, not yet confident enough to join them but perhaps imagining herself doing so at some point. I imagined along with her: all of them playing hopscotch, tag, duck-duck-goose. Popping in and out of each other's homes without having to take endless buses and Tubes, and my heart swelled with pleasure for her.

'Let's check out your new school,' I said to her one evening. One of the friendly toddler mums had told me where it was. It was coming up to eight and the sun was setting. I pointed the school out to her as we walked past. The playground, the statues, the warm red-brick walls, all glowing in the last of the light.

5

There'd been a delay on the District Line and now Zoë would be late. Grand Rounds started at seven and this morning it was her doing the presentation: Methaemoglobinaemia in Pregnancy. They'd all be sitting there, waiting, sipping lukewarm coffee from those tall plasticky flasks where you had to press the button down, and the drug rep who had sponsored the croissants and been there since six thirty setting up the laptop and PowerPoint screen would be trying to entertain everyone, anxiously wondering where she was.

Well, let them. She didn't care.

It was hard to stay motivated since Jeremy had abruptly dumped her.

'We're moving too fast' was how he'd put it. After three years.

The familiar dreary *ping* in her gut. Everyone thought she was so focused and proactive. She'd got her consultant post last year, aged only thirty-one, but triumphant as she'd been at the time, since Jeremy had ditched her it had felt like a hollow victory. And frankly, although she loved her job, becoming the boss had catastrophically affected her social life because now she was expected to keep a distance from the trainees and hang out with the other consultants, who were mostly in their forties and fifties. Couldn't even go to the Spotted Merkin after work any more.

Not that she wanted to, she supposed. She was past falling out of bars with directionless twenty-somethings, but it was one more avenue closed.

Jeremy had dumped her in March, six months ago. Since then, on the advice of friends, she had half-heartedly tried OLD but was finding it hard going. The dick-pics, the last-minute cancellations, the no-shows. Another one yesterday who'd seemed pleasant . . . she'd allowed herself to hope, but within five minutes . . . I mean, she wasn't super-choosy, she was willing to give people a chance, but they had to at least know what the word 'obstetrician' meant and how to pronounce it.

And that was without the married men posing as single, the serial killers . . .

The train lurched and got going. Zoë sighed. You couldn't even talk about it; that was half the trouble. Not properly. If your date stopped calling the day after you'd slept with him you had to laugh and say, 'At least I got a good shag out of it!' People expected this. They'd breathe heavily and say, 'You're *so* lucky! What *I'd* give to be free and single!' And you had to say, 'Oh God, yes, definitely!'

Well – she didn't enjoy it! *They* might, but she didn't. She'd only slept with that last one because he'd seemed so keen and after the obligatory three lunchtime dates followed by an evening at a 'non-mainstream' music venue it seemed like the logical next step. She was the one, not him, who had to worry about chlamydia and blood clots from the Pill and her biological clock running out. One-night stands had never done it for her. But oh no, if you said that, you were needy, neurotic, old-fashioned. God forbid you might be looking for something 'meaningful'. A *relationship*. Her mate Naomi, who was pansexual, was scathing. Just enjoy the bloody sex, she'd say. Don't be so patriarchal and heteronormative.

Ridiculous because your biology was your biology.

Zoë wanted to be married. With children. There – she'd said it. She wanted to get on with it, to stop having to fret about her ovarian reserve and move on to the myriad other things she would much prefer to focus on. Her proteomics Ph.D., the overhaul of her trust's Gynae Oncology services. Jeremy, that wanker, upping and leaving her like that had thrown a massive spanner in her schedule.

Anyway, biology aside, what was so wrong with wanting to get married? Wanting to share your life, to have someone looking out for you in this cold, pushy world? Why did you have to hide it, to pretend? Zoë did want it. Her *mother* wanted it. Zoë was the only one of the family left with no prospects. Her younger sister, heading for partnership in her Silver

Circle firm, was getting married next month. Zoë would be the oldest bridesmaid . . .

At Embankment she bought an almond latte and followed the signs for the Northern Line. It was still early, not yet peak rush hour. She found a seat and fought the urge to snooze. Since Jeremy had left, the energy had just . . . leached out of her. Not physically, but mentally. It wasn't just the fact of being dumped – and she had liked him, she had cared about him, so there was that. But even when the shock had eased and she was able to go about her day without wanting to throw up or hear 'their' song without feeling the urge to scream, there'd been all the other stuff. The having to move out and rent a poky flat in Pimlico while Jeremy carried on living in the concierge-serviced flat in Islington with his family money (property, apparently) though she was far brighter than he was and worked harder and contributed more to society but for far less pay. The simple but devastating loss of trust. The sense of the rug being pulled out.

'I haven't been sure for a year,' he'd said casually while she gasped in disbelief.

So, all the time they'd been holidaying together in Ibiza and Japan, all the times they'd talked about whether they should get married abroad, all those trendy nights out and cosy nights in, the night they'd been to the Mayor of Scaredy Cat Town, going through the fridge . . . all the times she had thought they were happy and secure, it had all been a lie. An illusion. It made the world feel less safe. Would she ever trust a man again? Would she even get the chance? She was nearly thirty-three – not old; not even halfway through. But here in London everything always had to be so current and fresh and new. Ads everywhere for Botox clinics and facelifts. Child-faced interns and student nurses crowding up behind her, their dewy cheeks as yet unmarked by the hours of Call and 3 a.m. crash sections . . . sometimes at work, surrounded by bright-eyed, wrinkle-free juniors, she felt about a hundred.

Obsessed. She was obsessed. She was sick of it. She was a cliché. She was a Disney princess past her prime, she was Bridget Jones fifty years on, she was Mrs Bennet from *Pride and* –

BEEEEP! A piercing shriek and a bellowed *Mind the doors!* Her stop! She grabbed her briefcase and shot from her seat. She was about to leap out on to the platform when she discovered that she was only holding one briefcase handle – a discovery which took place when the other half of the briefcase flopped open and the contents fell out all over the carriage. For fox's sake! Her stuff was everywhere, under legs and seats and wheelie-cases; she wouldn't make her stop now, she'd miss Grand Rounds, and being five minutes late was one thing, but not turning up at all – there'd be emails galore and official complaints. And, oh *fucking* hell – some of these were patients' notes she'd sneaked home illegally for an audit . . . if any of them went missing or some concerned busybody handed them in to the hospital . . . the GDPR . . . visions of GMC fitness-to-practise meetings swam before her eyes.

'Here.' A bulky shape in beige chinos was crouching beside her. 'Let me help.'

Quickly the shape began to scoop up papers. He dumped a pile of them out on to the platform. A breeze threatened to scatter the ones on top.

'You go out,' he told her. 'Put a foot on them and I'll pass you the rest.' Dazed, she obeyed.

He ducked in and out of the carriage, gathering sheets and notes, ignoring the doors that threatened to guillotine him. He went on handing her pages and charts and folders until everything was out.

'Thank you! Thank you!' She was stuffing them all into the briefcase, barely seeing him. Feet scuffled past as more passengers arrived, taking advantage of the few seconds' delay to speed up and sprint on board.

More beeping. The doors crashed together. The train whooped and screeched off into the tunnel. In the aftermath, in the beat of silence where her eardrums seemed to pop outwards, when she looked up, her knight in shining chinos was still there.

'This wasn't your stop,' she said. 'Was it?'

'Not to worry.' He shrugged. 'I'll hop on the next one in . . . er, let's see . . . one whole minute. Life will go on.' He grinned down at her. The platform was already filling up again.

'I'm so sorry!' Zoë climbed to her feet, hampered by her pencil skirt and heels. Firmly she screwed shut the catch on her briefcase. 'But equally – thank you so much. Well . . .' She gestured vaguely. 'I'd better . . .' Could she just leave? She did have her meeting.

'You're a medic.' The man nodded at the NEJM under her arm.

'Yes.' Surprised, she looked at him again. He was quite good-looking. Tall, fair-haired, well-built. Along with the chinos he wore hiking boots and a thick green fleece.

Abruptly she asked, 'Where are you from?'

'Ireland.' The tunnel began to roar. 'Well,' he said. 'This is me. Better let you go and save some lives.'

'Okay. Thanks so much again.' He definitely was attractive. Not obscenely so – not the sort to spend hours in the gym or in front of a mirror – but well north of average. His hands were in his pockets so she couldn't see if there was a ring. Dear Lord, there she went again. It was exhausting, it really bloody was. 'I'm very grateful,' she said. 'I'd have been in the . . . in some difficulty if some of this stuff had been lost.'

'No problem at all. Glad I could help.'

The way he stood there. So relaxed and at ease. She found she was smiling at him. Making way too much eye contact in fact, but he didn't seem to mind; he was doing it right back at her. Oh, for goodness' sake. The chances were she'd never see him again. What did she have to lose?

'Odd question,' she said, 'but if you're new here and you'd like some-one to show you around . . . I mean, if you fancy a drink sometime . . .'

'What?' He looked surprised.

'Just a suggestion.' There hadn't been any way to ask that without sounding forward. Of course he'd have a girlfriend. Or boyfriend. Prob-ably boyfriend: he really was very nice-looking. Well, she'd tried. And now could put a line under it and get on with her day without having to waste it on yet more tiresome what-ifs.

'Right,' she said. 'I'll just –'

'Wait!' Smiling now, he was rummaging in his pockets. He came up with a pen and what looked like a crumpled-up shop receipt. As the rumbling in the tunnel grew louder he smoothed it out quickly, bent, and scribbled on it, using his knee as a desk. 'Here,' he said, straightening again. 'My number. Or if you'd prefer, text me your number and I'll call you.'

He was holding the receipt out towards her. With his left hand. No ring.

She took it. A mobile number followed by a name.

'Great' – she re-checked the name – 'Paul. I'll send you my number.'

'Fantastic . . . and, er . . . ?'

'Zoë,' she shouted, because by then the train had reached the platform. Her elbows bumped and jerked as people pushed past her towards the doors.

'Zoë! Okay!' A quick salute. 'Talk soon, Zoë.'

He stepped on to the train and looked back. His smiling grey eyes met hers and her insides sucked together. Then the doors shut and with the usual dramatic hissing and screeching the train was gone, busily clattering into the tunnel. She stared after it, the breeze lifting the ends of her hair, like a girl in a war film. The scrap of paper with his number on it tingled in her fingers. Had that just happened? He had seemed so normal. Just two normal human beings, meeting and connecting. Sometimes you forgot that this was how it happened.

6

As you know, one of my main concerns about moving to Dublin had been how Lexie would take to a new school. Especially given the issues she'd been having in London. To add to my worries, we'd had no choice about where to send her. Your mum had been right about the baby boom. All the other schools were full and St Catherine's National School, being in our parish, was the only one obliged to take us in. Accustomed to obsessing over Ofsted reports and league tables, I fretted about what we'd been landed with, but early impressions were reassuring. I liked the quaint red-brick buildings, the green-clad, well-behaved pupils, the statue of Mary, blue-gowned and serene, holding her hands out towards the children. Single-sex, which neither of us had a problem with.

It was a small school though, just two buildings linked by a prefab tunnel which unfortunately took up quite a lot of the playground. Due to the lack of space there were a lot of rules: no running, no balls, no chasing, which must have been frustrating for the younger children. Extracurriculars were non-existent. Difficult not to compare it with Lexie's old school, Caldwell Manor, with its tennis courts, hockey and soccer pitches, music rooms and dance studio. But I swatted the comparison away. Caldwell had been a hothouse, toddlers doing Kumon maths, six-year-olds aiming for the Olympics or a seat in Parliament. This cosy, down-to-earth school with its Let Children Be Children ethos would be good, I thought, for our shyer, more sensitive child.

Hats off to her, Lexie gave things her best shot. Remember

how she was first out of bed every morning even before the alarm went off, to pack her melon-patterned lunchbox and her panda pencil-sharpener. She liked her uniform and her teacher and her classroom.

A few girls were mentioned regularly. Polly Mayhew was a name we heard a lot. Polly Mayhew could hoot through her thumbs; Polly Mayhew could do both types of splits; Polly Mayhew had a glittery see-through backpack; that sort of thing.

'There's Polly,' Lexie said one morning, pointing.

Interested to see this paragon, I followed the direction of her finger and saw an attractive blonde child in a blue puffy gilet laughing with some other girls. 'And Tabitha. And Mabel. And Sadbh.' Lexie watched them wistfully. 'They're all best friends together.'

'You'll get to know them. It'll take time.'

But even for my shy Lexie, things seemed to be taking longer than I would have expected. By the end of October I noticed that she was still hanging back alone in the playground while the other girls played together in large, shrieking groups.

'They go to each other's houses on Fridays,' Lexie said. 'The mums are all friends with each other and arrange it.'

The mums . . . okay. I hadn't had a chance to get to know the other parents well yet. I'd had unpacking and paperwork to do, and although I did smile and say hi to whoever was nearby, I'd been too preoccupied with plumbing issues and setting up bank accounts to hang about long enough to see the same person more than once. Now, looking at Lexie's hopeful little face, I acknowledged that I'd been neglecting the situation and would have to put myself out there a bit more.

I began to pay more attention to the parents. There was a handful of fathers and childminders, but the vast majority doing the school run appeared to be mothers. Lexie pointed them out, matching them up with their daughters: Tabitha with the pale green jacket, Sadbh with the strawberry-blonde curls, Mabel with the trainers that lit up.

Oh, the dreaded small talk! Is there anyone who doesn't find it excruciating? Still, for Lexie's sake, it had to be done. 'Morning,' I said, smilingly walking up to join Mabel's (or Amelie's or Ava's) mother instead of scarpering as soon as the leenas went in. 'I'm Sara. My daughter has just started in Amelie's (or Ava's or Mabel's) class.'

Most of them were perfectly pleasant. 'Oh, you're from England? Which part? Lovely.' Then their gazes would drift. 'Karen – sorry, Sara – *Karen!* Have you heard? Denise is bringing the buns on Friday!' They weren't excluding me intentionally. It was just that they had made their friends already. Put the effort in during the Reception years, painstakingly chipping away at the ice, finally breaking through to the warm sea of effortless conversation. Now here I was, hauling them out again to the frozen floes of banality.

In fact, as time went on, standing listening to the conversations around me, I began to realize that many of them knew each other not just from their children being at school together but from way before that.

'Yep,' you confirmed. 'You'll find that quite a few of them went to school at St Catherine's themselves. And then married men from the boys' school down the road. You'd wonder what the point is in half of them being educated at all if their only goal in life is to produce more pupils to re-enter the vortex.'

Dublin being a capital city, this hadn't occurred to me. Certainly, I had expected it to be less transient than central London, but Dublin – or this part of it, anyway – seemed more like some Puddle-on-the-Marsh hamlet where the locals had lived since the Domesday Book and were suspicious of newcomers. All those misty-eyed tales your friends had told me about the wonderful Irish sense of community had, I realized, helped to build up a fantasy in my head that this would be a place where everyone helped each other, where everyone was magically embraced and included. Laugh if you like, though I think 'laughter' at this point would be like the part in a horror film where the tinkly music suddenly changes key. But anyhow, that's what I had naïvely thought. Here, however, just as with any other community, making friends was going to take time and perseverance.

One afternoon Lexie and I were walking home through our estate when she hissed at me, 'There's Polly!'

A hundred metres or so ahead of us was the blonde child in the blue gilet, accompanied by an older girl and a woman who looked to be Filipino. They were walking up the avenue between the cherry trees.

'She lives up there,' Lexie said. 'At the top of the hill.'

'Not far from us then.'

'And they've got a DOG!'

'Lucky Polly!'

A couple of mornings later, walking to school, Lexie grabbed my sleeve and hissed again, 'There's Polly's mum!'

At the St Catherine's gates a woman in a mint-coloured rain-coat and white baseball cap was shielding her eyes against the drizzle as Polly ran into the playground. It was November now, and the glorious weather had turned.

Lexie pressed up against me, whispering into my ear. 'Will you talk to her? Ask if Polly could come over? Since they live near?'

'Sure. Okay.' It would be something more to say than 'Rainy today, isn't it?'

It was only as I came nearer to the woman that I recognized her. The haughty expression, the too-dark eyebrows . . . it was the coffee woman from Lexie's first day! I faltered, then made myself continue. Chances were, she wouldn't even remember.

If she did, I would simply apologize again and enquire as to whether she'd got the stain out.

'Hi there!' I said as I reached her.

The woman turned, her coat rustling. Rain dripped from the brim of her baseball cap. Close up, she was the same age as me or a couple of years older. Her eyes were pale blue and very round, like marbles.

Grace! I thought. A tremendous flash of heat swept over me. It *is* her! Grace Gillespie's daughter is in Lexie's class! Involuntarily, I stepped back. The heat intensified, spreading up my neck and into my face. The woman was frowning, her lips moving, though I could hear nothing through the roaring in my ears. 'Hello?' her mouth seemed to be saying. 'HELLO?'

Not her! The heat and roaring receded. It wasn't Grace. It was just the eyes that were the same – almost identical, in fact, but everything else was different. This woman's hair was blonder and straighter. She was thinner, with thinner lips. She was not Grace Gillespie, who lived in a different country, hundreds of miles away. She was just a normal Irish mum, slightly harried by the rain, waving her child off to school.

My hearing came popping back.

Weakly, recovering, I said, 'I hear our daughters are in the same class.'

'Oh?' She pronounced it *Ew?*

'Yes. We've just moved here. I'm Sara.'

'Vanessa. Pleased to meet you.' Her voice was soft and sweet and slightly squeaky, more like a child's than an adult's. If she recognized me from that first morning, she gave no sign. Encouraged, I soldiered on. 'I've heard Lexie, my daughter, mention Polly a couple of times. I think we might be neighbours. I've seen Polly walk home near our road.'

'Oh, you're in Brookview too? Which part?'

'Halfway up, near the green. Brookview Terrace.'

'Ah.'

'I wondered if Polly might like to come over to play with Lexie sometime? Since they live so close to each other.'

'That would be super.' Vanessa was looking towards a group of women across the road. 'Sorry – I don't mean to be rude, but I actually just need to catch these people . . .'

'Of course! Lovely to meet you, Vanessa.'

'You too,' she called, clutching her baseball cap and hurrying across the road.

'Did you ask her?' Lexie was waiting for me at the gate.

'I didn't have a chance. But I will next time.'

Not long after that, the three of us went to Sunday lunch at your parents' house. It was the first time since we'd moved here. Your mum had gone to a great deal of trouble. Crystal-cut wine glasses, gilt-edged plates, linen napkins, all set out in the good front room with the pelmeted curtains and the thick cream carpet, which I prayed Lexie wouldn't drop gravy on.

While your dad mixed me a gin and Schweppes I studied the semicircle of photos on the sideboard. You, aged eight, freckly and sanctimonious in your First Holy Communion outfit: brown shorts and waistcoat with a white rosette. You and your brother in helmets and salopettes, arms around each other, against a backdrop of snowy peaks. You in a black gown and tasselled hat holding your commerce degree scroll, Breda beside you, radiant in royal blue: *I couldn't have a better son if I'd knitted him myself.* Our wedding, the two of us smiling broadly, me lifting a hand to keep my hair out of my eyes, Lexie barely visible under my long cream dress.

'*Slainte!*' Breda beamed, raising her G&T. Ice cubes rattled. 'To Adam! Finally coming back home!'

What age is she, your mum? Seventy-one? -Two? She could pass for ten years younger, trim and fit in her pink ribbed sweater. Every time I see her a vision springs to mind, of swirly-patterned brown carpets, glass cases filled with golf trophies and a large, printed notice: 'Members must NOT Remove Towels from the Changing Room!'

'And what have you been up to, Sara?' Breda asked. 'While Lexie's at school? Now that you're a lady of leisure?'

'Well' – I took a sip of my drink – 'we've had some issues with the plumbing. And I've had a lot of admin to do. But I've done some exploring too. It's wonderful to be so close to the sea. Yesterday I swam at Seapoint.'

'Lovely!' She was trying her best to look interested, but her neck bulged as she stifled a yawn.

'Oh.' She swivelled back to you as soon as I stopped talking. 'Adam. I meant to tell you. Cathy Morley got engaged!'

'Who?'

'You know. The Morleys. They used to have that house at the top of our road. The one the Finnertys bought when John Hennessy died.'

'. . . Okay . . .'

'Yes, marrying a barrister. Very bright, I believe. One of the Kellys from Carrickmines. The dad owned three restaurants but lost them in all the lockdowns. Very sad. Of course, you know he –' She lowered her voice and mimed raising a glass to her lips.

'Mmmm.' You were hungry and your lips were thin. Despite your working flat out, CareyComp was still very slow to get off the ground. When you weren't travelling you were holed up in our bedroom, tap-tapping away on your laptop or having agitated conversations on your phone. We were beginning to worry about finances. Dublin was more expensive even than you had expected and, with me not earning, and you minimally, our savings were haemorrhaging faster than either of us had anticipated. That was the week you had reluctantly taken on the lodger in the Vauxhall flat, so at least a mini tourniquet had been applied there. Even at the best of times I'd noticed how you could be irritated by your mum, by the way she persisted in seeing you as the teenager you had been twenty years ago instead of the person you were now.

'She thinks I've never left Stillorgan,' you grumbled. 'How the hell am I meant to know who all these people she keeps talking about are?'

You perked up when the food was served. Roast beef with three different types of potato.

'His favourite,' Breda mouthed at me over the scream of the electric carving knife.

Her cooking was superb and she was a solicitous host, constantly popping out of her seat to offer food or top up glasses. At times her behaviour bordered on the tense.

'But it's from Avoca,' she said, staring, when I declined the apple crumble.

'It looks delicious. But I couldn't manage any more. Really.'

'That must be why you're so thin.'

'*Mum!* She said no!'

Breda looked affronted but put the crumble back on the sideboard.

'Now,' she said. 'I've spoken to Elaine Montrose. She's captain this year, and Declan's going to write your proposal letter.'

'I don't play golf.'

'Well, you should. It's very good for connections. Only last week Declan played twelve holes with Tony Merriman.'

'Golf with politicians?' Your eyebrows rose. 'Is that how business is still done in Ireland?'

Your tone was so scathing that she was silenced. After a moment she turned to Lexie. 'How's school going, pet?'

'Okay.'

'How's the Gaeilge going? *Cailín maith? Cad is ainm duit?* No?'

'It's early days,' I said, seeing Lexie's expression grow anxious.

'Of course, of course. Plenty of time. Your dad was wonderful at languages. Remember all those prizes you won, Adam? That school was lucky to have you. I always said to your father, it's *them* who should be paying *us*! And of course' – nodding significantly at me – 'Adam was on the team the year they won the Senior Cup!'

'The . . .'

'The Leinster. Schools. Senior. Cup?'

'Oh. Wow. I haven't heard of that, but it sounds fantastic.'

'You mean Adam never told you?'

'Mum.' You put your fork down. 'Seriously. It was over twenty years ago.'

'What?' She seemed startled and confused, as if trying to calculate in her head. I looked at Lexie and wondered if I would feel that way about her one day. If all my memories of her would stay as fresh and close and precious as they were now. Typically, she had dripped apple sauce all over her T-shirt. I passed her a napkin and motioned at her to wipe it off.

'. . . think she'd remember.' Breda was hissing to Jim at the other end of the table.

'I wouldn't take it personally, love. Schools rugby isn't as big a thing over there.'

Your phone vibrated, crawling towards the Royal Doulton carrot bowl. 'Sorry, everyone.' Tersely you scooped it up and pushed back your chair. 'I need to take this.'

There was silence after you left. Smiling, I said to Breda, 'You must have been very proud of Adam. Winning the Leinster Cup.'

'It was a significant achievement,' she said stiffly. 'Several of those players went on to play for Ireland.'

'That's impressive! I'm sure Adam never told me. He always underplays everything.'

She dabbed at her lips, mollified. 'He also won the overall school trophy for Player of the Year.'

'I'm sure Lexie would adore to see that.'

She rose, folding her napkin. 'All right.'

'Oh no – I didn't mean right now. You haven't finished –'

'No, no. You stay there. I'll see if I can find it.'

She headed for the door. You were still outside somewhere on your phone. At the top of the table your dad went on eating, rhythmically raising and lowering his fork, wholly focused on his food. Lexie and I shrugged at each other and grinned.

From the top of the stairs Breda called. '*Jim!*'

'Oh dear.' He hadn't finished, but he climbed to his feet, rotating his belly out from under the table.

'Oh, no. Please –'

'No point in arguing,' he said, good-naturedly. 'Herself has spoken.'

You passed him in the doorway on your way back in. 'For God's sake. What now?'

'It's like Musical Chairs here,' Lexie giggled. From the ceiling came thumps and bangs. 'Not that one!' Your mum's voice floated down through the rafters. 'Try over here!'

Moments later, she reappeared in the doorway.

'Found it,' she said breathlessly. 'It was in the guest room. Under the spare towels. Anyway. Here we are!'

Her arms trembled under the weight of a crystal plate at least twenty-five inches in diameter. Two muscular, shorts-clad men were carved into the centre along with a rugby ball etched with names and dates.

'Gosh.' I didn't know what to say. 'That's incredible.'

'Take it with you,' she beamed. 'Display it in your sitting room!'

'Mum – no! Look at her face! She thinks it's hideous. Anyway, where would we put it? We haven't got space for half our stuff in that bloody box we're . . . Sorry. Sorry, Mum! I'm being a dick. I'm shattered. Work's been a bloody nightmare.'

'Oh, Adam.' Breda put the plate down and hurried around the table. 'I *completely* understand. I know how hard you work. And trying to support a family on top of everything . . . Sit! Sit down! Relax. There's fresh coffee on. Sara, you'll have a cup.'

Behind her back you shook your head vigorously and pointed at your watch. I felt caught. The coffee did smell good. More to the point, if we walked out now, your elderly parents would be left to clear all the lunch stuff from the dining room by themselves and cart it down the hall to the kitchen. You frowned, poking again at your watch. Your eyes looked strained and hollowed. I guessed that the phone call must have been more bad news. Lexie, too, looked worn-out. School in the morning.

'I'm so sorry,' I said to Breda. 'Next time. But thank you for a really lovely afternoon. And delicious food.'

'Sorry, Mum.' Off the hook, you strode to envelop her in a hearty hug. 'Love to stay longer, but you heard the old ball and chain.'

Breda's face fell as she glanced towards me.

While you and Jim were saying goodbye, Breda approached me carrying what appeared to be an enormous pile of towels. 'I've wrapped this up for you.'

'What?'

She said in an angry whisper, 'You can't have everything your way, you know. He has a right to display it. It's his house too.'

7

Lexie, I was discovering, was more than just a bit tense about her Gaeilge. In fact, she seemed highly stressed by it.

'I can't do this,' she said at the kitchen table, her sleeve in her mouth.

'Don't eat your uniform. Come on. Let's do this. *Gúna* is the Irish for . . .'

The Irish language was bizarre, random extra letters and prefixes all over the place, but I found I was quite enjoying learning it, following the goings-on of Siofra *agus* Seán as they played a hurling match, bought tickets for a music concert and went to the beach for a picnic. It was our language, completely unlike any other, our ancient secret code, survivor of years of suppression, older than any Magna Carta or Roman coin.

Lexie, her hair in her mouth, put her head on the table.

'Stop *fidgeting.*'

We'd been at the table for an hour, and she kept writhing and scratching, lying sideways on her chair, anything instead of getting on with her homework. Yes, the language was new to her, but she seemed to be making much more of a meal of it than was warranted, not even trying to give it a chance.

'Lex,' you called. 'Forget that crap. Come on in and watch *The Simpsons.*'

Lexie glanced at me. I chose not to contradict you in front of her.

'Go on,' I told her. 'It's nearly bedtime.'

She hopped off her chair. Tidying away her books, I heard

the two of you next door, 'You're much too pretty to learn Irish,' and Lexie giggling in response.

But later in bed she said glumly, 'I wish it was Friday. And I didn't have school tomorrow.'

'Is it the Irish? Daddy's right. I was being too strict. You don't have to learn it if you don't want to.'

But she kept on pulling and picking at her duvet. 'I wish I didn't have school. I'm stupid.'

'No, you're not. Why would you think that?'

She didn't answer. She looked pale. Maybe she was coming down with something. Her forehead, though, felt cool. I read her a chapter of Hetty Feather and by the time I switched off her lamp she seemed more settled.

Downstairs I said, 'Lexie seems a bit uptight about school. I hope everything's okay.'

'Aren't you being a bit OTT about the Irish? She's just started here. Give her a chance.'

I left it there. You had enough on your plate. Anyhow, I didn't know how to explain it. It wasn't the Irish itself that was the problem. It was the fact that she seemed so stressed out by a couple of words which she should have known didn't matter as she was new to them and which tonight hadn't even been that difficult.

The following morning, I went up to Ms Brennan on the steps.

'Do you mind if I have a word?'

'Well, if you're –'

'I'll be quick. I know you're busy. I just wanted to check how Lexie is getting on.'

'Oh.' Her flustered expression relaxed slightly. 'Very well. A lovely child. So polite and helpful.'

'She seems rather anxious about her Irish.'

'Well, we haven't been putting pressure on her. She's never learned it before so it's bound to take a while.'

'Yes, of course. And her other subjects are okay?'

'Yes. *Well.*' A little hip-hop, side-to-side head motion. 'Possibly a tiny bit behind in some things, but –'

'Really?'

'Yes, but then again, she's ahead in others. So it's only what you'd expect. Different schools do things at different paces. She's very diligent so I'm sure she'll catch up.'

'That's good to hear.'

'Yes. I mean, while you're at it, you could encourage her to pay just a *little* more attention in class? She can be quite fidgety at times. Goes off into her own world. But apart from that she's doing very well.'

'I'll tell her that. Thank you.'

Later, walking home, I passed the message on to Lexie. 'I met Ms Brennan today and she told me you're doing really well. The only thing she said was, if you could try to focus a bit more during class. Not fidget so much – remember, we spoke about –'

I turned. Lexie had fallen behind. She had stopped walking and was chewing her sleeve again. Such a bad habit. I went to her and gently removed her hand. Two large holes in the cuff. We'd had that in London too.

Schoolwork excluded, I'd been wondering if the trouble might be with friendships. I knew she missed Lilah and Jasmine, her two besties since her Manways creche days, but even though we'd been in Dublin for nearly three months now there was no sign of their being replaced. And it wasn't that she didn't want to. Quite the opposite. I saw the yearning in her eyes as she watched the other children in the playground. Despite her shyness, friendships were important to Lexie. She was far more sociable than I. But something wasn't clicking for her. Possibly, I thought, it was her air of desperation that was putting people off.

Obviously, you and I were biased, but both of us thought that if Lexie had been a child in our class at school we would have liked her. She wasn't the coolest kid on the block or the life and soul of the party, but she was emotionally intelligent, perceptive and kind, genuinely interested in other people. She didn't whine or tell tales. When relaxed, she could be merry and very funny. She was shy, but not pathologically so; she might be slow to make the first move but would respond readily to another child who did. So then, what was the problem? Yes, there was that Domesday Book vibe from some of the mums – but surely that shouldn't be a factor for an eight-year-old?

I tried talking to her about it. 'What games do you play at breaktime?'

She shrugged. 'A lot of the times the girls just sit and talk.'

'About what?'

She shrugged again.

'About maths? The government?'

'No!' She giggled.

'Then what?'

She sucked her hair. 'They talk very quickly,' she said. 'A lot of the time I don't understand what they're saying.'

'Yes, Irish people do tend to speak –'

She interrupted me. 'There's Polly!' Across the Green, Vanessa, wearing a sleeveless long cream coat and sunglasses, was walking along, talking into her phone. Behind her, Polly, looking bored, snapped leaves off hedges.

'Polly,' Lexie called. Then immediately shrank against me as if she couldn't believe what she had just done. But she went on staring at Polly with an undisguised adoration that made me hold my breath for her. How would the uber-cool Polly recip-rocate? Lexie was youngish for her age; Polly looked to be nine going on sixteen. The hero-worship, I was pretty sure, was entirely on one side.

Polly turned. 'Hey!' She grinned. 'Lexie!'

Lexie's face lit up. At once she left me and flew across the grass, looking happier than I'd seen her for quite a while. Strolling after her as she and Polly greeted each other, it occurred to me that she was one of those people who does better in smaller groups.

Vanessa ended her call and looked about her, rather irritably. I waved, pointing to the girls on the Green. She stopped and waited, her bob sitting just so to her chin. Her trainers were toothpaste-white. I had just been for a windy walk on the beach and felt conscious of my parka – that you hate, I know – and my battered hiking boots and my hair falling messily out of its bun.

Polly called as I reached them, 'Can Lexie come and play?'

Lexie gasped and swung to me. 'Mum! Please!'

I grinned at Vanessa. 'I don't mind if you don't. Or Polly could come to us, if that's better? We're just down that way.'

'I'm sorry.' Vanessa seemed confused. 'Have we met?'

'Yes. I'm Sara. Lexie is in Polly's class. We spoke at the school the other day.'

'Oh, yes, of course. I'm so sorry. I'm terribly bad at faces.'

We were all standing together now in a group, Lexie looking from face to face, her eyes shining with pleasure.

'Polly is very welcome to come and play,' I said.

'You're very kind, and that would have been lovely. But unfortunately, Polly, you've got homework to do.'

'Aww.'

'What about Friday?' I suggested.

More gasps. The girls danced about, clasping their hands. 'Pleasepleaseplease.'

'I'll just need to check,' Vanessa said. 'I think Polly *may* have a dental appointment.'

'Really? Do I?'

'It hasn't been confirmed yet. Can I let you know – um . . .'

'Sara. Of course. Do you need my number?'

'Did Erica not add you to the class WhatsApp?'

'Yes, she did.'

'Super. I'll find you there.' Vanessa smiled. She was being perfectly pleasant but she had just the teensiest air of being in a hurry so I called Lexie off the Green.

'Aww. Five more minutes. Polly's found a centipede.'

'We need to go now. But hopefully you'll see Polly on Friday.'

We parted company with lots of *Very kind*s and *I'll let you know*s, but by Thursday evening I still hadn't heard anything. I sent Vanessa a reminder – *Tomorrow still ok for Polly to come over? Sara* – but heard nothing in return, even though I could see from the blue double tick that my message had been read.

On Friday afternoon we saw Polly leaving the school with a group of other girls. 'She's going to Amelie's.' Lexie watched, disappointed, as the girls piled into a huge shiny black seven-seater that looked like a hearse.

'Her mum must have forgotten,' I said. Vanessa did strike me as the flaky type. 'Never mind. Another time.'

'Next Friday? Will you ask her?'

'If I see her.'

'But Polly'll get booked up. She's really popular. You have to get in early.'

Now she was making *me* anxious. I pushed it down. 'Come on. Let's stop at Spoon for a bun.'

I didn't see Vanessa again for a while. Usually it was their child-minder who did the school run, but she had a timid demeanour and something told me she wasn't in a position to make these kinds of decisions. I had Vanessa's phone number, but it seemed she didn't get around to responding to messages. I decided to simply wait until we bumped into each other, which was bound to happen soon. Sure enough, the following week,

I saw her waiting at a traffic light in her gleaming white SUV with her window open. I waved, but the light changed and she accelerated off without responding. Didn't see me, I thought.

A couple of days later I was in the shopping centre when a woman in a mint raincoat came zipping past. Vanessa! Again, I lifted a hand to greet her, but again she looked through me and disappeared into a nail bar. She must have had something on her mind. Or else she really was incredibly bad with faces.

Half an hour later, however, heading towards SuperValu, I spotted her again, approaching from the opposite side. We reached the doors at almost the same moment. I stopped and, just in case she was the shy type, gave a friendly smile. 'Hey! Vanessa!'

'Sara,' I added firmly in case her eyesight was the problem and she didn't have her contacts in. 'From the school. Lexie's mum.'

'Of course! Hellew.' I don't know what might have happened next, but just then her phone, always in her hand, began to ring.

We both looked at it. Vanessa made an apologetic little face. 'Mind if I –'

'No, no, please. Go ahead.'

She was already pressing the button. 'Hello? Oh, *hiii*!'

I waited. It seemed rude to walk off just as we'd been in the middle of greeting each other, but on the other hand I could hardly stand there eavesdropping for the entire conversation.

'Oh my God, that's *hilarious*! Did you hear what she said at Pilates?'

I began to edge towards the doors. Still not getting it. Still expecting some sign, some regretful little moue: *Sorry! Be with you in a second!* But when I glanced over my shoulder not only was there no rueful catching of the eye but she had turned and walked off altogether, still talking, her mint coat vanishing down the escalator.

I went around the aisles, picking out items. Tomatoes, rice, washing powder. Through my discomfiture a picture was slowly dawning. *A . . . dental appointment. Do I?* The blue ticks and the no reply. The persistent prosopagnosia. And now, finally, the step-up in rebuff as, obviously, I was too dim or socially clueless to take the hint. My face burned as I took down a bottle of shampoo. It had taken me a while, but finally I'd got there.

Lexie, unfortunately, wouldn't let it go. You were in London so it was just her and me for the weekend. She was bored and kept pestering me about Polly.

'Did you see her mum? Can you call her?'

'No answer,' I lied. 'I think her phone might be broken.'

'Can we call to her house? She lives just up the hill.'

'We've arranged to visit Nanna,' I improvised.

As luck would have it, as we were walking down the hill to the bus Vanessa and Polly hove into view, approaching from the Green. I waved. Vanessa gave a polite little nod. Then, lest there be any lingering misapprehension that I was being over-sensitive, she slowed, touching Polly's elbow to keep her back, so that Lexie and I would be obliged to out-pace them. It was definitely not my imagination.

'Look!' Lexie hauled on my arm. 'There she is! Can we walk with them? *Please?*'

I made some excuse about not wanting to miss the bus and kept going.

Lexie was sullen with me for the rest of the day. I knew she blamed me for keeping her and Polly apart, but how could I tell her the real reason – *Polly might be nice but her mother is a rude cow* – in case she repeated it at school? My initial embarrassment was replaced by irritation at Vanessa for putting me in this position. What was her problem, anyway? Polly and Lexie liked each other. They'd been delighted to see each other on the Green. Why be

68

so obstructive? Because we were foreigners? Because our house was too small? Or perhaps Vanessa simply didn't need any more friends, didn't want to draw a newbie on herself that she mightn't be able to shake off – okay, great, understandable, but what about her daughter? What if *she* wanted to make a new friend? Well, it was going to be very awkward, us living so close and passing each other all the time. And how exhausting for Vanessa to have to keep her head down every time she went to SuperValu.

Whatever; I wasn't going to get any answers, so we'd have to move on. There were twenty-three other girls in Lexie's class; there had to be someone more normal she could connect with. The trouble was, the brief, superficial school-gate conversations I'd been engaging in still weren't getting me anywhere. There were only so many times I could say 'I love your daughter's trainers' or 'Do you live nearby?' to people I saw one day then didn't see again for three weeks. The forcedness of it made me sound boring and insincere. What did people SAY? Why was it so hard? At work in London there were always a thousand things to discuss, but here the most banal utterings seemed to lurch from my mouth and plop to their deaths on the tarmac.

Despite my concerns, I rarely saw Vanessa. Her childminder often did the school runs so it was only occasionally that I spotted the mint raincoat under the murky sky as she joined her group of friends in their spot in the middle of the playground. But when she did, they all talked and laughed easily, their faces turned to Vanessa like flowers to the sun. None of them seemed to have a problem with her, nor she with them. Was I the problem? Was I doing something, or failing to do something, that made them not want to associate with Lexie or me? Standing on the edge of the effortlessly chattering groups, I had the sinking feeling that I was letting Lexie down.

*

69

A few days later a message appeared on the third-class parents WhatsApp group.

Ladies!!! Volunteers needed to clear out the storeroom to make way for the new Sensory Room. Reminder: ALL PARENTS are requested to take turns to help out at school events during the year!!!!!! Thanks. Erica.

I signed up at once. In my experience, the best way to get a conversation going was when everyone was busy doing something.

Five mothers, including me, showed up for the clear-out. One of them was the pale woman, Edel, whom I'd met on the first day. I'd seen her about a few times since, but we hadn't been close enough to speak and she never seemed to catch my eye. Yet another person who had given me the brush-off – however, in her case, I suspected that the motive might be different. She was always in her long black coat, fully zipped up, looking vaguely disorientated, as if she had just landed from a different dimension. I wondered if she was depressed. Another woman, tall and elegant in a pale grey trouser suit, was new to Dublin too. She had two children – one, Mia, in Lexie's class – and had just moved here from Kilkenny. She introduced herself as Eva.

Dervla, of the maroon hoodie and auburn ponytail, was in charge. She collected the keys from the secretary's office and led us all down the Junior Corridor to the storage room.

'Now. What we have to do is put all useable books into these red boxes, and all broken items and rubbish in these plastic bags for recycling. Here are the plastic bags and here are the boxes. Whatever you do, do NOT mix up good books with damaged ones.'

The room was filled with years' worth of junk. Rusty chairs stacked in corners, dusty books crammed on to sagging shelves, loose pages marked with footprints strewn all over the floor. Various indeterminate plastic and electrical items lay randomly about.

'Where do we put these?' Edel asked, looking all around her. 'Here?'

'No. NOT there.' Dervla held her head. 'Okay. I'll go through this again. This is important, guys, so listen up. The USE-ABLE books go in the RED boxes ONLY.'

'Oh dear,' murmured Luisa, the fourth mother, beside me. She and I had ended up working as a pair, owing to the fact that we worked at a similar pace. She passed useable books to me; I scooped broken items and rubbish back to her. She had long dark hair and a rock-chick style of dressing, artier than was typical at St Catherine's: leather jeggings, sleeveless black T-shirt with a skull on the front, huge, dangly dreamcatcher earrings. I kept wincing in case one of them caught on a rusty chair leg and ripped her ear off. She said little but had a sort of quirky twist to her mouth; whether because she was privately amused by something, or because that was just the way her face was, I couldn't tell.

Now she grinned over at me. 'So, who is your child?'

'Lexie. We're new here. Who's yours?'

'I have Alejandra. She's my mad girl.'

'I don't think I've seen you around.' I liked her casual, don't-give-a-shit attitude.

'No. I never see *anyone*. I'm usually at work. I show my face once a year here, you know, get it out of the way. Then I don't have to go through this torture again.'

'What job do you do?'

'I own an alternative-health store. I had one in São Paulo, but now I've closed it and re-opened here in Ireland.'

'Wow! Good for you!'

'. . . email the principal,' Dervla was saying to Edel. 'I've been on to her three times already.'

Eva, wrinkling her nose as she held a partially melted plastic Moana lunchbox between finger and thumb, said, '*I'm* a bit annoyed, actually. I'm supposed to be at work today. I thought we all had to do this, that's why I came. That WhatsApp message was quite threatening, I thought. Who is this Erica person? Surely she should be here?'

'Erica Laffey,' said Dervla, thinning her lips as she moved some of Edel's books to a different box. 'Happy to tell us what to do, but you won't see her and the rest of the BMs slaving away in here.'

'The who?'

'The Beautiful Mums,' Luisa said. 'The ones who take up the centre of the playground every morning so the rest of us have to go the long way around.'

Edel said, 'I overheard Vanessa saying it was great to have sheep doing the donkey work.'

'The absolute cheek.' Dervla looked annoyed. 'Typical!'

'Who's Vanessa?' Eva asked.

'Vanessa Mayhew. The head BM.'

I listened, intrigued. So it wasn't just me. Not every parent in third class was a blue-tick Vanessa fan.

'Mayhew?' Eva looked interested. 'I've heard of her husband through work. Isn't he a partner in that big investment firm, Murphy & Mayhew?'

'Does Vanessa work in finance too?' I asked, thinking of her childminder.

'Not her.' Luisa shook her head. 'She's the type who feels sorry for women that have to work. You didn't marry a successful enough man.'

'She lives near us,' I said. 'I tried to invite her daughter over, but I don't think it went down too well.'

'Of course it didn't! You've just moved here. You could be anyone! Alejandra and Polly used to play together when they first started school. Then one day I saw Vanessa pull Polly away and say to one of her friends, "So funny who they like, isn't it? So peculiar."'

72

'There's always one,' Dervla said. 'In every class. They go out of their way to leave people out.'

'Hardly on purpose, though,' said Eva.

'Oh, it is,' said Luisa. 'It's all part of the frisson. Because where's the fun in being *in*, if no one is *out*?'

'Well, I think she looks nice,' Eva said. 'I'm sure she and her friends have no idea people think about them like that. In fact, I probably know quite a lot of people her husband knows through work. I've been meaning to talk to her.'

Luisa caught my eye. 'Well, if your husband is important enough, you'll be approached.'

Eva bristled. 'I'm a senior manager in my company! And you're in management too. In retail, didn't I just hear you say?'

'Owner, actually, but it doesn't matter what *you* do, it has to be your husband.'

'There's nothing wrong with my husband.'

'I didn't mean . . .' Luisa gave a sigh. 'Look. Vanessa and her friends are entitled to be friendly with whomever they like. Schools are for the children, not the adults, no? But unfortunately this bad dynamic seems to spread to all the girls. Alejandra stays out of it now. She hangs out with our neighbour from the class ahead. Far less drama. We're unlucky with our class, I think. Anyway.' She climbed to her feet, brushing dust off her jeggings. 'I think we're finished here. I have a work meeting.' She grinned at me. 'Nice to meet you, Sara. Maybe I'll see you again next year!'

'Leaving the rest of us to lock up,' Dervla said disapprovingly when Luisa had left. Clearly mistrust of Vanessa was the only thing we all had in common and the temporary bonding session was now over. Eva, Edel and I stood in a semicircle, watching Dervla lock the door. Then the four of us walked together with the key to the secretary's office. Dervla had a complaint to raise with Mrs Bakewell so she stayed behind while the rest of us exited into the bright, damp morning.

'It does seem quite hard to meet people here, doesn't it?' Eva said as we walked across the empty playground. 'These Dubliners do seem a bit cliquey. Mia hasn't really settled at school yet.'

'Would Mia and Imogen like to come to play with Lexie on Friday?' I hadn't heard Lexie mention either girl, but all the more reason to get to know them.

And so Imogen and Mia came to us. I tried to contact Luisa too, to invite Alejandra, but unfortunately she appeared to have removed herself from the third-class mums WhatsApp. The other girls, however, seemed to enjoy the afternoon. Imogen became angry when the spoon in her ice-cream tub was blue and she had wanted red, but Lexie, always easy-going about things like that, swapped with her and it was fine. Mia spent most of the playdate staring at her feet, but on the plus side she was polite and sweet and seemed happy to do or eat literally everything that was offered without complaint.

Lexie was over the moon with the whole thing. She was in a wonderful mood that night. You were home and commented on it. We made popcorn and hot chocolate and watched *Paddington 2* together. Despite all the difficulties about school and work and money, it was the most relaxing evening we had spent since moving here and I remember feeling glad that the initial snags and glitches of our bedding-in stage seemed finally to be coming to an end.

8

The very next day she texted him. Literally no point in hanging about.

Hi there. Zoë here from W'loo station. Thanks again for your help! Look forward to repaying you with that drink.

What did she have to lose? Apart from her life, obviously, if he turned out to be a murderer.

Then she waited. Going by previous experience, there'd be the usual multiple messages back and forth before they got around to meeting. Train-related jokes and memes and so forth. But three or four days went by and there was nothing. So there it was. He'd changed his mind. She'd caught him by surprise on the platform; he'd been too chivalrous to refuse but upon reflection had come to his senses.

Briefly, she burned. Then she got over it. Life was busy. She had a triplet IVF Caesarean section coming up and a woman with severe aortic stenosis approaching her thirtieth week.

On the Thursday evening he phoned. Actually phoned! No preliminary text, no heads-up. Didn't he realize that this was not how it worked?

It was just past nine, but she was already in bed, getting an early night in before the triplet Caesar the next day. She shot up, her heart gathering speed, staring at the screen. She cleared her throat a couple of times and stretched her lips before speaking. Then decided not to answer. She was tired. She wasn't ready. She'd see what he said on the voicemail, call him back tomorrow. No, she wouldn't. She knew she wouldn't! The moment would have passed. Oh, for heaven's sake!

'Hello!'

'Hi there.' Deep voice. 'Is that Zoë?'

'Paul!' No point coming over all bashful, coyly asking, 'Wh–who's this?' when his name was right there on the screen. 'Lovely to hear from you!'

75

'You too.' His pleasure sounded genuine. 'Still on for that drink?'

'Of course.'

'Saturday?'

Just like that. No games. No multiple texts, no: *Next week? Sorry, can't. The following Tuesday? I'm away. How about eight weeks' time?*

'That would be lovely,' she said. 'Oh, though. Just give me a sec . . .'

'Busy social life?'

'No.' She laughed scornfully at the thought. 'Just making sure I'm not on call.'

'Ah. I know *that* feeling.'

'Are you a medic too?'

'Yep. GP.'

'Oh.' She was surprised. And then again, she wasn't. Perhaps this explained the familiarity she had felt between them on the platform. The sense that there was so much to say.

She wasn't on call on Saturday, just working until lunchtime, so they arranged to meet at Borough Market after her morning theatre session. Three ERPCs and a C-section. She must look frazzled, but hopefully Paul would understand. Presumably he knew what it was like to spend several hours standing in a hot room wearing the equivalent of a J-cloth on his head. At the last minute she ducked into a pub toilet for a quick re-grout. The walk from work had brought a glow to her cheeks. Despite the J-cloth, her hair was behaving itself, swishy and dark blonde rather than limp and mousy. She smudged on some eyeshadow with her fingers, swept her fringe to the left and smiled at herself. She looked fine. She looked . . . *good*, in fact.

Entering the market with its echoey voices, its smells of cheeses and focaccia and the shafts of sunlight spiking through the arched glass roof, she looked about for him. Now was the bit where, when she spotted him, he'd have a strange leer or be excavating his ear and peering at the contents. But again, no. He looked just as good as she remembered. Better! She watched him for a moment, tall and broad in his dark green fleece, as at home by the Parma ham and mozzarella stall as if he were running it

76

himself, and felt again the slow internal thump she'd felt when their eyes had met at the Tube station. *Careful, Zoë. Don't get ahead of yourself here.*

'Hallo!' She waved at him above all the heads.

'Hey!' He straightened, his eyes brightening, taking her in. Clearly happy with what he saw.

She walked calmly to meet him. *Rule number one: DON'T talk about Jeremy!* One of her OLD dates had practically backed away, then run for the hills while she was in the loo. It seemed that after a couple of drinks she'd lost sight of where she was and had mistaken him for actually *being* Jeremy, like in those therapy sessions where people are encouraged to scream and shout at cushions.

It was early October and still warm enough, just about, to sit out-doors. They found a table on a pavement, surrounded by steaming open-air woks and blackboard menus.

'This is so strange,' they kept joking. 'I can't believe we're doing this. We could be anyone!' People did say Ted Bundy had been charming, so Zoë made sure to mention that she'd taken the precaution of letting her sister know where she was.

Naturally, they talked shop. Paul was a GP in Cork, in Ireland, but was currently taking a career break. He was here in London because he was working on a project, a new artificial intelligence diagnostic system that he had designed and patented and was hoping to market.

'That's so impressive! Would you leave medicine altogether? If your robot thingy worked out and you became a mogul?'

'Maybe.' He shrugged. 'I've always been interested in the entrepre-neurial side of things. Anyway' – flicking at a beer mat – 'it suits me to be away from home for a while.'

'Oh dear. Recent break-up?'

'Is it that obvious?'

'Oh God, me too.' *DON'T talk about Jeremy!*

They sat there for so long that they ended up ordering an early supper – though neither of them ate very much of it – but Zoë didn't push things. She was conscious of a tension within herself. She was still waiting for the shoe to drop, for him to say something stupid – that Hitler had been misunderstood or that he'd never heard of guacamole. She wanted the date to end before he could do that so that she could go home with this feeling, this song in her heart, just this one time.

Shortly after coffee she told him she had to leave. She had to work tomorrow anyway. He asked if they could meet again and she said yes. He walked part of the way home with her along the South Bank and there they sealed the deal, just beyond Blackfriars Bridge, the sun orange on the water. People must have brushed past them, jostling them as they kissed, calling to one another down the long promenade, but she neither heard nor saw them.

She googled him, naturally. His GP practice in Cork, Ireland, did exist, so that was one thing. Then she looked up his name on the Irish Medical Council website. There he was. Going by his year of graduation, same as hers, they must be of an age. None of this proved that he wasn't a serial killer, but at least it would be easy for her family to track him down after-wards and retrieve her mangled corpse.

When he called her again, it was as if they'd known each other for years.

They met after her work the following Wednesday. He lived quite near to her hospital so when he suggested they walk to his place for coffee she was happy to agree. The conversation bounced between them as they strolled along. She enjoyed his witty comments, the easy right-back-atcha banter, so rare to find. He was renting a room in a flat in Vauxhall.

'Ooh!' She gazed around her at the full-height windows overlooking the Thames. 'Swanky.'

'My landlord is some finance guy. He's hardly ever here. We both travel a lot so we rarely overlap.'

While he was figuring out the coffee machine in the kitchen she relaxed in the living room. On the table in front of her was a maroon-coloured Irish passport. Just sitting there on the edge. As if he expected her to check on him. Casually she leaned forward and crooked it open with the tip of her finger. There he was. The photo was an old one; in it he looked several years younger than he did now. But there were the same scrubbed pink cheeks, super-healthy, as if he milked cows and drank cod liver oil every day. The name was correct, and he was indeed thirty-two years old. Footsteps sounded from the hallway. She removed her finger from the passport. Sat back again and smiled at him as he came in.

9

Sometimes these days I catch you looking at me with a troubled, haunted expression and I know what's going through your mind. You're afraid of what I must think of you.

'How can you bear it,' you whispered that night, the night it happened, your hands shaking as I helped you to unbutton your shirt. 'You don't deserve this. Don't try to share the blame.'

But I'm not. Or rather, neither of us is to blame because we had no choice in what happened. She gave us no choice.

The sun is sinking behind the trees. The days have shortened. Summers in Ireland are more fleeting than in London. School starts back tomorrow; can you believe that? There is a crispness to the air, a hint of new shoes, sharpened pencils and blank copybooks. As a small child, I used to love this time of year. This, rather than January, was always the new year for me. A fresh start. Everything so hopeful.

By the end of November, now that Lexie had finally made some friends, she seemed happier. At drop-off, she ran to greet Imogen and Mia in the playground and didn't cling quite so tightly to my hand as we walked down the hill. The sky was an eerie ochre behind witchy black trees. There were crunchy leaves on the pavements and a bite to the mornings that I found energizing.

Catching sight of Edel and Eva in their east-facing spot by the wheelie bins, I steered Lexie in their direction. They were deep in discussion about Ms Brennan's Ancient Egypt project.

'It's completely inappropriate,' Eva was complaining. 'I

mean, does she think parents have nothing to do all day but sit around making pharaoh masks? I *work*. What's wrong with them just drawing them in their copies?'

'It's ridiculous,' Edel said. 'Dervla's going to email Mrs Bakewell.'

From time to time at these drop-offs I looked out for Luisa, but she never seemed to be at the school. Obviously, she hadn't been joking when she'd said 'See you next year.' Lexie was gazing longingly at something over my shoulder. I turned to look. The Beautiful Mums were gathered as usual in the centre of the play-ground in their identical long duvet coats and cropped leggings. It wasn't that other people *couldn't* stand there with them, but the force-field of weaponized politeness – the thin smiles, the vague, non-committal responses, the not-quite eye contact – gradually, subtly, repelled. Beside them, in a scaled-down version, the daughters – Polly, Amelie, Mabel, Tabitha, Sadbh – stylish and confident with the latest fidget toys and hair scrunchies, also just out of reach, an invisible cordon around the brightest and shini-est girls in the class, which couldn't have been much fun for the other children who had to sit with them every day.

Lexie was still staring over at the shiny girls. Polly saw her and smiled and waved before one of her friends tapped her arm, drawing her attention away.

'Probably planning another one of those showy playdates,' Edel said. 'I couldn't be doing with that kind of malarkey. I'd hate the mess in the house.'

'I don't do playdates full stop,' Eva said. 'I've made that clear to my two. I've more than enough to do.'

'Weekends are probably easier for you,' I said, remembering my London days of working long hours.

'No. Weekends are *my* time. I do my fill during the week. I've no intention of spending my weekends babysitting other people's children on top of everything else.'

'Well, look,' I said, 'I'm not working at the moment, so the girls are welcome to ours any time. In fact – what about this Friday?'

Eva said, rather grudgingly, 'As long as you know I won't be able to pay you back.'

'Fantastic!' I didn't care who went where, as long as Lexie was happy.

Things might have improved for Lexie, but it was around this time that I had begun to notice a change in you. You were becoming more and more irritable. I was sympathetic: the red-eye flights, the Zoom meetings at all hours, the constant worrying about whether it had been premature to leave Bragger & Flasher. The financial situation we were in. We had overestimated how easily I'd get a job in Dublin. I'd had no luck finding anything so far, particularly as I couldn't commit to anything for longer than a few months. I knew you were under pressure and I tried to be understanding, but at times your moodiness could be wearing. One morning, I remember, you were particularly agitated. I returned from taking Lexie to school to a fraught-sounding phone call up in the bedroom.

'There *was* a final instalment!' Your voice came heatedly through the door. 'You know perfectly well there was. Don't you read your emails?'

I climbed the stairs quietly with your coffee from Berry Nice. It didn't help matters that when you were in Dublin your 'office' was a wobbly desk in the corner of our bedroom, surrounded by unpacked boxes with nowhere to put the contents.

'No, *you* educate yourself! Try reading your bloody emails for a –'

You were interrupted by tripping over a pile of towels. I put the coffee down and hurried to gather them up, piling them on the bed to give you space. You stepped over me and resumed your call.

'I've a good mind to get a solicitor. That'll . . . what the –'
You held your phone out and stared at it in disbelief. 'He's hung
up. Bastard has hung fucking up.'

'Adam.' I looked up from the towels. The party walls were
thin. Angela, our neighbour, would purse her lips at me over
the buxus. She'd already told me not to park in front of her
driveway (we didn't have a car yet) and had made Lexie move
her penny-board off her section of the pavement.

'*Wanker!*' you shouted, and hurled your phone across the
room.

It was unusual for your anger to turn physical. Normally you
controlled your fury, turned it inwards, became snappy and
avoidant. But it wasn't unknown for you to lash out. There'd
been that time in London when Lexie was a baby and that man
in the park had accidentally kicked his football into her pram.
Fortunately, the temperature being below twenty degrees, she
was covered in a huge pile of blankets, like the pea at the bottom
of the princess's bed.

'Oy!' you shouted as I flew to pick her up. 'There's a baby in
that pram.'

'Just throw the ball back, mate.' I didn't think the man was
being intentionally aggressive. He was one of those faulty-
brake types who blunders through life, rear-ending everyone
on the way. He could see that Lexie was unharmed and was
bristling at having to take a dressing-down from Dad.

'You could have killed her, you muppet.'

'Then just get yourself another one.' He looked at me with a
leer which was designed to provoke, and you of course rose to
it and went for him. Punched him hard in the face, and down
he went like a skittle. Blood everywhere.

'Adam!' Horrified, I'd dragged you off. I was relieved to see
the other man sit up again, holding his hands in front of his
nose. I guessed he wasn't the type to bother with the police, but

if he'd had a couple of mates nearby you'd have been in trouble. Once you'd calmed down you'd been shocked at yourself too.

This morning you had, I knew, intended for your mobile to land on the carpet. Unfortunately the door to the en suite was open. The phone sailed through and crashed on to the tiles.

The air in the bedroom turned properly blue.

'Take it easy,' I sighed, going to inspect the damage.

'Probably completely banjaxed now, thanks to that . . . that *helmet*.' But predictably, now that you'd popped your valve, you were starting to simmer down.

I knelt to pick up the phone.

'It's okay,' I said. 'It's still working. Look, a message has just come through.'

You were beside me at once. 'Give it here.'

'It's from –'

'I said, give it to me!' You snatched the phone from my hand.

'Hey,' I said, startled, shaking my wrist. 'Don't –'

'Then don't read my messages. These are important work calls I don't need to lose. Okay?'

And you stamped off out of the room, leaving me staring after you.

It was on the first Friday in December that I finally realized what had been going on with Lexie. I remember the date because it was the afternoon we had Imogen and Mia over for that second playdate. I had taken them to a playground, where they climbed and screamed until the rain meant they could no longer safely grip the bars. Now we were on the upper deck of the bus home, heat blowing up from under the seats. It was after four and almost dark. Christmas trees had begun to twinkle and shimmer in windows. The girls sat in a row and chattered.

'. . . So Ava thinks she's so great. Just because she got a new Bichon Frisé.'

84

'Wait, what?' Lexie asked.

'A Bichon Frisé.'

'Oh. They're lovely. One of our neighbours got a Labarra.'

'A what?' Imogen asked.

'A Labarra.'

'Do you mean a Labrador, Lexie?' Mia asked.

'Yeah.'

'Why didn't you just say that then?' Imogen asked.

I was noticing something. In fact, in retrospect, I had probably been noticing it for quite some time without fully registering it, but there in the rainy dusk it finally pushed itself to the fore.

'What's your favourite dog, Lexie?' Mia asked.

'I like . . . um . . . Crocker . . .'

She meant cocker spaniel of course. She was obsessed with them. We thought it was sweet the way she kept mispronouncing the name.

'*What?*' Imogen said impatiently.

'I don't know,' said Lexie after a moment. 'I don't have a favourite.'

'You probably don't know much about dogs,' Imogen said. 'That's because you're from London. My mum's friend says everyone there lives in apartments so no one has pets.'

She and Mia talked on. Lexie remained silent, gazing out at the white-topped sea. She probably knew more about dogs than the rest of us put together. Crawling along the coast road, rows of red lights blurring in the windows, was when it hit me. *Something's not right.*

At home, fussing over wet coats and spaghetti Bolognese, I found myself listening, on edge. Once I had seen it, I couldn't unsee it. I listened to her trying to describe some event that had happened or how something had made her feel, heard how when she hesitated the others would jump to finish her sentences – not always in the way she had intended, but she didn't object. *That's not what you wanted to say*, I felt like shouting.

'Knock knock,' Mia said.

'Who's there?'

'Interrupting cow.'

'Interpreting cow w—'

'MOO!'

Mia and Imogen laughed, and so did I. Lexie didn't. She simply looked baffled.

A lot of the time I don't understand what they're saying.

Moving Imogen's schoolbag from a chair, I spotted a book poking out. I took it out. Amelia Fang – a favourite of Lexie's that I often read to her at bedtime. Because she was too young, I had always assumed, to read it herself.

'Are you reading this?' I asked Imogen when she came in.

'Sure. I've read them all apart from this one.'

'Me too,' Mia piped up. 'They're really popular in our class. Lots of girls have read them.'

Lexie hadn't. Lexie would no more be capable of reading Amelia Fang by herself than I would Newton's *Principia Mathematica*.

'Lexie can't read,' I said flatly to you later.

'Hmm?' You were slumped on the sofa, your socked feet on the coffee table. 'Of course she can. She reads her homework, doesn't she?'

'She can stumble her way through a couple of sentences. It's not proper reading. Not the kind the other girls do. I saw the books they had in their bags.'

'You were snooping in her friends' bags?'

'Yes.' I was sitting upright in the bobbly mustard armchair, tapping my nails on my teeth. 'I'm thinking I should make an appointment to see her teacher.'

You yawned. 'Whatever you think. I'm sure if there was a problem the school would have said.'

'You could come too,' I suggested. 'Seeing as you'll be here all next week.'

'Yes – oh, wait. I'll be in London. I'm meeting Zoë.'

'Who?'

You didn't respond. You had started to scroll rapidly on your phone. I waved my hand in front of your face.

'Earth to Adam. Who's Zoë?'

'Hmm?'

'Just now you said you were meeting a Zoë.'

More intense scrolling. Then you looked up, your face clearing.

'Oh,' you said. '*Zoë*. Just a client. Just need to go through a contract.'

Homework at the kitchen table.

'Hexa,' I said. 'Gon. Put them together and what do you get?'

Usually when she stumbled on something I said it for her and moved on, assuming a lapse of concentration. Tonight, at the back of my mind, there was a kind of low hum of panic which I tried to ignore.

'Hexa,' I repeated. 'Gon. What is it?'

She pushed her shoulder to her ear.

'It's easy. Look. Say *Hexa*.'

'Hexa.'

'*Gon.*'

'Gon.'

'Good! Now, put them together. Hexa. Gon. And you get . . .' Silence. 'Come on, Lex. You must hear it.'

'I don't hear anything.' She was writhing, fiddling with her pencil case, chewing the end of her plait, looking everywhere but at the page. 'I don't know what you're talking about.'

This was ridiculous. She had to be doing this on purpose. 'Lexie, for goodness' sake. Stop messing about and just *say* it.'

'I don't know. I don't know.'

Something in me clicked. The hum of panic rose. My fist slammed on the table, making her pencils jump.

'HEXAGON,' I shouted. What on earth was she playing at? Didn't she care if the other children pulled ahead of her, left her behind? Was this what she *wanted*?

'It's HEXAGON.' My face in hers, right up close. I saw the love and fear in her eyes and for a fraction of a second I felt something like blind rage.

'I'm sorry.' Instantly, it left me. 'I'm sorry, Lex. I shouldn't have done that.'

She shrank back. She whispered, 'I don't want to do this any more.'

'What's going on?'

You in the doorway. The darkness outside had turned the patio door into a mirror. I saw the picture we made: Lexie cowering, me standing over her, hair straggly, red-faced, like an ogre.

'Come on, Lex.' You held out your hand. She slid from her chair and you steered her from the room. You didn't say a word. In a way it was worse than if you had.

At bedtime, filled with remorse, I tried to make it up to her. I read her two extra chapters of Hetty Feather. But all the time the fidgeting and the tension and the hands to her mouth.

She whispered, 'I hate bedtimes.'

'Why, sweetheart?'

'School.'

'What do you hate about school?'

'I get pain in my tummy. I feel afraid. Like something bad is going to happen.'

'What could happen? Is it the teacher? The girls?'

'I don't know. I don't know, but I feel like it is.'

I stroked her apple-scented hair. I went on stroking until she fell asleep, until her eyelashes stopped moving against my skin. Her warm, limp body was heavy on my arm. I lay beside her, staring at the dim squares around the curtains, the smudgy outline of her chest of drawers covered with dog stickers. How could I have done that? The love and pain in her eyes when I shouted at her. The emotion I felt that I had thought was rage but now recognized for what it had really been. Not rage but fear.

Something bad is going to happen.

Vanessa and the BMs again in the playground, curled in their tight little circle, spines outward. In the mood I was in it irked me. It was Grace Gillespie all over again. Our primary school in Surrey had been a happy one until Grace had arrived in Year 6. After that there had been rules. Places you could go or not go depending on what Grace decided.

I exited the playground and crossed the road. Why was I being so triggered by the BMs, who, after all, were doing nothing more than talk harmlessly among themselves? I hadn't slept well; perhaps that was why my head was filled with unhappy childhood memories I hadn't thought about for years. But I knew there was another reason too.

My brother Steve had had trouble reading. Like me with Lexie, my mother had seen nothing, noticed nothing. Steve – or I – could have grown an extra eye and she wouldn't have noticed. She'd been a shell since Dad had gone off with Michaela. A depressive loner, mostly quiet and withdrawn, watching TV in her dressing gown with a glass of wine in her hand, but occasionally – and we never knew what would bring it on – there would be bursts of rage. Exactly like I'd had with

Lexie. Episodes out of nowhere; only she would know what had caused them. Then she would scream into our faces, her mouth twisted, her unwashed hair hanging in clumps while Steve and I stared in uncomprehending terror at her contorted expression, the spit on her lips.

Worse than that, though, were the periods when she would stop talking to one or other of us over something minor – once, I remember, it was because I had innocently told her I'd over-heard a neighbour saying: 'Those poor kids' – but it could be anything.

'I'm not speaking to you,' she'd say, and she wouldn't. For days, sometimes weeks, at a time.

There was one time she must have been particularly angry, I don't know what about, but what I remember is that she made both Steve and me go to bed every day straight after school. For a month. Every morning we would put on our uniforms and go in and interact with our teachers and classmates as if everything was normal, but as soon as we got home we had to go straight to bed and stay there until the morning. Steve was maybe eleven at the time and I ten.

At the end of the school day my stomach would begin to churn as I saw all the other children skipping off with their mums, laughing and sharing tales about their day. Steve and I would walk home behind our mother in silence. She would open the front door and, without a word or any eye contact whatsoever, point to the stairs. She'd have left water and a sand-wich by our beds and we would have to make sure to go to the bathroom before we went in. That was it; that was the last we would see of anyone until the morning. She'd lock our doors to stop us sneaking out to comfort each other. This was back when Steve and I were still close.

That closeness had faded. In his teens, Steve had turned so angry. He did worse and worse at school, attended less and less.

'School's not for me. I'm too thick,' he would say, and even when we loved each other I agreed with him. His school reports were abysmal. 'What on earth's the matter with you?' our mother would snap, slamming the phone down after yet another call from the school. 'Are you doing this on purpose or are you really that stupid?' And when, increasingly, we fought, I would imitate, in my own anger and unhappiness, what everyone else said; our mother, his teachers, the other boys. 'You're stupid,' I shouted at him.

I never see him now.

Ms Brennan sat at her desk in a billowy, puff-sleeved dress printed with daisies. I hunched on one of the diminutive children's chairs, surrounded by a display of wobbly motte-and-baileys made from upturned cereal bowls. Around the walls were rows of self-portraits: smiley crayon faces, scribbly hair, uneven eyes. Lexie's contribution was by the whiteboard, quite a decent likeness of her in her favourite tie-dye T-shirt: *This is Me. I have yelo Hair. I live in Dudlin.*

'As you can see,' Ms Brennan smiled, passing me a folder with Lexie's name on it, 'you have nothing to worry about. Lexie is doing very well.'

I took the folder. Far from being reassured, I was shocked. This was worse than I had thought. The Irish – obviously. The spelling I had more or less expected. But the maths . . .

'How can you say this is doing *well*?' I asked.

'You should be proud of her. She's one of the hardest-working children in the class.'

'Then why isn't she doing better?'

'Mrs Carey, Lexie is a perfectly average student.'

'Average students make an average effort. You've just said she's one of the hardest-working children in the class. There's a mismatch, surely, between that and these scores. Which, unless I'm missing something, are well *below* the average class score.'

'It's early days yet. She's still adjusting to –'

I was staring, puzzled, at the maths paper. Lexie was good at maths. I knew she was. You knew she was. She was quick to figure things out. How much to pay in a shop – she'd get there ahead of the till. She recited her tables while bouncing on the trampoline; she knew them backwards; she even knew the multiplication ones, well ahead of time. Seven plus four plus nine – how could she have got that wrong?

'Carelessness.' Ms Brennan pursed her lips in a rueful way. 'Doesn't read the questions properly.'

I looked again at the question. *Paul owns seven footballs. Ahmed borrowed four hockey sticks. They meet Siobhan, who inherited nine tennis racquets. If they put them all together how many pieces of sports equipment will they have?* Words, words everywhere. My heart sank.

'She tends to zone out,' Ms Brennan was saying. 'Often comes up after the lesson to ask questions that show she hasn't been listening.'

'Because she can't understand what you're saying.' I looked at her in frustration. How could she not see it? 'Could she have some sort of – I don't know. Language issue?'

'Well, now that's a leap.'

'But –'

'Look.' She eyed the clock. 'I can see you're concerned. And now that you've raised it, I promise we'll keep an eye. In the meantime, I realize you have high expectations of Lexie, but as I'm sure you'll agree, Mrs Carey, it is important to let children be children. Pressurizing your daughter really isn't going to help.'

'See?' You forked basmati into your mouth.

I had been waiting all day for you to fly home so we could discuss the Ms Brennan meeting. At bedtime I had asked Lexie about it. 'Can you follow what people are saying? Do other people seem to understand things you don't?' Lexie had gone very still. She said that whenever Ms Brennan made an announcement to the class Lexie would lose track after the first couple of sentences. She'd have to look at the other girls to see how they were responding, what they were doing. It was the same in the playground. It wasn't that she couldn't *hear* the words, it was that they didn't make any sense. It was like one of those films, I imagined, where all the characters mumble unintelligibly so you have to strain to follow the plot, then somebody shouts, 'Upper virus fishmonger C45,' and everyone leaps up and starts shooting. It's English, Jim, but not as we know it. No wonder she'd been so tense and unhappy but unable to tell us why. She didn't know why herself. She simply had no way of knowing that other people didn't experience what she did.

'She's really behind, Adam.'

'So, reading's not her thing.' You went on shovelling in rice, one eye on your phone, which kept lighting up with message after message. 'So what? She's good at other stuff. Art. Sport. She's a doer, not a reader. The bookworms of this world will be reading about *her*.'

'It's not just reading, though. She struggles to get her point across. Change makes her anxious because her processing is off.'

'If she is . . . *anxious*' – a little twirl of your fork as if to say you weren't mad about the term but okay, whatever – 'surely the teacher is right and you piling the pressure on isn't helping? I hate to bring it up again, but the way you were shouting at her the other night –'

'I know.' I twiddled the stem of my glass. Yet another person telling me I was pressurizing Lexie. But if *I didn't* pressurize her – if I let it go, if I shrugged and said, *Oh well, she mustn't be that bright*, when really I knew she was – wouldn't that be failing her too? The frustration of not knowing what to do made me want to snap the stem of the glass. Grind my teeth on the shards. This must be how poor Lexie felt, constantly gnawing at her nails and sleeves.

'Just because she's not as swotty as you were,' you said, 'does there have to be a reason? A label?' At the word 'label' you crooked your fingers in the air in a way that I suddenly found intensely irritating.

'It's a fact, Adam. I've been reading up on it. Language issues. Dyslexia. Whatever. If you think back, you'll remember. Every class had them. The two or three children who always sat at the back and never put their hands up. Never spoke to anyone. Like ghosts. It is a thing.'

You lowered your fork in a weary way. 'Do we have to get into this now? I'm literally just off the plane. I've been going all day.'

I saw how drawn and stressed-out you looked. Yet I couldn't help myself. My worry for Lexie overrode all else.

'She'll hide who she is,' I said, 'and go quiet. So all those other people who can talk and write, their stories will get told, but not hers, and that'll become the narrative she'll have to go along with. Her own personality and abilities will be trapped behind this . . . this *paywall*. My brother Steve . . .'

I paused. The time Steve had been arrested in his twenties after a man had been stabbed. We'd never heard Steve's side of the story. He had seemed overwhelmed, refusing to speak up or put up any kind of a defence. His own solicitor had been exasperated by him. He'd got six months.

'You always said Steve was a troublemaker.'

'I'm thinking now I badly misjudged him.'

'So you're saying it wasn't his fault he was a boozer and got into all those fights? Come off it, Sara. Anyway, I hardly think Lexie —'

'Girls don't get into fights. They take a different path.'

'What's that supposed to mean?'

In the garden something moved. It was night-time so the glass doors were lit up like a cinema screen, showing the movie of Adam and Sara eating their dinner in their overbright kitchen. But when I refocused, gazing through us at the darkness, we blurred and vanished.

'There was this girl at school,' I said slowly. 'Heather. A friend of mine.'

'You never mentioned a Heather.'

'No. She – we lost touch.'

Shadows shifting in the blackness. Branches swaying. Or ghosts. Becoming less and less visible. And by sixteen they had faded away.

'Anyway,' you said with your mouth full, 'Lexie's very pretty.'

'What?'

'Look, don't get me wrong, but lots of women – okay, you go to college, pass all the exams, beat all the men, blah blah blah – but then after a few years, what do most of you do? Get married. Get pregnant, and bingo! Meal ticket for life.' Facetious chuckle. 'Can't say I blame you! Do it myself if I could!'

I stared at you. 'You're joking.'

'I know, I know – you stopped work because we moved. But you always hated your job. Don't pretend you didn't jump at the chance to give it up.'

I couldn't believe what I was hearing. Was this really how little you knew me?

'I said I disliked *aspects* of Manways.' I spoke coldly. 'I never said I didn't want to work. I've been trying my best to find a job here. And – most women don't work? Really? Have you ever been in a school or a hospital? Seen a nurse? Heard of Angela Merkel?'

'Oh, for –'

'*You're* the one who wanted us to move here. I know you're doing your best, but I think I've been incredibly patient with our financial situation. I didn't ask not to be able to contribute, and I certainly haven't been sitting around having coffees and pedicures.'

'Christ, Sara. It was banter. What is wrong with you these days? Helicoptering around Lexie, medicalizing all kinds of perfectly normal childhood issues. You've got way too much time on your hands. Hopefully you will go back to work soon.'

'Of course I will! Everyone should be financially independent. In case they're not in the fortunate position of meeting . . . Mr Wonderful.'

I practically spat the last words out. *Who were you?* I remember thinking. Had you always been this boorish? I had always thought of you as being quite forward-thinking and egalitarian. Was this the real Irish you, re-emerging now that you were on your home turf?

'What if Lexie doesn't want to get married at all?' I asked. 'And the only job she can get is something crap and low-paying where she's exploited and treated like rubbish and paid a pittance –'

'Now you're catastrophizing.'

'Happens to millions around the globe. Life is tough, Adam. You wouldn't know that because you had a lovely, easy childhood. Everything handed to you on a plate.'

'Lexie will have that too.'

'You're spectacularly missing the point. What if you lose all your money? Get hit by a bus?'

'I'm insured,' you said, bored.

'Meet someone else on all your trips away?'

Silence.

Then, flintily, you said, 'What do you mean?'

I'd got you there. And I knew why. You were thinking of that time back when we'd been engaged and you had met Anja.

When I'd heard about Anja – not from you, naturally – I'd been utterly shocked. It was like something from some trashy, sensationalist magazine, not like something you, or any normal, stable person, could do. Meeting a woman on the very first evening of your mate's stag ski holiday, hanging out with her for the entire week, lying to her about being single. Introducing her to all your friends – not one of whom disillusioned her. On the flight home you sat beside each other, holding hands, making plans to meet the following weekend. At the baggage claim she needed to use the bathroom so you said you'd go on through Customs and meet her outside. And when you came striding out to the arrivals hall there I was, wreathed in smiles, holding up a giant joke greeting sign. You rushed over, all hearty hugs and greetings. I remember thinking you seemed in a tremendous hurry for us to leave.

I'd never have known if I hadn't received an email to my Manways work account. Somehow, she'd tracked me down. She described it all; how she'd hurried out of the ladies with her wheelie case after a quick spritz of deodorant and been slapped in the face by the sight of us kissing, then walking away with our arms around each other. She'd thought at first it must be a joke. You and your mates must be messing with her, videoing her reaction. It had taken her some time to accept that you weren't coming back.

You were abject, distraught. You'd panicked, you said. It was last-minute nerves, knowing that you would never be on a singles holiday again. But marrying me was your unequivocal choice. It was me and the baby you wanted, without a shadow of a doubt. On a bench in a courtyard off Embankment – a tiny hidden courtyard with plum blossom snowing down on the cobbles and buildings with crooked little doors where at any moment a wizened old man in a pointed hat might appear holding a secret parchment – we talked and talked, held hands, finally made a pact never to refer to it again. And, to be fair, we had never needed to. I could see you weren't happy to have it thrown up again now.

'*If* you met someone,' I clarified through gritted teeth, 'I would manage. I'd never be forced for financial reasons to depend on a person who didn't want me. Why wouldn't I make sure my daughter had the same privilege?'

A sound at the door. I turned. Lexie in her yellow pyjamas with 'Save Planet Earth' printed on the front, her long hair down her back.

'What's wrong?' Her voice trembled. 'Who's meeting someone else? Where's Daddy going?'

You looked at me in disgust. 'Fantastic, Sara. Nice work.'

I stood up and moved towards her. My gut hurt. You were right; something was wrong with me lately. Lexie upset yet again because of me. I reached for her. She was so precious. So precious. I would tear someone's heart out for her. But she brushed past me and went to you. You held your arms out and she climbed up on to your lap.

'I'll never leave you,' you murmured into her hair. She curled into you and you wrapped your arms tightly around her, each of you needing no one but the other.

'Sara . . .'

Another sodden December morning, no different to nine mornings out of ten here. Hoods and hats everywhere. Cars hissed past, throwing up spray. At the pedestrian crossing a dark-haired, pretty, plumpish woman pushing a buggy had turned to look at me.

'It *is* Sara, isn't it?' Droplets sparkled on her white wool beanie. 'Your daughter's in Mabel's class. I've meaning to say hi. I'm Isabel.' I knew already who she was; one of the Beautiful Mums.

'Hi,' I said, not really in the mood. But she had the Teflon confidence and superb social skills of her group.

'You're from London, aren't you?'

'Yes.'

I waited for her to come to the point. Probably she was looking for a volunteer for yet another school-related task. I could think of no way to end the conversation without seeming rude. Yet I knew that if it was the other way around and *she* didn't want to talk to *me*, I would have been the one made to feel stalkerish and intrusive.

'I lived in Hammersmith in my twenties,' Isabel said. 'Loved it! You must find it so quiet here.'

She chattered on, easy as pie. The child in the buggy, two-year-old Jake, snoozed with his legs akimbo and his head flung back, a large dinosaur-patterned dummy planted in the centre of his face. It turned out she had lived in San Francisco too for a while. She and her husband had got engaged on Alcatraz. Her brown eyes crinkled up when she said this. 'D'you think he was trying to tell me something?'

She was unexpectedly likeable. Having seen the way she and her friends fawned over Vanessa, I had assumed she would be as blinkered and insular as the others. But there was an edge to her that I hadn't expected.

'Vanessa and I were at school together,' she said. 'We've known each other since we were four. For better or for worse.' Again the mischievous crinkling of her eyes.

The lights changed and we followed the herd of woolly hats across the road.

'Well,' said Isabel, 'it was nice running into you, but I'll have to rush. I've an appointment with my older son's tutor.'

'Tutor?'

'Yes. He's dyslexic.' She rolled her eyes. 'Total pain in the arse.'

Just like that. No big deal.

'I'm thinking Lexie too,' I blurted.

'Really?' She looked concerned. 'Have you spoken to the school?'

'They said they'll keep an eye.'

'Mmmm. Unless things are really severe they can see you as a bit precious. You'll need to be pushy. But look, recognizing something's wrong in the first place is half the battle, so' – she reached out and rubbed at my parka sleeve – 'well done you!'

Her touch was so soothing. I felt like a patient in a hospital, having balm massaged in by a kind nurse in white until the ouch went away.

'She's my first,' I said, 'so it's all new. I've been building it up into this massive deal in my head.'

'Oh no. You shouldn't panic. It's very common. In the old days it wasn't a thing because everyone would have been out hunting or berry-picking and there'd have been a special person like a monk to write things down. But now everyone's supposed to be the monk. It doesn't matter if you're crap at music or maths or sport – you just don't do them – but if you can't get the hang of reading it can completely balls up the rest of your education. Here.' She rummaged in her oversized shoulder bag, finally shaking out her phone, which was tangled up in phone cables and hair elastics. 'I can give you a couple of numbers. If you want to get the ball rolling yourself?'

'I do! Thank you very much.'

And just like that, everything was reframed. Not just by the fact that now I knew where to go for answers but also from the sheer relief of having spoken to another mother who understood. And like one of Isabel's overstretched hair bobbins pinging back into place, I was back to my usual practical self. It was unlike me to have been so paranoid and emotional. So there was a problem – so what. There was also bound to be a solution, and whatever it was we would find it.

11

The very next day, as if the universe had finally decided it was
time to throw our family a bone, CareyComp got its big break.
This was, I think, the second Friday in December. Remember,
literally the previous evening, us thinking it was all over? Lexie
asking at dinner whether we were going to stay in Ireland for
ever and, if so, could we please, please, please, get a dog, and
me grimacing at you – we were still tiptoeing after our row –
saying we'd have to see. Then later when we were in bed, you
confessing that you had something to tell me. Moving to Ireland, you said, had not worked out. CareyComp was seriously
struggling. Lexie would not be getting a dog because we could
no longer afford to stay here, even for the year we had planned.
In January we would be packing up and returning to London.

Considering I had never wanted to come here in the first
place, I was surprised by my dismay. Now that Lexie was finally
starting to settle, I'd been hoping we wouldn't have to move her
again before the end of the school year. More disruption really
wasn't what she needed. But seeing how devastated you were I
simply said, 'I'm so sorry, Adam.'

'Yup, well. Moving here was a mistake. We should never have
done it.'

As it happened, I didn't agree. Lexie and I had been starting
to enjoy Dublin. You'd been too busy to give it a chance. But
there was no point in getting into that now.

'It was worth a try.' I touched your arm supportively. 'And it's
not the end. Is it? There's every chance still that CareyComp
will take off.'

You just shook your head. It was clear that you weren't keen to talk, and the conversation soon tailed off. You were tired and quickly fell asleep, but I lay on, wakeful, thinking in the dark.

Then early the next morning, completely out of the blue, your phone rang. Your burgeoning American unicorn that had been breadcrumbing you for months had abruptly, unexpectedly, decided to commit.

You whooped, literally whooped, when you came off the phone. 'This is it! This is *it*, Sara! We'll have contacts all over the States by next year. I was this close – *this* close' – making a rabbit face with your teeth and holding your finger and thumb a millimetre apart – 'to packing the whole thing in and crawling back to Bragger & Flasher.'

'Never! No way! I knew you'd do it!'

You were ecstatic, on a high. Both of us were. Lexie came running in to see what all the fuss was about and you picked her up and swung her around until she squealed.

'When do you sign?' I asked.

'They want some fine-tuning. Further discussions and guarantees, yadda yadda yadda, so there's still a bit to do before we sign. But nothing CareyComp can't handle.'

'And now,' I said, 'Lexie can stay in Ireland till the end of school year.'

'Oh. Yes. Sure.' You were miles away, your mind racing, already brainstorming with tech bros in some cutting-edge Austin boardroom. 'If that's what you'd both like.'

You took that weekend off work – fully off – for the first time in months. No travel, no Zoom calls, no 3 a.m. conferences. Just your full focus on Lexie and me. On the Saturday we went rock-climbing on the beach until it became too dark to see properly. You played with Lexie in a way I rarely did, messing about, pushing each other into puddles, while I, the sensible one, looked after the spare shoes and took the photos. Lexie lapped it up, loving every minute of your attention. *Click*: her blue bobble hat, her laughing, scrunched-up face. You were, I told myself, trying to help Lexie in your own way. We were looking at different sides of the same coin and both were of equal value. She needed both of us, good cop, bad cop, me to push, you to comfort. No matter what methods we disagreed upon, it was clear that our goal was the same: her happiness.

Later we went to Cornettos, which Lexie had been desperate to try every time we'd passed it. She thought the enormous domed wood-fired oven looked like a hobbit's house. She nagged me into exchanging my jeans for a red silk Isabel Marant dress I hadn't worn in years and oohed and aahed over it, insisting I add make-up and heels. One of the heels got jammed between the twelve-inch reclaimed floorboards as we were being led to our table, and the pizzas, served on pretentious wooden chopping boards, cost three times as much as normal ones – in other words, it was all wonderful! Wonderful to be out again, not to have to worry about money. We toasted Carey-Comp with artisanal gin, enjoying the crowded tables, the blazing spectacle of the pizza oven, the beer garden festooned with Christmas lights where people in puffy coats and woolly hats drank cocktails around the firepit. Lexie munched dough balls, tracing through the maze on the children's menu, candle flames dancing in her enormous pupils.

Returning from a visit to the bathroom, I caught you off guard. Your smile had faded. You were facing the window, but your eyes were not focused on the harbour or the lights strung along the pier, leading out into the darkness.

'Hey.' Sliding into my seat, I touched your hand.

'What?' You jumped and turned. 'Sorry! Sorry, I'm just wrecked.'

'I'm sure. And in case you didn't already know it, I'm very proud of you. Lexie and I, we both are.'

I smiled at you. You looked away, at Lexie's battered Golden Syrup tin filled with colouring pencils.

'I have to meet the Americans,' you said. 'In London, on Monday. I'll be there for a few days. But next weekend, why don't you take a break? Go to London, see your friends. I'll hold the fort here.'

Automatically I went to refuse, not wanting to leave Lexie. But then I stopped. Something English about the restaurant – or perhaps it was my dress – reminded me suddenly and sharply of nights out in London. Katie, Janina and I in our single days, heading out after work on a Friday, giddy with hunger and excitement. The lamp-lit awnings along cobbled alleys, the smells of beer, open grills and expensive cologne. The bursts of bass from nightclub entrances vibrating off towering, ancient monuments, the answering deep thump in my chest that said anything was possible, anything at all. How long had it been since I'd had a proper laugh with my friends? With any other woman? Lately I'd begun to feel rather isolated. The other day I'd left my phone at home on charge, and when I returned there were twenty-eight missed WhatsApp messages. Animated and intrigued, I'd clicked in, wondering what excitement I had missed.

Ladies!!!! Next Thursday is Pyjama Day!!! The girls have to bring in two euro for charity.

Super!! Thanks for letting us know.

Thanks Erica!

Thanks Erica!!!

Amazing, thanks Erica XXX

Thanks a mill Erica X

Peony is missing her tracksuit top. Age 8-9. If anyone finds it please let me know.

Brill, thanks Erica!!!

Siofra has nits. Again. Can everyone please make sure to check your daughter's hair as this is her third time this term.

I'm at the dentist and then going to Tesco but as soon as I'm home I'll check for the tracksuit top

Huge thanks Erica!!!

How much do the girls have to bring?

I have a tracksuit top here. Age 5-6.

Anyone know when is Pyjama Day?

How bad-tempered I had been lately with poor Lexie. Shouting and snapping at her over her homework. For something she could not help! My heart still hurt when I remembered the expression on her face. And you, too. I might not have been happy to hear it, but you'd had a point. Perhaps I was too invested in her, overly analysing and micromanaging her every move. Projecting Steve's and my childhood on to hers. I did have too much time on my hands these days, and little things were stretching to fill it; things I normally wouldn't think twice about – a crabby husband, an unanswered WhatsApp – were becoming personal insults. Unattached worries floated, searching for something apart from work to cling to. It was time for me to step back, regain some perspective.

'I'd love to go,' I said, and I meant it.

Afterwards we walked up the hill to catch the bus home, Lexie turning somersaults between us, hanging off our hands. The strings of coloured lights bobbing and swaying above the street. The frost in the air and the hope in my heart.

On Monday I rang the numbers Isabel had given me and had Lexie placed on a waiting list for assessment – a list which, it turned out, was several months long. Hanging up, I felt again the tension, the twist of urgency in my gut. *Relax, Sara! You've started the ball rolling now.*

Meanwhile, there were things I could do. Letting her know that help was on the way. That she wasn't alone. Taking away the pain in her tummy, the feeling that something bad was going to happen.

I was kinder and more patient with her during the home-work. I must have been making things ten times worse, making her associate it with me shouting and slamming down my hands. So I said nothing when she fiddled endlessly with her pencil case, ignored it when she mixed up her *b*s and *d*s, made no comment when she spelled the same word backwards after being shown the correct version three times in a row.

And for the first time in weeks there was no chewing of her sleeves, no look of anxiety and despair. At bedtime she seemed happier.

'Lots of people find words tricky,' I assured her. 'We'll sort it out. Don't worry.' She snuggled trustingly up to me, listening. Her gentle eyes, so close to mine – are gentle-looking people born with gentle personalities? Or do they become that way because of how people respond to the way they look? All those holes in her sleeves. Holes in her little life. She had never been a complainer; she didn't know how. Instead she had chewed through her emotions.

Chilling, how easy it is to mess with someone's head. To crush a person, like Steve had been crushed. True, my mother's behaviour had not destroyed me. But I hadn't had Steve's prob-lems. I'd been a tougher nut to crack. Not so my gentle Lexie.

You say, Adam, that I exaggerate her difficulties, am too obsessed with her schoolwork, but believe me, I know what happens to these people. I did well at school and I escaped our childhood. And Steve did not. Several months earlier he'd been found, hypothermic and intoxicated, sleeping rough in a park in Amsterdam. He'd told the police where to stick their nanny-state totalitarianism, that he had as much right as anyone to be there. They'd taken him to hospital anyway, but he'd absconded as soon as he could, ignoring all attempts by my mother and his ex-wife to contact him.

Lexie drifted off, arms and legs twitching, even in her sleep unable to be still. Gradually her breathing slowed. The rhythmic shushing lulled me, like ASMR. I felt peaceful. Optimistic. Things were picking up now. I was looking forward to my trip to London, to Christmas, to you spending more time with us. To new beginnings.

Inexorably, like a pendulum, my thoughts swung back. Steve. *Heather*. All the ghosts. I did my best to push them away.

12

During October and November Zoë and Paul fell into a pattern of seeing each other whenever he wasn't travelling or she wasn't working. He met her friends, Nicole and Sanjeev, who liked him. Also Naomi, who didn't, but that was no major surprise. 'Anyone who wears a fleece like that is a wanker. Got "Tory" written all over him. Or whatever the Irish equivalent is.'

It wasn't all hearts and roses. At times he could be out of sorts. He was working very hard, pitching his AI software to bioengineering firms who would demand endless tweaks and modifications, then change their minds. Occasionally, returning to London, he would seem edgy and downcast, but being with her always seemed to cheer him up again. He would briefly answer her questions about his latest meetings, then firmly switch the spotlight to her. What had *she* been up to? What kinds of films, music, travel and nights out did *she* like? He seemed fascinated by her responses. She energized him, he said. He was keen to explore 'her' London. After a couple of dates she had ventured to ask him about his ex-girlfriend. Again his reply was brief. They'd been together for a few years. She was a decent person but could be cold. Ending it had been the right decision, but he couldn't help feeling guilty.

Once more he switched the focus back to her. What about *her* ex? Zoë offloaded – cautiously. As it turned out, however, she needn't have worried because the urge to rant about dear Jeremy appeared to have plummeted. Since meeting Paul she had hardly thought about him at all.

Despite his occasional work-related irritability, she felt at ease with Paul. She could tell from the way he looked at her that he found her beautiful and desirable no matter how wrung out and knackered she often felt. When she was tired after a long shift he would call to her flat with food and they would spend hours comfortably arguing, lying in bed with their limbs hooked together. Which was not to suggest that things in the bedroom were always 'comfortable'. Paul had this way of looking at her, a hard, intent look that made her limbs loosen.

One weekend in November her mother came down from Cirencester to meet them for lunch at the Wolseley. Paul had a meeting so had to leave after a quick aperitif, but it was enough.

'Well!' her mother said, sitting up straight when he had left. 'He seems a nice chap. Brighter than Jeremy, wouldn't you say? And not at all bad-looking. And his Irish accent isn't too strong. What's his family like?'

'They're in Ireland. I haven't met them yet.'

Later she said to Paul, 'You got a gold star today.'

'I tend to be good with mums.'

Zoë said thoughtfully, 'I've never been to Ireland.'

'Really? Never?'

'What would have been the point? I don't get much free time. There were always more exciting and less rainy places to go.'

'You'll have to come to Cork then. Meet everyone.'

'Now that I've met you, I am more curious.'

She imagined single-toothed drunk men in tweed caps, donkeys wandering on narrow roads, but when she googled again she saw a normal, modern city. Lots of hills and church spires and seascapes. Rather pretty, in fact.

In December, Paul called, sounding elated.

'My AI diagnostic has found a home!' His deep, joyous voice floated over the phone, squeezing her heart until it felt as if bubbles were popping out. 'Couple of glitches to iron out still, but it looks like they're going to sign.'

'Paul, that is magnificent! Well done!'

'Let's celebrate,' he said. 'I've a meeting in Edinburgh this weekend but I'll be back in London on Monday. Could you possibly get away for a night or two? We could do something. Go to Bath or somewhere.'

It was a huge step. She felt it. They'd only been together for a couple of months, but already she felt as comfortable with him as if he were a mitten and she the snug hand inside. On the Monday she met him at Paddington station. 'This reminds me of our first meeting,' she said, unable to stop smiling when she saw him, her whole face splitting, and him too; she caught the way his expression changed when he saw her.

Bath was a wonderland, done up like some Mittel-European forest from a Grimms fairy tale. Wooden chalets selling crafts and gingerbread, pine trees sprayed white, Bath Abbey a suitably majestic backdrop. After checking in to the hotel – a converted stately home with a claw-footed bathtub in their actual bedroom – they wandered the streets under the twinkly snowflake-shaped lights. Paul took photos of her beside a stall selling candy canes that matched her pink-and-white-striped scarf. Then a passer-by photographed the two of them together, wreathed in the scented smoke from a chestnut brazier.

'Stay here,' Paul said at one point, holding his hands up. Then he ran back to the stall they had just passed.

Waiting, she found herself watching a young family. The parents were debating over something at a stall, but it was the child, staring gravely at her from its father's arms, who caught her attention. A round, fat ball of a baby, red-cheeked, in a puffy white snowsuit that made it look like a marshmallow. The thought popped into her head: *Our children will be clever.*

Paul returned with a paper bag patterned with reindeer. Inside, wrapped in white tissue paper, was a Christmas-tree decoration, a delicate glass globe enclosing two miniature snow people. Simple but beautifully made. Zoë was fussy about her Christmas decor. It meant something to her, getting it right, keeping it tasteful yet meaningful. She liked natural greenery, tiny, minimalist lights. Nothing commercial or wasteful, everything made to last. Paul knew her well. He had hit the mark exactly. The globe was perfect, magical, just right. She would keep it always.

The following Tuesday Paul came to hers, bringing one of those takeaway suppers that just needed to be finished off in an oven. It was cold and she had switched on the gas fire, drawn the curtains as rain pattered. Just another normal winter's evening.

'Oops,' he said as he came in from the kitchen. 'Need to send one last mail.' He entered his phone code and tapped away.

Afterwards he went to take a shower.

She lazed on the sofa in her silk camisole PJs, enjoying the feeling of being looked after and the glints of firelight in the blackish red of her wine. Michael Bublé sang 'White Christmas' on the Alexa, reminding her of her childhood, and again she thought of the baby she'd seen in Bath. From the kitchen wafted the smells of garlic and rosemary. Paul's phone was sitting on the arm of the chair. She realized that she hadn't seen the Bath photos yet. She knew his code; she'd just seen him tap it in. She'd take a little peek, perhaps forward to herself the photo of the two of them that the passer-by had taken.

There were two Bath photos. One of the abbey, the other of a stall selling hand-carved wooden toys. None, though, with her or Paul in it. Strange.

She checked the Deleted album. There they were. The ones of her by the candy cane stall with her pink-and-white-striped scarf, and the one of her and Paul together in front of the brazier. He must have deleted them by accident. She restored them to the main album. Then, idly, she scrolled back through his previous photos. Lots of dull scans of paperwork, screenshots of stock market indexes and business articles that meant little to her. She was about to shut the gallery down when a new photo slid into view. A girl, a pretty, rather watery-looking child of about eight or nine with long fair hair. He had a niece he was fond of; he'd mentioned that. His brother's child.

More photos. The child again. Doing a handstand, balancing on a rope swing with her arm and leg stuck out, beaming gappily, holding up a tooth. She meant something to him, this child.

She scrolled further. Was he a little obsessed with this girl? Tick-tick went her brain. Her mouth felt dry.

A recent one of Paul and the child together. Standing on some rocks in the dusk, the girl smiling in a blue knitted bobble hat. Paul's arms were around her. Zoë stared blankly at it.

Next photo. The child again, still on the rocks, this time with an older woman, forty or thereabouts. Tall and slim with blonde hair, wearing jeans and a berry-coloured parka coat. Quite attractive for someone her age.

Then a photo of them all together: Paul, the child and the woman. Paul was in the centre with his arms around the other two. All three of them were smiling. The date on the photo was the Saturday before last. When Paul had been away – at a meeting in Edinburgh, he'd said.

Paul came into the sitting room, naked apart from a towel around his waist.

'Your shower's very –' he said, and stopped.

Her voice came out high and piteous. She hadn't meant it to be like that. She loathed the way it sounded, but the question had to be asked.

'Are you married?'

Even as she said it she thought: *Dramatic much?* She was only asking so that she could be soothed and flattered and reassured. This was his brother's family. The man in the photos, in the poor dusk light – this man was, in fact, his brother. Paul would roll his eyes and chuckle at her mistake. *I told you we looked alike.*

But Paul just went on standing there, and after a moment something inside her seemed to break and fall.

'Yes,' he said.

13

A week after the Cornettos evening I found myself boarding the Friday late-afternoon flight to London, swept along on a tide of shoppers, wailing babies and stags in flashing reindeer sweaters. My seatmates were two hyperactive eight-year-olds, squealing through mouthfuls of Tangfastics about meeting their cousins and going to see *Cursed Child*. One of them kept jerking my elbow as I tried to drink my mini bottle of warm, vinegary white wine. I didn't mind at all. In the cheerful, mellow mood I was in I might have been in a five-star hotel sipping a Château d'Yquem. Katie and Prisha, my old Manways mates, had booked a restaurant near Covent Garden. I was looking forward to sitting under some huge, incomprehensible piece of wall-art, sipping a complicated cocktail and launching into a hilarious catch-up. Unfortunately, Janina, subsumed by a toddler and eight-week-old twins, couldn't make it up from Devon.

I had wondered if Lexie might be upset that I was leaving, but in fact she was over the moon that your mum, unable to bear the thought of you parenting alone, had invited her to stay for the weekend. Thrilled, she had packed her little bag, painstakingly folding in her slipper socks and her pug-patterned hoodie blanket. Then we dropped the bag up to Stillorgan. Your mum's house looked as if a tasteful elf's workshop had exploded in it. Swathes of fake greenery everywhere, curtains of gold lights cascading from the banisters, ceramic snowmen and silver angels dotted about like shrapnel. The front room had been taken over by an eleven-foot Christmas tree topped with the pottery angel with the melted eye that you had made at school thirty-five years ago. Most mind-blowing of all, in Lexie's opinion, was the super-sized selection box which your mum presented to her with a great deal of shushing and hammy glances in my direction.

'I just love Christmas!' your mum said superfluously, clasping her hands. On the hall table was a wooden crib with little painted figures. The decor here was more restrained than elsewhere; no gold ribbons or giant frosted balls, just a simple sprig of holly. The tiny wooden manger was empty. 'It's always been our family tradition,' Breda said, 'to pop the baby in at midnight on Christmas Eve. Adam and his brother used to argue over whose turn it was – remember, Adam?'

'Uh-huh.'

'I thought this year maybe Lexie might do it.'

'Me?' Lexie's eyes began to shine. 'Really?'

'And,' Breda continued, obviously having heard that there was an issue, 'I'm going to teach her some Irish!'

'Oh no,' I said, as Lexie's face fell. 'There's no need. Just enjoy the weekend together.'

'It'll be fun! I still have all of Adam's old books from when he was in Junior Infants.'

'No, please. Let's just wait for the assessment.'

'Assessment?' She was agog. 'What's this?'

So then the explanations, accompanied by an ostentatiously neutral 'no comment' facial expression from you.

'Goodness. I see.' An exchange of glances between the two of you, which, yes, I did catch. 'Everyone seems to have "learning issues" these days, don't they?'

'Your reindeer candle-holders are adorable,' I said, nodding towards a set of nested tables, and the rest of the visit passed smoothly.

The following morning at school I hugged Lexie tightly.

'Bye, sweetheart. Nanna will collect you later. Have fun, and see you on Sunday.'

'Bye, Mummy. I'll miss you.' She returned my hug, but her attention was already elsewhere, focused six hours into the future where an enormous selection box sat waiting for her on Breda's kitchen counter.

Leaving the playground, I spotted Isabel in a silver puffa coat with a white fur collar that gleamed in the winter sun. She was pushing Jake in his buggy, dino dummy plugged firmly in. I zigzagged back through the crowd to meet her.

'Hey,' I said. 'I made that appointment. Thank you so much for the tip.'

Her round, cinnamon-bun face lit up. 'Fantastic!' She manoeuvred the buggy around a traffic cone which was sitting for no clear reason in the middle of the pavement. 'I'm sure she'll be fine. Honestly, all those bookworm kids who do super-well at school, real life is an anticlimax for them. They're always wanting someone in charge to pat them on the head. Our kids will *be* the ones in charge. They'll hit the ground running, wait and see.'

Her optimism matched my buoyant, pre-London mood.

'Heading to Spoon?' I asked. The third-class Christmas coffee morning had been announced earlier that week on the class WhatsApp. I always went to these events to get to know the parents, but at times they could be laborious. With Isabel there though, I thought it might be fun.

'Oh,' she said. 'I'd love to, but . . . unfortunately I've something else arranged.'

'Okay.' I was disappointed. 'Next time.'

'Enjoy,' she said, patting my arm again in that warm, touchy-feely way of hers.

Still smiling, my arm tingling, I went on around the corner to Spoon. Then pushed open the door and exchanged the crisp sunny morning for the gloom and the hush and the smell of old food. Edel was sitting in the corner in her long black coat. I had never seen her without it, indoors or out.

'Hi there!' But as soon as I spoke I realized that my voice was much too loud and cheerful. 'I mean – hey.' I lowered the volume, dialling down the mood. It was clear that all was not well. 'Anything wrong?'

'It's Dervla. She's late. Again! We said eight-forty, and it's now . . .'

'Oh . . . er . . . just gone nine.'

'Typical! That's the problem with Dervla! So flaky and unreliable.'

Dervla arrived, bringing with her a blast of noise and light from the doorway. 'Hello! Hello!'

Coolly, Edel sipped her glass of water.

Dervla said sharply, 'Everything okay?'

'Dervla – sorry, but we did say twenty to? I've been sitting here on my own for the past twenty minutes.'

'Well, gosh. Couldn't you have read your phone or something?'

'That's not the point. It's if I'd *known*. I mightn't have rushed so much to get here.'

'The problem with Edel,' Dervla said in a low voice when Edel had gone to order a scone, 'is that she can be quite neurotic and controlling.'

'So!' I said brightly as Edel returned, 'Anyone doing anything nice for the weekend?'

'What would we be doing?' Edel asked.

'I'm going to London,' I said. 'Later this afternoon. Haven't been back for months so I'm really looking forward to it.'

Dervla made a face. 'Crowded cities wouldn't be my scene.'

'Easy known you've only the one child,' Edel said gloomily. 'When you've two, like I have, you never get to go anywhere.'

'Well, why don't we organize something some weekend?' I said. 'What about a cycle? The bicycle lanes on the coast here are great. You can hire bikes all along the route. I'm sure the girls would enjoy it.'

'Sounds very . . . healthy.' Edel looked doubtful. 'I'm not sure it would work though. How would we get there?'

'Just, you know. Meet at a point and hire the bikes.'

'I couldn't see it working.' Edel shook her head. 'It's just not that easy when you've two.'

'Right so!' Dervla clicked her pen. 'I'm trying to organize the school Gaeilge fundraising fair. The idea is, the girls bring in old toys or books, home-baked buns and so on, then on the day they bring in five euro and buy everything through Irish. Mrs Bakewell is *almost* on board with it. The major obstacle, apparently, to people bringing food in is allergies. Which I can understand, because Siofra gets terrible diarrhoea with kiwis.'

'Polly Mayhew gets anaphylaxis with nuts,' Edel said.

'She would!'

'No, I think it's genuine? I heard she had a major reaction and ended up being admitted to hospital a couple of times.'

More mums were arriving at the coffee morning, shuffling exhaustedly between the tables like extras from *Day of the Dead*, trundling huge buggies, weighed down with toddlers, bags, snack-boxes and other vast piles of paraphernalia. Hard to know what their true personalities were, so preoccupied with their offspring were they, whipping off and on nappies, tearing open snack packets, dabbing, snatching, leaping up mid-sentence. Focusing on the children's needs almost to the exclusion of all else. Had I been like that with Lexie? Tupperware snapped, crumbs sprayed, Peppa Pig snorted from phones. 'Anyone know the wi-fi code?' 'Violet, where's your other sock?' 'Fionn, oh my God, don't *do* that!'

'You've got your hands full,' I said to the frazzled-looking woman beside me. 'Can I help? Let me put those bags under the table.'

'Oh, that would be – Fionn, *no!* Don't eat that! Here, sit here beside Mummy and I'll get you a rice cake. No, please, not the . . . use a tissue . . . oh dear! Look, why don't you draw something? What about that stegosaurus you drew the other day? That was really excellent.'

'Full on, isn't it?' I said sympathetically when she drew breath.

'Don't tell me!'

'I remember those days with Lexie.'

'Mmmm. It's different with boys though. The problem is, he's so bright? Means he's constantly on the go.'

'That must be –'

'Mummy!'

'– must be very –'

'MUMMY!'

'Yes, sweetie?'

'What are dinosaurs made of?'

'See?' She looked triumphant. 'Boys are so much more, I don't know. *Curious* than girls? Dinosaurs were like *reptiles*, sweetheart.'

'What are reptiles?'

'Now, *reptiles* are . . .'

Back on my other side: '– a disgrace. I'm going to email her again. If we could get a few signatures together. Would you sign, Sara?'

'What? Sure.'

'I mean, it's so bad for the children's health.'

'Is it . . .'

'The rubbish some parents send them in with. If we could have at least one day when they bring in carrot sticks or tomatoes. My aim is to persuade Mrs Bakewell to promote Vegetable Thursday.'

'Of course!' I tried to mirror Dervla's enthusiasm. Since I had no real opinion on it, it seemed easiest to agree. I wished I could think these things mattered though, instead of always having to fake it. Perhaps then I'd find it easier to get those deeper conversations going. Dervla, for example, with her zeal for organization, her eye for the details that others thought beneath them; it was her thing, her essence, and she glowed with it. The only thing I could honestly say I had ever felt passionate about was Lexie. Again that feeling I sometimes had, that something was missing in me, like I lacked a soul or something.

Well, I *was* looking forward to this! The plane banked; ears popping, I pressed my forehead to the plasticky window. The Thames loops, slung like a pulley around the Millennium Dome, glittered in the evening sun. Finally, somewhere not constantly covered in thick grey cloud.

The Piccadilly Line was jammed and became more so the closer we came to town. I disembarked at Covent Garden, deep underground. Hordes of people crushed into the rubber-smelling lift, like the wildebeest stampede in *The Lion King*. Topside the air was cool, filled with the pleasurable evening sounds of music and footsteps and voices, the rumble of red buses, cleaner and glossier than the ones in Dublin. I stood and breathed it all in, realizing how much I had missed it.

Katie and Prisha had booked a restaurant I'd never heard of called Hubris. It was crowded – everywhere here was crowded – and buzzy, all gold velvet sofas, giant ferns in brass pots, a brown marble art deco bar with blue-lit shelves behind. The women's bathroom had pink marble sinks, gold grouting and a sparkly gold floor. Gaudy, pretentious, tacky and perfect! Emerging, I spotted Katie and Prisha semaphoring from a long table in the middle of the room. I'd thought it would just be the three of us, but there were at least a dozen women there, all super-stylishly dressed, all with shiny silk tops and dresses, shiny teeth and hair, shiny shiny shiny. Katie and Prisha introduced them. Over the thump and jingle of Ariana Grande's 'Santa Tell Me' I half caught names and occupations: a BBC reporter just back from the Sino-Russian border, a government public-health advisor I was certain I recognized from TV, various finance people involved with multimillion-pound contracts. The tasting menu had just arrived and was being passed down the table: crab pancakes, okonomiyaki, hot sticks, matcha ice cream. The conversation spun and sparkled with the beaten brass plates.

'– Ironman was tough but I –'

'– cycling in Northern Ethiopia, it was fifty degrees –'

'– negotiating with the Chinese, but they're –'

'– why I learned Mandarin, you can control –'

I sipped my jasmine and calvados, taking it all in, swivelling my head like a Wimbledon spectator. The snappy banter, the out-of-the-box thinking, the sheer confidence they all felt that the world was listening, waiting for their opinions. These highly driven Londoners, already with a weight of achievement behind them yet still pushing forward, constantly compelled towards some distant horizon. The Dubliners I had met, by comparison, seemed softer and woollier, content to consume rather than create. Londoners, of course, being far sharper and harder to bump into unless you had your own glittering armour.

'Enjoying yourself?' Katie shouted across the table at me. 'Hope we're not boring the pants off you.'

'Certainly not! It's a fantastic change from all the school mum-conversations.'

'Eek.' Katie wrinkled her nose. She had no children and no intention of having any. 'I can imagine.'

'I realize it oils the wheels of civilization and all that, but I seem to be utterly hopeless at small talk.'

'What do you mean?' said a spiky little person called Harriet beside me. '*Small* talk?'

'I mean at the school gates, you know, the day-to-day stuff. Whether the teacher would prefer flowers or a voucher for her Christmas present. Whether Tuesday should be tracksuit day.'

'But you specifically said just now "mum conversations".'

'Well, it is mostly mums —'

'So, if women do it, it's "small" talk, is it? What sort of weighty talk do men do, then?'

I'd forgotten about Harriet, always prickly, always having to analyse and politicize everything. Since I'd left, Katie seemed to have got more friendly with her.

'Do men not care about what their children wear?'

'They do. Probably. But —'

'Pay no attention to Harriet,' Katie advised. 'She's hamstered. Won't remember a thing about this in the morning.

'So misogynistic,' Harriet said to the table. 'But then Éire is very backwards like that. You'd never catch me living there.'

Several pisco sours later the lights seemed too bright and I couldn't feel where my lips were. It had been a long time since I'd drunk that much alcohol. They all kept talking about work and I began to feel out of things. Manways had moved on; new people and projects, new places to eat and go out. I'd barely left London and already my finger was well and truly off the pulse, as if I'd been living in that Tir na nÓg place I'd read about in Lexie's Irish books where three months equalled a hundred years in the human world. At two in the morning, out of the habit of staying up late, I called it a night and took a taxi to Vauxhall. Exhilarated and exhausted, I fell on to the waterbed and lay with one foot on the floor to stop the room from spinning.

14

I hadn't closed the bedroom blinds. A metallic glare drilled into my eyeballs. Queasily, I pulled the duvet over my face. It settled on my mouth, ballooning in and out as I breathed.

My plan for the day was to visit my mother. I had debated with myself whether to let her know I was in England, but in the end duty had won the day.

I had tried to persuade her to come up and meet me in London.

'I'll treat you,' I'd said. 'We'll go somewhere nice. Have afternoon tea.'

Silence as the suggestion fell, twisting and tumbling, into a deep abyss. What had I been thinking? She was not a scone and éclair type of mum.

I eased myself out of bed. Luckily, your lodger was away so I was free to shuffle to the kitchen in my underwear and make coffee. Magda had been in to clean since you'd stayed earlier in the week. The kitchen was spotless, as was the living area with its picture windows and clean grey light. Apart from your triple bank of computer screens in the alcove, there was little sign that anyone lived here. Sipping Nespresso, I ambled to your desk. Here, too, Magda's touch was evident. You were a messy worker, testily flinging papers here, there and everywhere during phone calls, but the desktop had been tidied, the ergonomic chair tucked in underneath, all papers and folders gathered in a neat pile. Something glittered, catching my eye: a small shiny object on top of the pile. Frowning, I looked down at it.

HOOONNKKK! Lexie had installed a ship's foghorn as your ringtone.

'All okay?' you asked when I located my phone. 'Magda been?'

'Yes. Everything very spick and span. How's Lexie?'

'Having a whale of a time with Mum. She wants to speak to you.'

'Okay. By the way – when's your lodger coming back?'

'Next week. I think. Why?'

'How long has he been away?'

'About a fortnight. Something wrong?'

'No,' I said. 'Just wondering.'

'Right. Well, I won't keep you. I'm sure you've got plans. I'll put Lex on to say hi.'

After chatting with Lexie I wandered to the window. In the daylight the shimmering fairy-tale bridges had vanished, replaced by a forest of concrete tower blocks. Without Lexie's toys lying about and her gaudy little drawings stuck with magnets to the fridge, the flat seemed lonely; sterile; more like a hotel than someone's home. Strange to think that we had ever lived here as a family. You and me I could still see, coming home late like I had last night, me kicking off my heels, you pressing up against me, pushing me on to the empty steel kitchen counter, grunting that it turned you on to mess up these perfect surroundings, my perfect dress – ultimately my perfect flat stomach with the pregnancy. But there the memories began to falter. I tried to picture Lexie in this corporate, climate-controlled space, high up here on her own behind the soundproofed triple-glazing instead of swinging from muddy ropes on the Green or cartwheeling on the smelly, rocky beach. Again, that dislocated Tir na nÓg feeling.

*

At Victoria I bought a bunch of winter lilies at a flower stall and caught the train to Leatherhead, where I exchanged for the bus to Flitston. My old hometown wasn't looking its best, tattier and more built-up than when I had last visited. The meadow behind the Georgian library had been obliterated by office buildings and a multistorey car park. But down the hill between the health centre and the Morrisons, my old school, St Ita's Catholic Girls' Primary (the boys' was next door) looked just the same. There was the wall with the spikes on top, the blue tubular steel railings and the playground with – just visible from here – the steps leading to the netball court.

Staring through the bus windows that smelled of halitosis, I found myself whooshed back in time. Although I had attended St Ita's since the age of four, the only memories triggered now by those steps were of Grace Gillespie, who hadn't even arrived until Year 6. See, from the day Grace had started there, those steps had been hers. It was she who decided each day which girls could join her there to view her collections of Pogs and scented erasers and which had to go and play elsewhere. Grace lived in the 'nice' part of Flitston, in a house with a large garden and a fishpond and a treehouse. She had been to Disneyland and had her own pink Game Boy. All of which would have been fine, except that Grace did not wear her good fortune lightly, more like a heavy backpack that swung when she moved, thwacking lesser travellers hard on the head. Grace had this – looking back now, I see it as an almost pathological need to control other people. She had landed in our previously docile and unworldly class like a bomb, exploding and shattering pre-existing friendships, rebuilding the pieces like Lego to suit herself. She was generous with gifts and invitations to her house to play with her treehouse and her Super Nintendo – but she had other methods of control too.

The first person to come to her attention in a negative way

was Lucy Wright. Prior to Grace's arrival, if we'd any kind of a leader, by default it was probably Lucy. Her parents had always been very enthusiastic and inclusive, going out of their way to include the whole class in birthday parties with chocolate fountains and magicians – I think now it was because Lucy was rather an awkward child, clumsy and over-loud, and they had worked hard to help her to overcome that. We girls had grown up with Lucy since we were babies, so if she was occasionally a bit bossy we were used to it and didn't mind. It didn't take Grace, the new contender for the top spot, long to detect the many flaws in Lucy's armour. She lay low at first, coiled and watching; a tiny sting here, a poisonous comment there, but when Lucy finally lost her temper one day and shouted at her – well, that was when Grace struck. Lucy had attacked Grace first – did we all see that? – and was dealt with, promptly and ruthlessly, like a plump, pale worm.

'She smells,' Grace said, wrinkling her nose. 'Of BO. Haven't you noticed? I mean, I'd never have mentioned it if she hadn't been so mean to me first. Screaming at me like that!'

'Cathy,' she whispered during a rainy breaktime in the banana-smelling classroom, 'did you know that Lucy tells everyone you're fat? I'm only saying it because I hate the way she pretends to be your friend. And Martha, I probably shouldn't tell you this, but she said your laugh was really fake and annoying.'

Cathy cried while Martha said, bewildered, 'I don't think Lucy would have said those things.'

'Oh, so you think that kind of behaviour is acceptable? You think it's fine to make Cathy cry like that? Well, whatever, but personally *I* think bullying is disgusting. It's okay, Cathy. Come to my house on Friday after school. A bunch of us are going to make Mr Frostys.'

Lucy didn't return to St Ita's after Christmas. I think her

family was moving house anyway, so probably it had nothing to do with Grace. But after that Grace's path was clear.

Although I was very aware of her – it was impossible not to be – I had little to do with her at first. My best friend, Moll, and I liked nerdy things: cycling to the field behind the Multiplex to feed the horses, lying in Moll's garden in dens made out of deck chairs and blankets reading Malory Towers and the Famous Five. We were quiet, swotty girls, as much above Grace's notice as below it. But one day I was on the netball steps – Moll was off school for some reason and I was sitting there on my own, humming and scratching my initials into the concrete – when Grace came up with her new best mates Leah and Joanna, two previously easy-going, gullible girls who used to giggle hysterically if anyone said the word 'knickers' but who now followed Grace everywhere, watchful as the abducted guard dog puppies from *Animal Farm*.

'Excuse me,' Grace said in her bleaty little voice. 'But can you go and do that somewhere else?'

Shading my eyes, I gazed up at her, at her puffy, petulant mouth and her round blue eyes.

'Move!' She made a shooing motion with her hand.

Politely I said, 'I was here first.'

Grace's eyebrows fused. Slowly she turned and, probably for the first time since she had moved here, gave me her full attention, looking me up and down, her top lip up, her teeth showing.

'I said *move*!'

'Nope.'

To this day, I don't know why I did it. I didn't even particularly want to stay on the steps; I could have scratched my initials as easily anywhere else. It was just that I disliked what she had done to the class. The whole feel of it had changed. Some of the girls I'd been friendly with since Reception barely spoke to anyone now except her. I wouldn't have said I was a confrontational child, but I could be feisty – far more impassioned than I am now, if I felt that something wasn't right. I wasn't afraid to stand up and state my case. And having once gone to the trouble of doing that, I was not inclined to back down.

Grace made an incredulous little noise. People were starting to gather, her friends, mine – other bookish girls like me – drifting across the playground. Joanna and Leah must have been sending out smoke signals: *Trouble a-brewin' at the Old School Steps.* A circle formed, with Grace and me at the centre.

'I don't,' Grace said, very slowly and distinctly, 'think you fully understand. These are our steps. We use them. So I'll give you one more chance to get off them.'

'Or what?'

I spoke confidently, but my heart had started to race. Something about her expression was triggering a drumbeat warning from the deep, animal part of my brain: *This is not normal. You don't know what you're dealing with here.* But what could she do? I was taller than she was and, I'd have bet, fitter and quicker. I scrambled to my feet, letting her see my height. The girls around us were silent. Grace's face had turned bright red, as much I think from humiliation as anger that everyone in the class had witnessed her failure to make me obey. Her fists clenched. 'Get. Off. MY STEPS!' With every word her voice rose, ending in a squeak of rage.

A teacher arrived, clapping her hands. 'Come along, girls. Bell's gone. Into class. *Now!* Grace Gillespie, are you listening to me?'

She gave me a look then, a look of sheer, cold hatred, way out of proportion to what anyone would expect from a simple childhood squabble over a step. 'Who do you think you are?' she hissed. 'You with your weirdo family. How *dare* you speak to me like that? You'll be sorry.'

Eyeballed by the teacher, she stamped off across the playground. My face and chest hummed as I made my own way to the classroom. From the back row behind me I heard the whispers, felt the stares, like fingers poking on my neck, fingers of spite and ill will. She wanted me to look at her, but I didn't. I sat as coolly as I could at the front on my own with Moll's empty chair beside me, but my fingers couldn't feel the pen I was holding. 'You'll be sorry,' she'd said. And believe me, I was.

The one time you visited my childhood home you commented that it must have been the inspiration for Harry Potter's house on Privet Drive. Brown-brick semi, brown-doored garage, diamond-paned PVC windows – in fact, the basic design was not unlike the houses in our Dublin estate, but where Brookview had brightly painted front doors and children playing and flowers growing, here in Surrey all was monochrome, with a dull, sidelined air.

My mother opened the front door. I hadn't seen her for several months, but she looked much the same; tall and rangy, and, in fact, quite healthy compared to how I'd often seen her in the past. A little faded and empty about the eyes perhaps, but then she was approaching seventy. Her grey hair was short, combed into a side parting that showed a lot of her scalp. She wore leggings, a hoodie and a navy gilet. Plain and functional but neat.

'Well,' she said in her usual brief way.

'How are you?' I reached to give her a tentative hug. Under the gilet she was thinner than I had expected. I handed her the lilies.

'Oh. How much did they cost? We've plenty of winter blooms in the garden.'

While she boiled the kettle I located a vase for the flowers. The orangey pine kitchen was very tidy and clean. The sitting room with its corduroy sofa and rose-patterned curtains was pristine too. In my childhood there had been mess everywhere, unwashed plates and glasses on the floor, meals rarely cleared away. Now all the debris had been removed, including all traces of me and Steve. No photos of us anywhere. No pottery angels with melted eyes and bright tinsel halos. Just bare surfaces, air-fresheners in all the sockets and a strong smell of pine. Was it always like this nowadays or had she tidied up especially for my arrival?

'Have you eaten?' she called over her shoulder, busy hanging teabags from mugs.

'Not yet.'

'Oh.' Doubtfully, she said, 'I think there's ham in the fridge. Maybe I should have got in something . . . but Alison and Geoff are coming later for cards and they usually bring a tray so . . .'

'It's fine,' I said. 'I'm not hungry.' I took the mug she handed me and sat at the table. 'Who're Alison and Geoff?'

'People I play cards with. We're in a club.'

'Ah.'

She sat opposite me with her own mug and a plate of Bourbons. One eye kept watering and she dabbed at it with a tissue. Her hand, though, was steady. If she was drinking these days, she was hiding it well.

'No tree?' I asked, looking around.

'What?'

'A Christmas tree? Even a little one from a garden centre?'

'Who'd see it?'

'Well – me? And your friends? The people you play cards with?'

'They see me all the time. I don't need to put on a show.'

The kitchen was quiet enough that I could hear the ticking of the carriage clock next door. I had tried to switch on the battered old radio on the windowsill but just got static.

'So,' I said. 'How have you been?'

She shrugged. 'I do my best. It's all anyone can do.'

'Heard anything from Steve?'

'No. He's not very good at getting in touch. Lisa was talking to him a couple of weeks back and said he seemed all right.'

'Good to hear.'

'By the way, Lisa's getting married again.'

'Really? Who to?'

'Some man she met at her gym. She didn't give much information.'

'Well,' I said, 'she deserves her happiness. Things with Steve can't have been easy. If you're talking to her, give her my best.'

'I will. Though if you ask me, we won't be hearing much from her from now on.'

'No. You're probably right.' The clock ticked on. In the distance a dog barked, a hoarse, monotonous, emotionless sound that went on and on as if the dog was tied up somewhere and desperately needed to hear something apart from his own breathing. Purely for something to do I took a Bourbon and snapped it in half, scattering crumbs.

'Adam's doing very well,' I said. 'He's been working all hours, but his new company is finally starting to take off.'

'Lovely.' A sip of her tea. You and she had never seen eye to eye.

'And Lexie's fine,' I went on, since she hadn't asked. 'Doing really well at her new school.'

'Ah, good.'

'She'd love to see you, Mum.'

'Well, you didn't bring her, did you?' She looked about her in an exaggerated way.

'No, but next time. Or you could come to us? See where we're living now?'

'Maybe.'

'Perhaps in the spring? You could show me the places where

you spent your childhood. I haven't seen much of Ireland yet outside of Dublin. It would be lovely if we could see it together. Travel around a bit.'

'We'll see. Flights cost money.'

'We'd pay. Come any time. Come for Christmas.' Suddenly I felt sorry for her, all alone here in her brown, pine-smelling house. 'You'd be very welcome.'

'What would I do there? I left Ireland years ago. Wouldn't know a soul there now.'

'You know me. And Lexie! Lexie would love to have you!'

She thinned her lips. 'We'll see. Not Christmas anyway, not at this stage. But maybe, as you say, in the spring.'

She was eyeing the biscuit crumbs and the ring of moisture my mug had left on the table as if physically holding herself back from leaping up to wipe them away. She was not just neater and tidier these days but obsessed with it. All the rage and fire from the old days had burned out, leaving only this hollow, ashy shell. I had felt sorry for her, but she didn't seem to feel it for herself. Maybe she was even perfectly content.

I took pity on her and allowed her to clean up while I went for a tour. My old bed was stripped, the coverless pillows and duvet folded on top. There were chips in the wall-paint where my Nirvana and Alice in Chains posters had once been. On a shelf in the otherwise empty wardrobe was a box with what was left of my teenage possessions. Some CDs, a couple of books, various certificates and class prizes. A photo of me, aged about eight, in the garden with Steve and my parents. The trees and grass were white. We had built a snowman with a row of stones for a mouth. All four of us were smiling. After my father had left a few months later there had been no more smiles, no more snowmen. Snowman-building sessions had ceased as abruptly and permanently as if they had never existed. I remember meeting him a year or so later at a rushed meal at a

Harvester – he and Michaela had come down from Scotland to tell us they were engaged – and thinking it was as if he hardly knew us, as if the person who had once laughed with us and tickled us and carried us on his shoulders had been abducted and replaced by an alien.

I left the house and went for a short walk around the enclave and down the bridle path where the branches met overhead and long straggly brambles hung down like the legs of giant dead spiders. Back in the kitchen, we had another cup of tea. This time I held the mug in my hand rather than leave a ring on the table. At four I said, 'Well, I'd better go. You'll want to be getting ready for your visitors.'

'You *could* stay,' she said. 'If you haven't any other plans.'

'I'm meeting friends for dinner,' I lied, because I had in fact left the evening free.

'Ah. Well then.' She seemed relieved.

Earlier than planned, we said goodbye in the porch and I repeated my invitation to come to Dublin. She seemed surprised when I hugged her again, standing stiffly in my arms; not as if she hated it, just as if hugging was this fancy thing people did now that they never had in her day and there was no need. Glancing back just before I turned out of the estate, I was surprised to see her still standing in the porch. Then I realized she was busy straightening the mat I must have nudged out of place.

On the train back to London I found myself wondering for the first time in my life what her childhood in Ireland had been like. Why she had never gone back there and didn't seem to want to, even now. Her parents were long dead, but even when they were alive she had never visited them nor they her. It had never occurred to me before to ask. Even if I had, I doubt she would have discussed it. I had never known her well and it was unlikely now that I ever would. I should have felt sad about it, but the truth was, I didn't. She was more like a distant aunt or a neighbour than a mother. My grieving had all happened a long time ago.

For my last day in London, I had arranged to meet Katie for lunch at Shepherd Market. My overnight knapsack on my back, I navigated the steep escalators and endless curving tunnels leading up from the platform at Green Park. Giant advertisements towered at every turn: BUY THIS! EXPERIENCE THAT! The gastropub Katie had chosen was quaint and festive with little Christmas trees everywhere and all the staff in Santa hats. The herring salad and hard seltzer were delicious and Katie was her usual lively self. But things were a little rushed as she was distracted by a work presentation she had to finish, and although my flight was still four hours away there had been announcements in the Tube stations warning of delays. So we skipped coffee and hugged each other and said we hoped it wouldn't be as long again before the next time.

As I turned left on to Piccadilly a man came racing around the corner, jacket flying, and almost smacked into me. He braked, his arms windmilling, leaning forward on his toes. 'So sor—' I began, but he swore, swerved around me with a filthy look and kept going.

When I first moved to Dublin a woman on the street had accidentally trodden on the back of my shoe. Expecting her to tut sharply and keep going, like a normal urban person, I was amazed when she stopped and came back to me. 'Sorry, love. I was in my own world there. Did I hurt you? Are you all right?' I'd thought at first that she must be taking the piss.

Walking back to the Tube station past the queues of black cabs and buses, the selfie-taking tourists, the sellers hawking Oxford University hoodies and Big Ben snow globes, just like that, the thought popped into my head: *London isn't home for me any more.*

15

'Yes,' Paul said simply. 'Yes, I'm married.'

Even through the sucking-in of air through a windpipe that seemed suddenly the diameter of a straw Zoë managed to lever herself up off the sofa, to stutter out the questions she knew she would want answers to later.

Not only, it seemed, was he married. With an eight-year-old daughter living in Ireland. It turned out he wasn't even a GP.

And his name wasn't Paul. It was Adam. He worked in finance. In RegTech – whatever the hell that meant.

'Zoë.' His hands were clasped behind his head. He looked as shocked and distressed as she felt. 'This is awful. I feel terrible. That day at the station . . . it was meant to be a joke –'

'A joke!'

'I didn't think I'd ever see you again. Paul – that's my brother who's the GP – so when I saw your medical papers his name just . . . But I never meant it to go further. I never meant to cause . . . *this*.'

'Put your clothes on, please.'

He looked down. His towel had slid off and lay puddled at his feet.

'Not that,' she said. 'Your proper clothes. I need you to leave.'

Since he seemed incapable of movement, she marched to the bathroom and fetched them herself. Her breathing still wasn't right. Her hands felt like giant mittens as she gathered up socks and boxers from the floor. She saw herself in the steamed-up mirror, blurrily holding his underwear, and thought in a panicky way, *What am I doing?* Was he for real? Surely this wasn't real. She'd nodded off while he was having his shower. Or this was a spectacularly ill-judged wind-up. Any second now he'd burst out laughing and shout: *Gotcha! That'll teach you to look through my phone.* The steam smelled of his cardamom-scented shower gel; she inhaled a draught of it and thought she was going to faint.

She sat on the loo seat, holding on to the edge of the sink until her vision came back. Then she returned to the sitting room and flung his clothes on a chair. The movement knocked his phone to the floor. That stupid, stupid phone! Why hadn't she left it alone? Minded her own business? They'd be eating dinner now. They'd be on their second glass of wine, laughing together under her potted Christmas tree with the delicate glass Bath ball hanging from its branch. She wanted to run at him. Claw at him. Rewind the past five minutes and beg him, beg him to forget.

'When you rang me,' Paul – *Adam!* – said, struggling to haul his trousers up over his damp legs, 'I thought I'd meet you just the once. I was swamped with work and a bit . . . lonely. I know how that sounds, but I honestly thought you'd be the same. That we'd both see it as a . . . I never thought we'd get on as well as we did.' He finished buttoning his jeans. Slumped his shoulders and said in a low voice, 'As we do.'

'No. We don't. I don't even know your real name! And don't give me that bullshit . . . *impulse*. You went to the trouble of getting . . . I mean, bloody hell . . . a *fake passport*.'

'It's not fake. It's my brother's.'

'Dear God!'

'It's not how it sounds. I only borrowed it.'

She flung his trainers at him. Hard. He brought his hands down quickly to intercept them.

'Please,' he said. 'Let me explain. The day I took his passport . . . I'd met you twice by then. And I liked you. A lot, in fact, but I didn't plan to see you again. Whatever we had, I knew for both our sakes it had to stop.'

'Just put your shoes on and go.'

'Then one day I was visiting my parents' house and happened to come across Paul's passport in a drawer. Out of nowhere – seeing his name – you were in my head. That day at the station . . . me writing his name on that piece of paper . . . us looking at each other when I got on the train . . . My God, Zoë, I thought you were –'

She remembered it too. Her chest tightened and she had to fight not to weep.

'I had to see you again. Utterly selfish as I know it was. I took the passport because I thought . . . Zoë's an intelligent woman, she'll want to check up on me . . .'

'And what about your brother? Didn't he need his passport?'

'He's not planning his holidays until August . . . he . . .'

'Oh my God, I don't CARE! Listen to yourself! You're a complete psychopath! I've had enough. You need to go.' Her voice cracked. 'Please.'

The sky was a black bowl with fuzzy orange edges. No stars, just orange clouds and a bad-tempered, thrusting rain. She handed him his jacket. She needed him out. Needed him gone before her legs gave and she sank to the floor.

On the communal balcony he turned, squinting in the glare of the security light. 'I thought it would fizzle out.' He had to raise his voice over the rain. 'We hardly knew each other. You're busy, I'm busy. But it didn't fizzle. It became stronger. I've lain awake at night thinking about it. All I know is, I didn't want it to stop.'

'You're married, Paul. Adam! *Married!* Your wife – I'll assume she's in the dark as much as I was. And your little girl . . .'

His colour rising, he looked away.

Slam the door, Zoë. *Do it!* But she couldn't. Her body yearned after him as he trudged down the balcony. She'd got used to seeing him here. Seeing him stride towards her in the evenings, his face alight with amusement, ready with some new meme or joke he'd heard that he knew she'd appreciate. She'd got used to thinking that he was hers. But he wasn't. He was someone else's, with his kind grey eyes. Eyes that made you think you could trust him. But it was just a trick of his genes, the way the pigment happened to be arranged in his irises.

At the top of the stairwell, he looked back. Pathetically, he called, 'I never meant to hurt you. I never meant it to end like this.'

'Don't be such a fucking cliché. How did you expect it to end?'

This time she did slam the door.

Then hung on to it, giddy and sick. She couldn't believe it. Couldn't believe it. The person she had grown to trust, the person who had done this to her, was the very person she would have wanted to tell about this. She wanted to fly out there and call him back. Desperately wanted to cling to him for comfort even as he was the one who had destroyed her.

16

Overall, the London weekend had been good for me. It had kickstarted my sludgy, silted-up brain, made me see things in a new way. And as so often happens with these things, one change led to another. Starting with what happened at the school gates the following morning.

Lexie was delighted to see me home. She'd had a 'brilliant' weekend at your mum's. They had baked cupcakes and next-door's elderly Jack Russell had come to visit. In the playground she raced off to show Mia and Imogen the gift I'd brought her, a pencil case shaped like a spaniel with long fluffy ears. I waved her off and turned for home.

Exiting through the gates, I was preoccupied, still thinking about certain aspects of the London trip, so it was entirely without thinking – almost a pure spinal reflex – that when a small neon-green blur came whizzing past me, heading for the road, my hand shot out and scooped it up just as a large van came flying around the corner. My hair blew back as the van roared past, directly over the spot where, a second before, the green blur had been. The van screeched around the turn at the end of the street and vanished.

It took a couple of seconds for my brain to catch up: *Okay, okay, woah, what's going on here?* Whereupon it promptly shut down for analysis, leaving me frozen to the spot with a howling, green-jacketed toddler in my arms. Then a woman came racing up and snatched him from my grip.

'Jake!' she screamed. She shook him, then pulled him close and hugged him. Then held him out and shook him again.

'How many times? How many *bloody* times? If this lady hadn't –' She stopped and stared at me. 'Sara!'

It was Isabel, wild-eyed and puce-faced.

'Sara! My God! He just yanked his hand away. He was gone in a second – if it hadn't been for you, he'd have been killed.'

'It probably would have missed him,' I said, though in fact I wasn't at all sure that was the case.

'No! Must have been doing sixty, easy, outside a primary school, the arsehole! If I'd got his number . . . Thank you, Sara! So, so much!'

I hadn't seen her like this before. Usually she was so placid and serene. She knelt to wipe the bawling Jake's nose and hoick his trousers up over his nappy. Every so often she gave him another little shake. '*Don't* run into the *road* like that! How many times? My God.' She put her hand to her eyes. 'It's like talking to the bloody schoolbag.'

She loaded him into his buggy and clipped on the straps while he writhed and complained.

'Don't bother! You're staying in there till you're twenty!'

She clambered back to her feet.

'Look. A few of us are having coffee this Wednesday –'

'The usual in Spoon?'

'God, no!' She gave a little laugh. 'No one normal goes to those!'

It turned out that even though Erica, as class PA rep, set up the Spoon mornings for the class, she and the rest of her group did their best to avoid them unless there was a specific reason to attend, like a fundraiser. Otherwise they held their own separate coffee mornings in a café further away or at each other's homes.

'Ah. Okay.'

'So.' Isabel raised her eyebrows at me. 'Wednesday morning at mine? I'll text you the address.'

'Sure. Yes. I'd love that! Thanks.'

'Great! See you then! And thanks so much again for snatching Jake from the jaws of death. I'm really very grateful.'

'Any time! Happy to help.'

She left, waving. I went my own way, wishing I didn't feel quite so pathetically flattered and grateful for the invitation. After all the grumbling I'd been doing about the Beautiful Mums, here I was jumping at the chance to join them as soon as they crooked a finger. I remembered too with a little inward squirm the other morning when Isabel and I had met, when she had declined my invitation to come to Spoon and smiled and patted me on the arm. 'Enjoy!' she had said kindly. How foolishly pleased I had felt, unaware of what was really going on.

I shook myself. Get over it, Sara. That was then and this was now.

I was a few minutes late arriving to Isabel's. There were no names on the streets and the house numbers weren't in order. Her house was in a terrace of Georgian cottages painted in pastel greens and pinks, separated from the pavement by spiked iron railings. Number fifteen had a pale blue front door flanked by two bay trees in pots. The paint on the door was peeling and the bay trees were tangled with bindweed. The shabbiness, however, merely added to the charm. In the sash window sat a stuffed blue rabbit threaded with a string of tiny, coloured Christmas lights. I pressed the doorbell and waited, clutching the box of macaroons I'd brought, conscious of a wheeling of butterflies as I wondered whether Vanessa would be there and how that might go.

'Sara!' Isabel seemed delighted to see me. 'Thank you so much for coming. Come in!'

The house was one of those which is larger inside than it appears on the outside. The narrow hallway extended a long way back, the black-and-white tiled floor littered with children's wellies, plastic dinosaurs and Mr Men books. An old-fashioned upright bicycle with a basket stood propped against the wall, half hidden by a row of coats bulging from hooks. There was a cosy smell of coffee and mince pies. Isabel led me towards the rear, pausing to shove Jake's pushchair under the stairs and scoop up a naked, headless Barbie doll which she held in a helpless way for a couple of seconds then tossed over the banister.

'Please excuse the mess, Sara.'

Down a short flight of steps was the kitchen, warm and cluttered in a charming, wholesome way, rather like Isabel herself. Blue-painted cupboards, crookedly draped with holly and tinsel, an oversized dresser stuffed with cookbooks, rosettes and jugs of dried flowers, a set of French doors leading to a tiny courtyard filled with pots of browning shrubs. The centre of the kitchen was dominated by a scrubbed wooden island, around which sat four women. Heads turned as we descended the steps.

'This is Sara,' Isabel introduced me. 'Some of you already know her from school – her daughter, Lexie, is in Ms Brennan's class.'

'Hi, Sara.' A woman with cropped dark hair gave me a friendly wave. 'Orla. I've heard Sadhbh mention Lexie a few times.'

Isabel introduced the others. Vanessa, whom of course I knew, deep in conversation with a slender, black-haired woman called Marina. They paused briefly to murmur in my direction, Vanessa once again showing no sign whatsoever that she recognized me. Perhaps she really did have a problem with faces. The fourth woman was Erica, the class PA rep. I saw her about most days but had never spoken to her as she was always rushing here and there, always with a dozen people to speak to and catch up with. She had at least four children, possibly five, all involved with multiple after-school activities, and of course she had her PA duties to attend to. 'Lovely to meet you.' She waggled her fingers at me, though her eyes didn't quite meet mine.

'Coffee?' Isabel asked.

'Lovely. Thanks.'

'I'll see if I can get this bloody thing going again.'

Orla smiled and patted the empty stool next to her. 'How's Lexie settling in?' From the far end of the island, Vanessa's cool voice floated: 'What's this, Isabel?'

'Be nice, Van!'

'I'm not sure I know what you mean?'

I refocused on Orla. 'Getting there, thanks. Slowly but surely.'

'We heard you saved Jake from being hit by a van.' Orla's hazel eyes were round.

'Literally,' Isabel called from the Aga. 'She was his guardian angel.'

'Oh, not really,' I said. 'Just a case of right place, right time.'

'Well, it's very lucky you were there.' Orla, like most of the other women there, was dressed as if she had just come from the gym: camo leggings, clean white trainers, pastel-coloured Lycra top. Erica and Vanessa could have been twins except that Erica's features were pointier and her blonde hair, cut in the same bob as Vanessa's, had a faint greenish tinge. Isabel had a more cosy, haphazard style and wore a long flowing skirt instead of the leggings. Only Marina looked completely different to the others. She wore the sort of clothes that if you closed your eyes you wouldn't be able to describe except to say that they were 'drapey' and 'grey'; the sort of fashionable but highly impractical clothes you might see on a runway. She had flawless, very pale skin and a bored, listless air, her eyes half closed as if she couldn't be bothered to open them all the way. She spoke very little and almost exclusively to Vanessa.

'So,' said Orla as Isabel placed a cup of rich-smelling frothy coffee in front of me, 'how are you enjoying Dublin?'

143

'I like it. Adam, my husband, is still travelling a lot with work, but I've been finding my way around.'

'What does he do?'

'He's in Compliance and Regulation. Used to work in London, but recently he's set up on his own.'

'Wow. Good for him! Why all the travelling?'

I took a sip of the coffee, which didn't taste quite as good as it smelled. Machine coffee, I always find, is never quite hot enough. 'He's in the process of signing up some international clients. Lots of conferences and meetings all over.'

It was at this point that I became aware that Vanessa was watching me. Erica was saying something to her, but she waved her off and leaned towards me, her eyes narrowed.

'Didn't I meet you . . . what's your daughter's name again?'

'Lexie.'

'Loxie?'

'Lexie.'

'Such a pretty name. It matches her.'

'Oh. Thank you.' I felt a warm glow. Perhaps I had misjudged her.

'You live in Brookview, don't you? Wasn't I meant to get back to you about something? A playdate or something?'

'I think so, but don't worry about it.'

'It's just I've been – Ew, my God, up to my eyes! Half the time these days I hardly know which way is up.'

'You've had such a stressful time,' Erica jumped in. 'I mean, that whole palaver about your kitchen. Whatever happened in the end?'

'Oh.' Vanessa sighed. She swivelled her stool towards my end of the island so that now we were six people chatting instead of two groups of three. 'The builders said they had a huge backlog after whatever the latest crisis was. Which of course I appreciate, but I said surely they could *prioritize* their clients? But there was one excuse after the next. Then the tiler, apparently, got cancer —'

'How awful.' Erica put her hand to her mouth.

'Well, of course. Of course, absolutely. And as you know, I'd normally be the first to drop everything and help, but . . . *but!* I'm afraid I have to say that my first teeny little Spidey sense was — *is this true?* Because they had used every other excuse under the sun by that stage. In the end I pulled out and switched to that amazing new Swedish design firm so, actually . . . anyway. It all ended up working out very well.'

'Well done you! Which Swedish firm? Elke Eberhard?'

'Who? No! Linnea Castell. They're internationally renowned; they only use solid wood and stone and natural pigments. I'm afraid I've never heard of . . . sorry, who did you say? Elky Bibbly-whatsit.'

'Jen Thompson said they did a lovely job on her conservatory.'

Vanessa made a little face. 'Well. There you go.'

I sipped my coffee, fascinated by Vanessa's absolute confidence in herself and her choices. Every decision she made was the very best; she seemed genuinely astonished that anyone could have a different opinion or worldview to her. Even her book club (hosted by one of Ireland's top authors) was the most elite and competitive that Dublin had to offer.

'Yes, Friday evenings, eight till ten. She runs it from her house — you know, that amazing white one down by the Dart? So convenient, as I can walk home if we've had a little drinkie. She's so gifted. We've become so close lately, it's amazing.'

'How did you get in?' Erica asked eagerly. 'I've been thinking of joining a book club myself lately.'

'Oh my God, Erry, that's amazing. I'd adore it if you could join ours. But unfortunately it's extremely difficult to get in and we're completely full.'

'Could you —'

'I'll definitely have a word, but there's an absolutely *massive* waiting list. Maybe try your local library?'

Isabel popped a fresh tray of tiny mince pies on the island.

'You're from London,' Vanessa said to me just as I popped one into my mouth.

'Oh . . .' I put my hand to my mouth. '. . . mmf . . . yes.'

'My friend Dilly who lives in Richmond – married to Oliver Reynolds – obviously, you know Oliver? – oh, I thought if your husband was in the finance world, but anyway – Oliver would be one of the most successful – anyway. Dilly goes to St Barts a lot and they bump into the Matthews all the time. Last month they were supposed to meet for drinks – it didn't happen in the end, I'm not quite sure what – but she sees them there all the time. You *do* know the Matthews?'

'Are they parents at St Catherine's?'

'*Pippa and James Matthews?* From London.'

Erica sniggered.

'Ah,' I said. 'I see.'

Isabel reappeared at my elbow with more coffee. She moved comfortably between us, refilling mugs, frequently stopping by me – a kind hostess, not just a polite one – to check if I was okay. Erica kept her focus wholly on Vanessa, nodding deeply at every sentence. Orla, too, seemed genuinely admiring. Marina was so aloof I hardly knew she was there. On the few occasions she did speak her voice was so low that I had to lean right in, straining to hear. Perhaps someone had once told her that a low voice was well bred and, a bit like Chinese foot-binding, things had got out of hand and she hadn't known where to stop. Or perhaps she was just shy. Next to her, by comparison, Erica sounded as if she was megaphoning from a ship at sea.

I'll admit it, that first morning I thoroughly enjoyed. The conversation flowed, effortlessly swirling from this to that. Light, easy topics, mostly about people I hadn't heard of – although I did learn that Vanessa and Orla had met in the waiting room at their antenatal clinic and Orla had been an absolute sweetheart on several occasions when Vanessa's childminders had let her down; also that Erica's husband was in the same golf club as Vanessa's. But I also picked up a lot of snippets relevant and interesting to Lexie and me. In an hour and a half I learned more useful information about Dublin than I had during the previous four months: swimming pools, parks, after-school activities. Orla kindly gave me the number of a karate class which her daughter Sadbh went to and enjoyed. Vanessa gave me the number of Dublin's top dentist and told me to be sure to mention her name when I phoned for an appointment.

I was careful not to outstay my welcome. After my second coffee I rose to leave.

'Lovely to meet you all. Happy Christmas, everyone.'

Vanessa, Marina and Erica nodded politely. Orla smiled and waved and said, 'Happy Christmas, Sara. See you at school.'

Isabel accompanied me to the door, tutting as she toed a badminton racquet out of my way. She picked my parka off a coat hook.

'Thank you so much for coming,' she said. 'I hope you enjoyed it. We can be a bit of an intimidating bunch, I know.'

'No, no, it was lovely. Thank *you*!'

'If Lexie's free, would she like to come here after school tomorrow? Last day of term and all that. Polly, Tabitha, Amelie and Sadbh are all coming.'

Lexie's face when I told her. It was like a song in my heart and the sun coming out.

17

The evening has come down now. The lavender grass is smudged with dew. Am I talking too much? It's easy to get bogged down in the little things. Descriptions of dinners and coffee mornings and people's hallways. I know you asked for every detail, but it's difficult to judge how literally you meant it. For my part, I'll admit that it's been an enormous relief to unburden myself. There's been so much I've wanted to say. But I know what you're really waiting to hear. How did it all go so wrong? What did happen the night of Vanessa's house party?

It's getting chilly. I can feel myself starting to shiver. Should we move inside? I'll take the plates; you take the bottle and glasses. Once we're in the kitchen we'll have another drink and I'll get to the party, I promise. But first can I give you just a little more about the background? Now that I'm in my stride I find myself remembering things I'd almost forgotten, things I feel are quite important and relevant to the story. I do think it's helpful to complete the full picture of what happened. Of how she was.

Vanessa's party was . . . when? . . . the second weekend in February. Prior to that, Lexie's first Christmas in Dublin went very well. I do remember you being very moody and distant again after the initial euphoria of the American phone call, but I tried to understand where you were coming from. The preparations for the contract involved an enormous amount of work and, as you had grimly remarked, *Many a slip 'twixt cup and lip.* So I jollied Lexie along and made sure to give you plenty of space.

Lexie, though. My God, she adored it all. From the day of that first playdate at Isabel's when she had come home with her eyes aglow, spinning, singing, walking on air, so happy she could hardly speak. The following evening she and I baked gingerbread people and wrapped gifts for your parents while Xmas FM crooned and jangled in the background and Lexie's Christmas pyjamas warmed in front of the gas fire. Our tree, small though it was, had turned out very well, decorated with the lanterns she'd made at school out of tinfoil and loo-roll inserts and the pinecones she and I had picked up on a forest walk and sprayed silver.

When she went to bed, however, I felt suddenly exhausted, a stray hubcap spinning down in her wake. I sank into the mustard chair, facing the row of stockings hanging from the mantelpiece. Three stockings. Our first pregnancy had come before we had even looked for it; a second had eluded us completely. This, we had been told, happened from time to time, for no clear reason. And we had both been so busy, working such long hours. One of the reasons – if I'm being truthful, the main reason – I had agreed to take time away from Manways and move to Dublin was that I'd hoped something might happen when things settled and you and I could relax and just . . . be. There was still time.

On Christmas Eve we took your parents' gifts up to their house. Your mum had lit a candle in the front window. The sight of it, so homely and welcoming, made me pause as Lexie ran on ahead to ring the bell. Breda opened the door, her arms wide, and Lexie flew into them.

I'll admit it, it took me aback. I knew that a bond had been building between them, especially since my London weekend, but this was my first time to really see it. They went off together, chatting, while you and I unloaded the gifts from the car – we'd bought the Peugeot by then. Later Lexie placed the baby in the manger, flanked by you and your mum – I think your dad had stayed in the kitchen to finish off the curry. Carefully, reverently, her tongue sticking out, she laid the tiny figure on his bed of straw. Breda had switched off the overhead light so that there was only a candle to illuminate the three of you, your faces softly lit. From the shadows at the bottom of the stairs I stood and watched you and I felt . . . I don't really know what I felt.

Lexie's elation continued into the new term. She raced through the school gates in the mornings to greet her friends, who now included Polly and Mabel and Sadbh, all the shiny girls. She was less anxious on Sunday nights, more animated walking past the Green in the mornings, past the leafless trees, still dark, the areas of bare mud, the empty swings hanging like gibbets, pulling out of my hand as she chattered.

'There's Teddy.' Pointing out various dogs we passed. 'And Digger.' Most mornings the school playground was like a kennels and she knew every one of the names. 'Can we *please* get a dog? I'm the only one who doesn't have one. Polly has Rocky and Tabitha has Jessie. Please? I'll walk them and pick up their poos and everything. I promise.'

I knew she would. Scatty Lexie, always dropping things and losing things, often overwhelmed, despite her careful planning, by the buttoning and unbuttoning of life. But a living, vulnerable creature dependent on her care – that she would not mess up. But of course there were issues to be considered.

'I'll have to talk to Daddy,' I said. 'We still need to decide our plans for next year.'

I was thoughtful as I walked home. What *were* our plans? I had agreed to give Ireland a year. My expectations had not been high, yet after a slow start things were going well. More than well. Lexie was happy here, much happier than she had been in London. CareyComp was finally on track for success. And now the year was almost halfway through, and schools and Manways and lodgers would all need notice of our return date.

That's if there was a return date.

I stopped.

'Sara! *SARA!*'

I turned. It was Isabel, bumping Jake's pushchair over the kerb.

'Been trying to catch up with you,' she gasped. 'Vanessa's organizing a ladies' lunch next Thursday.'

'Sounds lovely.' I was delighted, looking forward to another cosy chat in a bun-scented kitchen.

'In town,' she said. 'While all the little darlings are busy doing projects about the Vikings, we'll be sipping a nice vino somewhere adorable. What do you say?'

'Great. Count me in.'

'Wonderful! Erica's going to book somewhere cheap'n'cheerful. I'll text you the venue. Oh, and it's just for a few of us, okay? No need to broadcast it around, have all the no-hopers turning up. Only joking, they're all very nice. But you know what I mean.'

'No,' I said. 'No, no, of course.'

On Thursday, very much looking forward to the lunch, I dropped Lexie off and headed for the gates, aiming to do a quick shop before catching a bus to the city centre.

A face loomed into my field of vision. '*There* you are!'

It was Dervla, materializing with Edel from their dark spot by the wheelie bins.

'Where've you been?' she asked. 'We haven't seen you in ages.'

'Oh, just around,' I said. 'Busy with Christmas and all that, you know. Did you have a nice break?'

'Grand.' Dervla brandished a folder. 'Coming to Spoon? I'm

about to draw up the stall rota for the Gaeilge Fair. Mrs Bakewell has finally given the go-ahead. I was hoping to pick your business brain to help with the fundraising and finance side?'

'Oh – I'd love to help but, unfortunately . . . I've got somewhere I need to be.'

'Ah?' Dervla waited.

'Actually,' I said apologetically, 'I need to go now, or I'll be late. But definitely count me in another time.'

I hurried across the road, leaving Edel to lean in to make some frowning comment to Dervla. I wondered if I should feel guilty. They had been kind to Lexie and me. But Dervla and her daughter Siofra were never around – all of their free time seemed to be taken up with extended family – and Edel never wanted to do anything outside of school. I didn't owe either of them anything. It was time for Lexie and me to branch out.

By 'cheap'n'cheerful', I had imagined a trattoria or a traditional Irish pub with nooks and hot whiskeys and a stove, but I couldn't see anything like that at the address Isabel had texted. Instead, a passer-by directed me to an imposing Georgian building with red-carpeted steps leading up to glossy black doors. A man in a long overcoat with gold buttons enquired in a hushed voice whether I had a reservation before allowing me to enter. Inside, in a heavily curtained anteroom, were the others: Isabel in a slinky blue dress, Erica in a leopardskin-print jumpsuit, Orla in flared black trousers and a ruffled blouse.

'I'm so sorry,' I said, mortified, as the maître d' helped me out of my parka. 'I thought this was just a casual lunch.' I had put on a reasonably decent top and black jacket but didn't look anything like as polished and glitzy as the others.

'It *was*,' said Isabel. 'Erica had booked Thai Me Down. But Vanessa said it would be like having lunch in a Starbucks.'

'It was all I could get at short notice,' Erica said defensively.

'No, I know, don't get me wrong. No one's blaming you. I mean – who'd have thought we'd get in here? Normally they're booked up months in advance. But you can always trust Vanessa with these things.'

We had to keep pressing ourselves back against the curtains as more diners arrived and had their coats taken. We were causing an obstruction but for some reason the restaurant had a policy not to seat the table until the entire party had arrived, and as yet there was no sign of Vanessa. Erica kept going tensely to the door to peer out. Finally, a taxi pulled up and Vanessa, wearing a long cream belted coat and gripping several distinctive khaki and cream shopping bags, was helped out. Two women climbed out after her, one with a black fur collar who I vaguely recognized as being another St Catherine's parent.

'Where were you?' Erica hissed as they reached the top of the steps.

'Oh – sorry. Are you here long? We got delayed.' Vanessa giggled, holding up the bags. I suspected that shopping wasn't all they'd been doing.

'You went to Brown Thomas?'

'Just a v. quick pop in with Jill. To look at dresses for Milly's lunch.'

'But' – Erica attempted to block Vanessa from the rest of us and spoke in a panicky whisper – 'I thought *I* was going to help you with that?'

'Did you? Oh no! Oh my gosh, I didn't think you'd mind. You know I'd have loved you to be there, but you know the way you and Jill don't get on.'

'What?'

'Well, I assumed you didn't? After what she said?'

'What? What did she say?'

'Erry, seriously, do we have to discuss this now? We're all here to have some fun. Let's all just relax together and enjoy a lovely lunch.'

The young waitress who had been checking on our party now summoned us through to the restaurant. Hungrily we surged past the curtains. Our table was at the back, adjacent to the toilets but beautifully set with candles and round glass bowls filled with roses and baby's breath.

'Hold on!' Vanessa stopped. 'I'm sorry, but this is not our table? This is a special lunch for a group of friends. It's not appropriate that we sit there.'

'It's all we have,' the waitress said, looking apologetic. 'We've been fully booked since November. But we've managed to put this table together specially for your party and, as you can see, it's perfectly –'

'What about that table by the window?'

'I'm so sorry, but it's reserved.'

'I feel I should mention to you at this point that my husband is David Mayhew? He and his colleagues have lunch here all the time.'

'I'm very sorry.' The young waitress smiled nervously. 'But unfortunately that table has been booked for weeks, also by a regular client. I'm very sorry, madam.'

'Well, it's – look. Could you get your manager, please? *Would* you mind? Thank you *so* much!'

'There is zero point,' Vanessa continued as the waitress scurried off, 'in talking to someone like her. Can you believe the cheek of her talking to me like . . . ah, Barry,' as a harassed-looking man came hurrying over. 'How are you today?'

'Extremely well, Mrs Mayhew. Lovely to see you!'

'You're looking very busy this afternoon.'

'Yes, we are. Exceptionally so.'

'Wonderful you're doing so well. I was just wondering –

154

Barry – could you possibly find us a *slightly* better table than the one your colleague has been trying to give us?'

Barry hesitated. 'Normally I would, Mrs Mayhew, but today is particularly difficult. We have a very large number of book-ings dating back several weeks.'

'But I'm sure *you* can sort it out?' Vanessa said in her little voice. She placed her hand on Barry's arm. 'David will be so pleased to hear you could help.'

Barry stared at his arm. In a hypnotized way he said, 'Let me take a look.'

Moments later, he returned. 'This way, please.'

He led us to the table by the window. Several of our party had already seated themselves at the toilet table – one person had already buttered a bread roll – but now everyone stood up again, gathering their coats and bags.

'Thank you, Barry.' As the already overworked staff rushed to re-set the table we had messed up. 'This really is extremely kind.'

'You're welcome, Mrs Mayhew.' Holding out her chair for her. 'How is Mr Mayhew?'

'Very well! I'll pass on your regards.'

'Please do. And' – he lowered his voice – 'aperitifs, of course, are on the house.'

'Wow,' said Isabel. 'Thank you very much! Isn't that nice?' she said when Barry had gone. 'Well done, Van.'

'Oh, Barry is *such* a sweetheart. He knows it's the least he can do after that woman's behaviour. But you needn't have sounded so grateful, Isabel. Dave practically pays these people's wages. Orla – *so* sorry, but would you mind moving down to the other end? It's just I really need to speak to Jill. Thank you! You're an absolute pet.'

For the second time that day Orla picked up her bag and coat and changed seats. Jill and Erica sat on either side of

Vanessa. The aperitifs arrived – something sweet and fizzy – and we all held a toast to child-free lunches. Our original waitress was not seen again. I wondered where she was, as the place was not large. Washing the toilets? Sacked? Being dealt with by some people in a basement?

But our new waiters were super-solicitous, whisking around bottles of San Pellegrino and baskets of gourmet breads. Undoubtedly, we were the most glamorous party there. We were a well-dressed bunch (well, apart from me), and the conversation, led by Vanessa, was witty and entertaining. Other tables glanced at us curiously and enviously – I don't think I'm exaggerating this. We brightened the place up, added a definite *je ne sais quoi*. No wonder Barry had caved in and given us the table. The original party – some kind of corporate lunch, judging by their grey suits – had arrived ten minutes later and, too polite or meek to complain, were shown, blinking resentfully, to the toilet table, where they sat with their heads in their menus while our table laughed and chatted and clinked Prosecco flutes.

I sat between Orla and Isabel. Marina, sitting directly across the table from me, spent the whole time staring at Vanessa, slowly eating a spinach leaf.

'It's not you, don't worry,' Isabel whispered. 'She never talks to anyone except Vanessa. She comes from Money with a capital M – her grandmother was married to someone or other – and she's very conscious of who she mixes with.'

'Wouldn't she have felt safer at a fee-paying school?'

'No, she's an artist, so she wanted Tabitha exposed to all kinds of backgrounds while in primary school. You know – refugees or people on drugs or in prison. Instead, this being South County Dublin, she's meeting solicitors and dentists and pharmacists and they keep talking to her as if she's one of them. It's horrifying for her.'

The waiters kept refilling my wine glass so that I ended up

putting quite a bit away without noticing. I can't remember now what I ate, but it was lovely to be out and about in my new adopted city with this group of lively, vivacious women. At one point Vanessa caught my eye and called down the table, 'Delighted you could join us, Sara!' making me feel even more warmly and fuzzily included. She and I might have got off to an awkward start, but it seemed that was all forgotten. I was beginning to see why Vanessa was the leader of the BMs. With her at the helm they were in safe hands. Things would be done right; they would not be fobbed off or overlooked or overcharged. I could even understand her entitlement over the table. If her husband gave the restaurant a lot of business, then perhaps it wasn't unreasonable of her to expect some sort of acknowledgement. It was a status thing; I knew that from London. Businesspeople could be funny about their image.

It was only towards the end of the lunch that one small incident occurred that caused Vanessa's gracious facade to slip slightly. Like all of us, she'd had a few drinks by then.

It happened when the waiter came around yet again with the wine. The majority of the BMs seemed in no hurry to leave, but as I had to collect Lexie from your mum's I put my hand over my glass. Beside me, I saw Orla doing the same.

'Orla, get that hand off your glass,' Vanessa ordered.

'I'm going to have to call it, Van. I've an Uber on the way.'

'Oh, for goodness' sake, Orla. After all the trouble I went to! This is meant to be a fun lunch. Not people having cups of *tea* and leaving early, which, can I just say, totally kills the mood.'

'I'm really sorry, Vanessa, but I'm utterly whacked.'

'We all are. I'm exhausted after having to deal with the kids for the past fortnight.'

'Yes, but I'm about to face into a week of nights.'

Vanessa wrinkled her nose. 'Poor you. I forgot you have to go and clean bums.'

Orla said quietly, 'Among other things.'

'I'm sorry?'

Orla's voice rose a micro-decibel. 'I said, "among other things". As you well know, Vanessa. Working as I do in a cardiothoracic ICU.'

'You're so sensitive. What did I say? Did anyone hear me saying anything bad?'

Everyone concentrated on their cutlery.

'I'm so hurt you'd choose to take offence like that. Just because I don't know everything a nurse does, my God.'

Orla looked at the tablecloth. 'I didn't mean it to sound like that. I'm just tired.'

'We're *all* tired. It's not a competition. We should be supporting each other. You make me sound as if I'm denigrating nurses. I've done fundraising for your hospital. Dave's company raised eight thousand euro for cancer last year.'

'Nurses are amazing,' put in Erica.

Orla said nothing. Vanessa was pink in the face, her glass tipping sideways in her hand. Briefly, her gaze moved to me. It lasted for no more than a second before switching back to Orla, but all the same I had the thought that there had been something in it. That for some reason she was blaming me for Orla's nano-rebellion. That Orla would never have dreamed of speaking back to her like that if it weren't for me.

A moment later Orla took out her bank card. Vanessa was on to her like a cat on a mouse.

'What are you doing, Orla?'

'Paying.'

'No, no! I'm treating you. This is my treat! Where would we all be without nurses? I was teasing you just now. If you took me up wrong, it's because we're all a bit drunky and I haven't seen you for ages. C'mere . . .' She reached down the table for Orla's hand. 'When your week of night work is finished you're coming out with me for a lovely lunch and chat. Just us two. Promise? Prommy? Just you and me?'

'Okay!'

I looked at Orla. All her resentment had vanished. She was radiant, luminous, glowing like one of the candles in the silver holders on the table.

18

If all of this makes it sound that I was in some way fixated on Vanessa at that point, that wasn't the case at all. I'm simply outlining it to give you as much context as I can. In fact, outside of meeting Vanessa in a group situation with the BMs – coffee at Orla's one morning, a power-walk in the park another – we had little to do with each other. And that was fine! We were on good enough terms now that Lexie was happy, and that, for me, was all that mattered.

And she *was* happy! She was now being included in the shiny girls' circle, and she adored it. From the moment she came home she talked non-stop about what they had been doing. Polly this, Polly that – Lexie lit up when she mentioned her name. There was no doubt that, like her mother, Polly was in charge and all the others danced to her tune.

The hero-worship did worry me at times. Seeing her trot after Polly like a faithful puppy. The constant whispering and talking behind hands, the conversations in the back of the car on playdates.

'I'm going to a campsite in Spain for my holidays.'

'Oh, we went to Spain years ago. But we didn't stay in a campsite, we stayed in a five-star hotel.'

'Did you see that awful dress Ms Brennan had on yesterday?'

'I know! Bit old for it, isn't she?'

Sometimes it all seemed very competitive. What TikToks they had to watch, what online clothing brands they had to wear. Where was the imaginative play, the games of Hide and Seek and Detectives? I thought Lexie often seemed edgy and tense after these afternoons, but when I asked her how things had gone she said fervently, 'Oh, we had such fun!' Maybe this was what girls her age were like, and I'd forgotten. Janina, who was emotionally wise, had once commented, 'You have to let an awful lot of stuff roll off your back, otherwise no one would ever talk to anyone.' Lexie seemed happy so I left her to it. Stopped projecting, as you advised.

By now it was almost February, and her birthday was coming up.

'What would you like for your present?'

'*You* know!'

'Oh, Lex. The dog thing again. I told you we have to wait to talk to Daddy about our plans.'

'I know.' Deflated. 'I can still dream, can't I?'

But there it was again. The decision that had to be made. And the fact was that ever since Christmas, the more I had thought about it, the more I had begun to wonder: why wouldn't we stay permanently in Ireland? Lexie was happy here. She had friends now. She had the sea, the beach, the mountains within easy distance. And more importantly she had family here: her cousins in Cork; her grandparents.

I hadn't had a chance yet to discuss any of this with you. I knew that you hadn't settled here as well as you'd hoped. It was hardly surprising, given the crazy hours you'd been working. But once the American contract was signed my hope was that you'd be able to slow down. Spend more time with us, relax, get to know Dublin again. You were the one who had wanted this move; it was a shame you hadn't been able to enjoy it and see how much it was benefiting Lexie.

By chance, driving home from the shops that afternoon, Lexie and I passed a bus shelter displaying an ad for a dog rescue centre. The puppy on the poster had huge, sad eyes, peeking through the bars of a cruel-looking cage. Lexie's head swivelled to follow it as we passed, as if the poster was a magnet and her head an iron filing. We had nothing planned for that afternoon and on impulse I bypassed the turn to our estate and kept driving.

It was a clear, cold day. As we climbed a narrow road into the hills the grass became dusted with frost. The low white sun that occasionally annoyed me when I was driving or using my laptop had up here an ethereal beauty, like a fantasy orb gleaming through stark, delicate branches. When we drove through the gates of the dog shelter Lexie gasped.

'Just a visit,' I warned her. 'Just to look around and perhaps leave a donation.'

We waited with the other visitors at the reception area. On the walls were posters of abused dogs that I was sure couldn't be suitable for children; dogs with dreadful suppurating wounds, dogs neglected and starving with their ribs sticking out. I glanced at Lexie to see how she was taking it, but she was grave and calm.

She was utterly silent as we were shown into the dog shed, as hushed and respectful as if she was entering a church – which in a way she was. The shed was a long building with cages down the sides, two or sometimes one dog per cage. Cards on the doors gave the dog's name and a potted history. Underneath each was printed: *Suitable for a Home with Children?* with a box to be ticked *Yes* or *No*. Some of the dogs came to their doors to greet us, others ignored us, still others cowered, trembling, as we passed. These, I assumed, were the ones who had been abused. Their boxes were all ticked: *No. No. No.* Lexie, saying nothing, moved quietly from cage to cage.

And then we saw George, hovering anxiously just inside his door, a funny little creature with a long nose that gave him a doleful appearance and honey-coloured feathery fur. His card said he was about eighteen months old and probably a mix between a cocker spaniel and something else. As soon as he saw us he became enormously excited, panting and scrabbling at the bars to get to us. Lexie couldn't speak.

'Would you like to say hi?' The guide came over and unlocked the door.

The expression on her face as he exploded out of the cage and tumbled into her. Her mouth opened. She fell to her knees. Her arms lifted to receive him . . . her eyes . . . the joy, unaffected, unrestrained . . . I generally tried to be a good parent, which in my book meant a strict one, but in the moments when she looked like this . . . what would I not do for her, give to her . . .

'. . . treated well,' the guide was saying. 'His owner couldn't work from home any more so couldn't give him the company and exercise he needs. He's very active, as you can see, and he does love a cuddle.'

'So he's suitable for children?' I asked.

Lexie's head popped up, her eyes round with disbelief.

'Yes, but that means there'll be a lot of demand for him.'

'Ah.' As Lexie's face fell. 'Well, that's good to hear. For his sake.'

Politely, the guide said, 'If you'd like to be considered anyway, you can fill out the form on our website and email it in.'

On the way home Lexie kept saying, 'We have to get him, Mum. We *have* to!'

'He won't be available. You heard.'

'I think he will. I thought the lady sort of *looked* at us.'

'You know the rule. We'll have to discuss it with Daddy.'

'You always say that. But he's never here. And if he was he'd just keep saying *we'll see, we'll see, we'll see*. It has to be your decision, Mum.' Recently she'd started to drop the Mummy.

'Please? He needs us. He looked so sad when we left.' She was pinned to the window, her gaze fixed uphill to the spot in the trees where the rescue centre was.

'That's just his long nose,' I said. 'Plus he didn't want to go back to his boring cage. Anyhow, there's something else I've been wanting to discuss with you. How would you like a party for your birthday?'

She whipped her head around. 'Actually?'

'Of course.'

'At our house? Can I get a disco light? Can we make our own pizzas?'

'Yes, yes and yes.'

'Wow! Oh wow! Can Polly come? And Sadbh? And Mabel?'

'And Mia and Imogen,' I reminded her.

'Sure! Oh wow! Wow! Thank you so much!'

She spent the rest of the journey planning the party, the topic of George seeming parked for now. I was relieved, as I hadn't meant for her to get so invested on a first visit.

On the way home we called to your mum's.

'Hi, lemon puff.'

'Hi, melon brain! Any news?'

'Yes! We're getting a dog!'

'Really?' Breda's eyebrows rose above her reading glasses at the same time as I said, 'Oh, Lex!'

'We went to see him today, and his name's George.'

Breda looked at me, her eyebrows vanishing further under her fringe.

'Go on, Lex,' I said. 'Clear off and play in the garden.'

She stopped to give your mum a hug before skipping off.

'Goodness.' Breda popped the kettle on. 'A dog.'

'It was just a tour of the shelter. Nothing's been decided.'

'Would you even be able to have one in your London apartment?'

It was a day for impulse, clearly. I think it might have been the way she had put her arms around Lexie, so warmly. The words were out of my mouth before I'd thought.

'The thing is, you know – we might stay here.'

'What?' She wheeled. 'Stay in Dublin? But Adam's work –'

'Moving here was always his idea,' I said. 'It was me who wanted a trial period. But I can see why he wanted to come back. Lexie is very happy here.'

Breda's eyes were bright. The teapot in her hands shook. 'Jim!' she shouted. 'Jim!'

He was next door in front of the TV.

'You'll never guess! Adam and Lexie are going to stay in Ireland!'

'That's great, love. What time's dinner?'

'Six.' Breda returned to the kettle.

Sometimes I wondered about their marriage. Almost all of your dad's conversations seemed to revolve around food. 'When's dinner? What are we having? What butcher did you use?' Was it due to his stroke? Surely he couldn't always have been like this. To be fair, I always found him very good-natured. As long as things went his way and nobody rocked his boat. But what did your mum think? There was more to her than I'd first thought, a quickness I imagined she couldn't always have worked off by the ninth hole. Divorce was so much less common here than in London. Children spent their childhoods with both parents. This stability was a major part of the attraction for me. And you know your parents better than I do; you know what your childhood was like. An extremely happy one, as you've told me many times. You'd have had to look very closely at Breda to detect that she might have been suppressing another side of herself, like a badly behaved pupil, in order to put her children's happiness before her own. If indeed she even was.

Lexie was beyond excited about her party. And because I had now been invited to Isabel's and Orla's homes – and to Vanessa's restaurant lunch, if you counted that – I felt that it was time I reciprocated. So, quashing some qualms at the thought of Vanessa or Erica coming face to face with our anaglypta wallpaper, I decided to invite the mums along too for a light lunch.

Dervla and Siofra were attending Dervla's brother-in-law's forty-seventh birthday dinner that weekend, but Edel and Eva said they could come. Orla and Isabel were also happy to accept.

'Saturday week?' Erica said when I asked her. 'Isn't that the day after Vanessa's party?'

'Vanessa's . . .'

'Oh!' Erica's hand went to her mouth. 'You didn't know.'

'No.'

'Oh my gosh. Everyone's going, so I just assumed . . . How awful. I'm so embarrassed.' Watching me, though, in a satisfied way, as if pleased I was being put in my place.

'Don't mind her.' Isabel rolled her eyes as we left. So she'd seen it too. 'Vanessa's do isn't really a mum thing. It's a work evening for Dave. Mostly his friends and colleagues. Apparently there's some bigwig coming from abroad that Dave's keen to get to know.'

From the little I had heard about Vanessa's husband, Dave, I vaguely pictured him as loud and red-faced, slapping other men on the back and bellowing about rugby and shares. 'Vanessa managed to invite him through a contact. Lennox-something. A big deal in the finance world.'

The description rang a bell. 'Josh Lennox?'

'That's it! Do you know him?'

'Adam does.'

'Really? How?'

'Well . . .' I was about to explain that you didn't know him as such, you'd just heard him speak at a conference and mentioned that you'd been impressed by him, but then Isabel became distracted. 'Oh, Jake! Seriously? All over your hair?'

166

'Just from work,' I said vaguely when she'd finished wiping, and left it at that.

The next day I saw Vanessa leaving the school. I hadn't exactly been putting off inviting Polly to Lexie's party . . . just, I was still conscious of the rebuff the time I'd asked Polly to play . . . and now it seemed there was this event at her house that I hadn't been invited to. But Lexie's party was a separate matter entirely and I knew that she really wanted Polly to come.

So I approached Vanessa, irritated by the way my pulse immediately began to accelerate, as if I'd been summoned to the principal's office.

'Hi there,' I said.

To my surprise she stopped at once.

'*Sara!*' Huge beam as she lifted her sunglasses. 'How *are* you? What a coincidence! I was just thinking about you. Aren't you looking very . . . *natural* . . . in your boots and your jeans? How do you do it?'

Well, this was a turn-up. I'd never known her so pleased to see me. It certainly made things a lot easier.

'Lexie's having a birthday party,' I said. 'On Saturday week. She'd love it if Polly could come. And you're very welcome, too, for some food. Nothing fancy, just casual, really –'

'We'd love to!' She cut through my wittering. 'That sounds super! Definitely count Polly and me in!'

'Fantastic!' I was pleased. It wouldn't have been the same for Lexie if Polly wasn't there.

'Oh, and by the way . . . I've been meaning to ask you, but you know how busy things are . . . I happen to be having a little gathering myself that week. On the Friday evening, in my house.'

'Oh, really?'

'Yes! And you and your husband, Andrew –'

'Adam.'

167

'Adam, of course. Sorry! Anyway, you're both very welcome to pop along.'

'Thank you. I'll have to get him to check his schedule, but I'm sure he –'

'Well, let me know, won't you?' A little testily. 'For numbers. But do try, won't you? There'll be people there your husband might like to meet. It'll be an excellent networking opportunity for him. I'm sure he won't want to miss it.'

It was classic Vanessa. Assuming that because something suited her it must automatically suit everyone else as well. In fact, it did suit me because I knew you'd like to meet Josh Lennox again, and because – yes, I'll admit it – I was delighted and relieved to be included. But it was the way she did it. Rather like being forced at gunpoint into having a pedicure.

'I'm sure he will be free,' I said. 'In which case we'd love to! Thank you very much!'

What did happen at that party? I know you've always been per-plexed by it. If things had been going well enough between Vanessa and me for her to have invited me in the first place, what on earth could have happened to make it all go so wrong?

Well, you were there, Adam. Everything that took place that night, you saw and heard it all. I know you don't believe that's all there was to it. You're convinced that there must have been more to it for Vanessa to have ended up doing what she did. But, truth be told, there really wasn't. It was all exactly as you saw.

19

A few days after their split, just before Christmas, he phoned. Naturally, Zoë declined the call.

'How I behaved,' he said in his message, his voice subdued, 'was unforgivable. And I know I shouldn't be calling, but . . .' Heavy sigh. 'I didn't want to leave you thinking it meant nothing. I've never met anyone like you. Your energy . . . your passion for what you do. I wish –' Pause. 'Anyway. I won't call again. I wish you all the best. Everything that's good and happy for your future. I don't expect you to respond to this. I just . . . wanted you to know.'

More heavy breathing. Then silence.

As speeches went – and she had given and heard many – it was impressive. Short, yet heartfelt, ticking all the boxes, delivered with just the right touch of emotion. If it was anyone else she would have thought he had written it out first and rehearsed it. Practising his corporate skills: *How to appease an irate investor.* But she knew he hadn't. She knew how capable he was of speaking fluently in the moment, from the heart.

And she *had* invested in him! She had taken her emotions out of their long-term, low-yield account and plunged them all into this risky, high-stakes venture she should have known all along was dodgier than a bank email that started 'Dear Lovely Madam'.

The thing was – she understood about the Tube station. Why he had lied. Hadn't she done that kind of thing herself? Pretended to be someone else on a night out, just for fun. Just to stop people saying 'Eh?' when she told them what she did for a living. One time she'd pretended to be a hand model. Other times an Arsenal scout or a paranormal investigator or the voice of Siri. The resulting conversations had been far more interesting and entertaining than when she'd told the truth.

She'd been young then though. Not over forty, like Adam was (yet another thing, it turned out, he had lied about). And for him to continue the pretence while dating her was much harder to forgive.

On New Year's Eve she was on call in theatre doing an urgent C-section. The parents were around her age, so together, so happy. She could hear them whispering to each other behind the sterile drape.

'I think they're in! I can feel them rummaging! Can you see anything?'

'Should I look?'

'Just a quick peek.'

A blue theatre hat came bobbing up above the drape. Anxious eyes darted towards the wound.

'Actually, Zane, don't! Let's wait and see him at the same time.'

Quickly the hat bobbed down again. Zoë hauled out the baby, a bald, purple boy, too startled to do anything but wobble and hit out wildly at the air with his fists.

'Hello, world. Congratulations, everyone!'

It never got old. No matter how many times. She passed the baby over the drape. Heard the soft cries of wonder, the mother's shaky voice, 'Hello there. Hello, little friend!' The father, staring speechlessly at both of them as if his heart would burst. As if he would destroy a mountain to protect them. Hormones, of course. The pituitary gland kicking in.

A couple of weeks later she phoned him.

They met in the park by Embankment station. It was mid-January, properly winter. He wore his hiking fleece with the hood up and a thick black jacket on top. She sat beside him on the bench in her pink-and-white-striped scarf, warming her hands on a takeaway coffee.

'What a mess.' His grey eyes were sad.

A *mess*? Zoë frowned. Had someone knocked over a juice carton? Spilled wine on a top? Adam looked so youthful. It was hard to believe he was so much older than her. So much older than what he'd said.

'Why are you meeting him?' Naomi had said in disgust. 'You know what he'll say. He's very sorry. His marriage is dead. He wishes he'd met you first. But he can't leave because of whatshername's mental health. Or whatever he thinks will get his end away.'

Zoë said bluntly, 'What does your wife think about all of this? This *mess*, as you call it? Or didn't you happen to mention it over the Christmas turkey and pigs in a blanket?'

'No, I did not. I'm ashamed of how I treated you. Both of you.'

'Do you love her?' She was curious.

He folded his arms. 'You called me a cliché. But things are only clichés because they're true. My wife is a good person. An excellent mother. We have a daughter together whom we both love. But as far as Sara and I are concerned . . . zilch. She has little interest in me, or at least only in relation to how it affects our daughter. It took me a long time to realize it because she's a very independent person. That's what I liked about her when we first met. She wasn't needy or clingy, she had her own life. But there's independence and there's . . . apathy. Coldness. The lack of emotion did start to get to me after a while, but I thought it was normal. The way all relationships go after a few years. A cliché, like you said. I said to myself, just get on with it, that's life, that's how people are. And then,' he said simply, 'I met you.'

Zoë said nothing.

'If it wasn't for my daughter – but there you go. My only regret about all of this is for your sake. That I dragged you into it and I hurt you.'

Her chest ached. She'd had to see him. One last time. She'd tried so hard not to, but she'd been so unhappy. But now she was here it seemed so futile. She sat forward to hide her distress, crumpling the empty coffee cup in her hand. There was the bin. Over there by the trees.

'Well.' She started to push herself off the bench. 'I'll just . . .'

'I can't leave my wife,' he said abruptly.

Startled, Zoë said, 'Of course not.'

'If I didn't have a child . . . But I do. I've thought and thought since I've met you about what to do. I've thought: Leave. But that would ruin my daughter's life. Stay until she's older – but then she'll look back and her childhood will have been a lie. And I'd have lost you by then anyway. I'd ask you to wait – but obviously that's impossible.'

She said nothing.

'Or . . . Or! We could just continue to see each other. Without my daughter knowing. People do that, you know. All the time. But I know you'd never agree to it and I know I can't ask it of you, so . . . it's not a runner. So there you have it. They're the options. None of them good.'

She nodded. She placed her hands on her knees, preparing to stand.

Fiercely, looking hard at her, he said, 'Whatever about me, I never thought *you'd* care this much. You're nearly ten years younger than me and so beautiful. So *alive*. If I could just give you one piece of advice. You are truly amazing. You could have anyone you wanted. Just don't make the mistake I made and marry someone you don't love.'

Rows of trees, black against the white sky. Beyond them was a bronze statue of a woman weeping against a plinth with a man's head on the top. *Walk away*, her brain advised coolly. *Walk away. There's nothing for you here. No wedding in a country church with bunting in the porch and sweet peas tied to the pews. If that's what you want you'll have to find it with someone else.*

But who? How, now, could she ever settle for anyone else? These last few weeks had been very difficult. Whether she believed him or not about how he felt about her – and why would he continue to lie now that he'd been found out? – it felt *right*, being here with him. Here on their bench with her breath coming in clouds, the flower stalls under their green umbrellas, the queues of woolly-hatted people at the coffee kiosk. Anywhere with him was the right place to be. She'd never felt that about anyone before. Even with Jeremy there had always been something missing, a sense that he just didn't get it. The conversations over all those trendy candlelit dinners that she'd tried and tried to breathe life into but that flopped and shrivelled like balloons in the cold. She had often been impatient with him. No wonder, she acknowledged, that he had left her. She should have let him go sooner, but she'd got used to accepting that if she wanted children with a partner she'd have to stop seeking perfection. And now that she'd found it, what should she do? Was half a good man better than a whole second-rate one? You only got one life. Why this . . .

this misplaced loyalty to a woman she'd never met, who didn't even live in the same country as her? This meeting of the minds didn't happen every day. If ever, for most. If you were lucky enough to experience it, you didn't just wander off and let someone else have it. Someone who didn't even want it! You fought for it. Or you let it slip from your grasp and you settled forever for a grey half-life.

'I wish I'd met you first.' Adam was watching her. His gaze so open, so tender.

'I wish I hadn't met you at all,' she said, honestly and hopelessly.

Gingerly he reached for her hand. She ignored him. Looking over at the weeping bronze woman, she said, 'Why do I think I'm her?'

'You're not. You're nothing like her. You're wearing far more clothes, for a start.'

She gave a snort of half-fake laughter.

Adam said bleakly, 'It's not much to offer.'

'I haven't said I'll accept, have I?' She looked down. Their hands were tightly clasped.

20

Initially I wasn't at all sure that you'd come to Vanessa's party. Since Christmas you'd been moodier than ever, one day on a high, sweeping Lexie up and making her giggle, the next crashing down again, irritable and withdrawn. We didn't know from one day to the next what we'd be facing when you came home. We hadn't had a proper conversation in days, weeks even.

'Take a break,' I begged. 'This constant work and travel can't be good for you. Your blood pressure must be sky high.'

'Can't,' you said curtly. 'I've a million things to do before the contract signing. If the Americans think we're not ready they could still pull out. These things don't happen by themselves, you know.'

Believe it or not, I did know. I wasn't an idiot. But even on the rare occasions you were at home you were increasingly distant and unavailable. We went to bed at different times. You worked while we were asleep and slept while we were awake. As a family, we were completely out of sync. I made an effort with cooking when you were home, but you just inhaled the food, thumbing your phone. Or said you'd had a sandwich on the plane so that I ended up eating alone. If I did manage to persuade you to join Lexie and me for a walk, you lagged behind, focusing on your screen. Or else strode ahead impatiently as if you had somewhere to be and we were holding you up. Again, out of sync. There, but not there.

One night you were awake, restless beside me, thinking yet again about things you wouldn't tell me about. I touched your foot with mine. Then, gently, trailed my toes up your calf. You lay for a moment, then shifted your leg away. Thinking you hadn't understood, I exchanged my foot for my hand. You rolled to face the wall. 'Tired,' you mumbled. 'Do you mind?'

'Not at all,' I said lightly. 'You must be getting your supply in London.'

You didn't reply. Ungrateful, I thought, angry now. Ungrateful for my lightness, my humour, my pretence that your rejection, on top of all your other behaviour, hadn't hurt. I'd been blaming your workload, but this indifference was just rude. We never touched any more. We barely spoke or even looked at each other. I was like a carpet to you, or one of the chairs. When had it all started? Had we been like this in London too? I had considered asking Breda to babysit and the two of us going out on a date, but frankly, the thought of us laughing together over dinner seemed like something from a million years ago. What on earth would we talk about? I wondered blankly. Yet whenever I asked you, 'Are we okay?' you kept saying, 'Fine, fine, fine!' How could I keep on asking without sounding nagging or mad?

You did, however, somewhat to my surprise, agree to come to Vanessa's party. I suspected it was the mention of Josh Lennox, as Vanessa had predicted. Breda was only too happy to babysit, so we were all set.

But on the Thursday morning my phone rang.

'Sara, I'm sorry, but Jim's breathing isn't good. I think it's his COPD again. I've had to get Colette from next door to help load him in the car. The GP wants to send him in for an X-ray.'

'Oh dear. Poor Jim. I hope he's okay.'

'I thought I'd better let you know. In case they keep him in. What will you do if I can't babysit tomorrow? Maybe Lexie could stay here?'

'No, no, you don't need that.' I was thinking. 'Don't worry. Someone at school will know a babysitter. You concentrate on Jim. Keep us posted.'

Orla had just arrived at the school, so I asked her.

'Know anyone who could babysit at short notice for Vanessa's thing tomorrow?'

'Ah, you're going! Great! Have a lovely evening.'

'Won't I see you there?'

'Nuh-uh.' Cheerfully. 'Didn't make the cut.'

'But – hang on, what?'

'Yeah, Vanessa's pretty strict about who gets to go to these things. It's a networking event for Dave, and my Neil doesn't come up to the mark. Biology teachers are no use to the finance world. She must have heard something good about your Adam. Or you yourself, of course.'

'Orla, I'm sorry. I didn't mean to – I mean . . .' I sounded like Erica now.

'It's fine. Honestly. I already knew about it before you told me. Look – why don't *I* mind Lexie for you? She can come here and have a sleepover. Sadbh would be thrilled.'

'Well, obviously, so would Lexie. But –'

'Sara – stop worrying. I don't take these things personally with Vanessa. I mean, yes, of course I'd love to go. I love a party. But *c'est la vie*. You go. Leave Lexie with us and make a night of it. Enjoy the glamour. Vanessa does know how to do these things well.'

In spite of Orla being so nice about it, I still felt uncomfortable. As if I had usurped her in some way – jumped into her grave, as my mother would have said. And I was still extremely surprised to have been invited when she hadn't been.

If I was the woo woo type I'd have thought that fate must have been trying to tell me something, because it was on the following afternoon, the very afternoon of Vanessa's dinner, that you and I had our Huge Row, our worst yet.

You're shaking your head now at the memory. Believe me, I'm not trying to make you feel bad by bringing it up. You were under a lot of pressure at the time and probably both of us were to blame. I only mention it for context, for completeness. In case the lead-up to the dinner might have had any bearing on what followed.

The row, as I'm sure you remember, took place in our bedroom. I had just dropped Lexie to school. Orla was going to collect her from there later and keep her at her house for the night. Lexie was so excited about the sleepover she could barely breathe.

Back at the house I handed you the croissant and americano I'd picked up for you at Berry Nice.

'Lexie's on cloud nine,' I said. 'Her party tomorrow – and now a sleepover as well. Such a shame you'll be away for her party.'

You rubbed open the croissant bag. 'Hard to believe she's going to be nine.'

'I know! Oh, and by the way – you won't believe this, but the dog shelter just phoned. They've said we can have him. Tomorrow, if we want.'

'Have who?'

'George! The dog!'

You frowned, your lips shedding pastry flakes. 'We're getting a dog?'

'Remember, I told you. About Lexie and me visiting the shelter. I didn't think we stood a chance of getting him so possibly I didn't make too much of it . . . but the thing is, now it seems that someone has backed out and, apparently, we're next in line. And since it's Lexie's birthday tomorrow I . . . well . . . I just went for it. I said yes!'

'Sara.' You put the croissant down and spoke in a very slow, clear voice. 'How can we get a dog if we're moving back to London?'

'Well, our moving plans are something we need to discuss. But even so it makes no difference, because even if we do go back we'll have to sell the flat and move out of London, so –'

'Move out of London?' You stared. 'Why?'

I stared back. Surely it was obvious?

'Well,' I said. 'Obviously, we can't go back to Vauxhall.'

'Why not?'

'There's nothing there for Lexie. It's not suitable for a child. And now George –'

'Who?'

'The dog.'

'The dog.' You were standing now with your arms on your head, something I always recognized as a sign that you were getting angry. 'A decision *you* made. Without even bothering to check with me.'

'I didn't intend to. It was just sprung on me.'

'But with no prior discussion –'

'There *was* prior discussion. You just didn't listen. Just like you haven't been listening to anything lately. You've been refusing to talk to us or take your head out of your phone –'

'That's because I've been *busy*.'

My own anger rose, but I forced it down. Now that I finally had your attention there was no point in having yet another argument with nothing being decided.

'So, then, tell me.' I spoke calmly. 'What *are* our plans? Ireland or England? School finishes in June. We need to decide where Lexie's going next year. And I need to tell Manways if –'

'I can't.' You looked away. 'Not yet.'

'Why not?'

'I need to know . . . more.'

'More what?'

'Just . . . more.' You wouldn't meet my eyes. I was baffled by your evasiveness.

'I'll tell you what I think,' I said after a moment. 'I think we should go on living here.'

'*Here?*'

'Yes! Why the big surprise? Isn't that what you wanted?'

'Staying here long term was never the plan. You know that.'

'That's not what *I* understood! I was the one who wanted the trial period. But I like it here, and so does Lexie. And Carey-Comp is doing well now; you've got more work than you can handle.'

'That's the point. I can't handle it all from here.'

'Yes, you can! You said so yourself at the beginning. No matter where you were based, you said, you'd still have to travel, so it would make no difference. And things are going well here for Lexie. She's got friends now, she's happy. And with your dad not being well . . . and your mum adores her; you were right about that. She was over the moon when I told her we were staying –'

'You told my *mother*? Sara, what the fuck?'

'Don't speak to me like –'

'What *is* it with you?' You were properly furious now. 'First you didn't want to move here. Now you don't want to move back.'

'I could say the same of you, except the opposite direction.' I was thoroughly bewildered. What was all this stonewalling, this caginess, this rewriting of things we'd both said? This absolute refusal to decide what needed to be decided? What were you waiting for? Work was going well. Lexie was happy. I was happy. What other issues weren't you telling me about that had to be factored in? I understood that for you Dublin was a step back that you maybe hadn't been prepared for, but surely you could throw off the shackles of childhood and start afresh. Treat your mother as an equal instead of you sulking and her fussing all the time. Retrain her so you both saw each other as adults. But you hadn't even tried. You hadn't given Dublin any kind of chance. The narrative about being so stressed because you were doing everything for us was wearing very thin. I would have been more than happy to get a job and contribute financially, but how could I commit to anything when you kept blocking all discussion of our future plans? *You're pushing it now, buster*, I thought. I had uprooted myself for you. Now it was your turn to ask what *we* wanted, Lexie and I. You weren't the only person in this family.

That was when you flung in your little zinger.

In an extremely nasty tone you said, 'If you have so little regard for my work or my opinion, Sara, maybe you should leave.'

'What?'

'I've had it up to here,' chopping towards your neck, 'with your lack of support. I've been working my ass off, taking huge risks, while you've been nothing but critical and dismissive. Getting a *dog*, knowing we have nowhere to put him. Deciding over my head to sell *my* flat in London that *I've* owned for years, long before I ever met you. I'm beginning to feel totally pushed out of this family. And if that's the way things are going to be, we should probably face facts and call it a day.'

'Adam, what –'

But you were gone. The bedroom door slammed. The walls shimmered; two books slid off the shelf. I was dumbstruck. What was all this? I didn't recognize any of the things you'd said about me. How had we gone from a discussion about a dog to – had you really implied that we should split up?

My ears were still ringing from the slam. No, not the slam. It was your phone, switched to vibrate, buzzing under a pile of papers. The pages trembled, threatening to slither off the table. I went to them and stabbed my finger down, stilling the phone underneath. But almost immediately it began to buzz again. Some pushy client, unable to accept that now was not a good time. I snatched up the phone, intending to switch it off completely, but as I did so the caller gave up and a moment later their text message lit up the screen.

We didn't speak for the rest of the afternoon. Once I had left the bedroom you returned to it and stayed there with the door shut, making angry-sounding phone calls. I didn't know if we were going to Vanessa's party and, frankly, I didn't care. I felt sick. Were things between us really that bad? Were we really heading for a separation?

And I'll admit it, Adam, in the moment, my main thought was: did I even care? With the way you'd been behaving lately, self-absorbed, self-important, showing not one jot of gratitude for the way Lexie and I had uprooted our lives to facilitate the ambition of the Great and Wonderful Adam Carey. I'd got used to managing here without you. Lexie and I had been happy on our own; happier than when we had to tiptoe around you and your pall of grandiose gloom. Your attitude was well and truly giving me the arse. Maybe I should call your bluff and tell you to go right ahead and pack.

But Lexie – Lexie would be distraught.

This travel, this distance, was killing us – but how could I pull you back? Throw myself on your mercy, say that I loved you and couldn't live without you? Ask you if you still loved me? But what if I didn't like what you replied?

And again, the angry thought: *what if I didn't care?*

Shortly after six I heard the en suite shower begin to hiss. The scent of your shower gel came wafting down the stairs. It looked as if we were going out after all.

Dressing dully and dutifully, I studied myself in the mirror, remembering a time when I had worn this dark red dress and you had come up behind me and pushed your hands up so that the skirt rose to my waist.

'So lucky,' you had said softly. 'So lucky.'

I couldn't imagine you doing it tonight. And I wouldn't have welcomed it if you had.

21

You and I walked up the hill to Vanessa's house, the scrape of my heels carrying in the cool air. The sky was a dull brown, the colour of a bruise. Crows cawed from the massive trees, early nesters getting ready to eat the other birds' eggs. This was the older part of the estate, the houses here fifty or sixty years old to our ten. And these houses, in turn, new relative to the grounds in which they stood, the demesne of a stately home hundreds of years old which had long since crumbled. Here and there were still the remnants of the thick walls, covered in ivy and ferns.

Being outdoors calmed me, as it always did. Took away some of the sick, knotted feeling from our row. I saw you walking beside me in your jacket and tie as if you were a stranger, as Vanessa and her friends would see you. You looked good. You always did. Your expression was still dour, but perhaps being outdoors had calmed you too because as we neared the house you cleared your throat and said in a grudging way, 'I'll finally get to see Cruella in the flesh. What's her husband do again?'

'Partner in Murphy & Mayhew,' I said eagerly. We had to get through the evening, and even if this truce was for the sake of appearances, it was a start. This party might be good for Carey-Comp. It might even sway your decision towards staying here.

'Oh yes. I know them. They're pretty big. For Ireland, anyway.'

Teslas and Porsches lined both sides of the road as we reached the summit of the hill. Around the curve was a series of large detached mock-Georgian homes with fluted plaster pillars. Vanessa's was third on the right. The electric gates stood open. Every window was lit. The circular driveway was dotted with candles in giant chrome lanterns. Through the windows and the open front door could be seen crowds of well-dressed people clutching champagne glasses and talking continuously, *bzzz bzzz bzzz*. The noise as we entered was deafening. The hall had a white marble floor and huge canvases on the walls: studio photographs of the Mayhews dressed in matching black against a white background, posed in various formations: holding hands and jumping all at the same time, lying on their tummies and laughing with their heads thrown back. Double doors on both sides led to large, white-carpeted rooms. Triple-wick scented candles burned everywhere.

A bow-tied teen took our coats. A woman in a white apron approached with a tray.

'Champagne?'

'Thank you.'

You accepted a glass too, though I knew you'd have preferred a beer.

Vanessa appeared, svelte in a backless black sequinned dress, her hair as sleek as if she hadn't moved a muscle since her blow-dry. Her forehead looked unusually smooth and youthful. I was struck again, as I hadn't been for a while, by how much she reminded me of Grace Gillespie.

'*Sara!* Wonderful to see you!' Double air-kiss. 'And this is your husband?' A penetrant head-to-toe sweep.

'Yes. Adam. Adam, this is Vanessa.'

'How super.' More air-kisses.

A man was beside me. 'Hallo there. Dave Mayhew! Nice to meet you.'

'Sara.' We shook hands. He was different to what I had expected. I had envisaged an arrogant, entitled alpha male, but he was thin and quiet and serious-looking, with grey eyes and hair the colour of dust, as though Vanessa fed off his blood.

His voice was soft and courteous. 'And Adam. You're both very welcome. Proper drinks through there if you'd like anything.' In the room to the left was a bar, surrounded by a crowd of mostly men with pints in their hands. Your face brightened.

'See you later,' Vanessa cooed, taking your fingers and giving your hands a little shake. 'We'll have a lovely chat.'

'She seems nice enough,' you said as we went through to the bar. 'Nicer than I was expecting. From the way you've been going on, I was expecting snakes in her hair.'

'She's not as bad as she was at the beginning,' I said. 'It was kind of her to invite us.'

'She's obviously done this before.' You nodded towards the caterers with their trays of canapés, the wandering trio of violinists playing Coldplay's 'Viva la Vida', the tables laden with cake stands and platters and tureens. 'This didn't come cheap. Murphy & Mayhew must have had a good year.'

At the far end of the room another set of doors led to a marquee with flashing coloured lights and a dance floor. Somebody backslapped you, shooting you forward so that your neck snapped back.

'Adam Carey! As I live and breathe!'

'Jesus! Decko McGinty!'

'Haven't sheen you in yearsh! Come and meet the ladsh!'

The man propelled you along, his arm around your shoulders. It shouldn't have surprised me that you'd meet people you knew here. Shouts rose from the bar as you approached. I shook hands and tried to keep track of the names: Fish, Boner, Sponge. They must have been the same age as you, but most of them looked older, yellower of tooth and bigger of belly. You looked fitter than all of them. Always a good mixer, you were soon in the thick of it and I could tell you were glad you had come. I saw Erica in a spangly tasselled dress laughing loudly at something a tall man was saying. Isabel, giggly in silver, waved me over. I could turn it on as well as anyone and after another glass of champagne soon I was smiling and laughing too.

'So what's the plan?' Boner/Sponge/Fish asked. 'You guys moving back here permanently or what?'

'Still deciding,' you said, not meeting my eye. A passing waiter topped up my champagne glass.

Boner tapped the side of his nose. 'Give you the name of a pal of mine, he'll look after you. Put your wife there down as your secretary. She sends an email here and there – nothing too tricky' – he gave me a wink – 'and you pay her a salary and knock it off tax.'

The talk to the left of me was about a legal case.

'. . . Gaffo in a spot of bother again.'

'What this time?'

'Hit a cyclist on the Rock Road. They're saying he was speeding.'

An intake of *ffff*s. 'Those speed limits are ridiculous. Thirty per hour, sure you're hardly moving at all.'

Vanessa's voice rang out crisply. 'It's no wonder the roads are so congested.'

'Absolutely.' Isabel was nodding, joining in the chorus, seemingly oblivious to the cognitive dissonance. No matter what, the BMs and their circle always stuck up for each other.

'So what happened?' someone asked.

'Oh – sued, of course, wouldn't you know. But he didn't get too far with it. No light on the bike. And, would you believe it, turned out the fella was illiterate. Barely able to write his own name. Sure he probably couldn't even read the road signs.'

'Chancer!'

'Indeed. Backed off quick enough when Gaffo's team threatened to make mincemeat out of him in court.'

My headache was back. The room was very hot. The smell of freesia and tuberose was overpowering.

'Excuse me. I'll just . . .'

Out in the hall, someone was emerging from what looked to be a bathroom. I seized the opportunity and ducked in. The bathroom, the size of our kitchen, had baskets of rolled white handtowels, designer handwash dispensers, individually wrapped soaps. All very thoughtful, all the signs of an experienced hostess. I dampened a towel and held it to my face. More than anything, I wished I was at home instead of at this brittle, pointlessly networking woman's dinner, watching a movie with Lexie, eating popcorn and hearing about her day. I took the towel away again. In the gold-veined mirror my eyes looked puffy and swollen. I wiped off my smudged mascara and re-applied it.

Back at the party, the conversations had swelled to a shouty roar, HAAR HAAR, as if to block out the fact that they had no internal voice at all, that without constant external stimulation to keep them pumped up their brains would deflate like balloons. RAAAAAR. You were at the centre of a crowd and hadn't missed me, so I passed on by and went through to the kitchen. Another huge room with a granite-topped island down the centre like a post-mortem slab. There were people there – catering staff loading glasses into the dishwasher, smaller clusters of guests, but no one I knew. I continued to a dim utility room with a bank of washers and dryers and finally through a back door to the garden.

Tranquil. Cool. Glass in hand, I wandered. The garden was neat and well kept. Lots of timber decking and tidy shrub borders – and was that a hot tub? Not currently in use, however. Give it an hour. More chrome lanterns and a couple of gas heaters. Not many people out here, just the odd smoker or scented-candle refugee like myself.

At the end of the lawn their dog, Rocky, was lying on the grass, tied to a pole. He looked to be asleep but, as I approached, he lifted his head and licked my hand, seeming grateful for my company. His water bowl was empty so I filled it from a tap in the wall. He got up and drank, his feathery tail slowly waving. When I went to leave he whimpered, pushing his nose into my palm. I crouched down again, talking softly to him.

When I looked up someone was standing in front of me.

'Hello there,' said Dave Mayhew.

I climbed to my feet, straightening my dress. 'Hi! Sorry, I was just . . .'

'I came out for some air,' Dave said. 'And to give Rocky here some water. But I see you've done that already. Thank you very much.'

He patted the dog's flank. 'Hey there, old man. Found a friend, did you?' The dog panted and whined, circling Dave's legs, pressing against his knees. Polly had said her dad hit him, but I couldn't see it. Dave's hands were gentle as he pulled the dog's ears. She meant her mother, I thought.

'Sara, isn't it?' Dave looked at me, the lenses of his glasses glinting in the light from the house. 'Where are you from with that lovely accent?'

'I grew up in Surrey.'

'Ah. Super spot. I have an aunt in Sussex. Used to go there a lot. Petworth House is there, isn't it? And Hever Castle – or is that Kent? Anne Boleyn's place. I love all that history. England has some beautiful countryside. The Lake District. And Yorkshire. Now that's a dog-walker's paradise.'

'Like stepping back in time to James Herriot's day.'

'I hear it irritates the locals. They can't even get planning for a garden shed. But worth it, don't you think? Everywhere these days is so overdeveloped. Nice to see some places holding out.'

We stood companionably in the night air. There weren't many trees in the actual garden, but behind the rear wall a dark stand of oak shushed in the breeze.

A Vanessa-shaped silhouette appeared at the kitchen window, shading her eyes with her hand.

'Ah,' said Dave. 'Hosting calls. Nice to talk to you, Sara.'

'Nice to talk to you too.' And off he went.

That was it. That was the sum total of what passed between Dave Mayhew and me in that garden. I spent a few more minutes with Rocky then decided it was time to return to the house.

As I reached the back door a woman, quite heavily pregnant, emerged, then appeared to stumble on the step. She caught the wall with her hand, but hard, so that she gasped with pain and her drink splashed over her dress. She was obviously shaken. I went to her, took the empty glass and helped her to a low wall to sit.

'Are you all right?'

'Yes, fine. Just a bit – how stupid.'

'I remember that balance thing,' I said. 'I fell a couple of times when I was pregnant. Comes out of nowhere, doesn't it? How many months are you?'

'Seven.' She grimaced. 'Thanks for the help, but I'm fine now. Feel free to go back inside. I don't want to spoil your night.'

'I don't mind. It's nice out here.'

'Yes. Warm in there, isn't it? All those candles. I'm sure the chemicals can't be good for . . .' Her hands floated to her bump. 'But this is nice.' She breathed deeply. 'How come you're out here?'

'Same reason as you. Except I'm not pregnant. I was visiting the dog.'

She laughed. 'Ah, isn't he sweet? We have our two Schnauzers back in Boston. Miss the little critters.'

She was chatty in a nervous way. Her eyes were very bright. I could see that she was very tired.

'You live in Boston?' I asked. Her accent was Irish.

'Yes. We're just home for a few days. A work trip, mainly. For my better half. And to visit family.' She touched her bump again. 'Truthfully, though, right this minute I'd prefer to be sitting in front of a telly with my feet up. Boring, I know, but I'm wrecked.'

A shadow crossed the light from the kitchen. When I turned I saw that Vanessa was standing behind us. I hadn't spoken to her since she'd greeted us earlier in the hall. Obviously, she was circulating in that way good hostesses do to make sure that their guests are enjoying the evening. I turned further to include her in our conversation.

'Everything okay?' Vanessa smiled.

'Just getting some air.' The overly bright look was back on the pregnant woman's face. 'This party is incredible, Vanessa. It must have taken you weeks to pull this together.'

'Oh, we used the most amazing caterers! All the top firms use them. I'll give you the details if you ever need them. Tell Conrad it was me who sent you. He'll make sure you're well looked after.'

The woman looked from Vanessa to me. 'So how do you two know each other? Through work, or . . .'

'My daughter's in Vanessa's daughter's class. They're good friends.' I smiled at Vanessa.

'Yes,' the woman said. 'Orla did mention that some of the school mums might be here. Where is Orla, anyway? I've been looking for her all evening.'

Vanessa said, 'Orla?'

'Orla Mooney. Your daughters are good friends, and so are you, right?'

'You know *Orla*?'

'Yes! We were neighbours when we were kids. Best friends, actually – wow, way back! We lost touch when my family moved. But we reconnected a few years ago, and when I knew I was coming to Ireland we said we'd definitely try to meet up. I told Orla we were coming here tonight and she said that was perfect as she was expecting to be here too. Unfortunately, I haven't been able to call her since we came to Ireland as my phone fell into a loo and I lost all my contacts. It's been awful, as I'm sure she's been trying to reach me and wondering why I haven't returned her calls. But I thought, no worries, I'd catch up with her here . . . where is she?'

'She wasn't inv—' I began, at the same time as Vanessa said, 'Unfortunately, I'm afraid Orla had other plans for tonight.'

'What?' The woman looked dismayed. 'But . . . Oh no. We're leaving in the morning. I wish I'd known. I'd have made more of an effort to meet her before tonight.'

I interrupted eagerly. 'But there must be some mistake. Orla doesn't have any other plans. She told me she hadn't been invited.' I turned to Vanessa. 'Would she have missed your invitation, do you think?'

Vanessa shrugged. 'Possibly. Or else she mixed up the dates. It's unfortunate, but there we are. Now if we —'

'She didn't mix up the dates,' I said. 'I'm sure she didn't know she was invited. She told me herself she'd have loved to come.'

Vanessa said stiffly, 'I'm afraid you don't know Orla as well as I do. She's a sweet person, but she can be quite flaky. I'm sure *you* know that,' turning to the other woman, 'seeing as you two go back so far.'

'Is she?' The woman looked uncertain. 'I haven't seen her for a long time so maybe . . . anyway, it does look like there's been a mix-up. Such a pity my phone got damaged.'

I should have left it there. In retrospect, Vanessa's voice had sounded tight and funny. But I'd had a few drinks and I still had that headache. My sense of when to shut up was blunted. I just didn't want to leave Orla and her nice friend thinking they had let each other down.

'Orla's at home right now,' I told the woman. 'Babysitting my daughter. She only offered to do that yesterday when she realized she wasn't coming here. Here – take my phone if you'd like. Give her a call.'

'Are you sure?' The woman's face lit up.

It was only as I was handing over my phone that I became aware that we had an audience. Several people had come up to stand behind us. You. Dave. A heavyish balding man in a blue jacket.

Orla's friend squealed into the phone. 'Orla? It's Kelly! I KNOW! Are you still up? Oh my God! I'm just leaving. I'll be there right away.'

She ended the call, beaming. 'This is fantastic! Imagine I nearly didn't get to see her! We'll jump in a taxi and go right – Oh.' Her face fell. She turned to Vanessa. 'I mean – would you mind?'

Before Vanessa could respond, the balding man stepped forward and put his hand on Kelly's waist. 'I think it's a good idea,' he said in an American accent. 'We've got a long journey home tomorrow and my wife is exhausted. Vanessa, Dave – thank you! This has been a wonderful party, and I'm sorry it's still so early but I think we'll have to call it a night.'

'I hope you understand,' Kelly appealed to Vanessa. 'It's been lovely. I hope you don't mind us bailing. It's just, I did promise Orla I'd try to see her.'

Vanessa appeared to be having difficulty speaking. Dave stepped into the breach. 'No problem at all,' he said. 'Completely understood. There seems to have been an unfortunate miscommunication regarding Orla – a pity her invitation was mislaid, but these things happen.' I thought he gave Vanessa a rather odd look.

Kisses and handshakes and goodbyes. Seconds later Kelly came rushing back to me. 'Almost forgot!' She handed me my phone. 'Thank you so much . . . um?'

'Sara.'

'Sara! Thank you very much! Really appreciate your help.'

Then she was gone, along with Dave and her husband, leaving me alone in the garden with you and Vanessa. Vanessa stood holding her wine glass, as still as a statue.

'Gosh,' I said into the silence. 'That was unexpected. But it's nice to think they'll –'

In a very cold voice Vanessa said, 'I thought you told Isabel you knew them?'

'What?'

She turned and walked back to the house.

I was confused. 'Know who? Who were those people?'

'That was Josh Lennox,' you said. 'Didn't you say that was who the party was for?'

Josh Lennox. Josh Lennox. I tried to think. When had someone mentioned that name recently? And what, just in a moment, had triggered in me such a tumbling sense of dread?

22

That's it, Adam. That's my step-by-step recall of that night, everything I can think of that happened. I won't deny that it was awkward. The way Vanessa had flounced off made it clear that she wasn't happy about the Lennoxes' departure. And, incidentally, the mystery of why you and I had been invited to the party had now been solved. Vanessa must have been envisioning Manhattan shopping trips and cocktails on yachts with her new besties, Josh and Kelly, courtesy of you. But if I had caused her any difficulty or embarrassment – and I acknowledge that perhaps I had – it was a genuine mistake on my part. Nothing happened that night that should have caused any person to go on to do the things she did. Not any normal person, anyway, though at the time we didn't realize what we were dealing with.

When we returned to the house, I tried to find her but couldn't. You chinwagged some more with your ex-schoolmates and we sampled some of the beef stroganoff and cheesecake before, shortly after one, you'd had enough and we decided to leave. I tried again to locate Vanessa to thank her and to apologize if I had spoken out of turn, but I still couldn't see her anywhere in the crowd. It didn't matter, I thought. She was busy and had probably forgotten about it. I'd see her the next day for Lexie's party.

On our walk home we were quiet – still not speaking to each other away from the crowd. But I'm sure that if what had happened had struck us as being significant we would have mentioned it. I know that you thought no more of the whole business than I did.

The following morning I woke, muzzy and out of sorts and with a hollow sensation in my abdomen that I put down to too much champagne. You slept on beside me, snoring slightly. Lexie was still at Orla's.

At nine I sent a message to the Lexie's Party WhatsApp group I had created: *Lexie and I really looking forward to seeing everyone later.* Then I got up, washed down two Paracetamol with some cold water and went to the beach for a swim. When I returned, feeling a bit better, you were up and packing for London. You responded with civil surprise when I handed you your coffee, and we spoke, a little warily, about the previous night and the people we'd met. Neither of us mentioned the row. We did need to talk, but with a taxi due at any moment now was not the time.

'Give Lexie a kiss for me,' you said as the taxi arrived. 'Tell her good luck with the party. And with the dog, whatever his name is.'

I was surprised. 'So we're getting him?'

'It's not ideal, you know that. But it is her birthday.'

'Adam – thank you! She'll be so happy!' Tentatively I reached to kiss your cheek. 'I'm sorry if you feel it wasn't discussed properly, but you won't regret it, I promise.'

At least we were communicating again, I thought, filled with relief, as I waved you off. Once this contract was signed hopefully all this distance and bad feeling between us would come to an end. We were almost there. *Patience*, I told myself. *Have the patience of a fucking saint.*

After you left, I busied myself hanging bunting above the kitchen table and setting out bowls of Pringles and jelly snakes. Then I went to collect Lexie from Orla's. She came skipping down the stairs with Sadbh, full of beans, saying she'd had the best night ever.

'Thanks so much!' I said to Orla. 'I definitely owe you!'

'No problem. She was a pleasure.'

'Vanessa's was fun,' I said. 'Mostly work people, as you predicted. I met your friend Kelly.'

'Yes. She called here on her way home.'

'I'm glad. She was so looking forward to seeing you.'

'Yes.'

'Right. Well.' I lifted Lexie's backpack from the newel post. 'I'd better get going, but I'll fill you in later over coffee.'

'About that.' Orla took a breath. 'Unfortunately, I won't be able to make it. My mum's fallen and hurt her leg and I need to call and check on her.'

'Oh no. I hope she's okay. Would it help if I minded Sadbh for you?'

'Thanks, but if you don't mind I think I'll just take her to my mum's. They haven't seen each other for a while. I'm sorry Sadbh will miss Lexie's party, but at least they had their sleepover.'

'Yes, of course.' Orla seemed a little abrupt, I thought. I wondered if her mum was more unwell than she was letting on. But then it occurred to me that perhaps she mightn't want to sit and listen to everyone banging on about a party she hadn't been invited to. If so, I couldn't blame her.

Eva and Edel had replied with thumbs-up emojis to my message on the Lexie's Party WhatsApp group. Nothing yet from any of the others. They must still be sleeping off Vanessa's bash. I bypassed the entrance to Brookview and turned on to the N11.

'Where are we going?' Lexie asked.

'Wait and see!'

Her face when she realized where we were headed. Even more so when we arrived at the shelter and saw George being led into Reception with his lead and his adoption pack.

'No way! No *way*!' She was utterly overcome.

196

George flew at her as if he'd known her for years. *Where WERE you? I've been waiting AGES!* He squeaked and panted as he threaded through her arms while she stroked him, flabbergasted, too happy to speak.

We bought some basic supplies from the shop, the staff handed us a folder with instructions about vaccines and worm tablets, and we were off. George sat on a towel (just in case) in the passenger footwell, shivering with excitement, eagerly licking Lexie's hand whenever she touched him. 'Hey, gorgeous,' she cooed. 'Hey, long-nose. Maybe we should call you Nosey! Wait till my friends see you. I can't wait for my party! This is going to be the best day ever!'

As we pulled up outside the house my phone chirped. Isabel: *Really sorry, Sara, but I'm going to have to give today a miss. Hangover from hell here! And sadly Mabel seems to have come down with a tummy bug so will keep her at home just in case. Muchos apologies to Lexie and will give her her present on Monday.*

I was surprised. I didn't remember seeing Isabel drink that much. She was a spritzer sort of person. I went to message back to see if she was okay but before I could my phone chirped again. Erica: *Sorry Sara. Unfortunately, something has come up. Won't make today.*

I frowned at the phone.

Lexie settled George into his new home, prattling non-stop as she led him on a tour. 'This is my room. And our garden. And over there's the Green — you can go there when you're older. And oh, wow, my party table — I LOVE it!' She went around inspecting all the bowls, giving the thumbs-up to each one. 'Do you like crisps, George? Do you? I bet you'd love some chocolate, but sadly dogs aren't allowed.'

On the kitchen counter were the bulging paper bags I had picked up from Berry Nice with lunch for the adults: olives, dates, sundried tomatoes with pinkish oil leaking from the tub, crusty baguettes. In the fridge were salads, cheeses, mush-room soup and a spinach-and-feta quiche. I'd bought way too much food if it was just going to be Edel, Eva and Vanessa – however something told me that I would not be seeing Vanessa.

Uneasily I unpacked the bags and stored the excess in the fridge. It was coincidence, I told myself, nothing more. But I remembered again Vanessa's coldness after the Kelly/Orla incident. Surely it couldn't be that? And if it was, why would the others be involved? I removed some of the settings from the table, rearranging the remaining ones so that it wouldn't look so bare.

At two thirty Edel and Eva arrived. Mia and Imogen rushed straight through to the garden to see George.

'What's this?' Edel wrinkled her nose at a bowl on the counter.

'Red pepper hummus.'

'Oh. I'm not a fan of Spanish food.'

'Nothing for me, thank you.' Eva patted her slender waist. She looked at the mounds of food. 'Are we the only ones here? I thought Vanessa and all those were coming?'

'They were,' I said. 'But things came up.'

Every time we heard a noise outside or the sound of a car Lexie ran to the front door, but there was no sign of Polly. Each time, her face fell, but she did her best to stay upbeat for Mia and Imogen, who were enchanted by George. We sang 'Happy Birthday', me performing as enthusiastically as I could to make up for the lack of numbers, and she blew out her can-dles. George with his merry eyes and overly long nose was a huge hit; Mia in particular seemed very taken with him, and overall, I thought, the afternoon had gone well.

But when the others had left, Lexie asked quietly, 'Why didn't they come? They promised they were going to come.'

'I told you, sweetheart. Sadbh's grandma hurt her leg and Mabel wasn't well. These things happen.'

'But why didn't Polly come?' she kept asking. 'Why didn't she tell me she wasn't coming? She said she was looking forward to it. I had everything ready.'

On the Sunday I took flowers and a thank-you card up to Vanessa's. No reply when I pressed the buzzer so I rested them against the electric gates. By nightfall there was still no response or acknowledgement that she had received them.

On Monday I spotted Isabel leaving the playground with Jake in his pushchair.

'Hey,' I greeted her, falling into step. 'Great party the other night.'

'Yes, it was lovely. Look, sorry, Sara, but I can't stop. I need to get Jake to his pre-school. They keep getting annoyed with me for being late.'

'No problem. See you later.' I watched her hurry across the road in her silvery coat.

At the entrance to Brookview I saw Vanessa, wearing her oversized sunglasses even though the morning was gloomy. I caught up with her.

'Vanessa, thank you so much for Friday! What a fantastic night! You must be delighted with the way it turned out.'

She just looked at me.

I said uncertainly, 'Has something happened? Are you all right?'

A little noise. 'I'm not listening to this.'

'Listening to what?'

But I was talking to myself. She had turned and walked away.

What on earth was going on? Was it the Lennox thing? Clearly from Vanessa's reaction there was an issue – but what? Had Dave lost business because of what had happened? Had I cost him some kind of deal by causing the Lennoxes to leave early? My heart sank. That must be it. Now I remembered the way Dave had looked at Vanessa, the odd glance he had given her. How humiliating for her to have to deal with that in front of all her guests.

I had no idea how to handle this or what to do next. I gave Orla a call.

'Are you free tomorrow? Quick coffee after drop-off?'

'I've a lot to –'

'Please. Just a quick one. I need to ask you something.'

Only then did it occur to me to wonder if I'd got Orla into trouble too. Kelly had left the party to meet her, after all. But when we met she seemed calm. Spoon was quiet, the other tables empty, the hard white light from the door illuminating the ground-in crumbs and fluff on the carpet. I bought us both a coffee and we sat.

'How's your mum?' I asked.

'My –'

'Her leg?'

'Oh. Yes. She's fine, thanks. It was just a sprain.'

'Thanks so much again for minding Lexie on Friday. She had a brilliant time.'

'She was no trouble.' Orla's voice warmed up a notch. 'She's always a pleasure.'

'Your friend Kelly seemed very nice.'

'She is. Thanks for lending her your phone, by the way. She said you were very kind.' Orla seemed more herself now, less formal and stiff, turning in her chair towards me.

Cautiously I said, 'You might have heard that it led to some upset with Vanessa. I didn't realize Kelly's husband was the guest of honour.'

'Well, me either,' Orla said. 'I've never met him. Such a pity. If I'd known how important he was to Vanessa's evening I could have introduced them all properly; it would have been lovely. Vanessa was very sweet about it the next day when she called. Apparently, she'd automatically assumed I'd be at the party. She couldn't believe I'd thought I needed to wait for an official invite.'

'Right,' I said. 'Well, I'm wondering if perhaps Dave missed out on a chance to do business with Josh because they left early.'

'Oh, surely not!' Orla looked at me. 'He'd hardly change his mind about working with someone just because his wife was tired?'

When she put it that way, it did sound unlikely. I paused, unsure of what to say next. Orla didn't seem aware of the confusion that had taken place at the party over whether or not she'd made other plans and I certainly wasn't going to put my hand in that blender.

'I just wondered,' I said, 'because Vanessa does seem upset with me about something.'

Orla moved a crumb around the table with her finger. 'Vanessa can be funny at times.'

'Isabel seems a bit off too,' I blurted, realizing as I said it how paranoid it sounded.

'Well, you know. She and Van have known each other for so long. If there's a conflict of interest, she'll always take Vanessa's side.'

Conflict of interest? My head snapped up. What was this? There had to be more to this than a pregnant woman leaving a party because she was tired.

'Orla – what's going on?'

Orla fiddled some more with the crumb.

'Is Vanessa annoyed with you too? Because if so, I'm really sorry but –'

'It's not that.'

'Then what?'

Orla's body cringed into a pretzel shape.

'You really don't know?'

'No.'

'Vanessa mentioned . . . she said . . .'

'Ye-es?' I resisted the urge to make a winding motion with my hands to reel the words out of her mouth.

'She said you made a move on Dave.'

'*WHAT?*' I was stunned. I hadn't seen this coming at all. 'Where did she get *that* from? I didn't even speak to him. Except to say hello at the start.'

'She says you were seen with him. Alone. At the bottom of the garden.'

'But I . . . wait. Yes. The dog. I was patting their dog when Dave came to give him some water. I'd forgotten about that.'

Orla said nothing.

'We exchanged a couple of words. But it was a minute or two at most. How on earth could that be built up into me making a move on him?'

'You were standing very close together,' Orla said. 'Tousling his hair and touching his face. And your hand was . . . apparently it was on his . . . belt.'

'*What?*' My face grew hot – though with shock rather than the thought of Dave's belt. 'That did *not* happen. No way. Why would someone say that? Whoever saw us must have been drunk. Or it was dark or, I don't know, but it didn't happen. It just didn't. I wouldn't do that. I honestly don't know what else I can say.' I was practically leaning over the table by this time, right up in Orla's face. 'You believe me, don't you?'

A pause. 'Yes.'

She didn't sound very sure.

'Does Vanessa really think that? No wonder she's so angry. But why *would* she think it? Just because some drunk person . . .

but why would she believe them? Over her own husband, if not me? Surely she's asked *him* what happened?'

Orla said miserably, 'The thing is, Dave has form. There's been trouble before. With women – well – stalking him.'

'Stalking *Dave*? . . . I mean . . .'

'Yes, women from his work, mostly. Vanessa says it's because he's so successful. It's been very difficult for both of them. And Adam travels a lot, doesn't he? You're on your own here quite a bit.'

'Yes, but that doesn't mean –'

'No, I know. But if there's been trouble before, it's how Vanessa might see things.'

'But I didn't do anything. And even if *he* came on to *me* – which he didn't – that's not *my* fault, is it?'

Orla's eyeballs oscillated as if she was wondering how much she should say.

'The thing about Vanessa,' she said finally, 'is, she might look as if her life is perfect, but there are a lot of things going on that people don't know. Her and Dave have nearly split up a few times thanks to the women at work. It's no one's fault, but I mean – poor Van. You can see why she gets so stressed. It's put a lot of strain on them. One of the children mentioned at school that Vanessa and Dave had been shouting and throwing things, and once Dave broke a chair.' Orla looked alarmed. 'You didn't hear that from me, by the way.'

'No, no, of course.' It put a new slant on things. Clearly Dave had a rampantly wandering eye. And probably lots of other wandering body parts too. If what Orla had said was true, I could almost feel sorry for Vanessa. Almost.

'I'll have to tell her,' I said. 'I'll have to call her and explain.'

Orla shrank back. 'That's up to you.'

'What do you mean?'

'It might be better to lie low for a while. Let things settle.'

'You mean I should say nothing? Let her think it's true?'

'No, not that. I just meant, not straight away. Give her time to cool down first. Vanessa can be . . . and you know, Polly being at school with . . . they can . . . Vanessa can be funny about things. You know?'

I took the long way home, hardly seeing which way I was going. *Lie low*, Orla had said. But was I supposed to just let Vanessa tell everyone I'd perved all over her husband and have them think it was true?

I was so agitated that it took me a moment to recognize that the woman I was obsessing over was walking mere feet ahead, streaky ponytail bouncing, a pale pink scarf looped about her neck.

I upped my pace. 'Vanessa!'

She kept going, but I followed her and came around. Yet again she was wearing her large sunglasses and now I wondered if it was to hide eyes that were red and swollen from crying.

'Vanessa,' I said wearily, 'can we talk? Please?'

'There's nothing to say.'

'Whatever someone thinks they saw, nothing happened between Dave and me. It was a couple of minutes of conversation between host and guest. Nothing more.'

She huffed a disbelieving little laugh.

'It's true. I'm sorry, but I just wouldn't –'

'*You* wouldn't?' She stopped and lifted the sunglasses. No swollen red lids under there. Just eyes that were icy cold, like peeled grapes from a fridge. '*YOU* wouldn't?'

'Nor would he either, I'm sure,' I said frantically, floundering. It was like talking to a ping-pong ball. The conversation was starting to bounce in directions that made no sense. 'Look, the point is, whatever you were told was not correct. It was a three-minute conversation about your dog. Nothing else. From either of us. Truly.'

'Let me pass, please.'

I began to feel exasperated. 'Vanessa, it was a lovely evening and I'm sorry if I overstepped with the Lennoxes. But you can't go around saying things about me that aren't true. It's ridiculous –'

As soon as I said that I knew it was a mistake.

'Ridiculous?' The peeled grapes bulged. *RIDICULOUS?* I'll tell you what's ridiculous. Me trusting you. After all I've done for you. Welcoming you to this area. Going *out of my way* to include you in school events when you knew *nobody*. Inviting you to my home to help your husband with his struggling business because I felt *sorry* for you. And this is how you repay me. Coming to my home with your superior attitude. Getting so drunk that you make a show of yourself. Driving away my guests . . . oh yes, don't pretend you don't know exactly what you were doing. And how dare you say that *I* don't know what *I* saw in MY! GARDEN!'

Her neck was taut and stringy, her face maroon. All her gracious sweetness was gone. With no one around to see, she was free to drop the fluffy candyfloss exterior, exposing the jagged hate-filled spike beneath.

'You know what?' Her eyes narrowed. 'I've always thought there was something weird about you. Stay away from me, stay away from my family.' And she marched off up the hill, leaving me swaying with shock.

Lexie came home that afternoon very upset. She had asked Polly why she hadn't come to her party.

'Me and Mabel spent Saturday together,' Polly had told her. 'We couldn't come because we went swimming and had pizza.'

'Oh, sweetheart.' My stomach flipped. 'I think there must

have been a mistake. The mothers must have got the dates mixed up. I'm sure the girls would love to have come if they could.'

Lexie, her shoulders slumped, trudged off to play with George, but I circled the kitchen, folding tea towels, moving plant pots, scraping cold candle wax off the counter, anything to distract me from the way my insides kept folding and churning. Orla had warned me that Vanessa could be tricky, but I found her behaviour utterly bizarre. And disturbing. Spreading those rumours about Dave with no basis whatsoever. And worse, doing what she had done to Lexie. Sabotaging her party. I had no doubt that was Vanessa's work. Polly and Lexie had been getting along perfectly well until now. Polly, of course, would do whatever Vanessa told her to do. The woman, after all, was her mother and she had to live with her.

Compulsively, I picked at the wax. The edge lifted off like a scab. Vanessa's irrational, disproportionate response was triggering memories decades old. The expression on her face in her garden the other night – now I knew what it had reminded me of.

In the days and weeks following my stand-off with Grace Gillespie on the netball steps she kept her word that I'd be sorry. My schoolbag had ink leaked into it. My books had pages torn out. My shoes went missing during PE and turned up in the toilet.

I never saw who was doing it. Obviously, Grace was behind it, but she couldn't have done it all by herself. She had got other people involved so that now I didn't know who to trust.

I knew better than to tell the teachers and there'd have been no point whatsoever in mentioning it at home. So I gritted my teeth and put up with it, taking the view that she'd get tired of it after a while. But she didn't. It was as if all along she had been searching for a target to replace Lucy Wright and now she'd found one she was going to lock on tight.

My old friend Emily walked straight past me one day in the playground as if she hadn't seen me.

Moll said, 'You know Emily's scented pencils that went missing? Grace told her she saw them in your bag.'

'What? That's a lie! Why didn't Emily ask me about it?'

'Grace told her not to. She said your mum couldn't afford things like that, so it was best to ignore it. Grace gave her a brand-new set and Emily was delighted.'

'But I didn't take them! I don't even like those smelly pencils; they don't write properly. And even if I did, I'm not a thief!'

Other things were being said about me, Moll said, embarrassed.

'What things?'

'Grace told a bunch of us she saw you picking your nose and wiping it on Nat's coat when you thought no one was looking.'

'You're joking! That's disgusting! I've never done anything like that.'

'I know. But it's what she's saying.'

Moll was doing her best to help, but I couldn't help wondering when she would begin to worry that Grace might target her too. I tried to reverse the damage but since I didn't know half the things that were being said my hands were tied.

23

I decided to take Orla's advice and steer clear of Vanessa. No point arguing with crazy. I was conscious, though, of the ongoing damage to my reputation. The BM ranks had well and truly closed. At drop-off Erica looked right through me. Marina too, though that was nothing new. Isabel did wave, but she always appeared in a hurry to be somewhere. I couldn't seem to get close enough to any of them to give my side of the story.

Edel said in a thrilled whisper, 'What's happened to the Beautiful Mums? Has there been a row?'

'Why? What did you hear?'

'On Vanessa's Instagram. It looks as if there's been some drama.'

As soon as I got home I looked up her profile. I braced myself to read my name, but she was too canny for that. There were, however, hints aplenty for those in the know.

Living my truth, in spite of those who try to hurt others.

When strangers let you down, real friends gather round.

Family is everything. Accompanied by photos of Vanessa and her family on a white-sand beach. Footprints. Dunes. Vanessa laughing as she roasted a marshmallow. Vanessa and Dave kissing in front of a sunset.

People – Erica, Jill, Marina, others whom I didn't know – responded with heart and flower emojis and Kahlil Gibran quotes. *Stay strong, Van xxx*

She can't keep this up, I thought. The truth would come out soon enough. Rushing to emotionally engage would only add fuel for those who thrived on the drama. Unfortunately, I was battle-hardened in these matters.

So for the moment I concentrated on keeping Lexie distracted. Here George rose to the occasion, getting us out of the house and into the fresh air. Despite his doleful appearance he was an extremely cheerful little creature, happily sniffing and trotting about, always flatteringly delighted to see us. I didn't anthropomorphize his behaviour. We controlled his food and his brief moments of freedom; he had no choice but to 'love' us. But during those days and the darker ones that followed I don't know where Lexie would have been without him.

The next drama, in March, was Polly's tenth birthday party. This had been in the planning for months and Lexie had been on the guest list since Christmas. She came home from school one day, worried and deflated.

'Polly won't talk about the party in front of me,' she said in a small voice. 'I don't think I'm invited any more.'

I cornered Isabel in the playground.

'Is Polly's party still on this weekend?' I asked.

'Yes.'

'Isabel – can I say something?'

'Well –'

'I think it's important that you know that nothing happened between me and Vanessa's husband.'

'Gosh, it's not really any of my –'

'I'm sorry, but I think it is. I don't know how to convince you, or anyone, except just to keep repeating that it didn't happen. I don't know why Vanessa is so convinced it did, but it didn't. And that's really all I can say.'

Isabel ducked her head, zipping and re-zipping Jake's hoodie. 'Vanessa has been under a lot of pressure lately.'

'But not from me. And the problem is, Lexie is being dragged into it.'

'Well, I don't think it's advisable to involve the –'

'Exactly. That's why I'd like to clear all this up as soon as possible.'

Isabel visibly squirmed. 'There's really no point involving me in this. Vanessa's the one you need to talk to, but you'll have to wait till she's ready. I'm sorry, but that's the only advice I can give you.'

Another with the *let it be*. But none of them – except, not very convincingly, Orla – was coming out and saying that they believed me. *If there's a conflict of interest, Isabel will always take her side.* Perhaps if they knew me better . . . but how was that going to happen if they wouldn't give me a chance? And no matter what any of them thought I'd done, how cruel to take it out on a child.

Well, it looked like this particular party was blown and we'd have to suck it up. On the day, Lexie sat miserably at the front window, watching as the shiny girls played rounders on the Green then raced up the hill together to Polly's house. I swallowed my anger and called her away.

'Remember, they've all known each other since they were babies,' I said. 'You're still new. These mix-ups will happen for a while until you're fully settled in.'

George and I lured her away for ice cream and a walk on the beach. We gave George a trial off the lead and he promptly repaid our trust by chasing a Dart and becoming a dot on the horizon, necessitating a lot of panicked shouting and running after him. Then he swallowed a plastic bag. By the time we returned home it was past six and Polly's party was almost certainly over. Hopefully Vanessa had finally made her point. A vindictive, unpleasant way to go about it, but now it was done.

I let George go to bed with Lexie. I hadn't planned to allow him up on the furniture, but she needed this.

'You're my true friend,' I heard her whispering. 'You'll never let me down.' When I peeked in he was lying with his head on her tummy, gazing up at her, his velvety little head furrowed, whether because he wanted food or because he genuinely thought she was unhappy and in need of comfort. I like to think the latter. He was a very sweet little animal.

On Monday, however, she came home from school very upset again.

'There's a new club and I can't be in it.'

'Why?'

'You had to score enough points to get in. You had to know a secret word and I didn't guess it.'

'Oh, sweetie. Maybe you can try again tomorrow.'

'I *can't*. Today was the day to guess and they all knew the word from the party and I didn't. I can't play with them any more. I'm not *allowed*.'

'But when –'

'*EVER!* That's what they said! Today was the only audition for the club and I didn't get in!'

She went up to her room and slammed the door.

Later when she came, red-eyed, to dinner, I said calmly, 'I don't know how long this club business will last. But surely the whole class can't be in it. Just find someone else to play with. Step away from those girls for a little while. They'll fight among themselves, you'll see, and the club will end. Meanwhile, why don't we invite Mia and Imogen over this Friday?'

She nodded sadly, picking at her food.

Step away. It was the best advice I could give her. Standing up to my own school bully had only made things worse. Drawn her upon me like a snake on a rat. If Vanessa and her daughter were cut from the same cloth, the only thing to do was to disengage. Orla had advised it. Isabel too. They knew Vanessa very well. Confronting this kind of person was not wise. I of all people knew only too well what happened if you did.

Grace, too, had invited the whole class to her birthday party except me. I tried to ignore it. Such a pathetic and obvious thing to do. The party was the talk of the class. There was going to be a karaoke machine and a nail bar. Moll said she didn't want to go. She wanted to refuse the invitation, but I insisted that she accept. Otherwise I was afraid that she might start to resent me.

On Moll's twelfth birthday I gave her a keyring with a sparkly silver M on it. Grace gave her a Body Shop perfume and shower gel set and an inflatable backpack. Moll told me that the perfume had given her a rash and she much preferred my gift. I appreciated that she'd said it.

I was relieved when the summer holidays came. Grace had ruined my final year of primary school, but it was over now. In secondary I could start afresh. Grace would not be there; word had it that she was going to an independent school in Kent where they went on trips to Chile and Kenya. Sadly, Moll wouldn't be joining me either; her family was moving to Germany. Visiting her for a final goodbye, seeing her noisy, excited family, the packing boxes in the hallway, the empty living room with the clean squares on the carpet where the furniture had been, Moll's bedroom cleared of all the books and pictures and ornaments that were as familiar and dear to me as my own – all of it made me feel bereft. We promised to write, but I knew in my heart it would never be the same.

I spent a lot of that summer alone. My mother was in her own world. Her rages of a couple of years ago had subsided into lethargy and she spent much of her time asleep, huddled under a blanket on the sofa with the curtains drawn. Steve was the snappy one these days. I kept myself out of the house, away from the pair of them, cycling for miles. I read dozens of books, lying in the sunshine with no one to bother me. I didn't see Grace once, and by the time September rolled around I'd had enough of my own company and was looking forward to starting secondary school.

On our first morning, I and a few other early birds loaded our books into some empty desks by the window, then headed off to explore. Returning to the homeroom, to my horror and dismay the first person I saw was Grace Gillespie.

Later I heard that there had been some financial irregularity at her father's tyre-and-tube wholesalers firm, which may have explained why she hadn't gone to the Kent school after all. She must have been disappointed to miss out on Chile and Kenya. But she was keeping her chin up, making the best of things. Incredibly, she and a couple of other girls were unloading our books from the window desks, piling them on a desk near the door.

'What do you think you're doing?' My heart was pumping. 'We were here first.'

She eyed me with cool disgust. 'Well well, whaddaya know. Butt out, egg breath, and sit by the door if you know what's good for you.'

The other window-desk girls began to murmur and back away. Either they were natural pacifists, or they were timid, or some part of their brains had warned them that Grace was not a person to mess with.

Unfortunately for me, I hadn't learned my lesson the first time. I can only explain it by saying that for me Grace was a big red button marked 'Do Not Push', and back then there was still enough in me that I needed to push it. I couldn't go on tiptoeing around her. I needed to start in this new school by showing her once and for all that she couldn't go on treating me like shit on her shoe.

'Excuse me.' Deliberately I scooped her books up from my desk. 'I'm putting these back where they belong.'

She tried to snatch them from my arms just as a teacher walked in. 'What's going on here? Whose desk is that? Doherty, didn't I see you putting your books in there earlier? So you, what's your name – Gillespie? – move your things elsewhere. Now!'

Big mistake. Bigger than I could ever have foreseen. Grace was back in my life with a vengeance. And with a hatred and focus that I never would have believed possible. I still can't believe it now.

More rumours about me – truly bizarre ones – and this time no one knew me from before so they had no way of knowing whether or not they could be true. There was no one to keep me informed of what was being said, no Moll to support me and stick by me. The few girls there from my old school either kept their heads down or sided with Grace. She was so determined to teach me a lesson that if I did make any new friends she promptly intervened to put a stop to it, by lies, bribes or threats. It sounds crazy now to say that's what she did, but she really did.

During the summer holidays of the following year a new girl moved to my estate and we became friendly. It was a huge relief to properly connect with a girl my age again, to hang out with someone who didn't know yet that they had to avoid me. But within days of school restarting the new girl was steering clear and I knew that Grace had got to her. She sucked people into her orbit like a black hole. She poured prodigious energy into punishing me and never seemed to tire of it. Her vindictiveness was bottomless and pointless, like that of a child who has been irritated by a fly and captures it and tortures it, slowly pulling its wings off, just because they can.

Some of the rumours I only came to hear about after they had got around most of the school.

'Sara's dad's in prison.'

'Sara's brother kills cats.'

'Sara kissed Mr Renfrew.'

With the Renfrew thing I found the anger once more to pull her up on it.

'You can't say things like that. You'll get me and him kicked out of school.'

'Say things like what?'

'That I had an affair with Mr Renfrew.'

'I never said that! My God! You had an affair with the geography teacher?'

Which of course made sure that even more people heard about it, if they hadn't already. People looked at me oddly or turned away when I walked past. No one would have believed that Grace could have made up and slyly spread the things she did. I was the crazy one if I tried to explain. What was I suggesting? That someone would spread these lies about me for no reason at all? Who on earth would spend so much time doing that? Was I mad?

And, true to form, after I dared to contradict her in public about Mr Renfrew, she stepped it up even more. The school was mixed, so boys were involved now too and things began to turn physical. My house was attacked with raw eggs, including through the letterbox. Dogshit was smeared on the seat of my bike. Someone's older brother stopped me in the street, warning me that I'd better not walk through a certain part of town or they'd 'get' me. Grace took care not to dirty her own hands in these matters. She stayed safely at home, knowing that if I was to accuse her of having people follow me home in the evenings, throwing rubbish at me from behind a wheelie bin, I would look completely insane.

But by then I was finally starting to cotton on. Standing up to someone like Grace was like pouring petrol on a fire. She loved it. *Needed it.* She thrived on the drama, the confrontation; it was oxygen to her, and eventually I realized that the only thing to do was to shut it off.

I saw her disappointment almost immediately as I opened the lid of my desk to find the word 'Freak' Tippexed on the inside, and simply closed it again and sat down. I invested in a padlock after that and locked everything away, including my coat and PE kit. Everywhere I went I took my bag with me. I spent lunchtimes in the library, away from her and her henchmen. If I or my family was insulted to my face, usually by her male friends — *Your brother's a paedo. Your mother's a whore* — I simply stared into the distance, then walked on when they had finished.

And slowly, gradually, it worked. With most of them, anyway. A shrinking hard core continued, but I kept on with my shutdown and, finally, a full three and a half years after I had first defied Grace Gillespie on those netball steps, she got bored with me and moved on. Dating was now on her agenda, and I suppose she had to prioritize. A couple of final half-hearted insults, then she was done. The next target she locked on to was Heather Smith.

I still find it hard to think about Heather Smith.

Once it was clear that Grace was out of the picture some of my old friends began to re-emerge from the woodwork. I got invited to their homes or to Saturday trips to the cinema or to London. But by then, I think, the damage had been done.

Classmates I bumped into years later were surprised that I had been so affected by Grace. 'We didn't think you minded,' they said. 'You always seemed so confident and cool.'

Cool, meaning: never showing any emotion, good or bad. I was just . . . blank. I hadn't set out to be like that. Grace had stolen my smile.

From time to time, I've wondered if part of my brain was stunted during those years. If some vital pathways had never properly developed, if the person I should have been had shrivelled from disuse, the real Sara suppressed, a shadow me, trapped inside, capable of who knew what. All I know was, once Grace Gillespie came into my life, I was never the same.

'She was a bitch,' the classmates said. 'You were one of the few who wouldn't take her shit. We all admired you.'

That wasn't how I remembered it. I remembered them all dumping me like a hot potato when Grace told them to. I was glad to leave the lot of them behind when I took up my place at Cambridge, and I never looked back.

Nowadays, I can be more charitable. People had been frightened of Grace. She needed a victim like most people need food and no one wanted to be it. No one could get the better of her because they were not dealing with someone normal who played by normal rules. She did things that, if you tried to tell someone about them, they would think you were crazy.

I rarely dwelled on the past, or on her. You've asked me why, if she'd had such a huge effect on me, you'd never heard me mention her before, but what would have been the point? I had moved on. I was a grown-up now, a parent, and she was irrelevant to me.

I did look her up once. This was after I had bumped into one of my ex-schoolmates and we'd had the sort of conversation about her that I've just described. That evening I googled her and found her Facebook page. I clicked in and there she was – no longer living in Flitston but in a town not too far away. She looked different to what I would have expected. The strange thing is that Vanessa looked more like the Grace I remembered than the real adult Grace did. In her Facebook photo the adult Grace looked perfectly normal, pleasant even – a smiling, slightly overweight mum of three boys in a green jacket, her hair darker, her jaw soft. Was she still, to this day, a major player, now among the school mums, dividing and conquering, reliving the best days of her life? But the only reason I wondered that was because I knew her. To other people she would look utterly ordinary. Maybe mean, maybe not; maybe happy, maybe not. There was no way of telling from her photo that she had once caused such misery, and ultimately the death of another child in her class.

It's black outside now. Here in the kitchen a moth is flapping and banging against the ceiling light, desperate to be a part of its brilliance, too infatuated to realize the danger it's in or that the safest thing it could do would be to leave it and fly away quietly into the night.

I don't know why I've been going on so much about Grace Gillespie. I know what you're probably thinking: that in my head she and Vanessa are so alike that I've been mixing them up in some way. But I don't think that's true. In spite of a very occasional flash of resemblance, I have never, in some loss of touch with reality, thought that Vanessa actually was Grace. No one was Grace! Vanessa was just a spoiled and unhappy woman, angry because she had a cheat for a husband and looking for someone to lash out at. Highly unlikely, I thought, that there could be two Graces in the world and that I would fall afoul of one a second time.

24

A few days after Polly's birthday party I arrived at the school to collect Lexie and saw Vanessa, Eva and Edel deep in conversation. I'd never seen that before. They separated, Vanessa went off to talk to someone else, and Eva and Edel came towards us, flushed and beaming.

'Gosh,' Eva said. 'She's actually very nice, isn't she? Just goes to show, you never know someone until you talk to them.'

I said, 'Lexie was wondering if the girls would like to come to us on Friday after school?'

'Oh, sorry. They're going to Polly's. A bunch of them are going to watch *Wednesday* and bake cupcakes.'

Edel and Eva left, still flustered and delightedly waving. Lexie stood very still. 'They never went to Polly's before.'

'That's okay. We'll invite them another time.'

'They'll be Polly's friends now.'

'And yours.'

'No. It's Polly who decides.'

'Nonsense.'

I tried not to show my disquiet at how upset she was. Over the weekend, she chewed her sleeves harder than ever. Her stutter came back. In my panic I began to wonder if we'd be better off returning to London after all. When you came home again her distress penetrated even your ongoing self-absorption. You wrapped her in your arms and she snuggled in, leaning her head against you, picking at your shirt button, cherished and safe.

The one good thing about that period was that in spite of

your workload you noticed her need for you and made room for her, gave her your time. There were no more rows between us, no more talk of separation – or indeed any talk at all regarding our plans for next year. And since it was now I who was unsure of where we should live, I didn't push the topic. Why reignite the tension? It certainly wasn't what Lexie needed. Just park it for now, I thought. Focus on Lexie. It was perhaps for that reason too that I didn't tell you about the rumour Vanessa had spread about me and Dave.

You joined us on George's walks on the pale blue and cream beach, the watery sky reflected in the flat, shimmering pools, the tall chimneys in contrast with their red stripes, like a watercolour from a child's book. You helped her to teach George how to *Wait!* and *Fetch!* I thought you might even have started to warm to him a bit. This was around the end of March.

Your parents came to dinner, Jim still comporting himself gingerly after his recent health scare. Apparently, it had been his heart again, the same issue that had caused his stroke. His meds had been changed. Your mum was worried about him. Lexie was still quiet and sad.

When Lexie had left the room, Breda said unexpectedly, 'I agree with Sara. I do see that Lexie has some learning issues.'

'Really?' Sharply, you looked up.

I chose not to ask why you believed your mother, who had done Lexie's homework with her a couple of times at most, over me, who did it with her every day. But mouth, gift horse, etc.

'Yes,' Breda said. 'She reminds me of a girl I knew at school. She got smacked most days with a ruler for not knowing her spellings. One day I remember she was made to stand on a chair in the middle of the classroom with a sign around her neck saying "I am a bold, lazy girl." I feel dreadful now that I never tried to help her. At the time we all thought she *was* bold and lazy because that's what the sign said. I wonder what ever happened to her.'

Later I read Lexie her bedtime story. She curled up to me in her fleece pyjamas with her head under my chin. Wisps of her hair kept getting in my mouth.

'Would you like a turn?' I asked. 'I'll read a paragraph, then you. We can switch.' She shook her head, clutching the collar of my top, twisting her face into my shoulder.

'Won't you even try? You've been doing so well lately.'

'They let Imogen into the club even though she didn't know the password. It's a club for the clever girls, but they said I'm not one of them.'

'You are. You *are* clever! And what's far more important, trust me, you are so, so lovely.'

'They don't care if you're lovely. They don't even see me. I'm invisible to them now. I'm like the left hand. The ghost in their game.'

I massaged her slight shoulders, stroked her hair over and over until gradually her breathing deepened and she loosened her grip on my throat.

Heather, I thought. Eyes burning, I stared into the darkness.

25

Despite her best efforts, I was not completely friendless during the Grace years. There were a couple of people whom even Grace's tentacles could not reach – or more to the point, the people were so beneath her that she couldn't be bothered – and one of these was Heather Smith.

Heather was more vulnerable even than I was. Clever – when I came to know her, I realized that she was quick and observant, could notice things in a situation I would never have seen – but hopeless at schoolwork, bottom in every exam. At the time I didn't question it, why someone so perceptive and streetwise could perform so poorly in the classroom. Someone had to be bottom, and in our class it was Heather Smith. That was just the way it was.

People didn't bully her or dislike her or pick on her. Even Grace didn't, or at least not initially. She was just . . . invisible. Barely there. She came to class, said almost nothing, left again. She was never seen at after-school events or at weekends or even during breaktimes. Where she went, no one knew. Or cared, or wondered. Including me.

One lunchtime it was too warm to go to the library so I climbed the wall behind the science block and pushed through a gap in some trees to the meadow beyond, and there was Heather, lying on her back on the grass.

The uniform, as always, looked wrong on her, as if she was in some way unsuited to being a schoolgirl. The skirt was too short, the black sweater too big, with a stretched-out neck and sleeves that were rolled up yet still fell over her hands. Her small, pale face had a slightly receding chin. She was pretty in a heart-shaped, delicate way. She had dark curly hair and dark blue eyes with long lashes. I don't think I had ever properly heard her speak.

'Sorry,' I said, and moved a little further away before sitting down. She had raised herself on to her elbows as if to consider getting up and leaving but after a while she seemed to relax. She lay back down and we both stayed there with no further communication between us.

Next day, the same thing. And the next. Both of us there, several feet apart, not speaking, but there.

I finished my novel. About to put it away, I glanced at Heather.

'D'you like reading?'

She smiled slightly but shook her head. I put the book in my bag and took out another.

We began to nod, to say hello. Once I didn't want to finish my tuna roll and got up to find a bin. Seeing her stare at it, I offered it to her instead and after hesitating she accepted, saying she'd forgotten her own lunch.

Another day it was too cold to sit around and she got up. 'Fancy a walk?'

We went to the shop as I wanted some crisps. I assumed she'd buy something too as she'd had no lunch, but she said she wasn't hungry. So we walked back to school together, me munching my crisps alongside her.

I became intrigued by her, not because she was immediately intriguing in herself but because I had so few other people to be interested in. I was interested by the way she was so aloof, so indifferent to the rest of our class. Who *did* she have? Who was in her family? What did she do outside of school? Even I, pariah that I was, was a social butterfly compared to Heather Smith.

By that time my mother was out of it most days, snoring on the couch with stains on her clothes. Steve was rarely at home, out roaming and having fledgling brushes with the police. I prepared all the family meals, which my mother and Steve would sometimes eat and sometimes not. I cleaned the house and did all the shopping, using cash from my mother's wallet. Sometimes she'd turn nasty and accuse me of stealing but mostly she let me get on with it, provided I left her enough to buy wine or gin. That, she still had to go out and buy herself as I was too young to be served.

Heather and I began to ask each other what we were doing at weekends. Then occasionally to meet on a Saturday to wander around the high street. I bought her the occasional sausage roll or packet of crisps – she rarely allowed me to do this, but when she did, clueless as I was, even I noticed how she could barely restrain herself from cramming them down her throat. Sometimes if it was raining, I treated us both to a two-for-one cinema matinee deal.

We continued to see each other during the summer holidays. Heather was always quiet, seeming content in my company but without needing it. It was almost always I who suggested we meet. Eventually, however, one sunny afternoon, sitting on the wall by the river, eating a 99 I'd bought for her, she opened up a bit.

She hated school. She could barely read – she'd never managed to get the hang of it for some reason and now she was too far behind to catch up. She couldn't, for example, read everything that was written on the side of the lorry parked across the road, or on the ice-cream menu in the shop we'd just visited. She wanted to leave Flitston as soon as she turned sixteen and could ditch school but had no idea where to go or what to do. She said nothing about her family but by that time I'd suspected that things weren't great for her at home.

On one occasion only I went to her house. It was a Sunday

and we had arranged to meet. She knew a ruined old stately home where we could climb a fence into the overgrown grounds. There was a pagan monument there which, she said, had a peaceful, magical aura. The old house was close to where she lived so we agreed to meet at the top of her road.

She lived in a small estate, three pebble-dashed terraces arranged in a U shape around a central green area. Some of the houses were neat and well kept, others less so, with rotting window frames and clumps of nettles and lumps of dried dog-shit in the gardens. Heather had said to meet at the top of the road, but I was early so I walked down one side of the U. Number fourteen had a broken gate and a sheet of black plastic covering the downstairs window from the inside. I had to double check that I had the right house. Part of me was repulsed. I wanted to turn and walk away but instead I eased through the gate that was stuck halfway and rang the doorbell.

Heather answered. She didn't seem too pleased to see me at the door, but she let me in.

'Wait here in the hall. I'll just be a minute. My mum's upstairs having a rest. She doesn't like people calling over.'

'Okay.' Her mum sounded a bit like mine.

Heather ran upstairs. The narrow hallway had green mould down one wall and a smell of chips and vinegar and other things. To my right was a closed door, from behind which came the sound of sport on the telly. Ahead, through an open door-way, was the kitchen. The mess in there was much worse than in our house. Rubbish overflowing from a bin, a pool of old milk – or something dried and yellowish – on the floor, what looked like motorbike parts on the draining board beside the sink.

Heather was back downstairs. 'Right, let's –'

'HEATHER!' A bellow from behind the closed door. 'Where you off to?'

'Going for a walk.'

'Get in here.'

She pushed open the door. The living room was dark except for the TV. The black plastic bin bag taped to the window was presumably there to keep the sun off the screen. There were no shelves, books, lamps, pictures. Just an armchair and a sofa and a large TV sitting on a wooden crate.

'Who's your friend?' the shadowy man in the armchair asked.

'She's from school,' said one of the two teenaged boys on the sofa.

'This is my dad,' Heather said, 'and my brothers. This is my friend Sara.'

In the light from the television I recognized one of the boys. He was in Year 11, the year above us. I'd heard him talking in the corridors about his air rifle, which he used to shoot grey squirrels. 'To give the red ones a chance. They're our native breed.'

'Name?' Heather's dad cupped his hand behind his ear.

'Sara.'

'Speak up.' He beckoned with his finger, watching me as I approached. The brothers stared too. I felt very uncomfortable.

'Sara,' I repeated when I was standing in front of him, more timidly, as I hadn't come across this kind of behaviour in an adult before.

'And where are you off to?'

'Just for a walk.'

'Make sure you both behave.' Still staring at me. 'I hope you won't get Heather into any trouble. Are you a good girl?'

'I think so.'

'Speak up!'

'Yes!' I said loudly.

'Yes what?'

'Yes, I'm a good girl,' I said, then cringed as the words came out.

Heather, furious, grabbed my arm. 'Let's go!'

'Make sure you're back before dark,' her dad shouted after her, but she ignored him and slammed the front door.

The pagan monument was indeed very peaceful. It was a large rock, basically, covered with lichen and some marks which could have been ancient carvings but more probably were due to wind damage, but Heather seemed attached to it for some reason and there was something reassuring about its smooth, solid curves. We sat on the bank of a nearby stream with our bare feet in the water. Heather was still very angry and upset and tense. She said nothing for a long time, and I understood her in a way I never had before. The silence between us was gentle and kind. I knew that by simply being there I was helping her, and I liked it, this feeling of being needed. It made me feel tender and protective towards her. Took me out of myself in a way I hadn't experienced before.

That was probably the day when we talked the most. Heather said again how much she wanted to leave home as soon as she turned sixteen. It was her dream – but where, she wondered, would she go? What would she do? 'I'm not very bright,' she said. 'I'm useless at most things.'

I remember coming home as the sun was about to set, the sky pink over the fields behind our estate, the pale green leaves bursting from the tops of the hedgerows. I remember standing in the doorway of our sitting room, looking at my mother snoring on the couch and feeling for the first time a sense of separating from her, of stepping away.

The following term, two things changed. It was our GCSE year and Grace and I were mostly in different classes, which was a huge relief. I only saw her now in homeroom, but that was increasingly rare.

The second change was that Heather became friendly with someone new. A boy from a different school, Ryan. He had a weekend job at a local supermarket, as did she. He was a quiet, thoughtful person. Good-looking. Girls in our year often talked about him. Grace in particular went on and on about him, had his name written in swirly letters on her pencil case. It was assumed by everyone that at some point, when she was ready, Grace and Ryan would get together. And now here he was, strolling about town with Heather Smith!

The big news one Monday was that Grace had taken the plunge at The Fountain on Saturday night. Grace in her vest top, smelling of White Musk, her hair loose on her glittery shoulders, had walked up to Ryan and offered him a sip of her rum and Coke.

'Thanks,' he said. 'But I'm here with Heather.'

'But you're not *with her* with her,' Grace had laughed. 'You've just come together from work. Come over here and join us.'

But he refused as he said he had to walk Heather home.

Gemma Partridge was despatched to give Heather the heads-up.

'You know Grace Gillespie likes Ryan.'

'So?'

'So back off. Give her some space.'

'What if I like him too?'

'Seriously? You think *you've* got a chance with Ryan Evans?'

'Why not?' I imagined Heather would have said it softly but with the steadfastness I had come to know. 'Why not let him decide?'

At this point Grace took over, shouldering her way through the pall of dewberry body spray. 'You're deluded. I doubt illiterate munter is his style.'

Unluckily for her, however, Ryan had come looking for Heather and was at that very moment standing right behind her.

'You know,' he said to Grace in front of everyone, 'you're not half as hot as you think you are,' and he and Heather walked off together.

Grace was incandescent. Not normal go-home-and-sleep-it-off fury. But Grace fury. Malignant fury. Fury like melting tar that stuck to the skin and could not be shaken off.

'That low-class slag,' she raged. 'What does he see in her? If I shagged anything that moved, he'd be sniffing all over me too.'

At school she set about intimidating Heather – stopping square in a doorway, for example, and refusing to move aside to let her pass, but Heather, as always, didn't seem to notice or care what other people did. She simply waited politely until a teacher came along and ordered Grace to move. I saw how Grace watched Heather, her eyes narrowed, her lips drawn back almost in a snarl.

Unfortunately, even though Ryan seemed a decent bloke, if there had been anything more than friendship between him and Heather, it didn't last long. One Saturday night at The Fountain he was seen kissing Alison Edwards, and after that he didn't walk through town with Heather any more.

It was as if Grace had been biding her time, just waiting for Heather to be alone.

'Stinking cow.'

'Illiterate skank.'

She was obsessed. Heather was all she seemed to talk about. Heather was a filthy slut. She'd had a threesome with two Year 10s. She was thick as mince and even Burger King wouldn't employ her.

Heather wasn't in any of my classes so I saw and heard a lot of this second-hand or from a distance. I wanted to offer support but I'd only recently got Grace off my own back and I had my GCSEs to think of. Anyhow, what could I have done? I rarely saw Heather these days. I studied in the library now every lunchtime instead of going to the meadow behind the school. Grace would get bored, I reasoned, if Heather had the sense to do what I'd done and kept her head down. In the meantime, if I did happen to hear Grace or her cronies hiss something at Heather as she passed, I'd try to catch her eye in a sympathetic way. Likewise, if she opened her homeroom desk to find a used tampon or condom inside. Wiser than I had been, she never reacted but quietly removed and binned the item without comment.

Grace, however, wasn't happy with this. She had let me go eventually, but only after she'd had her fill. Heather hadn't given her anything yet. She needed Heather to know what she'd done. Humiliating her like that in front of everyone. She needed to make her pay.

She got a boy to pretend he liked Heather.

I didn't know about it at the time. What was being planned. If I had, I would certainly have intervened. Sam Lewis was one of the best-looking boys in our year, tall and fit and muscular, not unlike Ryan in appearance. Unlike Ryan, however, he did fancy Grace and was more than happy to help her out. He wasn't the cocky, macho type – a lot of girls went for that, but Sam's MO was Caring Empath. He looked deep into people's souls. His understanding knew no bounds. Whether a person liked gardening or tying fireworks to stray cats, Sam would listen and identify with their uniqueness and truth.

He and Heather went on a couple of dates. Apparently, she really liked him. She liked that he listened to her and cared about her as if she was someone. One Saturday night she was invited to a party. And to Sam's house afterwards, where some photos were taken which a couple of the other boys subsequently took charge of.

On Monday when Heather came into homeroom the noises started up from the corners.

'Tsss . . .'

'Slut!'

'How much?'

Heather stopped dead. Frowned. Then turned ashen as she realized. I thought she was going to faint. She made it to her desk. I tried to look at her, to catch her eye, but she had the lid open and was behind it. Then Mrs Giordano arrived for citizenship and I had to turn to the front.

At break Heather was gone from the room before I could reach her. Grace said in a light-hearted, musing way, 'Imagine if someone gave those photos to her brother.'

'Damien? Fucking hell.'

'Gillespie, you're a wench. Her dad wouldn't let her out for a year.'

'Vinnie – what d'you think?' Lightly, humorously, she brushed a finger over Vinnie's rookie biceps. Vinnie's face purpled. He'd have set himself on fire if Grace had told him to. A drooling lap dog but with sharp teeth and a vicious disposition.

'Will I?'

'My God, I was *joking*! I mean, do whatever you want, but it's got nothing to do with me. Although, if her dad did stop her going out, we wouldn't have to see her mug in The Fountain for a while.'

She touched Vinnie's arm again.

Grace never did like to get her hands dirty.

Shortly after that, Heather stopped coming to school. Just stopped one day, about the second week in April, and that was the last anyone saw of her. Pregnant, someone said. Someone else, however, said they'd heard she was unwell. A neighbour had mentioned that the family hadn't been seen outside the house for a while.

I wanted to contact her, but I was busy with my GCSE studies and we had no mobiles back then and I didn't know her landline number. If their house even had a landline. When the exams were over, I told myself, I'd call to her house. It would be awkward, as she'd said her mum didn't like people visiting. But if she chose not to answer I'd leave a note for her through the letterbox.

In early May, our local newspaper reported that the body of a teenage girl had been found beside Bedwyr's Grave in the grounds of Trendlingham House. Police were not seeking anyone else in relation to the incident. Hanged, people said – though the newspaper, unusually declining to use the details of a child's death to sell itself, did not elaborate.

It was a Tuesday when I heard for certain that the dead girl was Heather.

Grace's mates were all talking about it. Everyone was. Usually, other people weren't allowed to stand or sit in 'their' spot on the radiators at the back of the homeroom, but that day I marched right up there and joined them. I waited for her to notice me, to say something. Just waited. I felt that there was a space all around me, that people were leaning away from me, that I was like Moses in the Red Sea, a powerful magnet, repelling all around me, forcing them to make way. My breath came strong and hard and deep.

'. . . blah blah, Heather. Who'd have thought she'd do something like that? So sad.'

'Anyone up for The Fountain this weekend?'

'Oh, Grace. Come on.'

'What? I hardly knew her. What do you want me to say?'

It was bravado. Guilt. She knew I was standing there. She would not look at me.

'I'm starving,' she said. 'Who's coming to the canteen.'

She hoicked her bag on to her shoulder. Her disciples drew back, preparing to follow.

I was perplexed. This was not bravado. Grace genuinely had moved on. Heather was gone, vanished, severed from her mind as cleanly as if she had never existed. There was something wrong with her, I remember thinking in bewilderment as I watched her sashay, laughing, down the corridor. She was like a toddler who screams with rage when a toy won't do what it wants but forgets it within seconds when the toy is taken away and a new one appears. Or like an inanimate object, a rock that, once pushed, will fall and keep falling till it lands and crushes, then comes to rest in the sun but feels no pain, and feels no sun either.

That was almost the last I saw of Grace or of any of them. The following year I moved to sixth-form college and my life became crammed with study, weekend waitressing and saving. I no longer did anything for the family at home. I'd been doing all the housework, nagging Steve to eat properly, helping my mother off the sofa to dress and shower, getting up in the middle of the night to check that she hadn't choked in her sleep. Now I simply left them to it, focusing instead on myself and my university applications and funding.

The day Heather and I had visited Bedwyr's Grave, she turned to me as we were leaving and, completely unexpectedly, gave me a warm hug. 'Today was lovely,' she said. 'Such a lovely afternoon. I'll always remember it. We both come from a sad past, but we have a good future. I know it.'

'I have a sad past?' I was still taken aback by the hug.

'Your family is like mine. Well, not exactly, but neither of us is lucky like that.'

I was surprised. Heather was the first person ever to have suggested to me that my mother wasn't all she should have been. It had never occurred to me to think it. My home life was my normal, I suppose. When you think about it, fifty per cent of parents are below average. Why should it have been some-one else and not me? The trick is to realize that it's the parent's fault and not yours. That there is nothing wrong with you. That's what was in my head when I returned home and saw my mother in her grubby dressing gown and had that sense of stepping away from her, of becoming my own person.

Not long after I got into Cambridge I had a dream. I dreamed that I was at The Fountain the night Heather had been there with Ryan. The smells of cigarette smoke, cider and Impulse, the Spice Girls singing 'Viva Forever'. I floated beside her as she faced up to Grace and said, 'Let him decide.'

'You cannot do that,' I wanted to shout at her. 'Let him go.'

I led her away, to the safety of Bedwyr's Grave, where we sat with our feet in the stream.

'Let's never go back,' I said. 'Let's run away and leave here, and we'll always help each other,' and Heather agreed.

It was so real, so powerful. Waking up, I couldn't believe it hadn't happened. The pain did something to me that I couldn't bear; it shrivelled me and made me not want to see myself. A person can only save themselves if they are worth saving and so I made the decision not to think about Heather any more.

On the morning of the playdate you asked me on the phone why I was inviting Polly.

'You keep on complaining about those people,' you said. 'Why doesn't Lexie just find some other friends?'

But can you understand now why? As it turns out, you were right and I was wrong. But can you understand why I tried? I like to think of myself as a strong person. I'm aware that in your eyes I must have seemed like a grovelling sycophant, inviting my child's bully over to play. But this wasn't about me. That day with Grace on the netball steps, I'd only had myself to blame. But Lexie had done nothing to deserve this. This was *my* fault. I was the one who had drawn Vanessa on her and it was up to me to lure her away again.

People don't 'stand up' to earthquakes or viruses. They win no medals or respect for it. They only end up hurting themselves. People don't stand outside in hurricanes, shouting at the wind, 'You'll never take my freeeedommm!' No, they fortify their homes, and if the hurricane is coming from the east they fortify from the east. They do what the hurricane decides. If the monster snarls and lowers its head and paws at the ground, they flatter it and feed it honeyed treats until it becomes lulled. And as soon as the opportunity arises, when the monster's attention is on its treat, they take their child and they softly, quietly, slip away.

26

More quickly than she had expected, Zoë and Adam had fallen back into their cosy routine. If anything, this time round they were closer than ever. Adam was more open about himself now that there was nothing to hide and there truly was a sense that they were holding nothing back.

They talked about their childhoods. He spoke fondly about his mum, who Zoë privately thought sounded like a suffocating nightmare. Zoë's parents had divorced when she was six. Both had since remarried. It had all been very amicable.

Adam was interested in this.

'Do you remember it happening? Was it terrible?'

'No. It's so common now. More than half of my friends. It wasn't that big a deal really.'

Whenever he mentioned his wife and daughter she tried to respond lightly but something clenched inside her. Yet if he *didn't* mention them she felt awkward too because the very absence of mention seemed such an elephant in the room. She made herself ignore it. This was the deal she had struck, and she had no choice but to get used to it.

Close as they were, they didn't see each other anything like as often as either of them would have wished. For one thing, there was the wife/ daughter issue. For another, both of them were working extremely hard. Often Adam took his laptop to her flat and hunched over her coffee table, fingers flying, while she cooked.

One evening she showed him an article that she had screenshotted from the *Financial Times*.

'Look! You're famous. CareyComp is number 890 in the top thousand fastest-growing new companies in the UK.'

'How did you find that?' he said, smiling. 'How do you have the energy to read up on things like this, on top of all you do already?'

'It's interesting.' She meant it. 'I've always wondered who *does* this. Who *are* these people who start things. Run things. Change the world. And now I know.'

'See, this is what makes you so incredible. My wife would never bother to research or screenshot anything to do with my work.'

'Really?' Zoë was surprised. 'Even though she works in finance herself?'

'That's what I mean about her having no interest in me or what I do.'

Casually, Zoë grated garlic.

'In fact' – Adam leaned back, stretching his legs out, in rare reflective mode – 'it's this complete lack of empathy and interest in anything – except our daughter, to be fair – that ended up driving us apart.'

It was unusual for him to speak critically of his wife, or indeed to mention her at all. Zoë snipped cardamom pods, all the while holding her breath, listening hard.

'She's so detached,' Adam said. 'She had a weird upbringing, so maybe that's why . . . but she's so . . . blank. Like something's missing in her. It's not normal, I sometimes think.'

The woman sounded peculiar all right – but then he would say that, wouldn't he?

'And now she's at home all day with nothing to do it's worse. She can't seem to pick up any hobbies or interests, like the other wives do. She can see the stress I'm under but she just blames me for everything. My problems. Our daughter's problems. Her not working. But she was bored by work. She never had your passion for what you do. I couldn't see *you* giving up your career.'

'No,' Zoë said. 'But then I couldn't imagine spending a large chunk of my life doing something that bored me.'

'Hey.' He brightened. 'Did I show you this photo of Lex doing the splits? First time to do them fully. She was so proud!'

She had been zesting a lemon but now wiped her hands to come and look. 'Ooh. Bendy.'

'And this one.'

'Lovely!'

She found she was having to do this quite a lot. *Ooh* and *ahh*.

'Lexie would adore that beagle,' Adam would say whenever they were out and about. 'She's mad about dogs. Oh, look over there – that huge slide. She'd love that! Anything sporty, she's completely fearless. If only she was with us now.'

There were definitely three of them in this relationship. In many ways, when Adam had been Paul it had been easier, because then there'd just been the two of them.

Sometimes she wondered why she was doing this to herself. Adam was having his cake and eating it, and still he expected Zoë to solve his problems for him.

'Sara's saying now she doesn't want to move back to London. She wants us to stay in Dublin. She's been putting pressure on me to decide, and I have no idea what to say.'

They were in bed and he was stroking her abdomen, gazing at her with the hard look that made her insides feel as if they'd been put through a blender.

'Just say you'll stay in Ireland.' She shrugged. 'That's fine, isn't it? She'll be happy there and we can continue as we are here.'

'But then we'll hardly ever see each other. Anyway, London's better for me for work.'

'So, then, tell her that.'

'But the problem is,' Adam sat up, 'now she's saying if we *do* move back to England we'd have to leave London and move to some banal village somewhere.'

Zoë opened her eyes. 'Why on earth?'

'She says London isn't suitable for our daughter.'

'Nonsense!'

'I don't know what to do, Zo. I'm getting to the stage where I'm starting to think, if we can't even agree on what country to live in . . . I just . . . I don't know what to do.'

Zoë said nothing.

Zoë knew what he should do.

Zoë thought that he should leave.

From what he was saying, the relationship sounded dead in the water. The wife didn't sound as if she had any interest. Didn't even want to live in the same country as him! If she loved him, she'd move heaven and earth to be with him. And if they thought the child hadn't picked up on any of this they were deluded.

'Just play it cool,' her colleague Andrea had advised. Andrea had been in this very situation. 'It has to come from him or you'll always be the bad guy.'

So she refrained from giving any opinion apart from mildly remarking when he moaned on about how difficult things were: 'Maybe you should stop living your life for others and live it for you.'

'If it wasn't for Lex . . . You know that, don't you?'

'Sure.'

'But as things stand . . . and right now especially, Lex is having some problems at school. Reading issues – and there's been some trouble with another girl. She's very sensitive, my wife says.'

'Mm-hmm.'

For heaven's sake! The woman was ridiculous. No wonder Adam had checked out.

But for every low point there were ten highs, a hundred highs! He had his flaws – his impatience, his obsession with his work – but she understood them because they were her flaws too. They didn't have to hide anything from each other. Things were complicated, they knew that, but they'd get there. The main thing was that she knew he was committed, and more so every day. Whenever he was away, he messaged constantly and he called her every night.

'I miss you,' he said. 'I can't wait to – GEORGE! Get back here! Blinking creature.'

'You seem to be getting quite fond of him,' Zoë remarked, hearing the affection in his tone. He had taken to walking his dog every evening when he was in Ireland; it had become their time, when they could talk freely without fear of his being overheard or interrupted.

'He's not the worst. Sure you're not, buddy? No! No, you're not!'

'How can you see him? Isn't it dark there now?'

'I got him one of those light-up collars that flashes. They all have them round here, different colours so you know which one's yours. There's about a dozen of them here now, all going around in circles sniffing each other's butts. The park looks like a Coldplay concert.'

She laughed, picturing him walking in the darkness, surrounded by circles of coloured lights. She felt as close to him as if she were there, as if there was a thread between them, stretching to reach no matter where they were. She could talk to him for ever and never run out of things to say.

One morning they were taking a walk, just an ordinary walk, on their way to have breakfast. She was off work because she'd been up all night on call. Adam met her at the hospital entrance and they walked towards the river. A stiff late-March wind blew into her face. Euphoric from lack of sleep, she prattled on like a person on speed.

'. . . ambulance and got the baby out okay, but the mother was still haemorrhaging, and her blood pressure was through the floor. I honestly thought she was gone. I wanted to scream and run out of there, but I had to keep going. And then suddenly, I don't know how, the bleeding just – stopped. I'd brought it back under control. Sheer luck more than anything. Her partner was outside. They'd prepared him for the worst. When I told him . . . his face . . . they've got two other children . . .'

When she finally ground to a halt she realized that Adam was staring at her. Wearing his familiar intent look, but now there was something else there too.

'I love you,' he said.

It was the first time he'd said it.

She whispered, 'I love you too.'

The moment was like a cobweb, so delicate yet so strong in the silvery light.

Wistfully he said, 'I wish you and Lexie could meet.'

The child again. Could they not even have this one moment?

'She can stay with us,' Zoë offered. 'Any time. She sounds like a sweetie.'

Then she held her breath, aware that she had just spoken as if Adam and Sara were about to separate.

He said eagerly, 'She'd love that. I know you two would get on really well. But' – his face fell – 'Sara would never let her come.'

'She'd have no choice.' Zoë shrugged. 'She's your daughter. And she's a British citizen.'

'That's true.' He brightened. 'We could go for fifty-fifty custody.'

Zoë scrunched her face up at the river. But she said nothing. For now. She'd made some gains today. Planted some seeds. Now to stand back and let them germinate.

The child was going to be tricky. She sounded a clingy little creature. All ickle fairies and wrapping him around her little finger. Men were like that with their daughters while they were still young and sweet. They secretly thought that because this was *their* daughter she would be somehow better than other females. She'd stay young and adorable for longer and never turn into a Woman. But when she did – well, Zoë had seen it before. The interest often faded. Had happened with her own father. That was life, though. Things moved on. People needed to stop weeping and wailing and clinging on for ever. This Lexie was, what . . . nine? A few years of charm left – four, five tops. Then she'd be a teenager and want to go her own way. And perhaps by then – Zoë nurtured a secret hope – she and Adam might have their own child. And he would love the new one just as much. More even, because it would be younger and sweeter.

27

And so we come back full circle to the afternoon of the playdate.

All the while I've been talking you've been sitting with your chin in your hand, staring expressionlessly through the patio doors into the darkness. When I stop there's a gap before you rouse yourself and turn to me, as if the signals to your brain have been delayed. Your eyes have dark smudges underneath. Neither of us has been sleeping well. There's stubble on your chin. It takes days for you to grow even a shadow of a beard, but now here it is, making you look older, harder, less like a person who sits at an ergonomic desk or in an airport lounge in your Paul Smith suit and more of a rough sleeper, a soldier in the wild where the normal rules don't apply.

'Go on,' you say.

Get to the truly weird part, you mean. The part that ultimately led us to where we are now. But before I move on to that, what else can I say about that dreadful afternoon?

No one had been more surprised than I when Vanessa had actually taken me up on my offer to mind Polly. You can understand now, I think, why I chose to adopt a killing-with-kindness strategy to deal with the aftermath of Vanessa's party. It took a huge effort, but once I realized what I was dealing with, I made sure to greet her and her friends in a pleasant way whenever our paths crossed. Naturally, Vanessa ignored me, though her eyes made a brief movement that conveyed more than mere words ever could. One or two of the other BMs, however, did begin to respond. I got the impression that Vanessa was being forced to tone down her accusations, realizing how unlikely they were and how ridiculous she was making herself sound.

Lexie, however, was still miserable at school, and I had no idea what to do about it. Staying in Dublin no longer seemed as ideal as it had. Yet nor did I want her to go back to the flat in Vauxhall, so it seemed we were all at a bit of a stalemate.

And then came the fundraising morning at Spoon.

As I've said, I only made the childminding offer as part of my campaign to neutralize the situation and make things better for Lexie. I was astonished when Vanessa actually accepted. In the moment, she must have been truly desperate.

I can see what you're thinking, Adam. For all our sakes, if only she had not been.

After the ambulance had taken Polly away, Angela led me back into the house. She tried to persuade me to sit, but I kept on pacing, trembling, around and around like a hamster in a ball. Imogen and Mia's parents arrived to collect them. Angela met them at the door, located coats and schoolbags, delivered the handover. '. . . accident, but your child is fine. No, no further details at the moment.' Brisk and firm. I was glad she was there to do it.

'Tea!' she said when she returned, pressing a mug into my hands. Lexie had taken George out to the garden to do his business.

I took the mug, hot liquid slopping over the sides. Later I noticed a scalded patch at the base of my thumb, but at the time I felt nothing. 'Do you think Polly will make it?'

'She had a good pulse when they left. The adrenaline brought her blood pressure up nicely. Careful – your tea.'

I straightened my mug. 'Why would her blood pressure have been so low?'

'That I don't know. I'm thinking maybe an internal bleed. If she fell from very high up.'

Internal bleed. Dots marched past my vision.

'Don't mind me.' Angela touched my arm. 'I'm just thinking out loud. The important thing is, she did seem much more stable as she was leaving. So that's a good sign.'

I appreciated her directness. Angela, it turned out, had been a very senior nurse, running her hospital's entire surgical department. Used to crises, to dealing in hard facts, which, difficult as they were to hear, I much preferred to platitudes.

'I'm so grateful you were there,' I said for what must have been the hundredth time. 'If it hadn't been for you . . .'

But of course, we still didn't know how Polly would do. 'Internal bleed' didn't sound good at all.

It was Angela who broke the news to Vanessa. She had come screeching up in a taxi from her charity lunch, twenty minutes after the ambulance had left. I'd been trying to phone her, but with no success. I floated towards her like a wraith, but Angela touched my elbow.

'It'll be better coming from me. You see to her.' She nodded at Lexie, who was peering, white-faced, around the door.

I knew she was right. I took Lexie into the living room and we sat on the sofa, me rubbing my hand in circles on her back, as much to comfort myself as her.

'Did she die?' Lexie asked quietly.

'No.' Though at that point I still wasn't certain.

'Are you sure? She looked dead.'

'She's definitely not dead. They checked her heart and it was beating.'

If Polly didn't make it, I realized, Lexie would carry this with her for the rest of her life. She would never be persuaded that what had happened was not her fault.

'Maybe she'll get a plaster cast.' Lexie brightened. 'Maybe she'll let people write on it.'

'Maybe. Let's see.'

Murmurs from the hall. My ear felt as if it was trying to crawl out of my head to hear. No screams, no bellows, no thundering footsteps heading my way. But I couldn't make out any words, not unless I left Lexie and pressed my ear to the door. I closed my eyes and bent my head back to her.

Angela came in. 'She's gone.'

I shuddered. Angela turned to Lexie. 'Are you hungry, pet? I've managed to rescue one of the pizzas.'

Her pale face flushed. 'A bit.'

'I'll reheat it for you.' Angela led her to the kitchen.

When she returned she said, 'She's fine. Eating away and feeding bits to George.'

'How was Vanessa? What did she say?'

'Very calm. Very practical, you know. Just wanted the facts. What happened. Which hospital. She rang her husband and he came straight away to pick her up. They're heading there now.'

'Yes. She is practical.' I imagined Vanessa. Would she march into the ED, giving orders to the medical team, demanding answers? Or cry and collapse, her knees buckling, at the sight of Polly, her child, so lifeless and still.

'Thank you,' I said. 'For telling her. I don't know how I would have done it.'

'You know,' Angela said kindly, 'this was not your fault.'

'Of course it was. I should have been watching.'

'You were watching,' said Angela. 'I see you with Lexie and her friends all the time. You always watch. You're an excellent mother. Don't doubt yourself.'

My phone fog-horned, jangling my nerves all over again. I had tried to call you several times, but your phone, as usual, had gone straight to voicemail. I'd left a message asking you to call back urgently. 'It's not Lexie,' I had added, thinking of how you would leap, like I had, to assume the worst.

Now, finally, your name on my screen.

'What's up?' Terse-ish tone. I remembered you saying you had a complicated meeting that afternoon.

'Something awful has happened.'

'Lexie –'

'No. No! She's fine.'

I can't remember exactly how I told you. What words I used. Whole chunks of that evening are still patchy. I'm sure that whatever I said was garbled, but I remember feeling confident, even as I stuttered through the details, that you'd get it, that you'd understand. You were always sharp like that, quick to extract what was relevant, knowing at once what to toss and what to keep.

You were aghast, naturally, but also matter of fact. Your deep voice was a comfort.

'I'll be home in the morning. First flight I can get.'

'Thank you. Thank you!' I don't remember ever being so glad to hear you were coming home.

You spoke briefly to Lexie and she came off soothed too.

I got her to bed. She was exhausted and fell asleep more quickly than I would have expected. When I came back downstairs my phone was lit up with messages. Horrified texts from Eva and Edel. Mia and Imogen had filled them in. I responded with what little I knew: Polly was not dead. She was at the hospital. Vanessa was with her.

Angela slid a glass of wine towards me.

'I found this in your wine rack and took the liberty of opening it. Hope it's not a valuable vintage you were saving for your Oscar nomination.'

I held the glass for the ritual of it, the semblance of a normal social interaction, but my throat would not have swallowed it.

'You should go home,' I said.

'I'm fine. I've no plans. I'm happy to stay for a while.'

'How do you think she's doing now?'

Angela pursed her lips. 'Let me try calling.'

'No,' she said into the phone. 'No, not a relative, but I was a nursing manager there until five years ago . . . and I was the one who did CPR on the child so . . . You what? Right. I see.' She ended the call, rolling her eyes. 'Data protection,' she mimicked. 'No common sense at all.'

Then she brightened. 'I'll try my friend Liz in Bed Management.'

Liz was just coming off duty, but she'd heard about a child being blue-lighted in after a fall. She'd pop back now to see how things were going.

A moment later she called back. 'Mmm,' Angela nodded. 'Yes. Mmm.' Then she gave me a vigorous thumbs-up. Polly was alive.

'Thank God!'

She was in ICU, on a ventilator.

'Not so good.' My insides shrivelled.

'It's as expected.' Angela was calm. 'She was already intubated when she arrived at the hospital. Liz said her blood pressure was still wobbly and they've had to do some scans. But overall, she's reasonably stable.'

'What kind of scans?'

'Liz didn't know. But she's not going to theatre so there mustn't be a severe bleed.' Angela hesitated as if debating whether to add something difficult.

'A few hours will tell a lot,' she said eventually. 'Children are very resilient. There's every chance she'll make an excellent recovery.'

Out of nowhere, something struck me. 'Polly's bag.'

'Bag?'

'Her school backpack.' Suddenly it seemed imperative that I knew where it was. 'Did you notice it in the hall with the others? It's got see-through pockets. With purple glitter in the layers.'

Angela frowned. 'I think . . .' She got up to check. 'Not here,' she called from the hall. 'It might have gone in the ambulance. Or maybe Vanessa took it.'

'Probably.' I sank back in my seat. If the backpack was gone, that meant I wouldn't have to take it up to the house or Vanessa wouldn't have to call here for it. Not that she'd be looking for it anyway while Polly was so ill. What was I thinking? Everything was a jumble in my head. And so, the next time I spoke to Vanessa, we would know one way or the other how Polly was. Nothing to do until then but wait, as Angela had said. At least it was the weekend and I didn't have to decide whether or not to send Lexie to school tomorrow.

Unsurprisingly, I hardly slept. I missed you beside me, your large, solid presence, breathing steadily in the night. The following day I went through the motions of parenthood, opening curtains, pouring cornflakes, trying to keep things as normal as possible for Lexie. Rain or shine, catastrophes or internal bleeds, George still had to be walked, so we drove to Wicklow and watched him rush about ecstatically, dragging huge branches and splashing in streams. Up there in the fresh, earth-scented air the clouds still gathered, the planet still spun and George still hadn't learned that he shouldn't try to eat bees.

My phone kept lighting up. Erica: *Hi Sara!!! Just heard the news??? Oh my God??? Call me!!! Let's do coffee!!! xxx (bunch of flowers emoji)*

So now everyone knew. It was very uncomfortable to think that the St Catherine's community would all be talking about this – a very ill child in their daughter's school; of course they would – but also avid after the details, wondering what on earth could have happened, what degree of incompetence and negligence could have allowed this to occur. And in the middle of it all, my worry for Lexie, what all of this might mean for her. I forced down my dread – at least the outward evidence of it – and deleted Erica's text without responding.

When we got back, to my enormous relief, you were home. You took over dealing with Lexie while I allowed my fake cheer to collapse and sat slumped over a cup of tea listening to your rumbling voice in the next room and her high answering laugh. I can't describe how glad I was to have you in the house.

Later you asked me what had happened, and I told you, just as I'm doing now and have done many times since that day. You listened intently, taking it all in.

'What happened? Where were you? Then what?'

At the time I didn't fully appreciate why you wanted all the details, but the telling of it helped enormously, I don't mind saying. My insides began to loosen and some of the aching stiffness eased from my jaw.

I asked your advice about something I had been wondering. 'Vanessa isn't answering my calls. Should I keep trying?'

You considered. 'I would say, not at the moment. If she hasn't responded so far. Just leave a message saying you're thinking of them and you're happy to talk if she'd like.'

That I had already done. Still, I had wondered if I should persevere, or perhaps call to the house. But you were right, of course. What if I spoke to her and asked how Polly was and she said . . . no. *No!* Best to wait for some news first.

On Monday, after the longest weekend of my life, I took Lexie to school.

I quailed going down the hill in case I met Vanessa at the gates. Which just showed my state of mind, because I was almost there before I remembered that of course I wouldn't meet her as Polly and her siblings wouldn't be at school. Never would the sight of that mint raincoat taking up the centre of the playground have been more welcome.

'Will Polly be in today?' Lexie asked.

'No. I don't think she'll be in for a while.'

'Should I get her homework for her? And her books? So she won't fall too far behind?'

'Maybe not today, sweetheart. But in a few days, when she's had a chance to rest.'

She said nothing for a moment. Then in a small voice she asked, 'Will people think it was my fault?'

I stopped. I looked down at her unhappy little face and felt my heart contract. 'Listen.' I took her by the shoulders and looked her in the eye. 'This was not your fault. Polly was the one who climbed the tree. It was a very sad accident, and we hope she'll make a full recovery, but it was *NOT* your fault.'

I had a word with Ms Brennan, asking her to keep an eye on Lexie and listen out for what was being said.

'Of course!' She hadn't heard the news and was horrified.

Outside, I met Orla. 'Have you heard anything about Polly?'

'She's still in ICU.'

'Okay.' That didn't sound good.

'She's not waking up as quickly as they expected. They're doing tests to see why she collapsed. They're not sure it was a fall.'

My foot caught on the pavement. 'What?'

'Apparently the paramedics didn't think the tree looked that high. So they've been wondering if maybe she collapsed and *then* fell, rather than the other way around. A seizure maybe. Or some kind of heart issue . . . I'm not sure. But it's very worrying. She's still very unwell.'

'Okay.' I walked on, hardly seeing what was in front of me. I certainly hadn't expected this. I didn't know what to think. But there was no point in thinking anything at all until we knew more.

In a shop I bought a card and wrote in it, saying how sorry I was that Polly was so ill. If Vanessa wanted to talk, or if there was anything at all I could do, please would she not hesitate to call me. I climbed the hill to her house. No sign of her car, or Dave's. At the hospital, of course. I pushed the card into the letterbox on her pillar.

Still no response, but that was hardly a surprise. I tried to imagine how I would feel if it was Lexie in ICU on a ventilator. I would be traumatized, I knew, shutting out all else except her.

All this time, you were there, walking George, doing the housework and keeping Lexie occupied. You had never, since we had moved to Dublin, spent so much time at home with us in one go. Vaguely, I was aware that the American contract was due to be signed around now and that you must have postponed and rescheduled things in order to be here with Lexie and me. I can't imagine it was an easy thing to arrange. I was grateful, and still am. Having you there to look after Lexie meant I could step away for a while, be outside, have air and space, keep moving, keep thinking.

One evening that week – I think it might have been the Wednesday – I went for a random drive and found myself passing a sign pointing to Polly's hospital. On impulse I drove through the gates and found a parking space. The hospital entrance was busy. Lights, people, taxis, ambulances. Pulling my parka around me – the April evening was cool – I walked around the main building towards the rear, through a maze of prefabs and wheelie bins and outpatient departments locked up for the night. 'MORTUARY' read a sign.

I reached an almost empty staff car park where distant hospital sounds – voices and bells and clangs – echoed off the concrete, and there I paused, looking up at the tower with its rows of lighted windows and the shapes moving about inside. Was that a nurse hanging something? A visitor looking out?

Somewhere behind one of those windows lay Polly, attached to a ventilator. Not breathing. Not waking up; they didn't know why. *Still very unwell.*

I pictured her as I had first properly met her, skipping in circles on the Green with Lexie. The self-assurance, the confident, willowy gait. The girl in the sun, so loved and so gifted compared with Heather and the other invisible children. The ghosts.

And then, unexpectedly, I felt pity for her. Was Polly loved? She got lots of praise, certainly. The best of everything. The trendiest water bottle and backpack, the latest-model SUV with the large golden dog in the back and the window decal with the cartoon caricatures of all the family in descending order of size. The bouncy castles, the gold medals (Youngest Recipient Ever), the orthodontic smiles. The perfect family. Until they got home.

Shouting and throwing things, Orla had said. A dog who was tied up all day and hit. A mother who could see only her own needs, her approval conditional upon Polly doing what *she* wanted, feeling the things *she* felt. Polly's own self suppressed, a shadow person trapped inside her, capable of who knew what. At Polly's birth her fairy godmothers had showered her with every blessing – but then along had come the evil Queen: *You can have everything except love.* Then there was Lexie, who had been given all the love in the world but who could barely read. And Heather . . . where had her fairy godmother been? *On your sixteenth birthday you shall prick your finger and die.*

I'd been standing out here alone for too long. My mind was taking strange roads, travelling down dark passages. Time to go home to you and Lexie.

As I turned to leave I had a sudden sense that I was not alone. Someone was there. Someone was waiting, watching from the shadows. The feeling was so strong that I spun around.

No one. Nothing but the empty car park and the echoing, windswept concrete.

The following day Orla phoned.

'Polly's awake. She came out of ICU this morning.'

My knees turned wobbly. 'That's wonderful!'

'She's still very frail, but it's a huge step.'

'That's wonderful!' I couldn't stop repeating it.

'Yes, the Mayhews are so relieved.'

'Please tell them how happy I am.'

'I will.'

A beat. Then Orla said, 'There's just something I need to mention. Just, I suppose, a bit of a heads-up.'

'Yes?'

'They did a blood test. On Polly. And they think they know the cause of her collapse.'

'What?'

'They think she had a massive anaphylaxis.'

'An *anaphylaxis*?'

'Yes. They were surprised too. They only did the test the night she came in because of her history. They didn't expect it to show anything. Everyone was so focused on the fall. But the result came back today and it was positive. It looks like she mightn't have fallen out of the tree at all.'

'But . . .' In my head I was back in the rain-dark kitchen, triple-checking the labels on the pizza boxes. 'But how? She didn't have any nuts.'

'I don't think it showed nuts specifically. Just that there was an allergy to something, but not what. I'm not an expert on allergies though, so don't quote me.'

My brain ticked and whirred.

'I thought I'd tell you,' Orla said. 'Just in case Vanessa . . . you know. Asks.'

'Of course. Of course. It's good you did. Thank you!' Regardless of cause, we agreed, the most important thing was that Polly was recovering.

But obviously it was playing on my mind. The implications of it. When Angela happened to drop by that afternoon, I asked her about it.

'How accurate is the blood test?' I asked. 'In terms of showing what she reacted to?'

'I think, like your friend said, it just shows she reacted to something but not what. Are there other things she's allergic to, do you know?'

'Not that I've heard.'

Later again I discussed it with you. 'I thought I'd been so careful. There weren't even any nuts in the house. We so rarely eat them.'

'Might have been something else then. Like Orla and Angela said.'

'Maybe.' I chewed my thumbnail. 'It's just odd, because she hadn't eaten *anything*. I was getting the pizzas ready but they hadn't been cooked yet.'

I was still turning it over in my mind the next day – where exactly the girls had been that afternoon, what they'd done – when I saw Vanessa trudging across the Green, a plastic supermarket bag hanging from her hand. She was unrecognizably unkempt, dressed in a sloppy grey hoodie, her hair frizzy at the ends with dark roots showing.

'Vanessa!' I went to her, glad to finally have a chance to tell her in person how sorry I was. 'Vanessa – how's Polly? It's so wonderful she's out of ICU. I'm so glad to hear she's better.'

'Better?' Vanessa stared. 'She is *not* better.'

'Oh . . . isn't . . .'

'My daughter almost died. If it wasn't for your neighbour,

she would have. Her airway was swollen. She almost choked. Her kidneys were damaged by the shock. Her speech and memory have been affected. So she is NOT "better", as you say.'

'I'm sorry.' My arms dangled, gorilla-like, by my sides. 'I should have thought. I'm sorry.'

She went on looking at me.

'Why did you give her peanuts?'

'I didn't.'

'Well, clearly, since she had some, you must have.'

'But . . . if she did, I don't know how. I was very careful. We don't even have peanuts in the house. Did . . . I mean, what does Polly say about it herself?'

'She can't remember anything about it. You don't seem to understand. She's had a *significant brain injury*. She is still extremely unwell.'

'Vanessa – I'm so, so sorry. I really am. This happened while Polly was in my care, and I feel terrible. I can't imagine how you've been feeling. But regarding the peanuts – I'm honestly baffled. I just don't know how . . . could it have been an allergy to something else, do you think?'

'She's not allergic to anything else.' Vanessa's cold, peeled-grape gaze moved over me.

And that was when she said something strange.

She said, 'You know what I think? The more I think about it, the more I think you gave her those nuts on purpose.'

It took me a moment to comprehend.

'Sorry . . . what?'

'You heard me. I'll be taking this further. Don't for one minute think you've heard the last of this.'

'Toxic,' you said in disgust. 'Utterly toxic.'

I was still reeling. Vanessa had turned and walked off after

255

detonating her grenade, leaving me winded and struggling to process, any and all questions floundering in the vacuum.

'Told you,' I said dully from the armchair. There was no triumph in my tone.

'She's going to sue.' You were nodding, your lips clamped in a line. 'Wait and see. She's got wind that CareyComp is on the up and the bloody woman wants in on it.'

I should have been angry too. Particularly this coming on top of the Dave allegation. But my anger wouldn't come. Perhaps that part of my brain was still stunned.

'Polly's been seriously ill,' I said. 'Imagine if it was Lexie. How we'd feel. We'd be baying for blood too.'

'I have to hand it to you, Sara.' I remember the way you said it, the expression on your face as you stood by the window, looking at me. 'You were right about her. About how she was treating Lexie. I should have listened.'

Belated as it was, your solidarity poured strength into me. I soaked it in as if it was a balm. It had taken something terrible to make it happen, but here we were, allies again, like old times.

'At least Polly is recovering,' I said. 'Angela was very optimistic. She said children are very resilient. Hopefully, once the worst is over, Vanessa won't need to vent any more and she'll focus on her instead.'

Even then, there I was, still giving Vanessa the benefit of the doubt. Who could blame her? I thought. Her anger was rightful, even if there was no evidence that I had done anything wrong. Let her vent, let her use me as her emotional punch bag until Polly was out of danger. Even after everything, I was still that naïve. I still didn't understand.

28

The first indication we had that Vanessa was not merely letting off steam but meant everything she'd said came a few days later.

It was a Thursday. Lexie was at your mum's – it was the Easter holidays, so she was off school – and you were still with us in Dublin, working hard upstairs. At a loose end, I was mopping the kitchen floor. Again. It had been mopped just the previous day, but I liked the way that the white microfibre mop head still turned grey in a way that gave me a much-needed shot of dopamine. The doorbell rang. Through the whorled-glass door panel loomed two blurry fluorescent yellow shapes.

Perhaps, I thought as I went down the hall, they were fundraising. A sponsored half-marathon or bake sale. But I must have known, because when I opened the door and saw that they looked far too formal and serious for a bake sale I didn't immediately jump to assuming, as I might otherwise have done, that something terrible had happened to Lexie.

'Sara Carey?' one of them asked.

There were two of them, one male, very young and skinny and keen, the other a woman in her forties, blonde and top heavy with a weary, seen-it-all type of face.

'Yes?'

'I'm Garda Dermot Murphy,' said the young, keen garda. He reminded me of someone, but I couldn't immediately think who. 'From Blackrock Garda Station. And my colleague, Garda Lorna Casey. We've had a report of an incident and we're wondering if you'd be willing to answer some questions?'

'Yes, of course.' I sounded breathless because by then there was no doubt what this was about.

It seemed to be expected that I asked them in. With the two of them squashed around our table the tiny kitchen was immediately full. Bulky yellow jackets everywhere. Even if I'd wanted to, I couldn't get to the kettle. They'd have to go thirsty. I stood in the doorway and waited.

'There's been an allegation –'

Garda Murphy's voice cracked slightly and he stopped to clear his throat. Now I knew who he reminded me of – the teenage pizza delivery boy in *The Simpsons*. I had the impression that the older woman was supervising him, and this was his first go at being a garda on his own. 'And we're wondering if you might have information that could assist us in following it up.'

'Okay.'

'Would you happen to know a Mrs Vanessa Mayhew?'

'Yes.'

'A neighbour of yours, isn't that right?'

'Yes.'

'We have received a report that on' – he checked his notebook – 'Friday, 2 April this year her daughter was given at this address some peanuts or a peanut substance which caused her to enter into anaphylactic shock.'

A roiling in my stomach. 'That's untrue.'

'Just accidentally, was it?'

'No! She didn't have peanuts at all.'

'But it *was* after an incident at this address that an ambulance was summoned and a child of a minor age was transported to hospital?'

'Yes, but –'

'What's this?' You, behind me in the doorway.

'My husband, Adam,' I introduced you.

'What's going on?'

I explained. 'There's been an allegation.'

'An allegation.' You looked towards Garda Murphy, who cleared his throat again and repeated more or less what he had just said. An allegation had been made to the effect that on Friday, 2 April at this self-same residence your wife had administered a peanut or peanut substance to a child, causing said child to require admittance to a hospital with an anaphylactic shock reaction.

'Deliberately, I think they mean,' I added quietly, and it was as if my brain had just woken up and said, *hang on, what the hell is this?* and now I felt the first stirrings of anger.

'Is this true?'

Garda Murphy said, 'We're just following up on all —'

'So you're accusing my wife of attempted murder?'

The two gardaí looked at each other.

'We'd just like to hear your side of the story.' The senior Garda Casey took over.

'Well,' I said. 'I'm more than happy to clear up any —'

'No.' You put your hand up. 'You're not. I'm no lawyer, but I doubt you two have any business turning up here like this. Shouldn't my wife be told her rights or something?'

'If you'd prefer to —'

'I would prefer. This is a very serious thing you're saying. You must know that we'll need to get advice before we go any further. I'm sorry, but I'll have to ask you both to leave.'

'I understand.' Garda Casey gave me a quite pleasant smile. 'You can contact Blackrock Garda Station at your convenience when you'd like to chat.'

They left with you glaring after them, but they were almost certainly used to leaving homes under glares. Did it bother them? I wondered.

'What's that loon playing at?' you demanded, returning to the kitchen. 'I was sure she'd set her lawyers on us but — seriously?

The police? Does she really believe this, or has she completely lost her marbles?'

'I suppose with Polly so unwell she's not thinking straight.' *But Polly hadn't been unwell when Vanessa had accused me of trying to shtup her Dave*, I thought, and again the overdue flare of anger.

'So, what now?' I said flatly. 'I assume I can't just ignore this.'

'Better not.' You tapped your phone on your palm, thinking. 'A friend of mine from school did law. I can try and track down a number for him. See what his take on it is.' You began to scroll through your contacts.

'Where did she get the peanuts from?' I wondered aloud for probably the thousandth time.

'Maybe she didn't. Like Angela said, it could have been any-thing. Gardaí showing up here: *We've had a report of peanuts* – Jesus Christ!'

Not once, then or afterwards, did you ever ask, 'Are you sure you didn't give her a peanut?' You must have wanted to. It would have been a perfectly reasonable question and the fact that you refused to ask it gave me the sense of a rock behind me, a rock I had almost begun to forget was there but when the ground under my feet began to crack and crumble, there it was at my back to support me, solid and sure.

Your solicitor mate, Flannan O'Kelly, dark of tan and white of tooth and wearing a sky-blue golf shirt, had a habit of tucking in his chin when he smiled in a way that made him look jowly and self-satisfied. To be fair, my nervousness was making me hyper-critical. Vanessa's accusation seemed to me so outra-geous that I was sure no authority could possibly take her seriously, but I still felt that I'd prefer to be officially reassured.

When he called to the house the following evening there was a lot of initial fist-bumping and reminiscing between the two of you about people called Hammer and Monkey – did anyone you'd grown up with have a normal name? I wondered – and the insanely hilarious time Monkey had put a fish hook through his lip at Hammer's stag. Then we got down to business, Flannan in the mustard armchair, you and I side by side on the pleather couch.

'How seriously should we take this?' you asked.

'Mmmm,' Flannan dropped the toothy smile. 'Be better, obviously, if it hadn't happened. You were right to ask the gardaí to leave.'

'But . . .' This wasn't what I had expected. 'They didn't seem very concerned. They said it was just a few questions.'

'Which I'm sure it is. For now.'

'But what could they do? What could happen?'

'In a worst-case scenario you could be charged.'

'*Charged?* What with?'

Flannan shrugged. 'Poisoning. Endangerment. Where a child is involved, it's a serious matter.'

My ears were flaming. Dermot and Lorna had seemed so nice. I'd been about to offer them tea. 'Maybe if I'd just gone ahead and talked to them, this would –'

'Nope.' Shaking his head firmly. 'Never, ever talk to the police without a solicitor present.'

'Can't you trust the Irish police?'

'As we seem to be seeing, you can't trust anyone. The gardaí are not your friends. They're supposed to be upfront, but nowadays they're trained to be all approachable. Catch more flies with honey than vinegar. They can be sneaky, hoping it won't dawn on you till halfway through the interview that you're a suspect, and God alone knows what you'll have said by then. But look, the fact that you haven't been cautioned or arrested means they've no evidence whatsoever, and there's only one place they're going to get any. From you.'

'But what evidence could I give?'

'They could get you for anything. You wouldn't know what law you might admit to having broken. There are loads of them. There's a malicious motive here, don't forget.'

You interrupted. 'This is bollocks. Don't the gardaí have enough to do? Surely there must be some kind of filter? I can't believe something as preposterous as this could be taken seriously.'

'It is frustrating,' Flannan agreed. 'Is your neighbour in the habit of making preposterous allegations?'

'Yes,' I said angrily, thinking of what she'd said about Dave and me.

Flannan scratched his chin. 'My concern here is what they might be really after. Their side could have some ambulance chaser who'll completely twist your words around.'

'You keep saying that. Twist them into what?'

'They could look for evidence for a civil case. Try it on re: things like failure of duty of care to supervise or to maintain a safe environment, etcetera, etcetera.'

'You're not serious!'

'I've seen it all, believe me. They could tie you up for months. Cost you a fortune in legal fees. So. No talking to anyone without a solicitor. That includes Mrs Mayhew herself, needless to say.'

'Isn't this vexatious wasting of police time?' you said. 'Can't we counter-sue for defamation? I mean, what are our options here?'

'First things first.' Flannan patted the air with his hands. 'Let's try to find out exactly what she's been saying. I'll arrange for a criminal lawyer to –'

'*Criminal?*'

'Yes. Crim's not my speciality. I'm more commercial.'

'But . . .' I'd been under the impression that we had invited Flannan here to calm things down. Instead, the situation seemed to be escalating wildly out of control. Was this, in fact, his intention? Wasn't it in his interest as a solicitor to ramp up the drama, triangulate all parties in order to make himself indispensable, then charge for it? 'Wouldn't that just make me look guilty?'

'Why would it?' he said mildly. 'You think miscarriages of justice never happen?'

I opened my mouth. Then paused, remembering what Vanessa's friends had said that night at her party, about the cyclist who couldn't read and the implication that Gaffo's legal team would use that to 'make mincemeat' of him. All of a sudden I felt afraid. Vanessa knew a lot of people. *Significant brain injury*, she'd said. *Damaged kidneys*. Polly was not out of the woods yet at all.

'If Polly . . .' I swallowed. 'Suppose she . . . Could I be charged with murder?'

'It's possible they might try. But,' Flannan went on, 'that's exactly what I'm here to prevent. So let's get this nipped in the bud. Now.' He clicked his pen. 'Let's go through what kinds of issues might come up. First, the obvious. *Did* you deliberately give the child peanuts?'

'No!' I said, at the same time as you said, 'Jesus, Flanners!'

He spread his hands, the pen dangling from between his fingers. 'All right, all right. So then, tell me, what did happen?'

'Vanessa needed a childminder,' I said. 'So Polly came home with us from school.' I ran through the afternoon, the mug-painting, the garden. Me getting the pizzas ready until I heard the screams outside.

'Did you know she was allergic to peanuts?'

'Yes. Everyone knew. All the parents in the class, I mean.'

'And did you feel competent to deal with such an allergy?'

'I . . . think so. At least, as much as any parent could be. Polly had shown me how to use her EpiPen.'

'And you knew when to use it? What symptoms to look out for?'

'Yes.'

'So then why didn't you?'

'Because I didn't know she was having an attack. I thought she'd fallen.'

'Even though she had eaten peanuts?'

'She hadn't –'

'From the blood test' – Flannan looked apologetic – 'it would seem as though she had.'

I said helplessly, 'If she did, I don't know how. There weren't any in the house.'

'All right. So, since you *thought* there were no peanuts, and since you *thought* her attack was due to a fall, you didn't treat her with the EpiPen. Why did you think her attack was due to a fall? Had you witnessed her falling?'

'No. I just assumed she had. Wrongly, as it turned out, but –'

'Why did you assume she had fallen?'

'Because she was lying under the tree. And it was raining and the branches were slippery –'

'So there was a dangerous tree on your property?'

'It's not on our property.'

'But she had access to it. Did you make sure they didn't climb on it?'

'I told them not to.'

'But you didn't watch them to make sure? These are young children, after all.'

I said shortly, 'They were old enough to understand the warning. I was busy getting the pizza ready.'

'So: *not* supervising. A child in your care with a severe medical condition.'

'It wouldn't have been possible to watch them every single

moment. And regarding the peanuts at least, there weren't. Any. In. The. House.'

'In the whole house?' Sceptically. 'You went through every single cupboard?'

'Yes,' I almost shouted. 'Yes, I did!'

Flannan tapped his pen on the arm of the chair. 'I'm trying to help you here.'

'I know. I know.'

'You can see now why it's never good to just "have a chat". The gardaí, by the way, to put your mind at rest, won't be allowed to cross-examine you like I did there. But down the line, if things get sticky, a barrister just might.'

I rubbed my eyes with my thumb and forefinger.

'Really, we're just being cautious. The reality is that if someone successfully sued because of an allergy on a playdate no one in Ireland could ever invite a child to their home again. But let's move away from that for now. The real concern here is in fact that the child's mother seems to be saying you did this *deliberately*. Why, in your opinion, would she say that?'

'Because she's –' You swivelled your index finger beside your temple.

Flannan went on looking at me.

'I know she's upset about her child,' I said.

'But to accuse you of doing it deliberately . . .'

My fingers spliced in and out of each other. Flannan leaned in. 'Yes?'

'This is going to sound bizarre.'

'The woman is accusing you of attempted murder.'

'Vanessa had a dinner party at her house.' Awkwardly, aware that this was the first time you were hearing this, I described what Vanessa had been saying about Dave and me in the garden that night.

'But it was rubbish,' I said. 'Completely unfounded. I tried to tell her, but she wouldn't listen.' I glanced towards you to see how you were taking it, but beyond a derisive roll of your eyes you didn't seem unduly perturbed.

Flannan asked, 'Any witnesses? On the afternoon of the play-date or just in general? That might disprove Mrs Mayhew's claims or show that she has a habit of . . . misinterpreting things?'

Would Orla corroborate what she'd told me about Vanessa being overly paranoid due to Dave's history of being stalked by all the work women? Would it be fair to involve her in this?

Angela: *You always watch. You're an excellent mother.*

Flannan nodded as he wrote down the names. 'Good. All right.' He clicked his pen again. 'The facts seem to me quite clear. You did not give the child peanuts – deliberately or otherwise – and there weren't any in the house. You had there-fore no reason to suspect an anaphylaxis. As soon as you became aware that the child was unwell you called an ambu-lance and helped your neighbour, a nurse, to perform first aid – an action which almost certainly saved the child's life. That's it. That's all we need to say. If the gardaí haven't cau-tioned you, they have no evidence. In fact, they probably think the other mother is as batty as we do. Nothing more will come of this I'm sure. Unless . . .'

'What?'

Flannan narrowed his eyes. He leaned back, slotting his fin-gers together on the front of his golf shirt.

'This husband you mentioned,' he said. 'Just tell me again about that. Anything more to it? In case someone tries to make something of it.'

I explained in more detail about Dave's and my brief conver-sation in the garden and how shocked I had been to hear the rumour Vanessa was spreading.

'Were you making a move on him? Or him on you?'

'*No!* We spoke for a couple of minutes. Literally, that was it. I've never seen him before or since that night.'

'All okay with you two?' Flannan looked between us. 'Marriage going well?'

'Yes.' I looked at you, thinking of how supportive you had been lately.

'No rows? Bit of distance? Can happen to the best of us.'

'Adam's been very busy,' I said. 'A lot of travel this year so we haven't been seeing so much of each other.'

'Ah. And while he's been away, you haven't been lonely? Tempted?'

'No,' I said firmly.

'And you?' Eyeing you. 'Been behaving yourself on all these travels of yours?'

'I've been up to my tonsils,' you said shortly. 'Don't have time to have a slash, much less an affair.'

'Good to hear. Nothing going to pop up then that'll give anyone any ammunition?'

'No.'

'No.'

Flannan handed me the card of the criminal law firm he planned to contact. *Morris & Gorman. Expertise in all areas of criminal litigation.* The words underneath jumped out at me: *Violent Crime, Sexual Offences, Child Trafficking and Pornography.*

'Yes, so just put this all out of your mind until you hear from them,' Flannan said breezily.

You won't be amazed to hear that I didn't find it that simple. You continued to beaver away in the bedroom, but I spent the next few days ricocheting around the house like a trapped bluebottle, fearful of meeting anyone until I knew which way this was going to go. Fortunately for Lexie's sake, you and Breda were on hand to help with shopping and taking her for walks and swims. Every time my phone chirped, or a letter fell on the doormat, a cold liquid seemed to spread from my chest to my stomach. The only positive thing was that Orla reported daily that Polly was continuing to improve. She was eating normal meals now and going for walks with her physio. Every day was a step forward, small but sure.

The criminal solicitor, Breffni Gorman, made contact. I had expected a criminal defence lawyer to be youngish, alternative, perhaps to meet us at a hipster vegan café in an edgy part of town, but Breffni was dressed like Gomez from the Addams family and had an office in a Georgian building next to a steak restaurant. I'd been looking forward to offloading to someone kind and solid and sympathetic, someone who would reassure me, as Flannan had not, that this was a storm in a teacup, and everything was going to be all right. I was surprised at how vulnerable all of this had made me feel. I was a professional, used to being respected and believed; only now was I aware of how little influence or expertise I had outside of my own narrow field and how little I knew of the law, even in England. I looked forward to feeling about my lawyer the way I had felt about my midwife when I was having Lexie: protected, minded, cared for. Breffni, however, looked as if he was in need of care himself. He was heavy and sweaty with a jaded, weighed-down air, limp black hair and skin that appeared not to have seen a UV ray since the nineties.

'The gist,' he said from across his vast leather-topped desk covered with documents with harps on them, 'of what I've managed to squeeze from the gardaí is as follows. Mrs Mayhew has alleged that in spite of it having been specifically and clearly explained to you that the child had a life-threatening nut allergy, you went ahead and gave the child peanuts while she was at your home. Mrs Mayhew is of the opinion that it was deliberate and could not have been an accident.'

'And why,' you asked, 'does she think my wife – or any sane person – would do that?'

'According to Mrs Mayhew, there were problems between her and your wife right from the start. Sara, you always seemed jealous and resentful of Mrs Mayhew despite her doing her best to welcome you here –' he put his palm up at me. 'You got drunk one night at her home and, among other things, tried to . . . apparently, she uses the term "seduce" . . . her husband. When she finally withdrew her friendship due to this you became extremely hostile and confronted her in the street in a highly threatening manner. She felt uneasy about accepting your invitation to her daughter –'

'Why did she then?' you asked in disgust.

'– but convinced herself that she must be overreacting. She thought that if her daughter could get through just that one afternoon you might be satisfied and leave them alone. However, as soon as she heard what had happened she knew immediately that her concerns had been valid.'

My face felt numb. I was breathing as if I were the one having an allergy attack. 'Shouldn't we talk to her? Just sit down with a mediator or something and . . . and *talk?*' I knew I had tried, but this was different. This was huger than I had imagined, beyond all shred of reason. This was more than a misunderstanding, even a deliberately exaggerated one. This was something on a different planet.

'Under no circumstances.' Breffni Gorman shook his head. 'She's already implying that you've been harassing her. Do not talk to her, even by accident, without –'

'A solicitor present. I know.'

He just looked at me.

'So, what happens now?'

'We meet with the gardaí and give our side of the story. And hopefully that'll be it. From what I can gather, this was an accident, and no crime has been committed. So, let's keep things simple. No going off tangent during the interview.'

'How do you mean?'

Breffni advised that the gardaí might be over-friendly or overfamiliar to lull me into a false sense of security, but I was to ignore this. 'No chit-chat about how difficult it can be to get on with the neighbours or how hard it can be to supervise young children, if you get me. If they try on anything like that, I'll intervene to get things back on track. Or if any new information surfaces from either side that we haven't already discussed. You can stop to ask me a question privately any time. I'll be scribbling away in the background, but I'll be listening.'

I tried to take it all in. My paranoia was at mushroom-cloud level.

'You might prefer to give a pre-prepared statement. However, it might be better to answer any clarifying questions they have, reduce the likelihood of them needing to call you back. Of course, you can choose to say nothing at all. No inference is meant to be drawn from that. It always is though, quite frankly. So how do you want to play it?'

I looked at him blankly. 'I don't know.'

'I'll need to be instructed before I can proceed.'

Weren't we paying *him*? I thought, confused. The time I'd had my tonsils out my surgeon hadn't asked me for instructions on how to proceed. I'd heard the term 'instructed by my client' but never fully considered what it meant. Was it so that if something went wrong Breffni could shrug and say, 'Well, I was only doing what my client told me'? His gaze kept sliding to his phone. If he was so uninterested, I thought angrily, why was he agreeing to take on my case? But if we asked for a different barrister and word got out around this tiny little town, would we be seen as troublemakers? Flannan had said he knew his onions and we had to trust him.

'I'll answer the questions,' I said.

He bowed his heavy head. 'As you wish.'

On the morning of the garda 'chat' I went to the loo about eight times before we left the house. Breffni met us on the steps of the station under a pointy porch shaped like a pyramid. Inside, he disappeared to talk to someone, leaving you and me sitting on a bench under a poster that read, 'If You Love It, Lock It!' But almost at once he reappeared and lifted his chin at me. My insides flipped. I made a quick face at you, rose and followed him through a door. We entered a room like a bare office, furnished only with a table and chairs. The blonde-haired Garda Casey was sitting in one of the chairs, filling out a form.

'Hi there,' she said, looking up. 'Thanks for coming. Dermot's just gone to make tea. Would you like a cup?'

'No, thank you,' I said prissily, remembering Breffni's instructions.

Garda Murphy came bustling in, 'Hi there! Hello!' as if we were old friends. He and Garda Casey sat across the table from Breffni and me.

Garda Casey rattled off the date and everyone's names. Then she smiled at me in her pleasant, world-weary way. 'Now. The reason you're here is because we'd like to follow up on the report about an incident at your home where a child, Polly Mayhew, very unfortunately ended up in hospital. We'd appreciate hearing your side of the story. Just tell us in your own words what happened. Along with any other details you feel may be relevant. Garda Murphy will take notes as we go along and you'll have a chance to read those over at the end.'

Through a dry and clicky mouth I told them about the play-date, emphasizing that I had been no further than one room away from the girls at all times, that Angela and I had acted promptly, phoning the ambulance and starting CPR.

'And sorry, just to clarify, your neighbour – Angela Moloney? – was she there all along?'

'No, she climbed over the back wall between our gardens when she heard the girls screaming. She got to Polly a few seconds after I did.'

'Oh yes. Thank you.'

I continued. As there were no peanuts in the house I had no reason to suspect that the cause of Polly's collapse was an anaphylaxis. I had certainly not given her peanuts, deliberately or otherwise.

'Did the child eat anything at all while she was in your house?'

'Not as far as I'm aware.'

On Breffni's advice I minimized any negativity I might previously have felt towards Vanessa, only mentioning for clarity that Vanessa's suspicion regarding me and Dave was a gross misunderstanding on her part. You and I were a strong couple and there was no basis whatsoever to the accusation. The process was straightforward and took less time than I would have thought. Garda Casey didn't ask me any further questions, just occasionally requested that I pause or repeat what I had said so that Garda Murphy could write it down. Before I knew it, we were finished.

'Would you like to read it back and sign?'

I noticed that he had spelled 'anaphylaxis' wrong but thought it best not to mention it. Perhaps he was another Lexie. If so, I found it reassuring that he had become a garda and had a promising career ahead of him. *Good for you*, I thought.

Then you, Breffni and I were out on the street again, blinking in the daylight.

'That's it?' It felt like an anticlimax. 'When will we hear?'

Breffni shrugged. 'Depends. They'll proceed with the investigation. Compile their report. Then a decision will made on whether to take it any further. Could be weeks.'

'*Weeks?*'

'I'll follow up on it and keep you informed. In my view, the most likely outcome is that the investigation will be dropped.'

'Okay. Well, thank you. Keep us posted.'

'Will do.' He shook our hands, then lumbered, walrus-like, down a side road towards the car park.

29

After that it was back to more excruciating waiting. Polly was still in hospital. Continuing to progress, Orla said in her daily text, for which I was extremely grateful because otherwise I'd have had no way of knowing. Despite this, it was impossible not to catastrophize. Polly had not yet been discharged, which, given the pressure on hospital beds the media was always talking about, must mean that her doctors were still worried. If she was to have some sort of relapse and I was to be arrested for murder – I realize how awful it must sound to you that my first thought was not for Polly and her family but for me, myself and I, and most of all for Lexie. What would happen to her if I were to go to prison? Innocent people only ended up in prison in films, so I might once have thought, but from what Flannan and Breffni had said and from how very seriously they seemed to be taking all of this, that wasn't necessarily the case at all.

The middle of the night when you were asleep was the worst. That was when all the most morbid thoughts came crowding in with nothing external to push them back.

Does evil exist? From time to time this question would come to my mind whenever I saw or read some terrible thing in the news. My pragmatic answer had always been: probably not. A third party, observing us from a distant planet, would probably conclude that while what was good for one human might be bad for another, that didn't make a choice objectively evil. If there's only enough food for one person, another must starve. If a person is born without the ability to feel pain, how can they be expected to understand pain in others? Do we, after all, care about or even notice the animals we slaughter for food? The living bacteria we kill with antibiotics?

When I was younger, I had always felt that ultimately there must be some form of justice. Not necessarily from any court or judge but a more natural, organic kind, a yin and yang, a balancing out. Akin to: Eat all the cake and there'll be none left. Fail to study and you won't pass the exam. Night comes, but so does the morning. The children's novels Moll and I used to devour in our dens had always had a moral: how you treat others will one day come back to you. Only in my teenage years had I come to see this for the wishful, doomed thinking it had always been. Grace Gillespie, for example, had never experienced any justice. So ordinary and content as she was now. Or maybe that *was* her punishment. She would have wanted to be special. Maybe she thinks she still is. No – it's random people who pay for the sins of others, as if humans were interchangeable, as if the gods or those third-party alien observers think humanity must share a common brain. Dull people popping out for milk mown down by drivers high on cocaine. Toddlers bombed in wars started by narcissists. Polly in ICU, her organs damaged by shock. My terror when I had thought it was Lexie. *Please, no, I'll do anything. Anything at all.*

One night I had a terrible dream – one of many, but this one stood out. I was in prison, and you took Lexie away . . . or she had forgotten me and didn't want me any more . . . but when I woke I was drenched in sweat, feeling as if I was breathing inside a plastic bag.

One thing I knew, staring up at the pleated lightshade as my pulse recovered. No matter what the outcome of this, where we would live next year was no longer in doubt. That decision had now been made for us. Lexie couldn't stay here, at this school, on this estate. All the other nearby schools were full – I had enquired – and the Dublin housing market was so squeezed it would be a long time before we could move. And Dublin was such a small place and Vanessa's web reached everywhere. No smoke without fire, people would say. No one would believe, deep down, that I hadn't tried to destroy Vanessa's family – or at the very least been crassly and unforgivably negligent. Lexie would never be allowed to settle in Ireland. She would never be allowed to be happy.

Dropping Lexie off to school and picking her up, I found myself avoiding the other parents, partly not to have to answer questions about Polly but also because I was beginning to distance myself from people I would in all likelihood never see again once we moved back to London.

Surprisingly, Lexie seemed in much better form these days – helped, I'm sure, by you being around so much more – but also Ms Brennan reported that while Lexie was quiet in class she did not appear unhappy or upset. In fact, contrary to what I might have expected, given that Polly had been injured at our house, she was playing well with the other children and was no longer being left out.

Orla and Isabel came crowding up to me one morning at the gate before I could get away.

'How have you been, Sara?' Orla asked.

'All right.'

Orla seemed to draw herself up and looked in a meaningful way at Isabel, who said uncomfortably, 'Sara – I heard. About the gardaí being involved.'

'I'm sorry.' I didn't know what else to say.

'I know Vanessa is very upset,' Orla said, 'and of course it's understandable. Poor Van, I can't imagine . . . But it's not right that things have gone this far. Is it, Isabel?'

Isabel mumbled again, her gaze off-centre. As if she'd have much preferred not to be put in this position. Not to have to cast her die. But, for the moment at least, there she was. Standing with Orla in front of me. Not walking away.

The following day I met Luisa, who was much more forthright. I hadn't seen her since the day of the storeroom clear-out, but now here she came, making a beeline for me at the steps.

'It's so terrible about Polly,' she said, her long black hair flying in the breeze, 'and we all hope she is better soon. But that terrible creature, Vanessa, has gone way too far, I think. Getting the police involved! What a horrible thing to do.'

'It's been a difficult time for everyone,' I said diplomatically.

'But it could have been any of us. We all invite children to play. Why blame you for this?' Luisa looked flashing and indignant.

'I suppose,' I said wearily, 'Vanessa can't understand why I keep saying Polly didn't have peanuts when the doctors say she must have. It looks suspicious to her. I don't understand it either.'

'*Pfft*. What do the doctors know?'

'Well, I –'

'Doctors don't know shit. Trying to push their addictive drugs on us. Suppressing natural, ancient remedies just so they can make their profit. If it's not in the JAMA, they don't want to know – but who controls the JAMA? Tell me that, eh?'

'I w—'

'Who even says it was something she ate, anyway?'

'What do you mean?'

'Weren't they in the garden? It could have been an insect bite. Even a plant. My cousin nearly died from an allergy to a nettle. Who can possibly know with these things?'

'Could she be on to something?' I asked you at home. 'Do you think I should say it to Breffni?'

Luisa's suggestion had made instant sense to me. Why no

277

doctor seemed to have come up with the possibility I didn't understand – but then they weren't detectives and had probably forgotten about Polly as soon as she'd left the ICU and her bed was promptly refilled.

'Of course you should,' you said. 'Anything to demonstrate how many alternative explanations there are to that batshit woman's ravings.'

I braced myself. Phoning Breffni was always off-putting. The few times I'd called him he'd sounded as if he could barely bother to answer the phone, 'Breffni Goorrrmmm . . .' his speech tapering off as he ran out of exhalation and didn't bother to refill, as if I was too dull to even introduce himself to. I pictured him putting his head face down on his desk at the sound of my voice. You said his lack of interest was probably a good sign, that he didn't expect to make much money out of me or have me as a client for much longer. As it happened, when I phoned, his secretary said he was at a funeral in Wexford but she'd pass on my message.

Angela phoned that afternoon.

'Could you pop in to me?' Her voice sounded odd. 'I need to show you something.'

Angela's house – I don't know if you were ever in it – is a larger version of ours, with the staircase and living room the opposite way around. It's cosier and nicer than our functional rental; lots of plush carpets, squashy sofas, armchairs in warm pinks and golds. A teddy bear in hospital scrubs sat on a shelf beside photos of her late husband and her two grown-up children. On a table was a large photo of Angela and her cycling club, red-faced and beaming, at the finish line of their charity cycle from Malin to Mizen Head. Mittens, her cat, lounged fatly on the windowsill, half-eyed, with the sun on his stripes.

Angela, typically, came straight to the point.

'I haven't told anyone else this.'

'Told them what?'

'Remember the day of Polly's accident, you asked me where her school backpack was?'

I thought back. 'Didn't you say it had gone in the ambulance? Or Vanessa had taken it.'

'Yes, because I couldn't find it in your hall with the other children's bags. But as it turns out . . .' She held something up. A backpack. Purple, with transparent pockets with glitter floating in the layers.

I frowned. 'Where did you find that?'

'It must have been under my coat,' she said. 'That day. I'd dumped my coat at the bottom of your stairs and didn't bother putting it on again when I was leaving. When I got home I was tired so I just threw the coat on the bed in the spare room. The weather's been so mild I haven't worn it since. I only got around to tidying it away this morning and when I picked it up Polly's bag fell on the floor. I must have gathered the bag up in a bundle with the coat and didn't notice it because of all the padding.'

'Okay.' I wasn't sure where she was going with this.

'I was about to drop it in to you but thought I'd check first if there was a lunchbox or flask that might need a wash after so long. So, I opened it and . . . well.'

She held the bag up towards me. Various items – books, a transparent plastic lunchbox – were visible through the open flap.

'Sorry – what am I looking at?'

Angela removed the lunchbox from the bag and popped the lid. Inside was a crumpled wodge of plastic. A chocolate-bar wrapper, the mini kind that usually comes in a multipack. On the front was a cartoon of two smiling children and the name: ChockoFest.

'I'm sorry,' I said, 'I still don't . . .'

Patiently Angela took the wrapper and smoothed it out. 'There.' She pointed to the list of ingredients.

The second ingredient down was highlighted in bold: **Peanuts**.

'Oh. Okay. Wow.' I plopped down on the sofa.

Angela, grimacing delicately, sat opposite. 'I know the gardaí are involved. I'm guessing this wrapper might answer a few questions. But just to say to you now. In my own mind I am fully clear that you did the very best you could to supervise that child without being psychic.'

I looked at Angela's sensible, by-the-book, law-abiding face. What was Angela saying? Was she saying that she'd lie to the cops for me? Bin the wrapper and say nothing?

'I'm not sure this is the full story,' I said. 'Why would Polly have eaten this? Vanessa said she knew what to eat and what not. She's a clever child. She'd know the consequences. And how did this even get into her lunchbox? She wouldn't have got it from home, I assume, and we didn't stop at a shop.'

'That all being the case,' Angela said gently, 'I'm afraid it does look very much as if she did eat it.'

I nodded. It seemed undeniable.

'Pity she didn't wait till she got home,' Angela said, a touch acidly.

'Yes indeed,' I said with a little laugh. 'If only I'd been a bit quicker with the pizzas. Then she wouldn't have been hungry enough to go digging in her schoolbag. But if she *had* eaten the bar at her own house . . . you wouldn't have been around to do the CPR . . .'

Our smiles faded as the implications sank in.

I pulled myself together.

'Angela – thank you for letting me know. I appreciate it. But I didn't give this chocolate to Polly. I don't know where it came from or why she had it but I'm more than happy for the police to know about it.'

Angela nodded. 'In that case I'm just sorry to have been the cause of such a delay. It never occurred to me that her bag could be here.'

'Of course not, and again I appreciate your support. So do the Mayhews, I'm sure. I'm glad you found this. I needed to know once and for all what happened, and now I do.'

Wildly, phoning Breffni yet again, I wondered if he too might advise me to say nothing and bury the wrapper in a cemetery at midnight – thus ensuring that my supervision skills couldn't be called into question. His secretary, however, answered and said he had gone to another funeral but would get back to me at the earliest opportunity. I was at a loss then as to what to do with the wrapper so I put the schoolbag in a cupboard until some-one should ask for it.

I didn't have much time to wonder what the wrapper might mean for me because the following morning another piece of the jigsaw materialized.

Dervla approached Orla and me in the playground.

'Can we talk?' Hushed voice, looking all around her.

'Yes, of course.'

It was a Wednesday, not a usual day for coffee mornings and socializing, so we went around the corner to Spoon. Sure enough there was only one other customer there, an elderly man with a leaking nose slowly tearing open a sachet of sugar. Dervla watched him for a few moments before seeming to cross him off as a mole. She turned back to me.

'That Friday Polly went to yours,' she said. 'The day of . . . of the . . .'

'Yes,' I said encouragingly, not sure where this was going.

'Wasn't that the day of the Gaeilge Fair?'

I paused but Orla, quicker than I, said at once, 'Yes! Yes, it was.'

I was still searching back. My brain had never been picked so clean, so raw.

'That's right,' I said, remembering now Imogen's sticky Haribo packet and the grimy blue dog that Lexie had been so proud of.

Dervla gave a little moan and put her hands to her face. Through her fingers she said, 'I thought so. The truth is, it's possible that some peanut bars *might* have been brought in under the radar.'

'Okay.'

'I was supposed to be vetting, but people kept turning up late and dropping things in at random. I tried my best, but it was impossible to keep on top of them all and I kept randomly coming across items which were contrary to our Do Not Bring list – which, by the way, we had sent out on all the class Whats-Apps during the week AND put up on a big sign at the entrance –'

'I remember,' I said when she stopped for a raspy inhale.

'Yes, but the point is people just don't *listen*. No matter how many times you – anyway, we didn't know on the day the . . . the *implications* of it, so I just threw any prohibited items in the bin as soon as I found them. If I'd only known –'

'Me too,' I said. 'But we didn't.'

'I don't know what to say.' Dervla looked at me unhappily. 'I just heard recently that Polly's illness was an anaphylaxis, is that right? And now the gardaí are involved.'

Her freckles were popping from her pallor. I hated to upset her further but thought it best that she knew.

'Our neighbour did find a wrapper in Polly's bag,' I said.

Dervla whispered. 'What kind?'

'ChockoFest.'

She turned even more ashen. 'I think that might have been one of the ones I found.'

'It's not *your* fault,' said Orla.

'I know . . . but Mrs Bakewell . . . This is why she never wants any events at the school. Anything fun. I suspect it was a fifth-class mother,' Dervla said angrily. 'I saw her arriving in late and dumping stuff into the pick'n'mix. You'd think the bloody woman would know by now, signs up and everything, but *ohhh no*, she's one of those ones the rules don't apply to her. Vanessa will definitely sue the school for this, you wait and see. And if Polly –'

Orla said, uncharacteristically firmly, 'Polly is going to be fine. It was very good of you to tell us this, Dervla. I know you feel bad, but you did your best to make everyone aware of the rules and in my opinion people need to take responsibility for themselves too. This is very helpful for everyone. Everyone's mind can be put at rest that there was no negligence or . . . or anything else.'

Orla sounded so certain, both about Polly being fine and about this clearing my name that my heart couldn't help but lift.

'Yes. Thank you,' I said to Dervla. 'But – the only thing I still can't understand is why Polly would have bought a peanut-containing bar. Surely she knew to check the ingredients? She wouldn't have put herself at risk like that.'

'Yes,' Dervla said promptly. 'She would. Vanessa thinks the sun shines out of her arse, but she can be a right madam. Rules aren't for the likes of her.'

'But she'd been in hospital before with a serious attack.'

'That was when she was much younger,' Orla said. 'I doubt the child remembers. And she's been pushing the boundaries a bit recently. Isabel said she was on a playdate at hers a few weeks ago – I think Lexie was there too; she might have mentioned it? Isabel took them to Scrumdiddly's and Polly wanted to sprinkle rainbow nut mix on her ice cream. Got a bit upset when Isabel said no. Created a little bit of a scene, in fact; Isabel ended up having to get a tiny bit firm with her. Could something like that have happened, do you think?'

Shortly afterwards, Breffni contacted me to say that the investigation was being dropped.

'Insufficient evidence to proceed,' he said faintly. 'Mrs Mayhew can appeal, of course. But that's the situation for now.'

'That's wonderful!' The greatest joy is relief from fear. 'Thank you so much!'

'You'll probably enjoy a glass of champagne later,' Breffni managed.

I was beyond anything as wild and hedonistic as that. It was enough to simply sit in the mustard armchair and stare at the telly, knowing it was mine, knowing that I could change the channel or the volume whenever I wanted, not have to squint at a screen bolted high on a prison common-room wall, with Lexie coming less and less often to visit, slowly becoming a stranger to me.

And the next news, almost immediately after that, was that Polly was home.

The first time I saw her she was walking slowly around the perimeter of the Green, leaning on her childminder's arm, wearing leggings and a pink padded jacket. She looked thinner than before, paler and more serious. More adult. She now knew something that most girls her age did not: what it was like to face death and step back again. Seeing her made me realize that over the past few weeks I had been thinking of Polly not as a person but as a concept, an obstacle, a dangerous enemy even, standing between me and my freedom. But now here she was in the flesh, a human little girl again, slender and fragile, recovering from a serious illness. The pair of them turned and went on up the hill.

And that was that – until it wasn't.

*

As far as I recall, that was around the second week of May. I had assumed that now that Polly was finally home and Vanessa's bizarre allegations had been refuted she would cease her wild, unhappy lashing-out at us and redirect her turbulent energies to her daughter, and gradually things would return to normal. It would be a slow process – I didn't kid myself that it would happen overnight – but at least now perhaps some form of healing could begin.

And then something happened that gave us a darker and more chilling glimpse of what lay beneath Vanessa's poised, saccharine veneer.

Lexie had been at Sabdh's house for the afternoon and you had volunteered to walk George to collect her. At the last minute I went with you as I thought it would be a good opportunity to raise again the topic of where we were going to live.

Dublin was colder than the south of England, but occasionally the most beautiful golden day came bursting out of nowhere, and this had been such a day. Buds dotted the branches of trees, like stars in the gloaming. I was about to comment on this when a white Volvo SUV that had just roared past us screeched to a halt a few feet up the road. The passenger door flew open and Vanessa practically stunt-rolled out. She strode back towards us, very quickly, not her usual controlled self but clearly in the grip of some very strong emotion.

'This isn't the end of it!' she yelled, pointing at me. 'Don't think you're going to get away with this.'

She was almost vibrating with rage. Dave got out of the driver's side. 'Van –'

'Get off.' She turned and screamed at him. 'Don't you dare stop me! She's not getting away with this. She tried to *murder our child*!'

'Your daughter,' you said coldly, 'ate those peanut bars herself. My wife is not responsible for what your child buys for herself in her own time.'

'She would never have bought peanuts! Your wife knows what happened. Don't you, you murdering bitch?'

In a very calm, contemptuous voice you said, 'That's enough. I'm warning you now, if we ever hear you say anything like that again we will sue you for malicious defamation.'

'Oh, so that's your attitude?' Her shaking finger switched to you. 'Then let's see. Let's see how you like it when it's *your* child!'

'What?' You went still.

'You heard!'

'Come on,' I said to you at the same time as Dave said, 'Let's go, Van. This isn't appropriate.' His gaze skittered away from mine as he took Vanessa's arm and tried to steer her back to the car. She resisted, clawing at his fingers.

'Get off! You lying, cheating bastard, you never give me any support!' They grappled, she scratching and shrieking, he grim-faced, dodging her nails. George whimpered, his tail Velcroed to his abdomen. I gripped his lead more tightly.

Then suddenly Vanessa seemed to slump, her energy spent.

'I know she did it.' Her voice cracked to an angry sob. 'I *know* she did! Why won't anyone believe me?'

Dave led her back to the Volvo.

When their car had crawled up the hill the evening silence closed in again.

'Well, that was awkward,' I said, trying to make light of it, but my voice came out high and thin.

You hadn't moved. You were still frozen to the road.

'She's completely unhinged.' Your lips were white. 'If she hurts Lexie . . .'

'She won't.' I was crouched by the terrified George, rubbing his chest to comfort him. 'She just needed to say it. To get the last of it out of her system. It's done now. Let it go. It's over.'

30

After Vanessa's outburst, things went quiet. There were no more public confrontations, no more screeched accusations in the street. We didn't see Vanessa at all. Lexie continued to go to school. Polly continued to heal. Orla told me that the Shiny Girls had all been to Polly's for a playdate and Polly had been in rude health, bouncing and somersaulting on the trampoline. She had restarted her gymnastics training. However, as yet, she had not returned to St Catherine's. The plan, it seemed, was to home-school her for the remainder of the term. From the way Orla avoided looking at me as she said this I guessed that Vanessa had been proclaiming to all and sundry that she didn't want Polly to be in the same classroom as Lexie. And by the following September, of course, we ourselves would be gone.

Because, battered and bruised as I felt, I was busy working on our return to London. Documents were piling up on the kitchen table: Lexie's London school applications, Manways HR forms, lease terminations, tenancy deposit return forms, insurance forms. For every item I ticked off, two more appeared, Hydra-like. Had there been this much bureaucracy coming over? I'd been working full time then and had far less spare time yet I didn't remember it being this onerous. Perhaps my brain had atrophied since then. Manways, for one, had promptly replied to my back-to-work enquiry with a massive audit for me to get started on even before I left Ireland. There was so much to do that the idea of trying to find an alternative to the Vauxhall flat while I was still in Dublin seemed daunting. We would have to live in Vauxhall for a while until further arrangements could be made. Perhaps, I thought dully, we would get so used to being there that in the end we would never leave. A web page popped up on my laptop screen, a job advertisement I had clicked on a couple of times before. Chief Financial Officer sought for an Irish charity that specialized in education for adults who for various reasons had never completed school. The salary was one sixth of what I'd been getting at Manways, but with the new success of CareyComp it would have been more than enough.

I shut down the page. Anyhow, the sun was reflecting off the screen, making it difficult to read. It was the end of May now and Lexie was where she often was these days, out playing on the Green. People were being kind to her. She had made friends with several of the neighbouring children and had received lots of playdate invitations: Sadbh, Mabel, Alejandra, even Mia. Without Polly, the class seemed different, younger and more innocent. They held handstand competitions or made daisy chains and it didn't seem to matter any more what clothes people wore or whether someone had heard of a popular TikTok influencer. Soon the summer holidays would begin, long days in the parks and on the beach. But Lexie would not be there. She'd be back in the Vauxhall flat with whatever child-minder or nanny we'd managed to hire, sealed in behind the triple glazing, looking down over all the steel and concrete. Such a shame, the way things had turned out. If it hadn't been for Vanessa, we would certainly have stayed. My earlier decision to live here permanently hadn't been a hasty one. I had thought it through thoroughly. I had really felt that Lexie could have thrived here. I never would have considered it otherwise.

Earlier, even though I knew I shouldn't have, if ultimately the decision wasn't hers to make, I had asked her, 'Where would you live if you had the choice? Here or London?'

I expected her to pause, tilting her head with her tongue

sticking out while she considered the pros and cons. But without hesitation she said, 'Here.'

'Really?'

'Anyway,' she said confidently, 'we can't go back to London. George would hate having no garden.'

'We do need to go back, Lex. But it's okay, because we'll look for a house with a garden for him.'

'But what will he do in the meantime? Go to the loo on the balcony?'

'Nanna might take care of him for a little while.'

'You mean leave him *here*?'

'Hopefully it . . . well . . . just until we find somewhere suitable.'

'But where?' Drawing George to her, tears already glittering.

'In a nice town or village. There are some beautiful villages in England.'

'Another new place? But I wouldn't know anyone. I'd have to start all over again.'

'That would be okay though, wouldn't it?' Trying to sound positive, trying not to remember that if I'd thought Dublin was a closed shop, I'd heard the Home Counties were a locked and bolted MI5 dungeon, close neighbours still nodding politely and saying 'Good day to you' after ten years.

Tentatively, because I hadn't raised this with her before, I said, 'It's wonderful that Polly is getting better. But how would it be if you were still here when she came back to school? Would things be awkward between you?'

'Why would they? Anyway, I wouldn't care if they were. I have my own friends now.'

'But didn't you say it's Polly who decides?'

'I thought she did, but she doesn't. My real friends would stick by me. Like they did when Polly was being mean.'

'When?' I hadn't heard this.

'The day Polly said no one was to talk to me. Everyone was on one side of the yard and I was on the other side on my own. A few people were laughing at me. But Mia stood up for me.'

'She did?' I was surprised. Mia was so bashful. I couldn't imagine her squaring up to the confident Shiny Girls. 'What did she say?'

'Nothing. She just walked across the yard. And stood beside me and held my hand.'

Another peach-skied evening on the beach with George. We ate pizza slices at rough tables with water bowls scattered about for the dogs and the crackle of the tide on the pebbles. Breda was with us, stringing shells from a pile on the table. George was chasing a seagull that was wheeling low – deliberately, it seemed to me – just out of reach. Whenever George gave up, the gull alighted on the sand, hopping closer and closer until the tormented George couldn't contain himself and lunged again. Then the gull would take off, its screeching cackle bouncing off the rocks.

'He's laughing at you,' Lexie shouted gleefully.

Why were we leaving all this? Only one reason. One person, yet everything else was good. How much power did that person have, really? She had overreached and been exposed. People were starting to smell the coffee. Lexie had support now. We could weather this. There had been this trial, this test, and Ireland had passed. I knew I wanted to stay.

You and I still hadn't had the conversation. You had never settled here, and now, as far as you were concerned, there was all the more impetus for us to leave. You'd seen me fill out all the London school and Manways forms; it was not unreasonable for you to assume that the decision was made and no further discussion was required. But I needed you to know that this wasn't necessarily the case. I needed to let you know that despite everything, Vanessa was no longer a factor for me. And then – knowing that – if you still wanted to return to England, I would respect that and accept it. After all the support you had provided lately you had re-earned your right to have a say.

I kept almost raising the subject, then chickening out. We were being so gentle with each other these days, all bickering and irritability gone. I was reluctant to revive a potentially contentious topic. But it had to be done.

The night we finally got around to discussing it I remember clearly, because that was also the night that the first odd thing happened. At the time, however, although it was strange, neither of us thought too much of it.

It was the last Sunday of May. Lexie was in bed. I had ordered takeaway – Lebanese, your favourite – and driven to Blackrock Market to pick it up. Once home I called you downstairs and began to unpeel lids in the living room. Spicy smells floated out. George's nose came popping up over the edge of the coffee table.

'I got you six falafels,' I said. 'I know they're your favourite. And would you believe it, the off licence had a bottle of Ksara.'

You helped yourself to halloumi and falafels but then moved them absently around your plate, making no attempt to eat them.

'Everything all right?' I asked.

'Yes.' Deep breath. 'I'm back in London next week.'

'Ah.' I lowered the tub of hummus. 'Back to all the travelling.'

'It's unavoidable. The Americans have been very patient, but if I don't get this contract signed we'll lose them. I've done as much as I can from here, but now I need to go back.'

I nodded. 'I know. And I'm very grateful, believe me. Having you here has made a huge difference. Especially for Lexie.'

I went on unpeeling lids. *Say it, Sara.* The topic of work and travelling was as good an opportunity as I was going to get. I opened my mouth.

'You know – we should talk about our plans for next year.'

I closed my mouth in surprise. It was you who had spoken, not me.

'I've been thinking,' you said. 'And maybe you're right. Maybe Dublin is the best place for Lexie.'

'*Really?*'

Quietly you said, 'You've been a step ahead of me all along when it comes to her. And I know you want her to stay. Am I right?'

Carefully, choosing my words, I said, 'I just don't think we should automatically give up on Dublin. Just because of one single person.'

'Even after all that's happened?' You looked grave.

'Look. Vanessa will never win Neighbour of the Year, and I don't expect we'll be receiving any more dinner-party invitations from her, but we'll manage. Lexie and Polly won't be at school together for ever. We won't even be living here at Brookview for ever. I just don't think Vanessa should dictate any long-term decision we make. Lexie has your mum here, and all her friends. Good friends, from what she tells me. And she's getting help now at school and she's due to see that educational psychologist in a couple of weeks. Back in London, she'd have to go on a waiting list all over again.'

From experience, I kept expecting you to cut in and talk over me impatiently, as you so often did. But you went on listening, thoughtfully in that new way you had, rolling a piece of halloumi between your fingers. George, sitting in front of you, stared at it, shifting from one bum cheek to the other, as if ready to offer a body part in exchange for a sliver.

'All that off my chest,' I said, 'it's your decision too. Carey-Comp is a major consideration and if you genuinely think things would be easier for you in London, then that's where we'll go.'

I held my breath, waiting for your response.

'Don't worry about CareyComp,' you said. 'If staying here is what's right for you and Lexie, then that's what you should do.'

'Are you sure?'

'I'm sure. Hey! Georgie!' You held up the halloumi. 'Spin!' George circled frenziedly on the shag-pile rug. I couldn't stop smiling. Was George the factor that had changed your mind? Considering you hadn't wanted him in the first place, you seemed to have grown very fond of him. You had fallen into the habit of taking him for a long walk every night before bed, just you and him, no matter how much exercise he'd had during the day.

'Lexie'll be so happy,' I said as George's chops closed deliriously around the halloumi. 'She was so worried about where he'd go if we were in London. I really appreciate this, Adam. I know it'll be messy for you having to keep commuting – and we'll need to find somewhere more permanent to live here – but I have such a good feeling about this. I think it'll be very good for us as a family.' I couldn't believe how easy it had been. That the decision was finally made, with both of us on the same page. How ironic that we had Vanessa to thank for the fact that you and I were closer than we had been for months. Perhaps I should send her up a case of Veuve Clicquot.

'Sara.' You had turned on the sofa to face me.

'Yes?'

'There's something I –'

'What's that?' I jerked my head towards the window.

'What?'

'A bang. Like something hitting glass. Did you hear it?'

The curtains were drawn. I rose quickly, my pulse rate rising. I went to them and yanked them apart. I cupped my hand on the window, shading my eyes, but all I saw was the empty road and the necklace of white streetlights shining around the Green.

'Just my nerves,' I said after a moment. But now you were beside me, looking too, your body taut. I guessed what you were thinking. I could see it in the tense way you peered into the night. Neither of us had mentioned it again, that thing Vanessa had said about Lexie the day she'd come shrieking at us out of her car, but I knew it was on your mind. And mine too. Despite the fact that I hadn't taken Vanessa seriously, it still ... someone threatening your child ... it had not been a nice thing to hear.

'A bang on glass?' you said.

'I *thought* so, but –'

You left me, heading for the hall. The streetlight gleamed through the door panel, magnified and focused by the whorls so that it looked like an interrogation lamp. You flung the door open. Together we stood on the threshold. Stepped dark shapes of houses down and down the hill, dotted with lighted squares, the faint scent of grilling meat and, when I turned my head, some pleasant, night-flowering plant. The distant hum of traffic on the dual carriageway, accentuating the silence on our street. Mittens was crouched on the wall between our house and Angela's, staring at a brick.

'Let's face it' – I gave a little laugh – 'if someone had disturbed him, he wouldn't still be sitting there. He'd have given them the flick and shot up into a tree.'

You relaxed slightly. But I noticed how you cast a final look up and down the street before shutting the door.

Back in the living room the tub of hummus was missing and so was George. By the time I had located him under the kitchen table and managed to prise the tub back – too late – our dinner was growing cold.

'Better eat before anything else happens.' I began to uncork the bottle of Ksara.

'By the way,' I paused, mid-twist. 'What were you about to say just now? Before I interrupted you. Something about George?'

You shook your head. 'Nothing. I can't remember.'

'Not more work talk, I hope.' I poured the wine and slid the glass towards you. 'It's still the weekend. Give yourself a break.'

31

That was the first odd thing, even if, as I've said, we thought no more about it at the time.

But the following morning there was more. It started off so small that again by itself it was nothing, nothing anyone would pay any attention to. I rose as usual at seven thirty, heated Lexie's porridge, packed her sandwiches for school. You were still in your pyjamas but already firing up your laptop.

'Come on, Lex,' I called as she dawdled. 'Time to go.'

Her wail came floating down the stairs. 'I can't find my other trainer.'

'Oh dear. Maybe if you tidied your room occasionally.'

I went to help. Her duvet was in a heap on the floor. I picked it up and shook it out. 'There,' I said as her trainer toppled on to the carpet. 'And — what's this?' as a second item fell from the folds. 'Didn't we say no sweets in your room?'

'I didn't!'

'Then what's this?' I bent to pick up the object. A yellow packet of M&Ms, the peanut-flavoured kind.

'They're not mine. I never saw them before.'

The packet had been opened, then folded closed again. From the feel of it, it was still half full of sweets. They slithered and shifted in my hand. 'Perhaps it was one of your friends.' But what child would leave an open bag of sweets uneaten? You walked past the door just then and I held out the packet. 'These yours?'

'No. And if Lex doesn't get a move on, she'll be late.'

'Oh, okay. Come on, dude, let's go!' I looked forward to filling her in on our decision to stay in Dublin, but for now I just wanted to get her out of the house. We hurried downstairs. The M&M bag was still in my hand so I tossed it into the hall-table drawer.

When we opened the front door there were a dozen or so tiny brownish-red objects, like pebbles, scattered on the step and down the path, all the way to the pavement.

'What are *those*?' I asked.

'They look like nuts.' Lexie had crouched to examine them.

So they did; the kind you might find in a bag of trail mix. It sounds strange now to say that I didn't think more of it but, again, there were possible explanations. It had been windy during the night; it seemed likely that they might have blown from a bin. And when I came back from the school they were gone. I assumed that you had cleared them up on your way out for your run.

The next morning the reddish objects were there again, scattered on the step and all along the pathway. And again when I returned you had cleared them away.

The following day it was you who took Lexie to school. You opened the front door. Then, abruptly, you stopped on the step. I heard you swear under your breath.

'Hey,' I heard Lexie say. 'Who keeps putting peanuts in our garden?'

I joined you on the step. You looked irritated. I knew how you felt. Peanuts on your path might seem a small thing, but when it was happening every day it was surprisingly aggravating. In a low voice I said, 'Are you thinking what I'm thinking?'

'I hope not. Stupid cow.'

The following morning I saw you tense before flinging open the front door. But the step and the pathway were empty.

That, in fact, was the last we saw of the peanuts. And for a few days nothing else happened. I think we even began to forget about them.

You went ahead with your London trip as planned. The

weather grew warmer and warmer until, like caterpillars, we shed our coats and emerged in our light summer clothes.

On the second Monday in June, after school, Lexie skipped out to the garden to play. Then there came a cry. Not a distressed one – not like the day Polly had collapsed – but unusual enough that I dropped my onion knife and ran out.

She was standing by the trampoline.

'Look,' she said, pointing through the netting.

In the middle of the jumping mat was a small brown mound, spiralled like a 99 ice cream.

'George!' Lexie scolded. 'That's not where you go!' He looked agreeable and wagged his tail. I eyed him. He had never done anything on the trampoline before. In fact, he was a little afraid of it and scuttled to hide indoors if someone was bouncing on it. And he wouldn't have managed the ladder and certainly couldn't have unzipped the netting.

I said nothing, however, just fetched a bag and scooped and binned the 99. I cleaned the mat with a disinfectant wipe and zipped the netting closed.

As I knew it would be, the poo was top of Lexie's agenda on the phone to you later.

'You'll never guess what George did on the trampoline!'

'What's this about poo?' you asked when she handed over the phone. 'Can't we get her to close the netting properly when she's finished jumping?'

I took the phone to the kitchen.

'I don't think it was George.'

'How do you mean?'

'How would he have got up the ladder?'

You didn't reply.

'This might sound stupid,' I said, 'but remember those peanuts last week? It might be coincidence but . . .'

I didn't spell it out. I could hear your jerky breathing as you walked and the sounds of voices and steps and buses hissing in the background. I guessed what was going through your mind. How unpleasant to think that someone would keep doing this. Someone being focused on our home like that, like a locked missile, or melted tar on skin.

'I don't know,' you said. 'I mean – could you really see her doing something like this? Climbing over our wall, complete with bag of fresh poo? With her beige clothes and her blow-dry? Hardly the athletic type, is she?'

'No.' It was true. It didn't sound at all Vanessa's style. She was far more likely to get up a nationwide Parents' Association petition to have us deported.

'It must have been a fox,' I said, and we left it at that.

Another couple of days passed. Then the letter showed up. Or rather, the photo.

It was tucked into the letterbox when I came home from school with Lexie. Lexie picked it out and handed it to me. A plain white envelope with a single word printed on the front in capital letters: CAREY. Fortunately, Lexie was upstairs when I opened it.

Inside the envelope was an A4-sized page, which I unfolded. A pen drawing of a stick figure hanging from a scaffold – the sort of step-by-step drawing you see in the children's word game Hangman. Except that this drawing had a photo glued to the head. A photo of Lexie's face.

I recognized the source. It had come from a photo on the school website, of the third-class children planting daffodils in the school garden. Someone had printed off the photo, cut out Lexie's face and stuck it to this disgusting picture. There was nothing else in the envelope. No note, no message.

I screenshotted it to you immediately. But it was several hours before you got back to me.

'Sorry,' you said, sounding done in. 'Wall to wall here all day. Where did you get that horrible thing?'

'Lexie found it in our letterbox this afternoon.'

'Where is she now?'

'In the living room.' Through the half-open door I watched her ruffle George's throat while doing a jigsaw. 'She's fine.'

'Nasty little note,' you said quietly.

'Yes.'

'I know it's tempting to jump to conclusions. But to be honest, what this looks like to me is kids messing. Polly's sisters, maybe? Or one of their friends, playing a joke.'

'Poor taste if so.' I smoothed and re-smoothed the drawing. 'You think a kid put the poo on the trampoline too?'

'The poo was probably a fox, didn't we say?'

Lexie's photo, on a picture of a hanged child. Would another child really do something as vile as that? Stupid question. I knew very well that a child most certainly would.

'You're worried,' you said.

'I just keep on thinking. About what Vanessa said that day, about seeing how we'd like it when it was *our* child.'

'But didn't you say yourself you didn't take her seriously? That she was letting off steam, like a toddler who'd forget about us when we weren't right in front of her.'

'I know. I did say that.'

'If it makes you feel better, why not give the gardaí a call? See what they say.'

'I'd thought of that. But what would they do?'

'Talk to her. Tell her to fuck off.'

'She'll deny it.'

'It'll frighten her though. If it is her. She won't want a uniform at her door in front of the neighbours.' You were warming to the idea. 'Worth a try, I'd say.'

Later, when Lexie was in bed, I phoned you back. This time you answered promptly.

'Well?'

'I called them. They advised keeping a log of any incidents. And to keep any evidence, like the picture and the nuts.'

'Are they going to talk to Vanessa?'

'Well, it's like he said – the garda – at the moment there's no proof. To be honest, he didn't seem to take it all that seriously. Maybe I shouldn't have, but I told him what you said about it not being Vanessa's style.'

'Did you tell him what she shouted about Lexie that time in the street?'

'Yes. And he said if we were concerned we should think about putting up a camera.'

Silence. Then you sighed. 'Well, you know. He's probably right. Probably the best thing is to ignore it and, hopefully, whoever it is will get bored and move on.'

'I'll get a camera anyway, shall I?'

'Can't do any harm. We could probably do with one anyway.'

To my mind, this last comment lacked enthusiasm. I stared out at the violet evening. *Was* I making too much of this? I kept veering between seeing Vanessa as a threat to thinking: *Forget about her. Move on.* Despite what she'd said in the street that day she had never struck me as being physically violent. You were veering too but, I suspected, for a different reason. Now that you were travelling again you were back to being distracted, less concerned about what was happening in Dublin than you were when you were here with us. Put an ocean between yourself and your troubles. I could feel you, very gradually, beginning to slip away from us again. The way you had before.

On the Friday evening I went upstairs to take a shower. Lexie was watching her Netflix show about the teenage girls who turn into mermaids. She was fascinated by this and had taken to wrapping a blanket around her legs while she watched the show, tied at the feet with a scrunchie to make it look like a fishtail.

'Can you let George in?' I called down from the bathroom. 'He's scratching at the back door.'

'He's not,' she called back. 'He's in here.'

'Is there something rattling against the door then? It's breezy out. Can you take a look?'

'Muum . . . I can't walk with my tail on . . . and the moon's just coming out . . . the mermaids are about to be hypnotized . . .'

'Never mind. I'll do it.'

I came downstairs, wrapped in my towel. As I turned from the bottom step the doors to the garden were directly ahead. The moment I saw them I gave a shout.

Lexie came racing out of the living room, stumbling and tripping on her blanket tail.

'Mummy! Mummy, what's wrong? Are you hurt?'

'It's all right.' Seeing her panic, I caught hold of myself. 'I thought I saw something, but . . .' The garden was empty as far as the leylandii. Beyond that my view was obscured; however, the only thing behind the leylandii was the back wall.

'Was someone out there?'

'No. It was just a shadow.'

But Lexie was still distressed. I suspect now she had overheard more talk about the peanuts and the poo than she had let on or we had realized.

'Someone was there.' Her voice rose. 'Someone was trying to get in.'

'No, truly. I think it was the branch, look.' I pointed to Angela's pear tree, bumping gently off the fence in the breeze. The patio door was locked, the bolt fully down.

Unconvinced, she trailed back to her mermaids. I decided to skip the shower and get dressed. My phone rang in the living room as I was putting on my dressing gown.

'Mummy saw someone in our garden,' I heard Lexie say as I came downstairs.

'Probably one of those magpies.' She'd put you on loud-speaker. 'Or Mittens chasing a mouse.'

'No,' Lexie said indignantly. 'It wasn't a magpie. It was real. I saw him too.'

I stopped tying my belt and looked at her in surprise.

Your voice sharpened. '*Him?* What did he look like?'

'He was wearing dark clothes, like a shadow. He was trying to get in our house.'

'Put Mummy on, will you?'

I took the phone to the kitchen.

'What's going on?'

'I'm not sure,' I said. 'There may have been someone in the garden.'

'Doing what?'

'I don't know. I heard something and thought I saw a shape, but when I looked properly it was gone.'

'Male or female?'

'No idea. Male, *possibly*. But it all happened so quickly. I'm not even sure if –'

'Have you called the police?'

'No, because . . . I mean I thought . . .' I faltered. 'I didn't realize until Lexie said it just now that she saw him too.'

I could hear you breathing through your nose, the way you do when you're hungry. 'This is the second time this has happened.'

'Is it?'

'Remember the night we had that takeaway? The bang on the window?'

I paused, thinking back. 'You're right. I'd forgotten.'

'Call the guards. Now! Let me know what they say. Keep your phone with you and call me or dial 999 if anything else happens. Lock all the doors and windows. Check upstairs too.'

'I will. I know.'

Lexie wanted the phone back when I'd finished with it. She called you to tell you that the police had been informed, and you stayed on the line with her, both of you joking and messing about. It was a comfort to her to have you there. 'I'll take care of Mummy,' she said. 'I won't let anything happen to her.' Listening to the brave little voice, I remembered how she had come flying out of the living room when I shouted, determined to protect me, even though she had been terrified herself.

When I finally got her to bed – she insisted on sleeping in ours – she lay beside me in the lamplight, studying my face close up in that unnerving way she had, her perfect eyesight taking in my every flaw.

'Is that man going to come back?'

'No. And if you hear the doorbell, it'll be the police coming to check on us, like they promised. So don't worry.'

It took quite a while for her to fall asleep, but by the time I eventually called you back she was out for the count, snoring deeply as she had a cold.

'They came.' I spoke in a low voice, lying beside her supine, snuffling little form. 'Two of them.'

'And?'

'They took a good look around. Over all the walls as well. They said they'd had no reports of any other trouble in the area but they'd keep an eye.'

'Did you remind them about the letter?'

'Yes. And again they suggested the cameras. Cameras are the best thing, they said. And to keep a log.'

'We *are* keeping a bloody log.' Your voice boomed from the speaker. I rolled away from Lexie so as not to wake her.

'What else can they do?' I whispered. 'There's every chance no one was there at all.'

'Lexie saw him too. Why are you minimizing, Sara?'

I hadn't thought I was. But perhaps in my efforts not to sound as if I was crying wolf I'd ended up swinging too far in the opposite direction. My judgement was off. Little things seemed enormous and enormous things seemed little, as though I was Alice in Wonderland, switching between the bottle and the cake.

I said honestly, 'I think I'm scared. It's like if I say nothing's happening, then it's not. I'm thinking, if it's not Vanessa herself doing these things – and the shape in the garden did look a bit more like a man – then maybe she's getting someone else to do them for her.' Grace Gillespie, as I recalled, had never liked to get her own hands dirty.

'I'll be home tomorrow,' you said grimly. 'I'll call in to the guards myself. The response isn't good enough, quite frankly.'

'They did come round. And suggested the cameras. What more should they be doing?'

'I don't know, but there's a threat to a child here. When they thought we'd given Vanessa's kid a fucking peanut they were at our door in a second.'

Lexie still had lots of questions the next morning about the shadowy man in our garden. I reassured her that the police had done a thorough check and there were no reports of any burglars in the area.

'I think we must have imagined it,' I said. In the light of day, I really did think this. I didn't believe that she had seen anyone. We were both jumpy; it had been the power of suggestion. Either that or she'd been backing me up, defending me from your initial dismissiveness.

'And George didn't bark,' I added, inspired. 'So that just shows you.'

George wouldn't bark if we were all being disembowelled bit

by bit. But it cheered her up. The sun was out, it was the week-end and you were coming home.

By the time you arrived you had calmed down. You had a word with Flannan, who advised that you start by taking up the garda suggestion of the camera instead of charging straight down the station like an entitled knob. So, we bought the cameras and put them up. Front and back, and linked them to our phones.

'Now.' You stood with your knuckles on your hips. 'Now let her try.'

No more peanuts. No more letters or poo, no more faces at the windows.

'Maybe it *was* just kids,' I said.

'I hope so because I really need to get back to London. The contract signing is next week.'

'So go!'

'You're sure?'

'Go,' I said firmly. 'We'll be fine.'

'Any problems, you know where I am. And the guards — don't hesitate to call them.'

'I won't.'

When you were leaving you bent to give Lexie your usual goodbye hug, one eye on your overnight bag as you felt about for your passport.

'You and Mummy mind each other.'

'I will,' she said seriously. 'Don't worry. I won't let anything happen to her. You just concentrate on taking care of yourself.'

I smiled at how grown-up she sounded and looked towards you to share the joke. Then stopped, struck by your expression. You had stopped rummaging and were staring at her in an odd, intent way, almost as if you were memorizing her. You dropped your bag, took her in your arms and hugged her little body hard, your cheek pressed tightly against hers.

'Look after her,' you said, your voice unsteady when you released her.

'Of course.'

32

The first few days you were back in London you phoned each morning and evening and had long, jokey conversations with Lexie. Inevitably the calls began to dwindle, to one a day, then none as you became caught up again in work and everything you were juggling over there. I didn't envy you being in the city, away from the sea breeze. It was the warmest day of the year so far, twenty-five degrees. The leaves were limp, hanging from the branches like dusty green rags.

On the Wednesday of her last week at school before the summer holidays Lexie asked, 'Can I go out on the Green?'

'Well . . .'

'Please? All the other kids are out.'

What harm could it do? I thought. I couldn't keep her in for ever in this heat. From the living-room window, I could easily see most of the Green. There were people everywhere, children playing, parents strolling. It was like an ad for a Neighbourhood Watch scheme.

'Stay on the Green itself,' I warned. 'Don't wander off on one of the streets where I can't see you.'

She promised. She threw off her school uniform, hauled on her new dark pink hoodie that she was so proud of and dashed out. Fidgety Lexie who never walked if she could run. I cooked spaghetti Bolognese, her favourite, and whenever I checked at the window there she was, nattering to another child or racing about but always within sight, like the considerate, obedient child she was.

At six she came in, cheerful and grubby, with the flushed beginnings of a tan.

'You're filthy,' I said. 'What on earth were you doing?'

'Playing Oceans.'

'What's Oceans – no, tell me over dinner. Go and wash your hands. In fact, hop into the shower, and give me those mucky clothes.'

I followed her up and waited outside the bathroom. The door opened; her hand appeared in the gap, thrusting out shorts, T-shirt and hoodie.

'Here you go.'

I took the bundle from her. Then said in surprise, 'They're all wet.'

'Huh?'

Something dark and sticky was spilling down the back of her hoodie. I turned it over. More gloop poured through my fingers. The hood was full of it. My hands were red. The liquid had soaked through to her white T-shirt, turning it crimson.

'Lexie!' I jumped up and banged on the door. 'Lexie, are you okay? Are you hurt?'

'What? No! What's wrong?'

She opened the door again, a white towel wrapped around her. No blood anywhere, no redness. No sign of any injury. When she saw the hoodie and the dark liquid dripping to the floor she gasped in fright. 'I didn't do that! It wasn't me!'

More thick, red ropes, hanging down to the carpet. Lexie wailed in panic. 'What is it? Is it blood?'

'No,' I said as a familiar smell reached my nostrils. 'It's not blood.' I gathered the hood closed to try to contain the spillage.

'It's paint.' I looked up at her. 'It's on your hair too.'

She gasped again, putting her hand to her head. The hand

came away slippery and red. She gave a cry. 'What if it doesn't come out?'

'It will.' I hoped. 'Don't worry. It looks worse than it is.'

'But the carpet . . .'

'It's fine. It'll come out too.'

'I didn't do this.' She was very upset. 'I promise. I wasn't playing with any paint. I don't know how it got there.'

'It's all right.' I calmed her. 'It wasn't your fault. You're not hurt, and that's the main thing. Let's get your hair sorted before dinner.'

I had to work on it for quite a while, using lots of conditioner to separate the strands from the sticky paint. As casually as possible I asked, 'Did anyone come near you while you were on the Green? Who might have been playing with paint and accidentally spilled it?'

'I don't *think* so.' Her voice bounced on the shower tiles. 'But we were playing Sardines in the bushes by the white fence and there were people passing on the other side of the fence.'

I continued to work on the paint. It took some time but finally I was able to comb most of it out, though a couple of particularly resistant snarls had to be snipped out.

'There!' I gave her hair a final comb. 'All done!'

I was about to dump the clothes in the laundry basket when, remembering the advice about keeping logs and evidence, I dropped them into the bath instead. There they lay, red and stiffening, looking chillingly like the clothes of a stabbing victim – and that, I thought grimly, was exactly the message they were meant to convey. The paint, I saw, had been poured into the hood. Someone had opened the hood quite deliberately and poured the paint in so that she would walk around without noticing it immediately. Belatedly I wondered if I should have taken a photo of her hair before it was washed. But taking pictures of her covered in paint would have upset her even more.

At dinner I made light of what had happened, saying that someone must have been very clumsy and would be very annoyed when they realized their paint pot was empty and they'd have to buy more. This made her giggle. Afterwards, when she was watching her mermaid show, I forwarded a photo of the gore-spattered clothes to you. No response. Presumably you were still wrapped up in your preparations for the contract.

I stood at the window like an army wife during a war, waiting for you to call.

Could it have been an accident? you wanted to know when we finally spoke. Was I completely sure that Lexie hadn't been playing with paint and didn't want to say?

I knew very well what was happening. What you were doing. You were busy and really, really did not want to have to come home.

'She wasn't near any paint,' I said. 'This was deliberate. A message. You saw the photo of the clothes.'

'Yes.'

'I'm worried, Adam. This is a step up. I genuinely didn't think she'd get physical. What's next? An actual assault?'

That shook you, I could tell.

'What did the police say?'

'I think they thought what you thought. Just kids in the park messing. They said if we wanted, we could log it.'

'Log it.' You snorted. 'Jesus, what a shower of boggers. You know what? I think it's time for me to speak to that woman myself.'

I'd been wanting to confront her too but had decided against it, emotions running high as they were. On the other hand, I was curious to know what she'd say.

'Be careful,' I warned. 'If you lose your temper she'll say you're harassing her and we'll lose what little support we have.'

Afterwards, you filled me in.

'Hellew?' Vanessa had answered the phone in her breathy little voice with its undercurrent of solid concrete.

'This is Adam Carey. Lexie's father.'

'What do you want?' As cool and collected as if her shrieking accusations on the street had never happened.

'I'll tell you what I want. I want you to stay the hell away from my family.'

'I have literally zero idea what you're talking about.'

'Then let me spell it out for you. People snooping round our windows at night. Threatening photos posted in our letterbox. Paint being thrown on my daughter. Sound familiar?'

In a super-polite voice Vanessa said, 'I feel obliged to inform you that this call is being recorded.'

This, we agreed, explained the innocent *who, me?* tone, the sane, reasonable charade of the helpless little woman being attacked by the loud, aggressive man. Remaining coolly polite in the face of someone's legitimate anger is inflammatory; Vanessa would know this; if she hadn't read it, she would know it from birth, a power-play like that would be encoded in her genes. If I had heard her I would have stepped in, tried to warn you.

'Listen –'

'No, *you* listen! Don't you dare call this number again. Stay away from us. If I hear any more from you I'll call the guards and have you prosecuted for harassment.'

'You –'

Click.

You tried to phone her back, stamping your finger on the screen, but there was no response. 'I'll keep calling,' you said furiously. 'I'll call her all night if I have to.'

'Don't,' I pleaded. 'You heard what she said. Let's just talk to the gardaí again ourselves. Keep on at them, like Flannan advised.'

'What's the bloody point? Unless we solve the crime ourselves by filming it moment by moment as it happens they'll have nothing to do with it.'

'I'll call them myself tomorrow,' I said wearily. Anyway, your tone and attitude would have done you no favours at the station.

'How long?' you asked after a moment. 'How long is this going to go on? I can't keep doing this, Sara. Cancelling meetings and clients to spend time in Dublin. If this keeps up, we're going to have to reconsider whether Lexie can stay here. It's not safe for her.'

'No. I know.' Bitterly I said, 'So it looks like she's driven us out after all.'

'Well, what choice do we have?' To be fair, there was no triumph in your tone, no hint of I-told-you-so. The move back to London probably did suit you, but this, I knew, would never have been the way you would have wanted it to happen.

'I don't get it, Sara. I don't get how someone like her can get away with screwing up other people's lives with not one person, apparently, able to do a single thing about it.'

'There are people like this. Unfortunately,' I said tiredly.

Neither of us spoke for a while. I began to wonder if your phone had died.

'Friday's the big day,' you said finally. 'We're signing the contract.'

'At last! Best of luck with it.'

'Thank you.' Then you said, 'Look, Sara. There's something I've been meaning to say. I know I haven't been the easiest to live with lately, and you haven't deserved it.'

'I understand –'

'No. No. We need to talk. Properly this time. Once the contract's done I'll come home and we'll . . . we'll sit down together. Go through everything. I think there are things we both need to say.'

After you had gone I simply stood where I was in the middle of the kitchen, my mouth slack, my phone hanging from my fingertips. A heavy blanket seemed to have fallen upon me. I felt immobilized and overwhelmed. Even the decision of where to put my feet, which room to go into, seemed momentous and beyond me, and whatever choice I made was bound to be flawed. The back-to-London paperwork was still piled up on the end of the kitchen table. I had gladly abandoned it; now it looked as if I'd have to return to it again.

This was all wrong. All our plans destroyed. Lexie's cosy future here with her grandparents ruined. My anger rose. I got myself moving again, cleared the dinner things, folded laundry, got Lexie's uniform ready for school. Then, for want of anything better to do, I sat on the sofa and watched something on Netflix, though for the life of me now I couldn't tell you what it was. When it was over, I remained on the sofa, staring at the screen as if the film was still running. My phone rang.

This next part is hard to explain. I answered and was listening to the caller when, out of nowhere, a kind of chill spread over me. I can't describe it. It felt as if something was about to happen, worse than anything that had happened before. I felt as I had that evening in the hospital car park when Polly had been in ICU, that I wasn't alone, that someone was there with me, waiting to creep from the shadows. I started from the sofa and turned, taking everything in: the door, the room, the coffee table with tangerine peelings on a plate, the shelves crammed with books and toys. Then I looked at the window but saw in the dark, uncurtained glass only my own face, a pale balloon, featureless, with no mouth or eyes.

Afterwards I went around checking the rest of the house, all the locks and windows and doors. Everything seemed secure. Eventually the feeling subsided and I went to bed, but it took me a long time to fall asleep.

*

The following day at pick-up Lexie came out with a group of girls. When she saw me she came running over. 'Can I go to Sadbh's tomorrow after school? Please? It's our last day and she really wants me to go.'

'Not tomorrow, sweetie. Sorry. Another time.'

'Aww.' But, Lexie being Lexie, she didn't argue and skipped home beside me cheerfully enough.

'Where's George?' Always her first question when she came into the house, flinging her backpack on the stairs.

'In the garden.'

'I'll get him!'

She came back in.

'He won't come when I call him.'

We both went out and called. No sign of him on the grass or under the trampoline. The gap under the side door was too narrow even for squashy little George. Wasn't it? I remember looking at it, wondering if the door seemed higher off the ground than usual. He had tried and failed many times before to squeeze through.

'Could he have jumped over the wall?' Lexie chewed at her sleeve, a flush rising up her neck.

'Let's check.'

We asked Angela and the neighbour on our other side, then the neighbours whose gardens backed on to ours. No sign. We called for him on the Green. Angela came out to help. I took one direction, she another, and between us we covered all the roads leading off the Green.

Out of the side of her mouth Angela asked me, 'Would he have gone down to the main road?'

'I was wondering that. But he never goes down there without being on his lead. I think the buses and lorries would frighten him. Even on the lead he always presses in close to us.'

Angela said to Lexie, 'About once a year Mittens disappears

for a few days, then comes back. I never find out where he goes! The first time it happened I was so worried. And my daughter knew a dog once who vanished for a week, then strolled home in perfect health, cool as you like. Is George microchipped?'

'Yes,' I said. 'And my phone number is on his collar.'

'There you are! Someone will bring him home. Or he'll come back later himself when he's hungry.'

Unfortunately, however, he did not. Lexie was distraught the following morning.

'He didn't come home?'

'No, sweetheart, I'm sorry.' I felt so bad for her. School would be a washout for her today, all the fun things they'd planned for the end of the year that she'd been looking forward to for so long.

'Will you keep trying to find him?' she pleaded all the way down the hill.

'I will. I promise.'

Angela emerged from her house as I returned.

'Any luck?'

'No.'

'Let's give it another try,' she said. 'A really thorough tour of all the gardens, just in case he's got himself trapped somewhere, in a shed or something. He'll hear us calling and bark.'

We went around the estate, shouting his name. We were at it for over an hour. I know how it must seem to you. You can't understand how it didn't dawn on me what must have happened, why I went on calling for him just as if he were a normal lost dog, as if any other possibility simply hadn't occurred to me.

Angela had to go then to babysit her grandson. 'Someone will pick him up and ring the number on his collar,' she said, and I agreed. It was after she left that I found him. You've said you'll always be thankful that Lexie was still at school.

When Angela left I decided to go home and clear up after breakfast. The kitchen bin was full so I removed the bag and took it out to the wheelie bin. The morning was sunny. The bolt on the side door was warm to the touch. When I lifted the lid of the bin a swarm of flies rose into my face. There was a whiff of gone-off meat. Through the glittery black-and-blue cloud I glimpsed something large and hairy, taking up most of the top half of the bin. Honey-coloured, feathery fur ruffled in the breeze.

I dropped the lid. It landed with a slam. I leaned on the wall, paparazzi flashes going off in my vision. Then I straightened and made myself lift the lid and look again. A black cable-tie was looped around his neck, pulled tight, deeply embedded in the fur.

Once on a trip to France I had eaten snails. After an initial feeling of revulsion, I'd found them to be quite tasty. I had eaten about a half a dozen when my brain belatedly registered what was happening and I began to retch. Now, having looked my fill, having seen what needed to be seen, I gagged, saliva rushing, my throat swelling like a toad's. I dropped the lid again and bent forward, my hands on my knees.

Little dog. Had he known? How much pain had he felt?

'I'm sorry,' I whispered. My eyes filled with tears. 'I'm so sorry.'

33

The American contract was signed. CareyComp's future was assured. Your flight had already landed in Dublin. When you reached Brookview and discovered what had happened you were beside yourself with grief and rage.

'Where's Lexie?' you demanded.

'Still at school. But I've packed an overnight bag for her. As soon as school's finished I'm taking her straight to your mum's.'

'Good idea. She can't stay here any longer. Not with that . . . that *freak* on the loose.'

Outside, you kicked at the side door. 'Someone's been at this. Look. Planed an inch or two off the bottom. They must have lured him out underneath.'

When you saw him in the bin you swallowed, your eyes shining. Together we lifted him out and wrapped him in some towels and heavy-duty bin bags.

'Poor man.' You kept stroking him. 'Poor little man. I should have done something. I should have stopped this.'

You wanted to remove the cable-tie, but I stopped you. 'Let the gardaí see it.'

'And what good will that do?'

'It'll be a criminal matter now. Due to the violence of it.'

'Got it on camera, did we?'

'No, unfortunately. I checked the footage. They don't show the side alley, only the front and back doors, and there's nothing to see there. Whoever lured him out must have climbed over from Angela's side. But the police will have to take us seriously now. I can't see how they wouldn't.'

'Bit fucking late, isn't it?'

We photographed the body – I wasn't sure how long it would last in this heat. Then we finished wrapping him and placed him in the shed, between the lawnmower and Lexie's bicycle. I hoped the breeze blocks and tin roof would keep him relatively cool.

Gruffly you said, 'What will you tell her?'

'I'll think of something.'

After school I drove Lexie to your mum's. She asked again about George, whether he had come home. I hadn't planned what to say but in the moment found myself telling her a long story about how a kind lady had found him in her garden and taken him to a vet who said he had died peacefully from a heart attack. I don't need to tell you again what she said, how she reacted. We spent the journey remembering him. The way he had lain on her bed with his head on her tummy. His joy the day we had collected him from the shelter, the way he had flown at her as if he had known her always: *Where WERE you?* His long, dopey, doleful nose. Seeing her pain made me angry all over again, and my anger as I drove was like a sour wound in my centre.

'Come out,' I said to you when I got home. 'Please. You need some air.'

You were on your phone in the kitchen but put it away and came to your feet as I entered. I was struck, as you rose in the gloom, by how huge and restless you looked, like a wild creature that had no place in a tiny house.

It was almost nine. I had spent the evening at your mum's settling Lexie and filling Breda in on what had happened – or some of it at least. I had never told her much about Vanessa, apart from that Lexie had been having some issues with her daughter. Your mum had been so indignant on Lexie's behalf

319

that I hadn't told her the rest, and I knew you certainly hadn't; her fussing would have driven you up the wall. George's red harness and lead hung from the hook on the cupboard. Under the table was a chewed tennis ball, the outer layer hanging off like a half-peeled onion.

'Come on,' I coaxed, seeing your gaze linger on the ball. 'You'll feel better if you come for a walk.'

It was the last Friday of June – not that I think either of us will ever forget. The bright-dark sky was full of water. The air was warm and pungent, like the inside of a greenhouse. We took the route we had often taken on our walks with George: out of the estate, right on to the main road, down the hill towards the coast. We reached the entrance to the park and I thought, *He'll never scamper in there again.* He never would catch one of the squirrels he had so desperately wanted to catch, who had eyed him with such contempt from the tree trunks, inches out of reach. His time here had been so short. He had been rescued from a drab little start, given a few weeks of love and kindness, and that was it. It hadn't been much of a life. If he'd been with us he would have sunk to his haunches, scrabbling his claws on the pavement, begging us to turn in to the trees and the squirrels. But he wasn't here and so we passed on, continuing towards the sea. You walked beside me in silence, lethargically kicking a pebble.

We descended the steps and clambered over the rocks to the beach. We walked southwards along the strand. The beach was empty, presumably thanks to the incipient rain. In the gathering dusk white lights blinked on the two tall chimneys and the orange and red lights of the city illuminated the smoke from the waste plant. Discarded razor-clam shells lay everywhere. I trod on them, finding the crunch soothing. It occupied my mind like a game. If you get ten crunches in a row this will happen, and if not, that will happen. The air cleared my head a

little; probably yours too. But after twenty minutes the damp-
ness condensed into drizzle and we began to head back towards
the rocks. The tide was coming in, filling the pools and hollows
more quickly than one would expect. Ahead of us was a set of
metal steps leading to the Dart overpass. From the far side of
the steps a lone fellow walker was approaching, their pale coat
luminous against the iron-coloured sky.

I turned to you. 'There's something I need to show you.'

'What?'

'I didn't want to show you in the house. Remember the
sweets I found in Lexie's room that morning?'

You frowned, narrowing your eyes at the misty bulk of
Howth Head across the bay.

'The packet of peanut M&Ms,' I prompted. 'Lexie said she'd
never seen them before.'

'Oh. Right.'

'This afternoon . . . after George . . . I just had a thought. I
took the packet out of the drawer and had another look. And
they're not sweets. Or some of them aren't.'

'What do you mean?'

I took the packet from my pocket, emptied the multicoloured contents into my hand and passed them to you.

'I didn't know they did white M&Ms,' you said, looking at
the mound of sweets in your palm.

'They don't.'

'Then what are these?' You picked out one of the white ones.

I switched on my phone torch and shone it on your palm.
Drizzle tapped on my hood. I moved the light, focusing it on
the white pill.

'Lan . . . oxin,' you read. 'Where have I heard that name?'

'It's digoxin,' I said. 'I googled it. It's used for heart problems. It's highly toxic, especially to children. If she'd taken even
a couple of these, her heart would have stopped.'

'B–but . . . but . . . why did she have them in her room?'

'She didn't. She said she'd never seen them before. And I believe her, because if she'd eaten one of these we'd have known all about it.'

The rain grew heavier. My torch lit your face from below. Darkness surrounded you like a cloak. The other walker was climbing the steps to the overpass. The beach was empty again.

'So . . . how?'

'I couldn't say for sure. But I've been thinking. Remember the bang we heard the night we were having the Lebanese? I'd forgotten until you reminded me. Like something hitting glass.'

'Yes.'

'I found these sweets the following morning. We checked the living-room window that night and looked out the front door. But we never checked upstairs –'

By now you had joined in and were talking with me, over me. 'It was warm and the bedroom windows were open –'

You stopped.

'She was in her room,' you said. 'She was in her fucking room.'

This is what I remember. Seaweed, and the thousands of shells. The glistening black rocks. The worm casts and the tide lines. The whiff of algae. In my mind now it is still very clear. As it turns out, there were some things I missed, but only because it's impossible to look at everything at once. Those things I did see remain stamped on my brain. So much of what's happened – the playdate, Vanessa's subsequent behaviour – I've described over and again to police, to solicitors, to other parents, but this night was between us alone and I've never had to describe it to anyone else. Except you.

This is the best I can do. We had stopped walking just before the steps to the overpass, and now, the rain intensifying, we started towards them again. The overpass led across the Dart tracks to the road, a road that on that wet night would be quiet, everything shut except the petrol stations. It was hidden from us, however, by the overpass and the trees overhanging the steps. It was quite dark by now; I remember noticing because when I paused to bend down before the steps I could hardly see my shoe.

As we climbed the steps there was a sudden loud drumming of drops on leaves and metal, a sound which receded again just as quickly as we entered a bubble of hush, cocooned by the shoulder-high metal walls and the trees and the pebble-dashed backs of houses on the road. Someone was ahead of us on the walkway, about to descend the opposite steps to the street. It was the person in the luminous coat whom I had seen on the beach earlier. The person glanced over their shoulder just as the streetlights came on. It was a woman and it was Vanessa.

You stopped walking. 'What –'

'It's Friday,' I said meaninglessly. At least, it was meaningless to you, but I remembered her saying that her book club met on a Friday evening in someone's house by the Dart tracks. *I can just walk home if I've had a drinkie.*

As if in a trance, as if wound up and placed on the walkway, you began to move towards her.

'Adam.' My voice was alarmed. 'What are you doing?'

You kept going. Could I have stopped you? Did I know what was going to happen?

You can drive yourself mad if you ask such questions.

'Hey!' you shouted. 'Hey!'

Whether she heard you or knew who we were, I couldn't tell. She kept walking.

'*Hey!* Stop! I want a word!'

At that she turned.

'*Excuse* me?'

'Who was in my daughter's room?'

323

She stared at you in her exaggeratedly incredulous way. 'Are you on drugs?'

'Who killed our dog?'

She huffed out one of her disbelieving little laughs. There was a raucous quality to it. I could tell she'd had a few drinks. Her hair was straggly, her eyes slightly unfocused.

'I'm calling the guards.' She began to tap unsteadily on her phone.

'*Who was in my daughter's room?*'

She tapped on. You strode towards her. But Vanessa was not afraid of you. Men did not get rough in Vanessa's world. Vanessa with her well-connected spouse and her adoring parents who thought she could do no wrong. Men were respectful of Vanessa, and afraid. She and her lawyer buddies knew all their weak spots. She had nothing to fear from you or your chino-wearing ilk. She stood her ground, swaying slightly, and tapped away. You reached her, snatched the phone and hurled it to the ground.

CLANG it went as it landed. Drops blurred the lit-up screen. In silence we all looked at the web of cracks in one corner. It seemed such a huge thing, a line that had been crossed, a veneer that had been ripped away. Your breaths came hard through your nose; already, however, I could see that your rapid-on, rapid-off anger was starting to subside.

'How dare you?' Vanessa's mouth was an O of outrage. 'How DARE you! I'll have you up for assault.'

'*Assault?* You strangled my dog, you brazen, narcissistic loon.'

'You're crazy! You're off your head. Like your psycho wife.' She looked at me then and the sheer hatred in her eyes made me recoil.

'You listen –'

'No, *you* listen!' Her dander was well and truly up now.

Perhaps it was the alcohol. Or perhaps, again, with no one else there to see, she could finally let her sweet, fluffy mask fall away. It must have been exhausting, anyway, keeping it on all the time.

'You,' she snarled, 'and your weirdo family need to get the *hell* out of our neighbourhood and go back to where you came from.'

'Or what?'

She went for it then. She let it all come bursting out. She clenched her fists and literally screamed it into your face, 'Or you and your precious fucking daughter will deserve everything you get.'

That was when you grabbed her. Your face dark and suffused as the time you had punched that man's face in London. Vanessa's head flew back.

'Adam!' I shouted.

This next part is the bit that's difficult to describe. Not because I wasn't paying attention – in fact, everything seemed slowed down and forensically clear – but because I couldn't look in every direction at once. If I'd known what was going to happen, I'd have focused more on Vanessa's face, but the thing was, it was so quick. I wasn't just looking at her, I was watching you too. And the overpass, and the empty beach down the steps, half hidden by the pelting rain.

My shout brought you to your senses. With a shove you released her and turned away. My sense was that when you let her go she seemed to flail, confused, her hands out in front of her as if she didn't know what she was doing. But that's in retrospect and may be in my head. You half staggered to the opposite wall and leaned your raised arms on it, burying your head, taking deep breaths, stretching your legs like a jogger doing warm-ups. Trying to ease the crazy pressure in your head, the vice that had closed when you felt that Lexie was under threat. You succeeded; quite quickly, in fact. Your breathing slowed. You straightened and turned, already starting to speak. Then your words died away.

I saw your confusion. The way you looked at her, then at me, a few feet away, then back to her again. Expecting an answer to the puzzle. I was the observer, after all, the audience. But I was the equivalent of the driver who glances at their phone for a moment and when they look back up it's too late.

Vanessa was on the ground. Motionless, face down, her legs twisted, one arm out to the side.

'What –'

I dropped to my knees. 'Vanessa!' Sharply, like the afternoon I had spoken to Polly. 'Vanessa!'

I rolled her on to her side. Her breathing was odd, snorting and obstructed. The streetlight was daylight-white through the black, flapping leaves. Her chest heaved in a rocking motion. Her eyes bulged. Her face, wet and streaming, was a horrible dark colour.

'What happened?' you said, your fists opening and closing. 'What's going on?'

'I don't know. Maybe she fainted.' My hand shook as I felt her neck. 'I can't feel a pulse, Adam. I think . . . I think we need to do CPR.'

'CPR?'

'Help me, Adam!'

You sank to your knees. We rolled Vanessa further on to her back and I began to press on her chest. But without Angela there I couldn't even be sure I was doing it right.

'Help!' I shouted. My voice came out cracked and thin. 'Help us! Anyone!' But the flimsy sound reached no further than the steps before dissipating in the downpour.

'Run,' I said to you. 'Run and –'

Vanessa gave another long, funny snore, which was abruptly cut off. I leaned in, trying to listen through the rain and the whipping leaves, up down, up down. I bent my lips to hers and blew into her mouth, but her chest did not move. Before my eyes her face grew darker.

'Vanessa!' I shook her. '*Vanessa!*'

I'd been here before, with my knees in a puddle and the rain running into my eyes. Polly's face had been ghostly and doll-like and smooth. I had thought she was dead. I did not then know what dead looked like. Vanessa was neither ghostly nor smooth but greyish and mottled. Not like a doll but like a hideous alien with the navy sky in its marble eyes. Again, I tried to feel her neck for a pulse. Instead, my fingers sank into a deep hole in the side of her head behind her ear. Repulsed, they jerked themselves out again.

'What's happening?' You were utterly at sea. 'Why have we stopped the CPR?'

'She's dead, Adam.'

'But . . . how . . . I don't understand.'

I was looking all around me. There! Beside her head, a rock, about the size of a plant pot, that had somehow ended up here from the beach. The top half of it was narrowed to an edge, axe-sharp. The sharp edge and the hood of her mint raincoat were stained dark red.

You saw it too. 'Oh Jesus.' You jerked up and backwards as if the rock was alive. 'I've killed her. I've killed someone.' You put your hands on your head and began to walk in circles. 'I've killed someone. I've –'

'Adam. Stop.'

'What'll I do? What'll I do?'

'STOP!'

Something gripped me then. An urgency.

'Adam. We have to go.'

'Go?'

I knew it better than I had ever known anything. The knowledge sliced through the jelly of my panic like a shining spear, to which I clung fiercely because I had to. I had to. You were too shocked to comprehend the danger you were in.

'We have to call an ambulance.'

'It's too late for that.' I pushed myself to my feet. This was a public pathway and Vanessa was lying strung across it with her caved-in head and her cracked phone. We'd get no further than the road before someone would surely come.

'We have to call the police.' You were so huge and obstinate, like a bull refusing to leave a field. How on earth was I going to get through to you, get you home?

'If you want to go to the police,' I said, 'go tomorrow. It won't make any difference to her. But please, Adam. Think about it. What good would it do? Losing you too?'

Your eyes jittered.

'Someone will have seen.'

'No one saw.'

'My DNA will be on her.'

I hadn't thought of that. Wildly, I stared around the walkway.

'Then let's get it off.'

Lord, how long it took, to get you to understand, then to agree. And that was without the physical aspect of it. Bodies are so heavy, even organically fed, Pilate-d ones like Vanessa's. But finally we – or at least you – got her upright and propped against the wall. I leaned on her to take her weight while you bent to grip her calves.

One. Two . . .

'Don't think,' I ordered as you let out a whimper. 'Just *do*!' We had Lexie to think of. If someone were to come up those steps now, from either side . . .

THREE.

You gave a massive heave and, thankfully, miraculously, over she went, out into the rain. I had thought there would be a thud, some sort of heavy noise from below, but I heard nothing over the sound of wind and water. Pulling my sleeve down over my fingers, I scooped up her phone and flung it after her. Then I grabbed your hand and towed you towards the steps to the beach. Halfway down I risked a pause to look over the railing. Had she landed? Had she caught on something and was even now dangling from the bridge above the tracks? But no. There on the track, half on, half off, lay a dark, lumpen shape, only the faintest sheen of mint distinguishing it from a log of wood or a bin bag.

'Come on!' I half dragged you down the rest of the steps.

We were one step from the sand when a dull gleam caught my eye. I shrank in horror before realizing that the light was coming not from the walkway but from further down the track. A distant yellow dot enlarged, then split into two as it approached. There came the clickety-clack of a train, the rain before it illuminated in orange slashes, like a Van Gogh painting.

'They'll stop,' you said. 'They'll see her.'

But they didn't. The train kept going, under the bridge, green and green, on and on. No jolt, no bump. It was as if Vanessa wasn't even there. The noise filled my head. The more carriages that passed over her, I thought, dazed, the more the evidence would be destroyed.

I know how calculating that sounds. I'm not proud of it. I'm not proud of any of the things I thought or did that night. I was like a machine or a block of stone. I had watched a woman I knew – the mother of a child in my daughter's class – die a horrible death, yet my only thought was of how to get you – us – home. But what good would it have done to be otherwise? What had happened was terrible beyond belief. I would think of it afterwards, over and over. But it had happened; it was done; it could not be reversed.

It's been different since the shock faded. I've relived that night a thousand times since; it's the first thing I think of every day, and the last. Maybe it always will be. Would it have helped, though, for you to go to prison? Perhaps even me, too, since I was your accomplice. What would happen to Lexie? Who would help her to read and write, to navigate this world that truly does not give one shit?

So no, I will not lie, I will not pretend that I faltered or prayed or wept as the train clattered and clattered and a long horn sounded, its pitch rising, then falling as it passed.

When it was finally gone the silence dinged at my ears. Gradually I heard again the incoming tide, the wind and the rain – though now that was starting to lighten. My legs were weak; I realized that I was gripping the railing to stop myself from falling. Cautiously I hauled myself up a couple of steps and peered over the side. Nothing. Or . . . wait. Was that her? I squinted. That dark lump, thrown to the litter-filled undergrowth? Smaller now – but that would fit. Only then did I become aware that the train had, in fact, come to a halt, a hundred or so metres beyond the bridge. The sleepers were flashing: red, black, red. There were distant voices.

My fingers dug into your arm. 'Let's go!'

We slipped northward like eels along the deserted beach, keeping to the dark of the rocks, sliding perilously on the green patches.

'Wh—wh—'

'Shush. Not now. We'll talk when we're home.'

'I didn't mean it. I didn't mean to hurt her.'

'I know. Now come.'

Our breathing was hoarse and ragged. We tried to control the loudness of it. I kept glancing behind me. The further from the overpass we went, the less detached I became and the more my feelings returned, panic being the main one, prickling like pins and needles in my head and face. *We'll never make it! Someone will come!* But when they didn't, when the stretch of empty beach between us and the overpass grew and grew and the rain cooled my cheeks and the tide rushed in my ears and the wind swept my hair off my face I felt a surge of disbelief, relief, exhilaration. And a sensation of being alive, alive, alive, so that I wanted to run out and spin in the vast, shining pools.

Adrenaline, of course. It subsided and I was back to reality, back to the slippery rocks, our noisy breathing, you, traumatized, stumbling along beside me. We picked our way along the slimy gradient. I hoped that the soles of our trainers had a good enough grip. Now would not be the time for a twisted ankle or fractured wrist.

After twenty minutes or so we crossed another walkway over the Dart tracks and came down into a park where ducks shaped like fluffy rugby balls snoozed beside a pond. Then into a small housing estate with exits to the main road. We cut through an alleyway lined with wheelie bins. There was the smell of cut grass and rotting litter. I felt very alert, noticing everything, thinking ahead. Lights in some of the windows, behind curtains and blinds. An upstairs bedroom. A child, perhaps, being read to sleep, snuggling under the duvet. The doorbell ringing: '*David Mayhew? Husband of Vanessa Mayhew? May we come in?*'

Polly with her significant brain injury and her damaged kidneys being woken from her sleep and – Stop! Stop now! But my heart came back into my throat and raced and raced and raced.

By the time we got home I had pushed my agitation away again, pared all emotion to a cold, cold calm. Because one of us had to. My memory is of you sitting on the edge of the bed in the early hours, sweating and shaking as if you were having a seizure. I had never seen you like this, so terrified and out of control.

'Do you think she's definitely dead?'

'She wasn't breathing. Then she dropped from the overpass and a train hit her.' Bluntly.

You covered your face with your hands.

'It's cold.' I felt sorry for you. 'Let's get you into bed.'

I helped you to remove your shirt. Your entire body was trembling uncontrollably, the way George's had the time some teens had once set off fireworks in the park.

'Can I have some water?' you asked.

When I returned you were looking at your knees and talking to yourself. 'I've lost everything,' you kept whispering, over and over. 'Everything.'

I handed you the glass.

'Thank you.' Your teeth chattered on the rim. 'I don't seem to be able to . . .'

'It's the shock. You need to try to sleep.'

'I killed her.' You kept on saying it. 'I killed a person. But I don't understand . . .'

'Shhh. Shh.' I squeezed your arm.

'The police . . . We should have stayed. We shouldn't have left! They'll know it was us!'

'Let's hope they don't connect.'

'Of course they'll connect! We made all those complaints about Vanessa. We'll be the first people they think of. And the rock.' A convulsive movement. 'The rock she landed on. They'll find her blood on it. They'll know she died on the bridge, not on the tracks, they'll know –'

'Don't worry about the rock,' I said.

'What?'

'I took it with me. I dumped it way down the beach. The tide's fully in now. I should think it's highly unlikely that anyone will find it.'

You stared at me.

'*If* the police come,' I said, 'we'll face them. We'll give our side of the story.'

'*We?* You didn't do anything.'

'Yes, I did. I'm just as responsible as you.'

'How?'

'I could have stopped you.'

'You couldn't. How could you have? Don't try to share the blame.'

'There is no blame. It was an accident.' My mouth stung. I had bitten the inside of my cheek and also banged and scraped my forehead, presumably while getting Vanessa over the parapet. One of my sleeves was torn. I knew nothing about forensics. I had often walked George over that overpass and never seen a CCTV camera, but what if there was one and I'd missed it? Would all this effort have been in vain and we'd be caught anyway, and Lexie . . .

'I don't understand it,' you were saying. 'I know I shouldn't have grabbed her like that, but it was barely . . . I didn't . . . I don't understand.'

'I read somewhere,' I said, 'that if you put pressure on the neck in the wrong place – plus, I think she'd had quite a bit to drink. She must have got dizzy and fallen. Even by accident, if you get the exact spot on the carotid artery – it can happen very quickly. Seconds, even. She'd have lost consciousness almost immediately. She wouldn't have suffered . . .'

My voice had risen, cracking on 'suffered'. I heard the emotion in it, and so did you. It surprised you, I could tell. You lifted your head and stared at me again. In your confused state – mine too, I know – my attempts to reassure you seemed only to befuddle you even more.

For a while we lay in a punch-drunk silence. I thought you had fallen asleep but then you stirred and groaned and put your arms over your face.

'I'm a murderer.'

'Shh. No.'

'I am! How can you bear it? To be here with me. You don't deserve this. You or Lexie. I'll turn myself in. Tomorrow. I won't force you to keep this secret. It's not fair to you.'

I sat up on my elbows. 'What good will it do Lexie to lose you?'

'She doesn't deserve a father like me.'

'She doesn't deserve *not* to have a father.'

You groaned again into your arms.

I reached over to pull them away.

'Look at me. *Look* at me.' Reluctantly, you did. 'You never intended to harm her. She threatened Lexie, she – my God, Adam, she killed our dog. She tried to *poison our child.*'

'Exactly! That's why we need to tell them.' You began to throw off the duvet. 'I'll call Flannan. I'll ring him. I'll get on to him straight away.'

'Wait!' I clutched your arm. You resisted, trying to pull it away. 'Justice doesn't always happen. You *know* that. You heard Flannan saying miscarriages of justice happen all the time.' Your arm was still tugging against mine. I held on and spoke rapidly. 'They'll say we had no proof. That any of it was her. They'll say how could we be sure. And I know it was an accident – but the thing is – she's dead, Adam. A woman is dead. And we . . . we threw her over the bridge.'

Your breath came in hard bursts through your nose.

'I don't want us to lose you. *Lexie* to lose you. And what . . . what about CareyComp?'

You stopped tugging.

'You've only just signed that contract. All those hours and nights of work. All the risks you took. All that time you had to spend away from Lexie. But no smoke without fire, is what people will say. It'll all be for nothing.'

334

Still, you didn't move. Even your nose breathing had stopped.

'No one saw us on that bridge.' The more I thought about it, the more I was certain. 'If the gardai do come, we'll defend ourselves. Our daughter was in danger. Vanessa had threatened her. *Assaulted* her! She . . . you lost your temper. It was an accident. In the moment, we panicked and ran. It's true, isn't it? But Adam — just suppose they don't come? Why ask for trouble?'

A pause. Your breathing re-started. Slowly, muscle by muscle, you sank back down on to the bed.

I lay down beside you. I saw your profile as you looked unhappily at the ceiling. Your chin sagged, giving you a hint of jowl I hadn't seen before. You looked older. Vulnerable.

My voice came then in the darkness, a voice I wouldn't have thought was mine, harder and more implacable than I had ever heard it. I said, 'Vanessa brought this on herself. On *us*. So, don't talk about blame, Adam. You don't deserve to be punished. And if they don't find us, and if you say nothing, then neither will I. *Ever!* This will be our secret. Do you understand?'

The Irish rain, never far from us, was back, ghostly and insistent at our window. After a long pause, you whispered, 'I do.'

I reached for you. For the first time in a very long time we took each other in our arms. We held each other for a while, but the night was close and humid. At some point we became too hot and our breaths in each other's faces became too much and we had to separate again.

34

I doubt I slept for more than an hour or two, but I did sleep, because when I woke I was briefly confused. The curtains were open and the room was filled with sunlight. But why was I still dressed? Why did I ache from head to toe, all my muscles and the inside of my cheek? Why were you sitting on your side of the bed, facing the wall, looking so haggard and grey? And George. No George downstairs, claws pattering like rain as he waited to be let out. His loving, lively essence vanquished, the gap so tangible and painful I could almost feel the air shift to try to fill it.

And Vanessa! Like a lift plummeting the memory plunged back, sucking the air from my lungs. I sat up, hauling in breaths. Did her family know? Had they heard? And the BMs – she was their core, the engine that kept them running. They would hardly be able to believe it. Her death would stun everyone. The shock to South County Dublin would reverberate for a long time.

I thought of Lexie, asleep in your childhood bedroom with Breda down the hall. When she woke, her first thought, I knew, would be of George. She would lie there and miss him and grieve and pay her respects. Then she would get up and have her cornflakes and watch her mermaid show on Netflix and your mum would cheer her up, planning something nice for the day. Whatever she did, she would be safe. I wouldn't have to worry about her any more. Later today I would call her, just to hear her high, sweet voice on the phone. *I love you, Mummy*. The comfort and joy of it.

Movement on your side of the bed. I turned to you.

'The gardaí will be here today,' you said in a monotone. 'I'm just surprised they aren't already.'

Every time a car passed we both twitched. I was glad that Lexie wasn't there and we didn't have to pretend that everything was all right. Your phone rang almost continuously – work calls – until eventually I switched it off. You walked in figures of eight, cracking your knuckles. I was worried for you. I offered you coffee, but you shook me away. Voices burbled from the Alexa on the kitchen counter.

'*. . . death of a woman last night in Dublin . . .*'

You clutched me.

'Turn it up,' you said hoarsely. 'Alexa – Turn! Up! The! News!'

'*The turnip is a root vegetable . . .*'

I wasn't surprised she had misheard. 'Alexa,' I ordered, more coherently. 'Turn up the volume.'

The newsreader's suddenly loud voice filled the room.

'*. . . Dart tracks near Seapoint. Emergency services were called to the scene just after . . .*'

It must have been a slow news day because Vanessa was all over the airwaves. Hourly, Alexa kept us informed.

'*. . . local woman sustained multiple injuries after apparently falling from the Dart overpass . . .*'

'*. . . dead woman's family has been informed. Inquiries are ongoing. Gardaí are appealing for witnesses to contact them at . . .*'

'Her family knows,' you said wretchedly.

I concentrated on making us both poached eggs on toast for lunch. We couldn't have managed anything more.

'But why aren't they *here*?' More cracking and pacing. 'Any minute now they'll ring the bell. I wish they'd get on with it.'

But they did not. No one called to our door. Not that day, not any day.

'I don't understand it,' you kept saying. 'You made all those

337

complaints about Vanessa. Surely, they logged them, put them in their Pulse thingy. They were going to talk to Vanessa about George. I don't get it. They've been utterly useless from the start, but this is beyond even what I expected.'

I didn't understand it either. I'd have thought they would have at least asked us – asked all the neighbours – if we'd seen Vanessa out and about that evening. But there was no point in speculating.

I persuaded you to turn your phone back on. To keep things as normal as possible. You weren't up to taking work calls – your attention was all over the place – so I dealt with those. I took messages briskly and pleasantly, as if I was your secretary. 'I'm so sorry but he's at a meeting. Can you put that in an email and I'll make sure he gets back to you? Thank you *so* much!'

It wasn't as difficult as you might expect to keep up appearances. Often, when one person in a partnership falls apart, the other has no choice but to put their own feelings aside and step up to bat. Life must go on. It's always been the way.

Your mum kept Lexie with her for a few days, and I'll always be grateful to her for that. Not that she minded. Now that the summer holidays were here she jumped at the chance to have Lexie all to herself. I suspect she thought that you and I might be having a second honeymoon. Working on providing her with another grandchild. We joined them in Stillorgan for dinner a couple of times – I'm not sure if you remember; much of the time you were like a zombie – and we did our best to laugh and chat as if everything was normal.

One thing I had to do before Lexie came home again was decide what to do with George's body. No one had called or asked to see it – to your utter incredulity. I reminded you that perhaps the local gardaí had other things on their minds just now. But what did one do with a dead dog if one only had a tiny garden?

Eventually, one evening I simply put him in the boot and drove him to the Wicklow Mountains. I parked on a deserted grassy lane near a pine forest and tipped his body into deep undergrowth, set well back from the trail. It was a glorious, golden evening. From up here I could see all the way to the sea. I sat for a while by the dense ferns, the mossy fallen trunks, but I felt nothing. No sense of him, I mean. His sunny little presence was gone, as surely as if he had never run on these paths, never splashed in those streams.

I was glad. I wouldn't have wanted to think he was there with me now. *Pressure on the neck*, I had said to you. Something to do with the carotid artery. Both sides at the same time, it had to be, and if you did it correctly it would be painless. Consciousness would be lost immediately. There would have been no pain. I hoped, anyway.

Vanessa's funeral, I heard afterwards, was very well attended. Hundreds of people – family, neighbours, Dave's work colleagues, a large St Catherine's contingent – spilled out of the church and into the car park and the three pubs around. You and I of course did not attend. Instead, Lexie and I joined you on a trip to London. We visited my mother and went to see *The Lion King*, and she caught up with Lilah and Jasmine. We cleared the last of our belongings out of the Vauxhall flat. 'Bye, flat,' Lexie said, unmoved. 'I don't think I'll be seeing you again.'

Back in Dublin, I reached out to Orla to say how sorry I was for her loss. Vanessa's friends, Orla told me, were having a lunch in her memory and I was more than welcome to join them. I tried to refuse – I didn't think it right that I be there – but she was insistent.

Lunch was in an upmarket little bistro near the school, a place the BMs had often visited. It was very Vanessa: classy, tasteful, the best in the area. I was wary of intruding on their long-standing friendship and grief, but none of the BMs seemed to think it strange that I was there. Or perhaps they simply didn't have the energy to protest. Without Vanessa they had an aimless, wandering air as if their battery had wound down. She had been the load-bearing axle that kept the spokes together and the wheels on the road. Without her they were like sticks scattered in the dust: scatty Isabel, timid, low self-esteem Orla, Single White Female Erica, Marina a barely-there shell.

They spoke about Vanessa in a subdued way. It transpired that Dave, in fact, *had* been seeing another woman all along.

'Someone from his work,' Orla told us. 'It came out at the inquest. She just moved to their Dublin office last year.'

Whether Vanessa had genuinely thought that the woman was me or whether she had just used me as a convenient vent for her anger, I will never know.

It appeared that the night Vanessa died she had opened up to her book club about Dave's philandering. She'd had quite a bit to drink – several Hendricks and the best part of a bottle of Pinot Grigio – and it had all come pouring out. She'd told them she'd had enough of Dave's womanizing and was going to divorce him. She'd been very upset, crying and disinhibited in the way that people can sometimes be at book-club meetings. All that literature and drama. Several of the members, apparently, had worried about her walking home alone in the state she was in – there had been some discussion about it while she was in the loo – but the general feeling was that she just needed to sleep it off and she'd be fine.

At the inquest, Orla said, there had been mention of the stress Vanessa had been under, what with Polly's illness and Dave's cushion-humping tendencies. Friends, family and her book club had testified that she had been behaving erratically, drinking more than usual, even going so far as to accuse a neighbour of having tried to murder her child. The night she had died she had been intoxicated, rambling on about murder and revenge. The inquest declared an open verdict.

'The family is moving away,' Orla said. 'To Cork, where Dave's mum lives. Dave's in an absolute heap. Says the work woman was just a fling and Vanessa was always his true soul-mate. So sad for them all.'

'I'm very sorry.' I spoke up. 'I know Vanessa and I had our difficulties after Polly's anaphylaxis —'

'That wasn't the real her,' Orla said firmly. 'She was under so much stress at the time she hardly knew what she was saying.'

'I know. And there were times also when she was very welcoming to me. I'm sorry I never had the chance to get to know her properly. It's devastating for Polly. Lexie is extremely upset.'

'Gorgeous, kind little Lexie,' Isabel said tearfully, and Orla squeezed my arm.

'I'm glad you came,' she whispered when we were dividing up the bill. 'Keep in touch over the summer, won't you?' Orla is a good person, a thoroughly decent woman. I have always thought so.

35

That's it, Adam. That's all I can think of to say. I hope you can now understand how it all links together, how what happened on the bridge was not solely down to you.

I can see that you're exhausted. These days you are always exhausted, to the extent that I've wondered if you need to see a doctor. I had hoped that once the initial trauma had faded and the threat of the gardaí had receded you would begin to recover. But you remain depleted, a ghost of your former self. It will take time, I know. All I can do is support you.

'How did it come to this?' you asked earlier, bewildered, in the garden. 'So many lives destroyed.'

And again, when we were carrying the wine bottle and glasses to the kitchen: 'I still don't understand. Why the gardaí never came to speak to us. They must have known there was bad blood between us.'

'Well, they're not coming now,' I said. 'The inquest is over. Dave is the only person who might have been difficult, but I can't see that happening. Vanessa was the energetic one in that household.'

'What were their names?'

'Who?'

'The gardaí you spoke to about the harassment. The ones who called to the house the night someone was in our garden.'

'I can't remember now.'

'Did they give you a Pulse reference number?'

'I think so. Why?'

'It's just weird, that's all.'

'Adam.' I spoke gently. 'Let it go. It's over. No one alive knows what happened. No one but me.'

You looked at me strangely when I said that. I wonder what you were thinking.

36

Shortly after the 'I love you' conversation by the Thames between Adam and Zoë things in Ireland took a turn for the dramatic. A neighbour's child, it appeared, had been injured in an accident, and the police, most bizarrely, were involved. Adam had to spend a considerable amount of time in Dublin sorting things out.

Zoë tried hard to be patient, but everything she did, it was as if a piece of her was missing. The whole thing went on for far longer than either of them had expected. 'The kid's mother is being very difficult,' Adam said. 'She's a few olives short of a pizza.' It was, Zoë thought, very strange. Didn't the Irish police have anything better to do?

While he was there Adam had to do all the work for the American contract in his tiny Dublin bedroom, and it was driving him crazy. To add to it, from things his wife was saying, she seemed under the impression that Adam being at home so much more meant that their marriage was the best it had been in years. Which, Adam said, made him feel like a shit because nothing could be further from the truth.

Zoë wondered. But she said nothing. She couldn't. When this crisis was over and he came back to her, things would be how they had been. In the meantime, she must stay calm. Trust her instincts and all would be well.

On the night he finally came back to London after almost two months in Dublin, they went to The Fat Noodle, one of their favourites. Afterwards they sat on his balcony in the balmy dusk drinking whiskey and soda.

'I've missed this,' Adam sighed. 'So, so much. And being here with you.'

Zoë hugged herself. It had been a lovely evening. She needn't have worried. She'd been starting to doubt, even just a little, but this evening had entirely re-confirmed the bond between them. Adam seemed glad and thankful to be back. He had completed most of the work for the contract and they looked forward to spending a few lazy days together when Zoë could get some time off work.

But then came yet more drama.

'The kid's mother is harassing us. Notes through the letterbox. People hanging around our garden at night.'

'Why?'

'Who knows? She's barmy. She's been threatening to harm Lexie. The police are involved again.'

'And what do they think?'

'Not much, it seems. But my wife is very on edge.'

Quelle surprise.

As a result of all of this, Adam had to go to Ireland again.

Abruptly, despondently, Zoë said, 'We can't go on like this.' She hadn't meant to blurt it out, but the uncertainty was taking its toll. She couldn't help the niggly sense that the longer Adam spent in Ireland, the more his attention drifted and the less concerned he became about what was happening in London. She hated not knowing, not being able to plan. She couldn't help wondering if he was taking her for a fool.

Adam took her in his arms.

'I meant what I said, Zo. I want this to work. I know how ludicrous this allergy business sounds, but I've just got this . . . this feeling. I wish that woman didn't live so close to Lexie. I wish we'd never met her. There's something very off about the way she's behaving. Something . . . I don't want to sound melodramatic, but something evil.'

Zoë almost snorted. He was sounding as paranoid as his wife now.

'So you've decided you're moving back to England. But if your wife has her way, you'll all end up living in Cumbria or somewhere and I'll never see you again.'

'No. Listen. I've made my decision. It's time Sara and I talked about separating. We want different things and it's time she had all the facts. I

345

almost told her the other evening, but something interrupted us and I chickened out . . . no, Zo, *listen!* Next time I won't back out. As soon as the contract is signed, I'm going to tell her. I haven't been fair to her. She needs to be able to plan her life too.'

The day the American contract was signed – after all the hands had been shaken and the elbows had been gripped and the mini tacos and glasses of champagne had been consumed – Adam and Zoë embraced at the entrance to the Piccadilly Line to Heathrow.

'Good luck,' Zoë said, 'with the . . . you know. The reveal.'

They kissed, tenderly and deeply. She stood at the turnstile, waving him off until the top of his head had disappeared down the escalator. She knew he wasn't looking forward to the discussion with Sara. The effect it would have on his daughter. Zoë did feel guilty. She was not a monster. But this was life. And surely Sara must know anyway that things weren't right between them. She couldn't possibly be as oblivious as Adam seemed to think.

Later that evening her phone rang. She pounced on it.

'Ad—'

In a trembly, faint voice he said, 'Our dog's been killed.'

'Your –'

'That woman strangled him.'

'Strangled *George*? Oh no! Oh, Adam! But what –'

'I have to go,' he said abruptly. 'My wife's coming back.'

'But –'

'I have to go. I will tell her. I swear I will. But not now. Now is not a good time.'

She could hear from his voice how distressed he was.

'I understand,' she said. 'And I'm very sorry. About George. I know how much you loved him.'

'Zoë.'

'Yes?'

'You are . . . you are amazing. We'll talk very soon. I promise. I love you.'

It was the last proper conversation they ever had.

At first, she simply waited to hear back from him. The phone call had been alarming. So this neighbour woman had actually killed George. It seemed that Adam hadn't been paranoid after all. Or making excuses. The woman really was dangerous. When, by midnight, she hadn't heard anything, she sent him a message. *Thinking of you. Zx*

No response. Perhaps he was still overwhelmed by grief. She had an early start the next day so she made herself go to bed.

The following morning she messaged him again. By the afternoon it still hadn't been read. It was unlike him. Worried, she phoned him, but the call went straight to voicemail.

'Get in touch,' she told him. 'Even just a thumb emoji. Just to let me know you're all right.'

Still nothing. Now she was seriously concerned. Was he hurt? Ill? Had something happened? How would she even know? She googled the Irish news websites. Their hospital waiting lists were in crisis. A government minister was being questioned about deposits to his account. A woman had jumped off a bridge on to a railway track. Nothing, though, about Adam or any of his family.

That unglued neighbour, strangling his dog. What else might she be capable of? Should Zoë contact the Irish police herself? But then they'd want to know who she was, and if Adam . . . Anyway, if something had happened to him, or if he was missing, his wife would surely have reported it.

Wouldn't she?

The myriad possibilities ran through Zoë's mind.

Two days later, her phone rang, and it was him.

'Adam! My God, I've been climbing the walls! Where on earth have you been?'

In a strange, flat voice he said, 'I'm sorry. We can't see each other any more.'

It was such an odd thing to say that she presumed she'd misheard.

'What's happened? Did you tell your wife? Are you all right?'

Tonelessly he repeated it. 'I can't see you again. We're finished.'

'I don't understand. What's going on?'

The call ended.

Was he in trouble? She knew he was. He had sounded so lifeless, as if he was ill or drugged. She called him again, not caring if his wife heard.

'Don't do this,' she begged his voicemail. 'Please. Tell me what's wrong. Whatever it is, we can work it out.'

She called him again. All day. Called and called, but he didn't answer.

Finally, days later, drearily trying him yet again, she heard a click, then the sound of breathing down the line. She sat up.

'Adam! Adam, for God's sake. Thank God you're –'

'I'm sorry.' It was a woman's voice. 'But Adam is not available.'

37

You're fast asleep now, but I'm still awake. It's sometime in the early hours. I'm sitting up in bed, my arms around my knees. Through the flimsy, unlined curtains a streetlight illuminates your desk, just enough for me to make out the shapes of your laptop, your phone, your piles of paperwork. Soon you'll be opening your new office in Sandyford. You'll be glad, I know, to have space and privacy, a base for staff. A proper PA. Beside me you twitch and mumble. Your face, even in your sleep, is deeply troubled.

Earlier this evening you looked at me oddly and I wondered what you were thinking. Whatever it was, I know you will never say to me. Some things can't be said.

'How did it come to this?' you asked in the garden.

Well, as I've tried my best to explain – and I have told you, if not every single thing that happened, then at least as much as I thought you needed to know – what happened had its roots long before the playdate. Vanessa, as I think I have more than adequately outlined, played a major role with the way she behaved. Tragic as her death is, especially for her children, I won't pretend that St Catherine's won't be a gentler and kinder place with her gone. Lexie will be much happier. You see, I know what happens to these children, and how all it takes is one person to point the herd, to make everything so much worse. Grace, for example, destroyed Heather. And me too. After Grace, I was never the same. A part of me, I am convinced, failed to develop but instead became withered and lost in the shadows. Who knows what I would have been capable of? Instead, here I am, my smile unformed, my personality grey and passionless – and I can no more help being like this than Lexie can help being sensitive and clumsy and dreamy – or than you can help being a cheat.

That's right! You thought I didn't know, but I do.

It started when I saw the messages beginning to pop up on your phone that you so carelessly, thoughtlessly, left lying about. From time to time, you were stupid enough to mention her, desperate to talk about her, even to me.

At first, I thought she might be some deluded, far-off client or one-night stand. That, I could have coped with. You were travelling a lot, away from home, lonely. You're not a saint. But when I saw the earring that had been left in the Vauxhall flat on top of your pile of papers – did Magda leave it there on purpose? I wonder. She knew I was staying that weekend and she's never been your biggest fan. And so, when my mother didn't want to have dinner with me that Saturday evening and I found myself at a loose end, I came up with the idea of hiring a private detective to see what was going on. To see what I was up against.

Zoë. Clever. Pretty. And most of all, young. All those comments you'd been making lately about 'women my age'. And she lived just across the river from you. Convenient!

I could observe, gather knowledge, but it was still happening. I'll never know how far it had gone but, I suspect, quite far. Further than any of the others. Oh yes – Anja was the first one I knew about, but she certainly wasn't the last. The thing about you is you like the game, the challenge. You like things to be new and exciting. But the more adrenaline you crave, the riskier the games become. Games have losers, and because you're the only one who knows you are playing, the loser will never be you. We were heading for disaster, and I was filled with fear for my struggling little daughter.

The evening of the Lebanese takeaway, when we talked about staying in Ireland and you looked shifty and said you had something to tell me . . . did you really think I didn't know? What you were about to say? I was desperate, thinking of Lexie upstairs, so innocently asleep while her dad was about to destroy her life over a tub of hummus. I had to stop you. I would not listen. I had to think on my feet, and in the moment all I could come up with was inventing a noise at the window. But it worked, and you crawled back under your rock. For a little while.

But my private detective kept digging. And the call I got from him that night – the night before George died – confirmed that she was with you even as we spoke. In your flat! Mere hours after our daughter had been assaulted in the park! So agitated and worried as you were on the phone, but as soon as you hung up – *poof!* – Lexie vanished from your mind.

I knew then that unless I did something definitive you were going to leave us. Leave Lexie! It would have destroyed her. Something had to happen. Something enormous had to take place that would shear you off permanently from this woman, send you spinning away from her orbit.

Since Vanessa's death, I've watched the messages, increasingly frantic: *Adam. Call me. Please. Whatever's wrong we can deal with it.* I've watched this Zoë being ghosted and I've been glad.

You won't go back to her now, will you? You can't. You can't afford to upset me.

She deserves her pain.

A few days ago, she rang, looking for you. I answered your phone in my new capacity as your secretary.

'Adam?' Eager. Young. Quite rah. Public school, I thought, or at least grammar school in a well-to-do area. 'Adam, for God's sake. Thank God you're –'

'I'm sorry,' I said courteously, 'but Adam is not available.'

'Oh.' Pause. 'Well, can I speak to him, please?'

Crisp. That's the word. Despite a slight uncertainty, her voice was strong and brisk. A voice that was accustomed to people hopping to it when she said the word. *Forceps, nurse, quickly. Why aren't those lab results ready? Kindly get your husband on the phone.*

I said, very politely, 'I'm sorry to have to inform you that your services will no longer be required.'

Silence. And I knew by the shape of her silence that this was the last time she would call.

Don't be mistaken, Adam. Don't see this for something it's not. I'm not doing any of this because I love you. The truth is, I feel nothing for you. This last year has crystallized things about you that I had long been refusing to accept. On your home ground you are boorish, materialistic, selfish and violent. Even after Vanessa's death your main concern was what *you* had lost. Whatever was once between us is long gone. If it was just me, this Zoë could have had you, and welcome.

But this isn't about me.

Here's the thing, Adam. The part that complicates all of this, the part that makes it impossible for me to hate you. Through all of this – Polly's collapse, the police, the lawyers – you were so supportive, especially to Lexie. All the threats to Lexie that I told you about – the bangs on the window, the menacing picture through the letterbox, the paint poured into her hood. George's death – these things were what brought you back to us. The fear that Lexie was in danger. You are such a good father, an excellent father, in fact. Your love for Lexie made you drop everything, even Zoë, no matter how much of a hold she had on you. The only thing, I knew, that would.

But as soon as the danger was past you kept slipping away from us again. From Lexie. So I knew I would have to bring you back in a more definitive way. She is, I know you agree, the most important person in all of this. Sweet little Lexie – the best of both of us – whose gentle, sunny personality was being destroyed by bullies, like Heather's had been, like Steve's. By the sort of people who can do this to others and never, ever pay.

Did I, you asked tentatively on one occasion, know that Vanessa was going to be there that night? The question surprised me. Did I, did you mean, plan the rain, the empty beach? Did I plan for you to lose your temper just at that moment? For you to grab her and shake her like that, then turn your back so that you did not see what came next or what exactly happened to make her fall? Did I plan for someone to have carried a rock up from the beach and placed it at that exact spot beside her bleeding, caved-in head?

It would have been impossible. To have all those pieces in place in advance . . . no one could do that. But your temper, lately so easily triggered, meant that a tragedy could have occurred at any time. It was always there, your anger, low-burning, ready to be stoked, an accident waiting to happen.

The real tragedy of course is that it need never have happened at all. People were on our side now. Luisa, Orla, Isabel. Vanessa had lost her edge. Cracks had appeared in the BMs' loyalties. We could have left it there. If it hadn't been for Zoë, there would have been no need for Vanessa to die.

Grace Gillespie. Funny how I've kept coming back to her. I haven't thought about her in so long, yet tonight here she's been, popping up in almost every memory. Perhaps because I've been thinking about why I am the way I am. What happened to the part of me that was lost. Or perhaps was never there in the first place; who knows? The magazines I read as a teen, *Just Seventeen* and *Mizz*, used to tell us girls: *you can't help how you look but you can make yourself beautiful inside.* Of course, now I know it's the opposite. With enough money and determination, you can look whatever way you want to, but it's almost impossible to change your personality, except for very short periods. You're born the way you are, or made it from an early age, the way a plant in a pot is trained to grown in one direction or another and once the wood has hardened it won't bend back. All I know is that often I have felt as if I was looking at other people through glass, separate from them, bewildered by their passions and enthusiasms for the most trivial things, convinced they must be faking it. I go through the motions, but their pain and pleasure, their pointless scurrying and busywork, is a mystery to me. Even you I would have let go without much of a fight.

But then Lexie came. And I finally understood what others must feel. It can make you do anything, this zeal, this love. Build cathedrals, write poetry. Fly to the edge of the universe or to the core of an atom. Anything at all. There is nothing I wouldn't do for her.

Hormones, of course, this drive to protect our young. We're no better than bacteria in that regard. Clustering, protecting, sharing food, living off other species. Willing to kill to further our own genes. A primal urge dressed up as a great, great love. But there it is. And I know you feel it too.

This, Adam, is what binds me to you, and you to me. Nature brought us together and let us go again when she was made. But we're not finished, because Lexie still needs you. Lexie will not grow up without a father. Lexie will not one day meet you in a Harvester and see only a stranger. So don't worry, Adam. Your secret will always be safe with me.

Epilogue

This morning I feel so much better. It's been such a relief to have had this heart-to-heart with you – probably one of the most comprehensive we've ever had. Unfortunately, you fell asleep before I reached the final section of my narrative, but that's all right. Probably there are some things it's best you don't know. A little mystery is good for a marriage.

Today is Lexie's first day back at school. Here she comes, skipping down the stairs in her green tracksuit and neat plaits, so happy to have us both there.

'You missed my first day last year,' she reminds you. 'When you were working in London.'

I see the way you look at her, red-eyed and shadowed and unshaven. Still so subdued despite all I can do to try to convince you to move on. You hug her, your face crumpling. There are times I find I can still feel a fondness for you. After all, when it mattered, you stepped up for Lexie and me, and for that I am truly grateful. You and I were good together once. All may not be lost. Who knows what might have happened with this Zoe person in the end. It's possible she would, in time, have gone the way of all the others, that she was a proxy, a symbol of your yearning for your youth and your old life in London. But I'm tired of taking these risks. It's time for us both to focus on what we have and to be thankful.

It's okay. As long as we have Lexie, we'll be okay. It's not that I deludedly think that my child is better than anyone else's. But she has her strengths, of course she has. With all her difficulties and her shyness, she has a surprising inner confidence and a strong sense of herself – her passion for animals, her love of art, of other people. Being part of a team. Being kind, curious, sensitive. People like Lexie are a joy, worth saving. The world is a better place just because they are in it. She can simply exist, simply be; she does not have to hide who she is. To pretend. Like I have to. Whether born or made, I cannot unmake myself, and I'll spend my life tweaking and tuning myself so as not to drive people away. Vanessa, too, had to wear her mask and never ever let it slip. It is exhausting, I know.

'Muu-uum,' Lexie shouts. 'Where's my hockey bag?'

I shake myself. She hasn't played hockey since the spring.

'Under our bed. I'll get it.'

Rummaging in the under-bed storage I hear a crackle. And I freeze. Way down under the winter jackets something scrunches in my hand. How could I have forgotten? How could I have been so careless? In all the fuss and trauma, it had completely slipped my mind. I glance behind me, making sure you and Lexie are still downstairs. Then quietly, painstakingly, I draw out the item. A plastic multipack of mini chocolate bars with the label ChockoFest on the front. One of the bars is missing. I push the pack deep into my bag.

'Coming!' I shout.

On the way to school Lexie runs ahead of me down the hill.

'Hold up,' I call. There's a bin on the street. I remove the multipack from my bag and pop it through the slot.

Lexie hops impatiently on the pavement. The sun shines through her hair. It looks like a halo. In all my life, she's the only thing that has mattered. There is nothing I wouldn't do for her. Nothing at all.

The playground is filled with children, racing about, scream-ing and shouting in their Irish accents. Parents everywhere, mothers mostly, with their pushchairs and scooters and cocka-poos, all talking at once, their mouths opening and closing, a huge, multicoloured, bovine herd. For a moment I falter, feeling the familiar weariness.

But they're just mothers, after all. Doing what mothers do, clustering protectively around their young, swapping facts and tips, cooperating to make their children's lives better. I pull myself together and walk towards a group of fourth-class mums. They move aside to make way for me, their faces turning like flowers to the sun.

'Sara – wasn't it so terrible about Vanessa?' 'Sara, you're good at finance. Any interest in being PA treasurer this year?' 'Sara, can you sign this petition about sandwiches?' I smile brightly as their ranks close around me. 'Would Lexie like to come and play?'

Yes. Yes, she would. She would like that more than anything.

Acknowledgements

Thanks are due to the following, for whose professionalism and expertise I am very grateful. My inspiring and ever-patient agent, Marianne Gunn O'Connor, for never allowing me to give up and for her input on the first draft. To Patricia Deevy of Penguin Sandycove for her intuitive and perceptive editing – a light and humorous touch with a great deal of depth behind it. To Sarah Day for her astute copy-editing. To all the other members of the agency and publishing teams for the hard work that I know goes on behind the scenes. And to Cara Hodge for the photos.